NO LONGER PROPERTY OF
SEATTLE PUBLIC LIBRARY

P9-CJJ-132

RECEIVED
NOV 03 2018
Douglass-Truth Branch Library

PRAISE FOR *REVOLUTIONARY*

"This is a bona fide and unforgettable Revolutionary War novel. [An] approachable, imaginative novel, a tale of muskets and masquerade, of marches and mutiny, that is also as an evocative portrayal of life in the Continental Army...Remarkable."

—*The New York Times*

"A vividly detailed fictionalization of the true story of Massachusetts-born Deborah Sampson...*Revolutionary* succeeds on a number of levels, as a great historical-military adventure story, as an exploration of gender identity, and as a page-turning description of [a] fascinating life."

—*The Boston Globe*

"Deftly written...original and affecting."   —*Publishers Weekly*

ADVANCE PRAISE FOR *CONTINENTAL DIVIDE*

"Simultaneously heartbreaking and uplifting, *Continental Divide* is a deeply engrossing and insightful book about love, loss, and what it means to be a man, whatever sex you were assigned at birth. It's an important book for people of any age and any gender."

—Lisa Selin Davis, author of *Tomboy*, *Lost Stars*, and *Belly*

"A classic Western with a modern twist. Ron's youthful journey of self-discovery in the mountains of Wyoming is both gripping and heartfelt."

—Rachel Cleves, author of *Charity and Sylvia*

"*Continental Divide* puts a new spin on a familiar "boy goes west to find himself" coming-of-age story. Here the protagonist is a young transgender man. As he travels through the masculine terrains of wrangling and firefighting, he struggles with how much to reveal about himself. Suspenseful, gut wrenching, and honest, *Continental Divide* will open people's hearts."

—Elizabeth Reis, author of *Bodies in Doubt: An American History of Intersex*

"*Continental Divide* brims with insights about the trans-masculine experience in particular and the contemporary gender landscape in general, and it is a straight-out riveting read, by turns moving, funny, sexy, and suspenseful. The world desperately needs more compelling #ownvoices trans narratives like this. So well done!"

—Lisa Bunker, author of *Felix Yz* and *Zenobia July*

"In *Continental Divide*, Alex Myers paints a delicate, breathtaking portrait of a young man who is forced by rejection and circumstance to search for himself among the toughened ranchers of Wyoming. It's a novel full of adventure and love, but most of all, Myers offers us a fine glimpse into the mind of a trans person coming to terms with the contours of his masculinity, who must withhold his deepest truths to survive."

—Meredith Talusan, author of *Fairest: A Memoir*

"*Continental Divide* is a coming of age story of a young person, who in spite of family hostility, chooses to leave Harvard and go west in search of their identity. But this is no ordinary story. Born as a girl, Ron knows he is a man. And he needs to know if he can live as one. Facing hostility, prejudice, anger, and violence, he fights to live as he feels he must: truthfully. Freighted with honesty and transparency, *Continental Divide* teaches us that identity is indelible, and who better to teach us this than Alex Myers, who fearlessly speaks his own truth and experience with great intelligence and passion."

—Robin Oliveira, *Author of Winter Sisters, I Always Loved You*, and *My Name is Mary Sutter*

"In *Continental Divide*, Alex Myers weaves a brilliant story that explores friendship, love, adventure and identity. The unpredictable, riveting scenes unfold like a film. Vivid description, fascinating characters and a thread of humor carry the reader along with Ron as he navigates a windy path toward trust and acceptance. I couldn't put this book down."

—Cindy Pierce, author of *Sexploitation* and *Sex, College, and Social Media*

"*Continental Divide* explores the great American myths that divide us all: of binary gender, Western masculinity, and hyper self-sufficiency. Told in compelling, vivid prose, Alex Myers has fashioned in Ron a memorable transgender protagonist whose quest to find himself in the Great American West yields surprising and illuminating results. *Continental Divide* is a picaresque trans-Western for the 21st century."

—Dr. Jennifer Natalya Fink, author of *Bhopal Dance*
and Professor of English at Georgetown University

"A gripping coming-of-age story, brimming with heart and adventure, that explores an ultramodern theme: a sensitive 19-year-old informs his parents that he no longer wishes to live as the girl they bore named Veronica, but rather as Ron, the man he believes deep inside he was always meant to be. Unaccepting, the parents cut him off, forcing him to drop out of Harvard. Eager to prove that he can make it on his own as a man, Ron heads West where he can start afresh.

"In Alex Myers' caring, expert hands, Ron and the other characters in this story who love him, torment him or just struggle to understand him, all spring to life as complex, fully recognizable human beings. Bravo, Alex! This book will join the long line of adventure stories and coming-of-age tales that thrill us and comfort us as we all find our path."

—Alison Leigh Cowan former reporter for *The New York Times* and
editor of *How to Survive Your Freshman Year*, 6th ed.

CONTINENTAL DIVIDE

CONTINENTAL DIVIDE

A NOVEL

BY ALEX MYERS

THE UNIVERSITY OF NEW ORLEANS PRESS

University of New Orleans Press
Manufactured in the United States of America
ISBN: 978-1-60801-169-8

CONTINENTAL DIVIDE. Copyright © 2019 Alex Myers.
All rights reserved.

Book and cover design by Alex Dimeff

Cover image: "Map of Wyoming 44.500N 109.000W," United States
Geological Survey / Public Domain

Author photograph by Lexi Adams Wolff

THE UNIVERSITY OF NEW ORLEANS PRESS
unopress.org

To my parents, Sue and Doug, who have taught me much about both love and wisdom.

CHAPTER ONE

The bus slowed down, and I caught sight of the off-ramp sign: Cody, 2 Miles. My yellow pad was propped on my lap and I clicked my pen, thinking of what else I could add to my pathetic to-do list. So far, all I had was:

Find a job
Settle down for a year
Prove to the world (myself?) that I can live as a guy

I'm a sucker for lists. Sometimes I cheat, to make myself feel better, and generate lists like:

Get up
Eat breakfast
Brush teeth

That way I can have the satisfaction of crossing items off. But today, given that I was up, that I'd eaten a granola bar recently, and that I wasn't about to brush my teeth on the bus, there was little low-hanging fruit to add to my list, short of:

Breathe
Panic

Feel miserable
Realize you put yourself in this situation

And though all of those were done, none of them were helpful. I shoved the yellow pad away just as the bus pulled into the station.

I let the others get off first, hanging back to help an old lady with her bag, hoping for some karmic repayment (of course, hoping for such repayment probably undermines any karma coming my way, but whatever) and then trudged over to the racks of tourist brochures, looking for a map. A horde of pamphlet-eating locusts must have descended recently. Only a few Smokey Bear fire danger placards remained. Beyond the station's windows, yellow-tan cliffs rose up in the mid-distance, and dry scrubland stretched from the perimeter of the parking lot all the way to the cliff's base. I blinked, hoping the landscape would resolve itself into something familiar. Pine trees? A pond? Maybe a boulder or two? But it just stood there, mute and waiting, and I remembered that this had been the idea: to get off the over-crowded, everything's-been-discovered-already East Coast and head out West, where *real* people lived.

I tugged my button-down shirt and gave my chest a surreptitious glance to make sure my tits weren't apparent. Time to do what I'd done in all the other towns in Wyoming: walk down Main Street and see if there were any jobs. I hadn't even been on the road for a week, but my eyes felt gritty, my mouth dry, my spine a Gordian knot. Damn bus seats. Damn sleepless nights. Damn near-empty wallet.

I shouldered my backpack and headed toward the bus station's glass doors. Before I made it through, a hand landed on my shoulder.

"Jack? Are you Jack?"

I turned to face a man in his mid-thirties, broad shoulders, the physique of a high school athlete going steadily to seed. He was a couple of inches taller than me with a baseball cap shading his face.

"No, I'm not Jack." My lips gave a little quirk, but I pinched back the smile that wanted to come out. *Girls smile too much.* Laurel said that all the time. *Especially when they don't have any reason to.* Screw Laurel. She's why I was out here. (Okay, that's not fair, but my fatigue was making me melodramatic.) Plus, I had a reason to smile—this guy, this oh-so-typical man, thought I was *Jack.* So I smiled and—just to double-down on what Laurel claims girls do too much—said, "Sorry."

"You want to be?"

"That depends," I said. The man scanned the station, hands on hips, feet—in cowboy boots—planted wide. The stance of a man who owned this place.

At length, his gaze dropped back to me. "You looking for a job?"

"Sure am."

"Then you want to be Jack." He took the cap off, revealing light brown hair thinning at the front. He scratched his scalp, settled the cap again, and lifted his chin to peer at me. "You eighteen?"

"Nineteen." I knew I didn't look it. It used to drive Laurel nuts that, when I passed, she was often mistaken for my older sister rather than my girlfriend. ("The day I'm mistaken for your mother, this relationship is over," she had joked. But other causes had intervened.)

The man scanned the station again, but it seemed like nothing better had presented itself. "I run a dude ranch outside of town. Season starts tomorrow, and I need one more guy on staff. Work in the kitchen, do some maintenance. That was supposed to be Jack, and he was supposed to be here yesterday. But you're here now, and you look clean cut. You want the job?"

I thought of stories I'd heard passed around the dorms at Harvard—people who thought they were going on archaeological digs but were forced to be drug mules or worse. However, I figured the last couple of weeks had been shitty enough that I was due for something better.

"Sure," I said. "Sounds great."

The man held out his hand. "I'm Gus."

I shook, using the special technique taught to me by Ms. Jasmine, a drag queen I'd met at one of the first support groups I'd attended. (Laurel and our friend Jane conspired to force me there.) "See, honey," Jasmine had told me. "Hands and feet, they'll always give you away. Me too. So, when I shake, I offer just the tips of my fingers, and I turn my hand like this. For you, stick out your first finger, don't bend it." Her hands were huge—she always asked for drinks in outsize glasses, she told me, like the ones for margaritas or something. Jasmine had great tips, though she said there was no hope for my feet. "And you know what they say, honey: The smaller the feet, the smaller the dick." True, in my case.

At any rate, Gus crushed my fingers, Ms. Jasmine's advice aside. "I'm Ron," I gasped.

He led me out of the station to a white Ford F-150 with Bar T Ranch stamped in green on the door. I was really doing this. I was really out West, really in the midst of cowboys and ranches, that mythical land of masculinity.

"Toss your pack in back."

I swung it over the side, slid into the passenger seat, and clipped my seatbelt. Gus ignored his, turned the key, and gunned the motor. I wiped my palms against my jeans, wishing I could take out my yellow pad and enjoy the satisfaction of crossing off:

Find a job.

But somehow that didn't feel like a very masculine thing to do, and masculine things—very masculine things—seemed crucial right now. I considered unbuckling my seat belt. I considered belching. Or maybe scratching somewhere mildly inappropriate. I tried to remember all the things my mother complained about my brothers doing or not doing. But I didn't want to think about my parents right now, so I stared out at the town's Main

Street—Cody, was it? It hit me then that I was in a truck, with a man I didn't know, driving away from civilization. I should be scared (okay, I was a bit), but as Gus maneuvered the truck past the plate glass windows of Murray's Western Wear and the old-time façade of the Irma Hotel, I just stared.

This wasn't Harvard Square. This wasn't Boston. This was somewhere I had never been, never even really imagined beyond a few childhood storybooks. This was a place that had never imagined me either. And I was going to get a chance to escape my past, slip away from anyone who knew me, away from anyone who had ever heard the word "transgender." Get a chance to be me without all the jargon and explanation.

It wasn't until we were through town, blowing by big box stores, that Gus started talking.

"Where you from?"

"New Hampshire."

"In college?"

"Yup." I smiled, hoping he wouldn't ask where. But of course he would. Everyone always does.

"Whereabouts?"

For a moment I considered saying UNH. All I could think of was the old joke my freshman dorm proctor used to tell. It went like this:

Nosy Person: So, where do you go to school?
Harvard Student: In New England.
Nosy Person: Where in New England?
Harvard Student: Massachusetts.
Nosy Person: Where in Massachusetts?
Harvard Student: Boston.
Nosy Person: Where in Boston?
Harvard Student: Cambridge.

And so on. But I figured Gus didn't want to mess around, and I might as well get it over with.

Gus's eyebrows shot up when I dropped the H-bomb. "So what are you doing in Wyoming?" He said this in a way that suggested that everyone from Harvard should, during their summer vacation, be running a multinational corporation or campaigning for a Senate seat. Or maybe that was my own neuroses hearing things.

"I just needed to get away." I thought of New York City, of the sublet, of Laurel. I thought of Cambridge, and my academic advisor Kate's office, and the stack of papers forcing me into a year off. "I needed to get some space."

"You've come to the right place." Gus resettled his hat. "I did the same thing at sixteen, bought a motorcycle and headed cross country. By the time I had hit Pennsylvania, the bike was toast and I was hitchhiking."

"Well, you made it quite a ways."

"Nah. I grew up in Jersey. Made it about a hundred miles. I didn't move out here until a few years ago. What do you study?"

"History." The truth was more complicated. Kate had threatened to throttle me if I changed majors again. I'd been in biology, anthropology, environmental studies, and now history. Kind of. I'd intended to switch over in the fall.

Gus shrugged as if this was moderately acceptable, but he'd rather hoped that his new kitchen assistant would be in engineering or something. "Long as you're not a poet," he said and flicked the knob on the radio. Country music curled out of the speakers. "Three things I don't want on my ranch: poets, vegetarians—" I waited, clenched with the certainty that the third would be "faggots." "—and drunks," he finished.

Okay. I could live with that. "I love hamburgers," I said. He didn't need to know that I'd gone vegetarian three months ago. Besides, that had been Laurel's idea. And now one big existential question about myself had been answered. I suppose everyone wonders it: In the face of adversity, a challenge to self and beliefs, would I be the one to stand up for what I valued?

Hell no, apparently. I'd crumple like a cheap soda can. Bring on the beef.

Around a curve in the road, the land shifted, opening. All the stores tapered off, and in the yawning vastness ahead, cliffs swooped up. Behind them grayer buttes (Or mesas? Plateaus? I didn't have the words for this landscape), and beyond that, deep blue mountains. They seemed to march on into forever.

"Wow," I said, forgetting, for a moment, my attempts to project masculine nonchalance.

"You ever been West before?"

"Never." It was embarrassing to admit that I'd gotten on the bus in New York City with only the dimmest idea of where I was going. That I'd headed out here based on a desire to prove I could live as who I was, a man, and the only basis I had for that understanding of the West came from my father's collection of Landmark Books: Davy Crockett, The Lewis and Clark Expedition, Daniel Boone, The California Gold Rush, Kit Carson. I'd read them obsessively when I was a little girl. Even then, I'd wanted what they offered: a new start, a rugged life, a sense of the physical and real rather than the theoretical.

Now, almost twenty and a newly-minted man, I was finally in a position to get what they promised. I just had to head out West and do it. Laurel had laughed at me when I told her, but here I was.

"You'll love it. Take this highway for an hour, and you'll end up in Yellowstone and then Jackson Hole."

"Yellowstone?"

Gus laughed. "You have no clue where you are, do you, Harvey?"

I tried to match his light-hearted tone with a smile, puzzling over the "Harvey." Oh. Harvard, Harvey. But he was right: I had no idea where I was, just an idea of where I wanted to be and where I didn't want to be. The cliffs and the grassland blurred, and Gus tapped the steering wheel in time with the country tunes, humming along: "...*just like my dad said...*"

The lyrics caught me, and I pressed my forehead against the window, thinking back to the moment that had (I could say with the perfection of hindsight) started my trip out here: my father saying, "I've got five sons, I don't need another. You're my daughter, and that's that. End of discussion."

Horses, cows, scrubby bushes, cows. Gus let off the accelerator, and we drifted to a stop at a four-way intersection boasting a pizza place, a hair salon, a paint store. "Last town before the ranch. How do you say it?" He pointed past me at the brick post office, which read Wapiti, Wyoming.

"Wah-pee-tee?" I ventured.

"Just like a tourist. Say it 'whoppity.' Sounds like you're driving on a flat tire: *whoppity, whoppity.*" He hit the gas, and I lurched forward against my seatbelt. A frothing river kept pace with the truck, and my ears kept popping. I tugged at them, waggling my jaw.

"We're getting up there," Gus said. "We're at seven thousand feet or so. Not enough to make you sick."

I grew up in the White Mountains. The bald peak of Chocorua practically stood in my backyard. I'd always thought it was a pretty big mountain at three thousand five hundred feet. But this… Peaks piled up on the horizon, like ocean waves waiting to crash ashore. My gaze shifted between the distant summits and the river that rushed along beside the road.

Just last week, after my disastrous conversation in Kate's office where she oh-so-gently informed me that Harvard couldn't extend financial aid until I'd spent a year living independent of any familial support, I'd stood on the banks of the Charles River and contemplated launching a note in a bottle:

Help! I've been existentially marooned! I don't know where I'm heading, but please come save me!

I hadn't though—for fear of laws against littering, as well as, what's the point of a note like that? And now here I was on the edge of another river, a better river, with water that raged and foamed rather than slinking brownly along. I was out West. The land of the rugged individual. The land where you got a chance to prove what you were really made of. The land where men were men, or they got the hell out of town.

Gus swung the wheel, and I clutched the door handle for support as we pivoted onto a dirt road, rattling over a grate of metal pipes that made my teeth click.

"Cattle guard," Gus explained. "Keeps 'em in. They won't cross it." Sure enough, cattle stood in the pasture along the road, placidly chewing, making no move for escape.

The truck rambled up a slope, and Gus drew to a stop where the road made a Y. Two Western-style gates marked the arms.

"All right, Harvey. A little quiz."

People always did this, as if being a Harvard student meant I should know seven foreign languages and the capital of Guinea-Bissau. "Okay," I said warily.

"What's that animal?" He pointed to the right-hand gate, which had rusty wagon wheels pinned to the uprights and, on the crossbar above, a skull. Oblong, big eye sockets, large front teeth (What else can you say about a skull?) with two small antlers coming out of the temple region.

"Uh, muntjac?"

"I don't even know what that is," said Gus, sounding disappointed.

"Small Asian deer, like a duiker but—"

"Nope. That's a jackalope. Jack rabbit skull, antelope antlers. Put it up there to fool the tourists." He gave me a punch on the arm. "And the Harvard students."

With that, he pressed the gas, and gravel pinged against the truck's underbelly as we crossed through the left gate. Cresting the rise, buildings appeared amid pine trees. Gus pulled the truck up in front of a Quonset-style metal garage. I hopped out, the air surprisingly cool against my skin. Down the slope from the garage, a narrow dirt road wound through brown log buildings that reminded me of YMCA camp in New Hampshire. There was a bigger building, a barn, I thought, surrounded by fenced-in areas of hard-packed dirt. Beyond that, more of the desert scrubland, open range where cows grazed (On what, sagebrush? Dirt?). I could just see the highway Gus and I had driven on, a pitch-black snake that divided the landscape. I took a deep breath and gave my best, hopefully ingratiating, grin and turned to face the garage. Hanging from the middle of the corrugated metal, in the space between the two bay doors, another jackalope skull leered at me, its grin an eerie echo of my own.

CHAPTER TWO

"Leave your bag by the truck," said Gus. "We'll give you a tour before settling you in at the bunkhouse."

Bunkhouse. That had an ominous ring. I followed Gus along the gravel road, split rail fences lining both sides. I kept swiveling my head side to side, trying to take it all in. To the right, the land rose steadily, with a willowy thicket clumped about a hundred yards up the slope and, beyond that as the land grew steeper, pine trees, though thinner and more jagged than the white pines of New Hampshire. Little cabins, single story clapboard affairs, were spaced out along the road. Some had front porches with rocking chairs, others had decks with picnic tables. Past these, the road ended in a parking area bordered by larger buildings on three sides. Directly across stood a mountain lodge: rough-hewn planks and huge glass windows. To the right, set up the slope a ways, a more modern-style split-level ranch house stood, a spray of plastic toys surrounding it, a detached garage to the side. And to the left, a two-story house painted pale blue with a sign hanging from the porch railing: Office.

I had been the dorky first-year student with his nose buried in a campus map for my entire first term at Harvard. Not because I was always getting lost (only sometimes) but because I loved maps. Here's the thing: If you've been shown how to get some-place, you can retrace your steps pretty easily. If you're told where you're supposed to go, you can always stop and ask for directions. But if you have a map, it's all there, everything you don't know. All the streets, all the buildings, all the possibilities.

Inside the pale blue house, what might have once been a kitchen or living room had been converted into a large office space. Three big desks, a set of small cubbies holding keys, a cof-fee pot, a filing cabinet.

From behind one of the desks, a slight man stood up. "You must be Jack." Everything about him was neat and trim: a perfect flat top of dirty blond hair and jeans so crisp they looked like they'd been starched and ironed.

"Jack didn't show up. This is Ron. He goes to Harvard," Gus said, removing his hat and tossing it, Frisbee-style, to plop onto one of the other desks.

"Hi, Ron. I'm Steve." The trim man held his hand across the desk and we shook. I tried Jasmine's index finger trick again, and this time my knuckles remained uncrushed.

"You can call Jack and tell him he's fired or un-hired or what-ever," Gus said. He wandered over to the desk where he'd tossed his hat and picked up a pile of mail. "Any messages?"

As they spoke, I admired Steve's desk. It had everything a workspace should: green-shaded lamp, cup of pens, tray for files. I'm the sort of person who envies a tidy desk. No matter what sort of metal or plastic organizer I buy, I always end up with stacks of pages, crumpled bits of notes, papers skewing every-where. Each paperclip on Steve's desk had been corralled into a mesh bin. Anyone with a desk this neat couldn't be a bad person.

"All right, Ron. I'll show you around," Steve said. We stepped back out into the sunlight. "Gus tell you what you'd be doing?"

"Kitchen and maintenance." Steve, for his slight frame, had a mellow deep voice, and I felt suddenly conscious of the pre-pu-bescent (or so it would seem) quality of mine. "He was pretty vague."

"A little of everything. Pay's three thousand for the summer."

I tried not to think in terms of the Harvard tuition bill. I wasn't going to worry about that. Just here and now. "Okay."

"Half at the midpoint and half at the end." Steve led the way toward the huge rough-hewn building past a volleyball net, a horseshoe pit, and a set of large barbecue grills. From up the slope, I heard the squeals of children and turned to look. Beside the split-level ranch house, two kids played on Big Wheels, and a blonde woman standing near them waved at us.

Steve waved back. "That's Nancy, Gus's wife. They live there, and Gus's sister, Cassie, lives over their garage. And this is the lodge."

Up close, I could appreciate just how big the lodge was: The pillars of its wrap-around porch were literal tree trunks; its windows stretched nearly a story-and-a-half high. Pines marched up the slope behind the building, and I heard a whisking noise as we stood there. At first I thought it was the wind through the trees, but it continued, unceasing, and as I stepped up to the porch, I saw a river curling around.

"That's the Shoshone River, the North Fork." Steve held the screen door for me. "Don't let it slam. One of Gus's pet peeves."

I eased the door shut. Inside, the lodge opened into one massive room. Log walls, high ceilings with dark beams, and at the far end a stone hearth and chimney where three people were dusting and sweeping.

"Bet they don't have one of these at Harvard." Steve pointed up to where a massive chandelier hung: an old-style wagon wheel supported a ring of lights amid a tangle of elk antlers.

I had to laugh. "We actually do. In the Freshman Union— that's the dining hall for first-year students. It used to be Teddy Roosevelt's. I think he shot all the elk himself."

"Oh." Steve's face fell somewhat.

"But we don't have any of these." I pointed to a chair, the frame of which was also made from elk antlers and the upholstery from

stretched hides. Steve brightened, and it struck me as utterly crucial that I keep him pleased, as if this were some absurd vaude-
ville show: *Harvard Boy in Wyoming*.

"Hey, girls," Steve called. We walked toward the hearth,
dodging tables with checkerboards and bookcases with yel-
lowing paperbacks. "This is Ron." The three girls ceased in
their dusting and polishing. "That's Kara." Brown hair with
a big poof of bangs, she waved at me from atop a stepladder.
"And that's Belva." A blonde with a pixie cut and a sharp
chin.

"Hi, Ron," she said and waved a feather duster at me, loosing a
shower of motes in the air.

"And Melissa." She sat on the floor, also blonde but definitely
by way of peroxide and heavier than Belva. She had a huge silver
bowl on the low table in front of her, hands ensconced in pink
rubber gloves as she polished it.

"The girls do the cleaning and watch the little kids. What else
do you do, girls?"

"Laundry. Lots of laundry," said Belva with a heavy Southern
drawl that made three syllables out of the word.

"Right. So toss them your dirty clothes, and they'll get to it—"

Kara chucked a dust rag at Steve. "You wash your own BVDs,
buster."

"I'm just kidding," Steve said as he intercepted the rag and
tossed it back. "Ron'll be in the kitchen this summer and also
helping me. He goes to Harvard."

"Good. Then he's smart enough to work a washing machine on
his own," said Kara.

Steve beckoned me through a door in the far wall.

"Bye, Ron!" the girls chorused. I'd just stepped over the threshold and turned to shut the door behind me when I heard one
of them say, "He's cute." A sparkle of pleasure twitched through
my chest. I didn't give a hoot whether they thought I was cute.
(Not really. Not deep down. Okay, I did, a bit.) But I was eternally
grateful that I had passed.

Ahead of me, Steve waited in the dining room. "They're nice gals. Gus doesn't want any monkey business at the ranch though, so save the romance for your days off."

"No problem," I said. I had no intention of monkeying with anyone anywhere this summer. Celibacy was my watchword.

We passed quickly through the dining room with its dozen large round tables and wagon wheel light fixtures before Steve pushed through the swinging door to the kitchen where a blare of Top 40 radio greeted us.

"I didn't know you liked this stuff, Marc," Steve shouted.

A squat fellow turned around from the grill he'd been scouring, revealing a stomach that looked like he'd swallowed two basketballs. He glistened with sweat all the way from his receding hairline to the apron tied at his waist, his white t-shirt almost translucent like the wax paper around a greasy hamburger. Despite the balding and the extra weight, he didn't look all that old, maybe mid-twenties.

"I don't. But there's only two stations out here in Hickville, and the other one's country. Turn this shit off, Carl!"

An abrupt silence followed Marc's shout, into which only the watery *floosh* of the industrial dishwasher interceded. A young guy stepped around the corner, drying his hands on a towel.

"Okay," said Steve. "Carl, this is Ron." I shook Carl's hand, thinking he looked intensely like an otter: sleek black hair slicked flat to his head, big dark eyes, and dark skin, with an air of insouciant amusement around his mouth as if he was just waiting to cause some trouble but nothing serious.

"Hey, man," he said.

"Hey." I bobbed my head. Be cool. Act normal. (Whatever that meant here in Wyoming. Normal had never been my strong suit.)

"And this is Marc. He's in charge in the kitchen. Marc, Ron." He didn't offer to shake my hand, so I gave a lame wave and then let my arm flop to my side.

"Has he finished fourth grade yet?" asked Marc. "Or does Gus think I'm running a preschool?"

"He goes to Harvard," Steve replied, apparently unsurprised by Marc's rudeness. "He'll be with you for meals and then work with me after breakfast."

"You came at the perfect time, kid." Marc tossed a scouring pad at me. "Grill's all yours."

I snagged the pad and gave Marc a smile. "Okay, no problem."

"We've got to finish the tour, but I'll bring him back," Steve said.

Out on the ranch's road again, Steve walked me by the guest cabins back to the garage where I grabbed my pack from the truck.

"Marc's full of piss sometimes," Steve said. "But he's a good cook, and if you do the work, he won't bother you." He steered us downslope past two corrals, one on each side of the road, and beyond those, a barn. "Just built that barn last season." Country music wafted out as we walked by the thrown-open double doors. "Girls live in that bungalow, and the wranglers in the house past that. And you're over here." A path twitched right and led to an L-shaped log building. The spring twanged as Steve pushed the door open. "The bunkhouse."

A Quick Inventory:

A plaid couch in yellow, brown, and orange (think burnt sienna, my least favorite crayon color as a kid)

Blue-striped wingback chair, looking stiff and out of place

Formica table with four chairs, the sort you'd find in a diner

Wall décor: Western

-One stuffed fish, looking like it'd swum in a river of dust

-Antlers, various

-Spurs

-Another jackalope skull

Steve pushed open another door, which led to the longer spine of the L: a narrow, corridor-like room with five bunk beds pushed against the walls. One bed stood at each end, two against the inside wall, and one against the outside wall by the window. Shit. This wasn't quite what I had hoped for.

The bunk at the far end had been claimed by Marc, the one at the near end by Carl (or so I guessed based on the yellow and brown University of Wyoming quilt). I tossed my pack on the bunk nearest the window.

"Bathroom's over there," Steve said, pointing at a door near Carl's bed. "Be at the kitchen by four thirty. That gives you plenty of time to get settled. Welcome aboard."

The screen door wheezed again. I heard a few crunching steps, then silence. I stood, flat-footed, vaguely facing the window that looked out onto…what? Where? The longer I stood, the more it felt like I was dissolving, slowly ceasing to be—my joints loose, my limbs heavy, like they might fall off.

I mean, I'd just gotten kicked out of my family, been removed from Harvard for a year, dumped my girlfriend (though it felt like vice versa), and run away to Wyoming. How the hell else should I feel?

Pull it together, Ron. Unpack. Pretend that it's YMCA camp, where Mom sent you for a week every July and the first day felt like the end of the world.

The deep breaths stabilized me, and I made a mental correction. I had not run away. I had made a deliberate choice. And it was a good choice. No one was going to tell me I didn't belong, or I couldn't hack it, or I wasn't who I said I was.

I tentatively approached the bathroom. Two sinks. A urinal. (Useless. Jane was always trying to tell me about "stand and pee" devices, but they looked ridiculous to me, and all I could envision was an embarrassed Ron with a very wet crotch.) Two stalls. Two showers with curtains. Okay. Possible. Not easy but possible.

I heard Kate telling me to play it safe. I heard Laurel telling me that I had a ton of internalized homophobia, self-loathing that fed into a fear of being labeled "transgender." She thought I had an obsession with passing, with needing everyone to see me as a guy. According to her, if I insisted on being a guy, I was in denial; I'd always be transgender. Well, screw that. I had made it out here, and it would be fine.

Slowly—in the same manner as I used to remove Band-Aids when I was a kid, an agonizing millimeter at a time—I unpacked. Clothes in the bureau (barely filling two drawers). Books on the shelf by the bunk, taking up almost as much space as my clothes. Yellow pads stacked there too, pens nearby. Shoes under the bottom bunk. The mattress gave off that musty smell of heavy use followed by total disuse, and I stretched my sleeping bag out on it.

In the bottom of my backpack, I stashed my tampons, a set of "nice clothes" (chinos, Oxford shirt, tie) that I couldn't imagine needing at the ranch, and the almost-full yellow pad that had been my journal for the last few weeks, all before I shoved the pack under the bunk. Then I fished out my running clothes and was trying to decide where to change (Here in the bunkroom? Or in the bathroom? In a *stall* in the bathroom? How much of a coward was I?) when I heard the asthmatic spring of the bunk-house door.

"Hello-oo? It's Nancy. Can I come in?"

I stepped out to the front room. "Hi…"

"You must be Ron? I'm Nancy. Gus's wife? I just brought your uniform shirts." She passed me a stack of t-shirts, green with the Bar T logo in white on the front. "I wanted to make sure you had everything you need. Goodness, this place. It needs some TLC." She shook her head, hands on the hips of her tapered, acid-washed jeans. "That couch. Ugh. Now Gus says you go to Harvard?" I nodded. "That's so nice. Your parents must be real proud. What do you study?"

"History."

"How nice. You sure look young. The girls are going to eat you up. Mind that you keep the fooling off the ranch. I'm going to peek in the bunkroom, okay?"

She was already past me, a little blade of a woman, her blonde hair a tight helmet atop her head, and I was still absorbing everything she'd said, dizzied not only by the pace of her banter but also the swirl of her perfume, floral and thick.

"That must be Marc's spot down there?" She clucked her tongue at the rumpled bed. "No wonder that man's a bachelor. The kids do love their Uncle Marc, but I declare…" She turned to face me. "Gus tell you they're brothers?"

I shook my head.

"Augustus, he's the oldest, and Marcus Aurelius, he's the baby of the family, and their sister's here too, Cassiopeia. Their daddy was a classics professor, so he taught Latin and Greek? But you go to Harvard, you know that. Is this your bed?"

I nodded.

"What would your mother say if she knew you were spending the summer in a sleeping bag?"

I imagined my mother might have quite a few things to say, mostly on other topics, but Nancy plowed ahead.

"I'll send a girl down with sheets and a blanket. And I bet you need towels too. Maybe a pillow? Boys…" She put a hand on my forearm. "Gus would wear the same jeans for a month if I didn't make him put them in the hamper. It's real nice to meet you. You just let me know if you need anything?"

"Thanks…"

She had already left, the scrunch of footsteps receding, and I stood reeling from the mix of perfume and personality.

After a run along the highway and a shower—the bunkhouse empty and safe—I put on a fresh compression shirt, the spandex so tight I had to roll it down my ribs. Laurel had helped me find these after reading an article about how binders and ACE bandages can cause cysts. It was a good thing I wasn't heavy chested. The compression shirts worked fine.

Still, I checked myself in the bunkhouse mirror: pale, young, and scared. Damn.

CHAPTER THREE

At 4:20 I was in the kitchen, country music blasting as Carl chopped tomatoes.

"Hey, man," he said as I came in.

"About time," Marc called from the other end of the kitchen where he was breading pork chops. "Get some potatoes from the storeroom, and you two can start peeling." Carl put his knife down and headed toward the back of the kitchen. "There's aprons in the drawer next to the sink. You know how to cook, Roger?"

"Ron. Not really. I mean, my mom taught me a few things."

"Well, this isn't your mom's kitchen. I don't want things fucked up."

Carl dragged out a sack of potatoes, and Marc picked one up, speaking slowly as if he were instructing a pair of iguanas. He had the same bushy eyebrows as his brother, the same bald slope of forehead. But otherwise the two of them hardly looked alike.

"Peel them. Get all the skin off. Wash them. Then slice them like this. Thin and even." He demonstrated, defoliating the spud in no time, then whisking his knife through it to generate a dozen neatly eviscerated wafers. "They've got to be the same size if you want them to cook evenly, okay? I know you two college boys think you're hot shit, but this is my kitchen, and I want things done right."

He dropped the knife on the cutting board and went back to the grill. The peeling was easy—that I'd done before—but the slicing wasn't as simple as Marc had made it seem. I'd butchered one spud, turning it into pieces that were more like cubes than wafers, when Marc came over to inspect, heaving a huge sigh.

"Looks like I'll be running a culinary skills class. Take your knife. Set the tip on the board, then rock the knife. See how the blade is curved? Rock it. I shouldn't hear a sound. No chopping, no hacking. Rock the blade."

I picked up my knife and imitated him. It was easier that way. "Thanks," I said. "I think I've got it."

He shot me a skeptical look and swept my first failed potato into the trash, then went to check on the ovens. Carl and I set to slicing, chatting over the twang of the radio. Carl was from Powell, which was about twenty minutes on the other side of Cody though, truth be told, this information didn't mean a thing to me. I still had no clue where I was. But I nodded along.

"I'm taking a break," Marc shouted. "Don't fuck things up while I'm gone." The screen door *thwacked* shut behind him.

Carl gave a little smirk. "What an asshole," he said, then continued on with his story. He was eighteen, going to the University of Wyoming in the fall. Trying to save up money this summer, which he thought would be easier if he lived in the middle of nowhere. From there, he began to interrogate me about sports, especially football, and we commiserated over being from states with no NFL teams and therefore having tenuous allegiances. This was a topic I knew nothing about, but at least I could parrot what my brothers and father had said, privately reveling in this masculine line of discourse. Lesbians seldom talked about the NFL, at least as far as I had experienced.

"So yeah," Carl went on. "I root for the Packers 'cause my dad's from Wisconsin originally, but—"

"No smoking on my ranch!" someone shouted from outside.

The back door to the kitchen flapped open, and Marc stomped in. "The guests aren't even here."

"No smoking. Period. Shape up or ship out," Gus said, following him in.

"Yeah? You want to be the cook this summer?" Marc had stopped short and turned to face his brother, his heavy gut practically pushed up against Gus's lesser stomach.

"You're not irreplaceable. Just watch it."

"You going to go back to the bus station and find another wimpy teenager to cook here? You better watch out, or they'll think you're a child molester."

"Shut your mouth." Gus stepped to the side, blocking Marc from my view. "You just remember I'm doing you a favor." He banged through the swinging doors into the dining room.

Carl's wide eyes glinted with amusement, and I went back to meticulously slicing.

"The Packers, huh?" I said. "Everyone in my family is a Pats fan—"

"You two done yet?" Marc leaned over the counter. "Come on, girls. Less gossip, more work."

The "girls" caught me by surprise, the mild insult of it. I hadn't heard it used that way since…a decade ago? At one of my brother's little league games—I spent a lot of my childhood watching my brothers play little league—when the coach had said that his team was acting like a bunch of girls for not wanting to play in the rain. But I'd never had it applied to me. Well, not in this way.

"Set the tables for fifteen, Rob. Wash the mixer, Carl. Let's get moving. This is a job, not summer camp."

"It's Ron," I said, but Marc ignored me.

He jammed a toothpick in his mouth and started chewing on it. "Fucking Gus," he muttered. I set two big round tables with plates, silverware, napkins, cups. I opened drawers and checked cabinets, trying to find everything I needed, resolved not to ask Marc for help. Every now and then he'd push through the doors. "Don't forget bowls of applesauce." Or, "Put out salt shakers."

It wasn't—to steal one of Laurel's favorite expressions—rocket surgery, but I'd worked up a sweat by the time Carl stepped out to ring the dinner bell.

"Start carrying it out, Rick," Marc said to me, the toothpick bobbing in his mouth.

I gave up on the name and ferried trays of pork chops, plates of potatoes, and bowls of salad to the tables. Nancy and her two sons came in first, then Steve and Gus. The three girls sat down by Nancy, and I struggled to put names and faces together: Belva, pixie blonde. Melissa, the slightly heavier one. Kara, brown hair with big bangs.

Then two wranglers burst in, the building seeming to vibrate under their pounding footsteps. Tight jeans, tight shirts, sleeves rolled up. The taller and younger one had a mullet—New Hampshire had finally gotten over that hairstyle in the late eighties—and gangling arms, while the shorter fellow was tan and scrawny like a piece of beef jerky. He looked to be older even than Steve. No hats and no spurs, but both sported big belt buckles.

"Where's Clyde?" Steve asked as they sat down next to him.

"He's at the barn," the shorter wrangler said.

The one with the mullet laughed, a surprising almost-giggle.

I brought out two pitchers of water and was setting them on the tables when a third wrangler, Clyde, I guessed, walked in. He seemed to be in his late thirties, with the sort of lined and tan face you got from working outside. Though not quite as tall as the wrangler with the mullet, Clyde was thicker set with a barrel chest and broad shoulders. He had a bandanna around his thick neck, and his rolled-up sleeves revealed the faded blue ink of tattoos.

Drawing out the chair next to Steve, he gave the wrangler with the mullet a stare. "Get that goofy look off your face, J.T."

"Where's Cassie?" Gus asked from the other table.

J.T., the one with the mullet, gave his almost-giggle again. "At the barn? Maybe you know, Clyde."

Marc and Carl took the last chairs at the wranglers' table, and in the scrape and shuffle of them settling, I didn't catch how Clyde answered J.T., although I didn't hear any more giggling. I took a seat next to Belva, leaving a space between Gus and me.

"Food's getting cold," said Marc, shooting a glare at Gus.

"I know it." Gus cleared his throat. "Heavenly Father…" I bowed my head. "Bless this food we're about to eat…"

The sharp snap of the screen door and then a two-part step, heel-toe, heel-toe, echoed across the lodge floor.

"Bless the people here and keep us…"

Heel-toe, closer. "Amen."

The chair next to me slid out, and a woman, in one fluid motion, settled herself in the seat and forked a pork chop onto her plate before the rest of us had gotten the taste of Amen off our lips.

"Cassiopeia," Gus intoned. "You're late."

"Yes, Augustus," she replied, sarcasm heavy in her voice as she tapped out all three syllables of his name. "Are we being formal tonight? That Appaloosa you bought is trouble. Its eye's gone all pink and crusty—"

"Not at the table," Nancy shuddered.

"Pork chop?" Cassie passed the tray to me. Although I wasn't quite sure what an Appaloosa was, I admired Cassie's dry sense of humor. It made a nice contrast to Nancy's saccharine. Nancy had said Cassie was the middle child, but she didn't look all that much older than Marc, maybe in her mid-twenties.

"Thanks."

"Cassie, that's Ron. He's helping Marc," Steve said.

"Lucky you."

I took a chop and passed the tray, offering Cassie a smile, but she was already talking to Gus again. "Whoever shoed that horse last did a piss poor—"

"Language," Nancy shrilled.

Cassie's hair, in a low ponytail on her neck, gleamed golden-brown, the color you get when you're making caramel and you're just melting the butter and brown sugar together. I tried to see the family resemblance between her and Marc and Gus: broad shoulders, high foreheads (more pronounced on the men, whose hairlines were receding), blue eyes—but Cassie's were soft like washed denim, while Marc's and Gus's were smoky. She had an angularity to her that neither brother possessed: squarish chin, pointed nose, ears that stuck out a little, and a dusting of freckles over her cheekbones. She tapped the table with her fingers: no manicure, no nail polish, I noticed.

"Potatoes, Ron?" Belva nudged.

"Yeah, thanks."

"I saw you running today."

Small town life—just like Tamworth, where everyone knew within ten minutes if you'd bought a new car or had a relative visiting. (I wondered who had seen me come home last week, if any of our neighbors heard my father yelling at me in our front yard. I could still feel his fingers digging into my shoulder as he shoved me out the door, still see him cock his hand back as if he was going to slap me, only to let it fall to his side, telling me, *Get out of here. I don't hit girls.*)

"I just went along the highway," I told Belva. "I'd been on the bus too long."

"You on the running team?" Nancy asked. Before I could answer, she leaned toward Cassie. "He goes to Harvard."

"Nice. You ride at all?" Cassie asked.

"Horses?" I said stupidly. "Not since I was young."

"Look pretty young to me right now."

"I'm nineteen." I could feel a flush rising up my neck.

She cocked an eyebrow. Damn. I wish I could do that: a perfectly skeptical look. "Riding a horse is like riding a bike. You never forget."

"Ron won't have much time to ride. He'll be with Marc or Steve most of the day," Gus said.

"I hope they're paying you well..." Cassie muttered, and the attention moved away from me again, thank goodness.

I tucked into the food—it was good, I'd grant Marc that. Just as I'd finished the pork chop (my first meat in a few months; I hoped my stomach wouldn't rebel), Marc called over. "Carl, clear the dishes. And you get the pies, Ron." I hopped up.

"He's got you trained already," said Cassie, tilting back in her chair.

"At least he got my name right this time," I replied. She gave me a half smile and another lift of her eyebrow.

Dessert demolished, Gus stood up. "The season begins tomorrow. We've got how many coming for the first week?"

"Thirty-five," Steve said.

"Thirty-five dudes arriving. Cabins set?"

"Yes," said Belva.

"Kitchen set?"

"Yeah, sure," said Marc.

"Barn okay?"

"Still standing," said J.T., the wrangler with the mullet.

"Except that Appaloosa," Cassie murmured, but Gus ignored her.

"Breakfast at seven. We'll go to Cody and pick the dudes up and have them here by two. Remember: no smoking and no drinking on the ranch." Gus went over to talk to Steve, and I stood up to clear the dishes.

Nancy put her hand on my wrist as I took her pie plate. "Ron, honey, do you need anything from town tomorrow?"

"Uh. Stamps. And..." I wanted a map, or a guidebook. "Could I go to the library?"

"Isn't that sweet? Gus, can you spare Ron tomorrow morning? He wants to go to the library."

"There's plenty of books on the lodge shelves."

"He doesn't want to read Louis L'Amour," Nancy snapped.

"No, he probably wants a copy of *Moby Dick*," said Cassie.

"Please. There are children present," Nancy hissed.

"It's about a whale."

Nancy just glowered at her.

"It's fine," said Steve, clearly amused. "He can go as soon as breakfast is cleared up. He can help with the dudes' luggage when he gets back."

The wranglers were the first to leave the dining hall, and I started gathering up dirty dishes as the others left. Cassie added her plate to my pile. "Don't let my little brother bug you," she said. "And I mean it, I'll take you out for a ride if you want." She snapped me a wink, and I wasn't sure how to interpret it. Was the wink because of the comment about her brother? Or because she really did want to take me out on a horse? Or was she just being nice to the new guy?

"Thanks," I told her. "That sounds like fun." Lame, I know. But interpersonal relations are not my strong suit, especially when the other person is a girl I find good looking.

"You've got something in your hair," she said, reaching up and pulling something loose. "Potato peel."

"Your brother gave me a lesson in the art of peeling and slicing," I replied.

She flicked the peel onto a dirty plate. "Well, don't let him boss you around too much," Cassie said. "He's always trying that with me." She winked again and then raised her voice. "Right, Marc?"

I turned and saw that Marc was holding the kitchen door open, staring at the two of us. "Get to work, Ron," he said. "Those plates aren't about to wash themselves."

"See what I mean?" Cassie said, *sotto voce*, and then turned to walk away. Her footsteps echoed in the empty lodge as I grabbed a bowl and turned to the kitchen door.

"What were you saying to my sister?" Marc demanded, stepping close to me.

"Uh, nothing," I mumbled. "Just talking."

"Did you say something about me?" Marc leaned even closer.

I put a protective arm around the dishes I was carrying, the pile teetering. "No. She was talking about going for a horse ride."

"Don't even think about it. Don't even fucking talk to my sister."

"I didn't..." The dishes wobbled, and I hastily set them on a table. A half-dozen replies jumbled together in my mind, mostly in Jane's voice, mostly yapping about paternalism and the use of women to bolster men's feelings of self-worth. Not that I was going to say any of that to Marc.

"You hear me?" Marc persisted. "Don't even look at Cassie."

"Okay, okay," I said. "I got it. Isn't she with Clyde anyhow?"

"What the fuck do you know, Harvard?" He pushed me, hard, on one shoulder, and I stepped back, holding up my hands.

"I think he's right, man," Carl said as he edged past Marc, a bucket of soapy water in one hand. "The girls all say Cassie's with Clyde."

Marc grabbed a wad of Carl's shirt. "You shut up too."

"Take it easy," Carl said, clamping his hand over Marc's. I could see Carl's fingers flex against Marc's forearm, and Marc abruptly let him go, shaking his wrist.

"Fuck off," Marc said. He glared at me.

Carl and I cleaned the dining hall in silence, waiting for the sound of the screen door snapping shut to tell us that Marc had left. We stacked the clean plates and hung the pots and pans from their rack. Then Carl peered outside.

"I think he's gone, man," he said. "Sometimes he hangs around, like he wants to catch me slacking off."

"What got him so upset?" I asked.

"I don't know what the deal is with him and Cassie. You'd think Marc was married to his sister."

We hung our aprons up, and Carl checked again to see that the coast was clear before we stepped out into the cool darkness.

"Marc's mostly okay," he said. "I figure, I won't bother him and he won't bother me. So far it's been fine, except when he gets pissed off at Gus and then takes it out on me. Or pissed off at the wranglers. Come to think of it, he gets pissed off at pretty much anything." Pine trees swished around us, and the silhouettes of mountains marched across the still-twilit horizon, an abrupt reminder that I was in a foreign land.

"I'm gonna go see Belva. You want to come to their cabin with me?" Carl asked.

"No thanks," I replied. "I'm pretty tired."

"Suit yourself."

Carl turned down a side path, and I crunched along the gravel toward the bunkhouse, which was empty. I made my bed with the sheets Nancy had left and put away the rest of my things, glad for the privacy in which to remove my compression shirt (add that to the list of things I'd have to figure out how to manage) and boxers, polka-dotted ones. My first purchase of guys' clothing after I'd come out (I'd gleefully tossed out all my Hanes panties and sports bras) was made at Filene's in downtown Boston. A ridiculous excursion with Jane, we went to go buy one of each: boxers, briefs, and boxer briefs.

"You have to decide what kind of guy you're going to be, Ron," she'd told me. I decided I'd be a discreet guy and opt for the concealment a slightly baggy pair of boxers allowed.

All that seemed so long ago, even though it was less than a year. I climbed into my bunk, worried about whether I'd be able to fall asleep in such a strange place. Taking out my yellow pad, I stared at the list I'd made, drawing my pencil through the first item.

~~Find a job~~

I paused over the second item. Was I really settled here for a year? For the summer, at least. A quick edit fixed that.

~~Settle down for a year summer~~

But the third one:

Prove to the world (myself?) that I can live as a guy

No one had found out yet. Was that what this was going to be? A summer—a year—of worrying? I didn't want to be constantly divided, feeling like I was one thing pretending to be another. I wasn't pretending. This was who I was, a guy. Somehow those Landmark Books had never included any passages on the existential dilemmas of Daniel Boone. Did he ever worry about where he belonged? Did Davy Crockett spend even ten seconds considering his gender expression? No, they just went and did. Why couldn't I do the same thing?

My eyelids were drooping, yet my mind still buzzed, my pencil poised over the pad. I'd dozed on the bus earlier, but my last good sleep was back in New York City, in that sublet with Laurel. A night that had been sticky with humidity, the fan in the window hardly helping at all.

I'd already gone to bed, spread-eagled on the damp sheets, when I heard Laurel come home, heard her chatting with Heather, her roommate for the summer and a former teammate of mine. (We'd both been on the women's basketball team at Harvard before I'd come out as a guy and quit the team.) I couldn't catch all their words over the hum of the fan, but I heard the rise and fall of their talk, a few bursts of laughter. And maybe it was my imagination, but I thought I'd heard some warmth there, some easiness, that I hadn't felt from Laurel in a while.

I'd met Heather on one of my first days at Harvard, and she'd immediately recognized me as a lesbian, even though I'd just come out to myself. She was the one who brought me to the queer student group. That's where I met Laurel and Jane and a bunch of other lesbians. After the meetings, we tended to split up, the gay men heading off in one direction and the queer women in the other. I had been so ecstatic, after a childhood in tiny Tamworth, to be with this cluster of lesbians: some jocks, some artists, some butch, some lipstick. We went to poetry slams and protests and cooked messy brunches together.

There was just an easiness about the group—that's what I overheard in Heather and Laurel's murmured talk. And that's what had ended when, the following year, I came out as transgender. Everyone said it was great, wonderful even, that I was discovering my true self. But that togetherness—that acceptance—it faded. I wasn't a lesbian, I wasn't a woman. But I also wasn't a guy. I wasn't straight, I wasn't gay. They didn't quite push me out of the group, but it no longer felt like I belonged.

Maybe it was me, not them, I thought, rolling over so the fan blew on my back. I waited for Laurel to come in so that I could drape my arm over her hips, pull her close for as long as we could stand it on this humid night. But I fell asleep before she came to bed.

When I got up the next morning (Heather had already taken off for her internship), I cooked eggs and toast. Laurel emerged from the bedroom, her blue-green hair standing on end, wearing a baggy t-shirt. Her summer classes in fashion design wouldn't start until the afternoon. That was when she held out a brown paper sack, which I opened to find a bunch of syringes and a vial of greasy liquid: testosterone.

"Where'd you get this?" I asked.

"You can get anything at art school," she replied. "Go ahead. Take it. Then you can be a man, like you want to be."

"I am a man. You just don't see it."

She gave me that smirk that I used to find sexy (now it looked more than a little obnoxious) and said, "You're transgender. That's what I see. You're queer. You're dating me, and I'm a lesbian. Think about it. How are you 'just a man'?"

I shoved the bag back into her hands. "I am. I can do it without this."

"Yeah? Seems to me like you want to be a straight dude, like you have some problem with being seen as queer." She ran her fingers through her hair.

"I have a problem with being seen as a woman. Because I'm not. Been there, tried that, didn't work."

"I get it. But you don't have to run to the other end of the binary. You don't have to turn into some Frat Bro."

"So, what? You want me to be androgynous? Is this about how you won't be queer enough if I look like a guy?" I knew it drove her nuts when people took us to be a straight couple. The irony. I was always delighted when someone called me *sir* or *young man,* and Laurel was always cutting in with, *He's trans*, as if they'd take her queer card away otherwise.

"Oh no. Don't you try and put this all on me. You want to be a man, fine. That's why I brought you the testosterone. Go ahead and take it. Get over yourself and admit that's what you want." She shook the bag at me, the syringes rattling around.

I closed my eyes, trying not to let the anger I felt rise up and swallow me. I was enough. I didn't need to change anything about myself. "Don't force this shit on me, Laurel. I can do this on my own."

"So what's your grand plan?"

That moment was a quivering edge—what *was* my plan? I couldn't stay here and keep having this fight with Laurel. But there wasn't anyone I could go to who wouldn't think of me as Veronica, as the girl I used to be. As transgender. I was tired of carrying that around.

Laurel was shaking her head, the smirk still on her lips. "Don't do something stupid, Ron."

Stupid was staying here. Stupid was letting her, letting Harvard, letting my past tell me who I was. I'd show them.

"I'm out of here," I said, brushing past the bag of testosterone as I went to the bedroom to get my things.

"Where are you going?" Laurel asked.

But I wasn't dumb enough to tell her. I knew she would just laugh if I said, *I'm going West. I'm going someplace where no one's heard the word "transgender."*

"I'll write when I get there," I told her instead.

And now here I was. I shoved the yellow pad away and turned off the lamp by the bed. The pillowcase smelled of a strange laundry detergent. The air that seeped through the window screen felt cool, with none of New York's humidity.

So, I had a summer ahead of me in this place, and then the rest of the year beyond that, with a whole lot of something to prove. I was pretty sure Kit Carson must've once felt the same way.

CHAPTER FOUR

The breakfast dishes done, Steve retrieved me from the kitchen as Carl and Marc went through the inventory in the storeroom. "Just need a copy of your license, plus a few forms to make you official," he said, leading me to the blue office building.

I pulled out my wallet and handed him my New Hampshire license. Thank god I'd gone up in March and had my name changed legally.

Steve took the card, read it over, and then set it on the copy machine. "Birthday in about a month, I see. Going to be twenty... Shoot, you look more like sixteen."

"I know."

"Ah, well, so did I. At least you're fairly tall. I quit growing in the tenth grade, and I didn't have a whisker until I was eighteen."

I nodded, relief rippling through me. He didn't see anything except a young-looking guy. Steve filled in the paperwork and handed the license back.

It had been one hell of a day getting that thing, between the probate court and the DMV. First, at the court, it had felt so funny to be close to home without my parents knowing. I kept worrying that someone I knew would see me. I wasn't ready to come out to them. I thought I would wait until the end of the term. (I guess I should have waited a little longer. Like until graduation.)

Everyone had told me that a change of name was a simple matter. But the judge had questioned me up and down: *Are you changing your name or your gender?* He asserted that his court didn't have the authority to change gender (and that, in my case, a name change would imply a gender change) and suggested that I had malicious intentions, like applying to The Citadel or joining the Boy Scouts. I assured him that I only wanted a name change, insisted that "Ron" was a gender-neutral name, and vowed that I would never sign on with the Scouts, and he eventually acquiesced. I left the courtroom frazzled. (If only Jane had been there to argue that names didn't constitute gender, that cultural conventions ascribed such normative values. But if she had, I probably wouldn't have left with a court order in my hand.)

It seemed, though, that the unpleasantness in the courtroom had earned me some good karma at the DMV. The final clerk I faced there, an older woman with home-set curls, was just about to hand me my new license when she paused.

"Will you look at that? Just a second, dear." I cursed under my breath, wanting the day done, but she returned ten minutes later and handed the card over. "They had you down as 'Female,'" she said. "Honestly." She shook her curls in disbelief.

I had smiled, resisted saying, *Thanks for the sex change*, and sauntered out. And it was thanks to her that I hadn't just handed Steve a license saying "F."

The Cody Public Library had nothing on Harvard's Widener, except perhaps the view. It was only one story with industrial beige carpeting. None of the woodwork, none of the shadowy stacks. The shelves in Cody boasted cookbooks and large-font copies of romances (many with Western themes: *Heart Wrangler, Back in the Saddle*) rather than the latest monographs on the French Revolution.

Nancy had taken her sons to the children's room while I perused the shelves dedicated to topics of local interest, finding a field guide and a history of Wyoming. I wandered around, soaking in the comfort that books provided and, thinking of Cassie, grabbed a copy of *Moby Dick*. Just because. Then I queued up at the circulation desk.

"Look at all the books Ron is checking out, boys," Nancy crooned. "He's with us, Gladys," she told the woman at the desk. "He goes to Harvard. I hope he rubs off on the boys."

Be careful what you wish for, I thought.

Around the corner at a drugstore, I bought envelopes and a yellow pad (always good to have a few extra) and took a free area map from the tourist racks. Nancy, who had more errands in town, dropped me off at the airport where the ranch vans idled. Soon enough, the dudes arrived, some single guys but mostly families with kids. I loaded their luggage in the back of the vans, and then we were speeding down the highway, mountains whipping past, the dudes' heads swiveling as they took it all in, making me feel like an old hand already.

The Pattern of the Days:

5:00 a.m. Rise. Listen to Marc groan. Observe him shove the whiskey bottle (increasingly depleted) under his bunk.

5:15 a.m. Make forty or so packed lunches. Amuse self by betting on whether turkey will be more popular than ham. Realize that most people order the same thing for lunch every day of their stay. Wonder whether you would too. (Yes, you would.)

6:15 a.m. Set tables for breakfast. Remember butter! Remember syrup! Remember juice! Make a pot of decaf coffee. There is always one woman who wants decaf coffee. Except she doesn't want it unless you have failed to remember to make a pot of decaf.

7:00 a.m. Serve breakfast. Listen to the dudes mumble about early mornings, claim they feel great, and make resolutions to get up early at home. Meanwhile, be cynical and doubt their wherewithal.

9:00 a.m. Eat your own breakfast. Report for work with Steve. Follow Steve's whims for the next hour or three.

12:00-ish p.m. Run. Shower if no one else is in the bunkhouse or if Marc is deep asleep. Gauge this based on the quality and frequency of his snores.

2:00 p.m. Escape to riverbank to eat lunch and relish being in the West, the land of real men. Tell yourself you are one of them. Open the pages of the Louis L'Amour novel you took from the shelf in the lodge. Read carefully and try to memorize some of the better phrases the cowboys use.

4:00 p.m. Return to kitchen. Obey Marc. Note that at dinner he is testier than at breakfast. Note on note: Next time at the Cody Public Library, look up the word "testier" to see if it comes from the same root as "testes."

9:00 p.m. Done for day. Seek refuge in a book.

I set the yellow pad down and let my surroundings filter in: the little creek that flowed by my feet, the pine trees that rose, straight and skinny, all around me. I'd hiked a ways down the North Fork from the ranch and then followed this creek up the slope to where it formed a small cascade. Another hour and I'd be back in the kitchen. But for now... I leaned back and reread the letter I'd just written to Jane: *It's so nice being in Wyoming. The job is fun.*

I could just as easily have written the opposite. Could just as easily have told Jane that I was lonely and scared here. That every time I changed in the bunkhouse, I worried that someone would see something odd, that they'd figure things out. Or how much it grated on me to hear what seemed like every other word out of Marc's and Carl's mouths: *fag, gay, queer*—always as insults, of course.

In my bunk at night, I sometimes berated myself for not saying anything, even as I knew it would be pointless and would only bring down heaps of crap on me. *They don't hate gay people*, I'd tell myself. *It's just slang.* But I didn't quite believe that. I could have told Jane about how Marc had taken to pushing me around the kitchen or the bunkhouse whenever he was in a bad mood, and it seemed like he was always in a bad mood.

I could have written that letter to Jane. It would have been just as true as the one I had written. I wanted to be here; I was desperately out of place. I felt like I belonged; I felt like a shadow.

The creek riffed along and I stood up, brushing needles from my legs and butt. I folded the letter to Jane and followed the creek down to the Fork, the Fork to the bridge, the bridge to the trail, to the bunkhouse, to where I copied her Greenwich, Connecticut address onto the front of an envelope. And paused.

Until I sent this letter, no one knew where I was. Not my parents. Not my friends. No one. I wondered if anyone cared, if anyone had thought about me, worried about me. I sealed the envelope and realized I didn't know the ranch's address. How odd, to know where this letter was going but not where it was coming from.

Nancy sat at one of the desks in the office—on the spectrum of clutter, it ranked between Steve's tidiness and Gus's debacle—her two sons playing on the floor with staplers and hole punches.

"Hi, Ron, honey. What do you need?" she said as I walked in.

"I'm mailing a letter, and I realized I didn't know the ranch's address." On the wall above her head, a clock ticked loudly, ratcheting out the seconds.

She handed me a sheet of letterhead. "You writing your mother? You want to give a call? You can use the phone, Gus won't mind."

"Thanks. I'll stick to letters. I'm old-fashioned."

"Isn't that sweet?" One of the boys made a noise like an airplane landing and chucked the stapler across the room. "Ryan! Knock it off. If you take that to the mailbox now, it'll be picked up today. The box at the end of the drive?" She picked up a sheaf of paper and tapped it against the desk before slotting it into her "out" tray.

"I've passed it on my runs. Anything else I can take?"

"Aren't you thoughtful? You can take these two. Ryan! Chris! Go for a walk with Ron. They've been cooped up in here. Their Aunt Cassie is supposed to give them a riding lesson soon."

Outside, the two boys whooped along beside me, dodging off into the sagebrush now and then to chase after jackrabbits. The scraggly animals that skittered through the dirt looked nothing like the plump bunnies of New Hampshire. The rabbits of my childhood sat in the yard chewing clover and occasionally did damage to my mother's bean crop. These critters were lean and rangy. Instead of little hops, their bounds were low to the ground, efficient. I watched them shoot between the sockets of tan grass, the kids in hopeless pursuit.

"You ever seen a jackalope?" the older one, Ryan, asked when he returned, panting.

"Just the ones hanging up around here," I replied. When we reached the Quonset-style garage, we paused and took a good gander at the skull up there, its antlers and hollow eye sockets.

"Do the other rabbits like the jackalopes?" Ryan asked.

I considered that question for a moment as the younger boy, Chris, seized my hand and swung my arm.

"I think it's an even split. Some rabbits are afraid of them. Some are jealous. And some don't like them just because they're different."

Ryan squinted at the skull. "Yeah. Maybe that's why we never see them around here. Not alive, at least."

The boys scampered down the road. When I was their age, my brother Michael had teased me with scary stories about a massive coyote that lived in a cave on Mount Chocorua. I had nightmares about it, and the only thing I had to fuel my imagination was the howling and yipping we sometimes heard at night. I gave one last glance to the jackalope, its awkward overbite giving it a sinister look. Good thing, probably, that I hadn't grown up around here. My nightmares would have been even worse.

I posted my letter in the mailbox and then raced the two boys back toward the ranch. The little one got tired halfway back and begged for a ride, which made the larger one beg for a ride, which made me say no rides and instead we frog-hopped the last bit in—which was how Cassie found the three of us, ribbiting and squatting in the dusty road.

"Very nice. You learn how to do that at Harvard?"

"Beforehand. It's what got me in," I said as I stood up, brushing imaginary dust from my knees as I felt heat rise in my face.

She gave me a wink, the quickest snap of her eyelid. "So Nancy's got you watching her rugrats now?"

"Oh, I was just headed to the mailbox, and they came along—"

"Watch out or she'll have you at it every day." She pushed the brim of her cowboy hat up. "Then again, that might be better than working for Marc."

"Don't expect to find me ribbiting on the road with him anytime soon."

"I'd pay big bucks to see that. All right, you two squirts. Let's get to the barn. See you, kiddo."

I waved as they walked off, a little bothered by that "kiddo." I didn't want her to think of me as a child… I shook my head. What did I care? She could think of me as a baby so long as she thought I was a boy.

As I wandered down toward the bunkhouse, I could see Carl and Belva walking along the fence line below the girls' cabin. It made me miss Laurel, the easy way we once had of being together. I loved watching her sketch. I loved the way we would share a couch, our legs tangled up in the middle, each of us reading a book. I loved the long walks we'd take through Cambridge neighborhoods, and how she was either snapping pictures (she did a wonderful series on bathtub Madonnas, Virgins-on-a-half-shell) or scavenging items from the trash for "found" art.

The girls were nice, Carl was fine, even Nancy was okay… But I wanted someone who understood me. I scuffed at the dirt with my hiking boot, making myself remember Laurel's final words in our fight: She didn't understand me either.

A couple of days later, Steve and I were digging postholes near the guest cabins.

"Tonight's rodeo night," he said when we took a break. "We take all the dudes into Cody for the show. And while they're busy, a bunch of us sneak off to play basketball. There's a summer league. Carl's playing. You in?"

"Sure."

"You ever play?"

"I used to…" I left it vague, not wanting to lie but knowing he wouldn't believe me if I said I'd played for Harvard's team. Hell, he wouldn't believe me if I said I'd played for my high school's team.

He slapped me lightly on the shoulder. "All right! We'll get you in then."

I smiled, hoping I hadn't been foolish to agree. As a girl, I'd been an athlete, a classic tomboy jock: soccer, basketball, softball. All I did was play sports (and study). As a girl, I'd been strong and tall. You saw me, hair back in a no-nonsense ponytail, wearing my Harvard or Tamworth basketball sweat suit, and you had no doubt about what I was. I had no doubt about it either. Until I did.

But as soon as I came out and transitioned, I became average. At five foot ten, I wasn't short and I wasn't tall. I had puny muscles, narrow shoulders, a pencil neck—though I'd once been the girl with the third-best bench press on the team. (My friend Heather, Laurel's current roommate, had the first.) It may be the only thing I regretted about coming out and living as a guy. Not just the loss of status but having to give up playing sports, or at least renounce my identity as an athlete.

Still, a little pickup ball would be fun—definitely more fun than digging postholes.

That night, dressed in my running shorts, a tight compression top, my Bar T uniform shirt, and running shoes (I hadn't packed any other sneakers), I stood in the Cody High School gym, feeling the dry leather of a basketball for the first time in almost a year. It felt good. I took a shot while the court was still empty, listened to the slap of the ball on the floor after it had *shushed* through the net.

Carl jogged out from the locker room—I'd changed at the ranch, but the others hadn't—and then Cassie emerged from under the bleachers with the controls for the clock. I stretched on the sideline while she messed with the cords, poking the buttons with increasing violence as they refused to respond.

"Stupid piece of…" She brought her fist down on the corner of the panel. I gave a little jump at the crash, and she turned to look at me. "Aren't you going to tell me how to work this thing?"

I shrugged and looked at it. "I haven't got a clue. I'd probably just electrocute myself." As soon as I'd said it, I realized it was a really dumb thing to say. Any self-respecting guy would at least give the pretense of knowing how to fix it. Cassie was just giving me this little half-grin as if I'd said something really amusing.

I leaned over the board, staring at the mess of wires, hoping my cheeks weren't flaming red. "Oh," I said. "You didn't plug it in." I grabbed the cord and jammed it into the socket on the floor. The scoreboard bleeped to life.

"My hero," Cassie said, with only a little bit of sarcasm.

The other team came out, seven of them, and then our own three wranglers and Steve emerged. I'd never seen any of them without jeans and cowboy boots. They looked like wading birds out of the water, all long pale legs and awkward strides. J.T.'s mullet fluttered as he jogged across the court, white socks pulled high, Larry Bird style. Billy wore cut off jeans and still had his cowboy hat on—it gave him a good five inches of extra height—though when he reached the bench, he set it down reverently.

"Okay," said Steve, clapping his hands. "That's the Rimrock Ranch team over there. They've got one tall guy. Clyde, you cover him."

"I say we double-team him," said Billy.

"Sounds good."

A Rimrock fellow sauntered over. "Shirts or skins?"

"Ah, it doesn't matter," Steve said.

But I stepped forward, panicked. "Can we be shirts?" Only after I'd blurted it out did I realize how odd it was for me to make that demand. I sputtered. "I've got this top I've got to wear—"

"You Jewish?" said J.T.

"Mormon, you idiot," said Billy.

"No, it's Jewish. They wear those shirts," J.T. insisted.

"Keep talking," said Cassie. "Someday you'll say something smart. Maybe."

"Shirts it is," said Steve. "Clyde, J.T., Billy, Carl, and me will start."

In other words, I'd be on the bench, which was fine with me.

Cassie gave a blast on the horn, and the two teams lined up. I sat down, clamping my hands under my thighs, nervous until the play began.

It was like no basketball I'd ever seen—most of the players would have done better on horseback. I sat there, amused at the woeful shots (Clyde put up two air balls in a row) and Cassie's running commentary (*Sweet Jesus, did your Grandma teach you to shoot? My horse could dribble better than that!*). Rimrock's big guy landed one shot, another. Billy tried to play defense, arms waving like an air traffic controller, but the big guy just steamrollered him. J.T. managed a steal and then dribbled on his own foot. In the best play so far, Carl won a rebound and scored a layup.

Soon after, Billy wheezed over to the bench.

"You go in. I'm dying."

"Quit smoking," said Cassie, adjusting the score. Rimrock 10, Bar T 2.

I hopped up and joined the fray, jogging along the periphery until I felt warm and limber and then... I ducked in, quick, snagged the ball from a Rimrock guy, head-faked a defender, and went in for an easy layup.

Rimrock brought it down the court, and I dodged around Steve, who was huffing toward the net, swatted a pass down, and sprinted off toward the basket for another layup. They passed it in and Carl stole it, threw it to me, and I managed a fadeaway jumper over one of the Rimrock players. The ball swished through the netting. Carl gave me a smile as he jogged down the court.

For almost fourteen years, the court had been my turf. Veronica, basketball player, known to her teammates (and her brothers) as "Ronster the Monster," a regular in *The Ossipee Herald*, sometimes *The Manchester Union Leader*, and, once a season, *The Boston Globe*. When I'd quit the Harvard team this past year when I transitioned, I told my parents I wanted to focus on academics. But I'd missed basketball. I'd missed the feeling of natural competency. I hadn't realized how the weight of the basketball in my hands felt absolutely perfect until just now.

A few more possessions and I'd evened the score. Rimrock had figured me out though, so I started dishing the ball to Carl and J.T. After a while, sweaty and panting, I ran to the bench where Steve guzzled water.

"No way," said Cassie. "Get your scrawny butt back in there."

"Yep. No subs for you," Steve agreed.

Over his shoulder, I saw Marc heading toward the bench, a definite weave in his steps. He'd been in the van with us when we drove to the gym, and I wondered if he'd been drinking outside the whole time. I ran back onto the floor while Marc settled on the bench where he cheered loudly. (Well, calling it "cheering" might be a stretch. *C'mon, fuckers!* was his most common call, and I was pretty sure I heard him say, *Look at that faggot shoot*, after I'd nailed a three-pointer.)

The game was one thirty-minute period, and I managed to score a few more times—until a Rimrock guy landed an elbow in my solar plexus. I fell hard on my ass and then limped over, gasping, to the bench.

Clyde hopped up from where he'd been sitting beside Cassie with his arm around her shoulders.

"I'll cream that bastard," he said, slapping me on the back, which didn't help my breathing any.

"You deserved that, show off," said Cassie, nudging the score up by two for Rimrock. "Nice playing."

"Thanks," I grunted, taking slow breaths to stop my diaphragm from spasming. Despite the pain, her comment brought a smile to my lips.

Marc moved closer to Cassie. His eyes were glued on Clyde as the wrangler jogged across the court. "You sleeping with that jerk-off?"

"Don't let him hear you say that," she said.

"I'm not scared of him. He's stupid as shit and you shouldn't—"

"Don't you dare tell me what to do," Cassie said.

Before Marc could reply, time ran out, and she sounded the horn: Rimrock 22, Bar T 30.

"All right!" Billy shouted. "You owe us eight pitchers. We whomped you good."

The Rimrock team shambled over. "Yeah, well, you have a ringer," one of them said, pointing at me.

"He's no ringer. He's our dishwasher," said J.T.

"Dining Room Manager," I corrected, but no one listened to me.

"You don't like it, you bring your dishwasher next time," said Billy.

"Our dishwasher's a girl," the Rimrock guy responded.

Clyde laughed. "Yeah, well, we thought ours was too until tonight. Eight pitchers. Don't try to cheat us. Sunday at the Dollar."

"What's the Dollar?" asked Carl.

"Bar in Cody. Loser buys the winner a pitcher a point for the margin," Steve said.

But I was still stuck on Clyde's comment. They'd thought I was a girl? Not really, right? They'd just thought I was weak, or useless. Well, I wasn't, and I'd shown them that, right on the basketball court, which might not be as meaningful to them as on a horse... I stopped myself. Why the fuck did guys have to pump themselves up by putting women down? And since when had I become part of that system?

I sat down and started stretching my hamstrings, trying to let it go. *Keep it simple*, that was my motto. I wasn't out to change the world order.

"Let's get rolling, folks," Steve said and headed off to the locker room.

Clyde had flopped on the bench next to Cassie. "Whaddya say we head in to Gino's?" he asked her.

"Gus is going to want some help with the dudes," she replied, coiling up the clock cord.

"Aw, c'mon," Clyde said as he reached his arm out, wrapping it around her waist and pulling her toward him. Her ponytail swung forward as he kissed her, and I looked away, assiduously pretending to tie my sneakers.

But then Marc shouted, "Get your hands off her!"

"Oh for Christ's sake. Grow up," Cassie replied.

Clyde only laughed.

I risked a glance at them. Marc stepped close to Clyde, and Clyde almost lazily reached out a hand to shove him.

"You son of a—" Marc shouted as he stumbled back.

"Think twice before you finish that sentence," Clyde warned. He put his arm around Cassie and tried to draw her close, but Cassie pushed against his ribs.

"You two act like you're six years old," she said.

"He started it," Clyde said.

She rolled her eyes. "Case in point. Let's get back to the ranch."

Clyde gave Marc another hard shove, sending him sprawling. I offered Marc a hand, but he swatted my arm away.

"Go away, asshole," he said.

"That's right, you faggot," Clyde sneered at Marc. "Pick on someone you stand a chance of beating."

"Christ," Cassie said. "Can't you two leave each other alone? And leave Ron out of it?" She stepped over to Marc. "I've told you a million times, I don't want you protecting me or whatever it is you think you're doing." She grabbed his elbow and heaved him to his feet. "Get in my truck. We're going back to the ranch. Now."

"C'mon, Cassie. Let's head to—" Clyde started.

But she just shook her head and kept a firm grip on Marc's elbow. "We're leaving."

Marc followed his sister out of the gym, leveling a stare at Clyde as he walked past.

Clyde had a wicked half-smile on his face as he leaned close to me. "It drives him crazy to know that I'm fucking his sister," he said. "That's half the fun of it."

I nodded, watching Cassie half-drag Marc from the gym as he stared daggers at Clyde. There were some things—many things—I didn't think I'd ever understand about guys. But I did understand this: I definitely wanted to stay on Clyde's good side.

That night in the bunkhouse, with Carl gone to be with Belva and Marc somewhere else (probably with Cassie), I turned to a fresh page of my legal pad.

Ron's List of Guys: A Hierarchical Taxonomy

Clyde. It's not just the tattoos—anyone can get those. It's the simmering violence, the animal feel that he could snap at any time but doesn't need to. Just his presence is threat enough.

Gus. He owns the place and he knows it.

J.T. Not sure about this one, but the guy is kind of a loose canon, not afraid of doing what he wants, never tries to please anyone.

Marc. More bark than bite, but he can still bite.

Carl. He'll grow up to be something like Gus.

Billy. Too much of a follower to earn a higher rank.

I wasn't sure about Steve. He was tough in his way—he could fix anything and dig postholes all day. But he didn't have the wrangler swagger, and he could be downright gentle at times. I'd seen him blowing dish soap bubbles with Gus's kids. Was there just *one* way to be a man? A single standard of the masculine? I tapped my pen against my teeth. I didn't think so, or maybe I just didn't want to believe it because, wherever Steve fell on this list, I knew I was at the bottom.

CHAPTER FIVE

My basketball celebrity was decidedly short-lived. The next morning, it was back to packing lunches and helping Steve with maintenance. He handed me a list, which I determined to get through on my own, no asking for help. Here's what I learned over the course of the day:

1. A broken toilet can be fixed, at least sometimes, by:
   a. Someone who knows nothing about toilets
   b. Removing all parts that can be removed
   c. Cursing
   d. Praying
   e. Putting it back together

2. When removing a family of mice that has taken up residence in a couch cushion, it is best to place the cushion in a garbage bag before attempting to carry it out of a guest cabin.

3. When setting up mousetraps in a guest cabin to capture escaped mice (see item number 2 above), assure the children that they are "have-a-heart" traps, and tell the mother that they are "instant-death."

4. If the can of wasp spray suggests, "Wait until dusk before spraying the hive," follow that suggestion.

Kara heard me swearing at the wasps and came out from the next cabin over after I failed to adhere to item number 4.

"Stay inside for a minute," I called to her, running away from the pursuing hordes. I could feel my face and neck swell.

Kara watched from behind the screen as the wasps raged, calmed, and finally retreated to their nasty little nest. "You should put some ice on those, sweetie," Kara said through the screen. "And if you get milk and baking soda, I'll make you a paste to put on them, like my mom does."

"Thanks," I said, warily retrieving my stepladder from under the roiling nest. I'd be back at sunset.

By dinner time, the stings had congealed into hard red lumps, painful to the touch and itchy. I splotched spoonfuls of mashed potatoes from a massive pot into serving bowls and tried to resist the urge to scratch my face off.

"Nice pimples, Ron," said Marc. It was turkey dinner tonight, and he was grumpy from having spent his afternoon roasting and basting a bunch of birds. (Actually, he'd have been grumpy no matter how his afternoon had been spent.)

"They're wasp stings," I said as I handed the empty potato pot to Carl.

"You look diseased. The guests won't like it. Carl, you serve. Ron, you wash."

At the end of the night, I grabbed a jug of milk and a box of baking soda.

"What're you doing with that?" Marc asked suspiciously.

"Kara said she'd make a paste for my stings."

"Good excuse," he said with a snort. "I wouldn't mind Kara playing nurse with me. Maybe I'll find a wasp nest."

"I can tell you where a big one is," I replied.

Marc let the screen door snap loudly shut behind him as we all left the kitchen. "I wish I could watch the game somewhere."

"Well, drive into Wapiti. There's gotta be a sports bar there," Carl said.

"I don't have a car, dipshit. I lost my fucking license. That's half the problem. The other half is those wranglers. We're supposed to have a poker game. But those faggots canceled on me, saying there's some wrangler meeting. They're probably fucking each other up the ass. Maybe Gus will let me watch at his place for once."

He turned onto the road that led up to Gus and Nancy's house while Carl and I walked down the slope toward the bunkhouse. "That guy is screwed up," Carl said. "I've met some serious jerks, but he's the worst."

I kicked a rock and sent it skittering down the road. "I wish he'd lay off. I'm tired of being called a fag," I said, the word feeling heavy on my tongue.

"Well, get yourself a girl. Then maybe he'll pick a different word."

"I'm guessing his vocabulary's rather limited."

Carl made me wait for him to put on cologne and a fresh shirt. "Man, you should spruce up. Chicks appreciate that shit."

"I feel like my face is going to explode, I want to scratch it so bad."

"Chill out." He stared at me for moment. "I hate to agree with Marc, but it does look like a bad pimple breakout. Better dress nice to compensate."

"What's nice enough to compensate for this?" I grumbled. "I didn't bring my tuxedo out here."

He led the way to the girls' cabin, which was, unsurprisingly, much nicer than the bunkhouse, not that it took much to reach that standard. They had a living room with matching couch and loveseat, plus a TV and big framed photos on the walls: sunsets, mountain peaks. A little throw rug on the floor beneath a coffee table. And against the wall stood a mini fridge with a few boxes and bags of snacks stacked neatly on top.

I handed the baking soda and milk to Kara, who mixed them in a bowl while Carl and Belva sorted through a box of cassettes.

"This one," Belva insisted. "I'm so sad the Judds broke up, but Wynonna is great."

Carl snorted and kept digging through the cassettes. "Don't you have any Alabama tapes?"

By the time they'd settled on a selection, Kara had made a paste out of the baking soda and milk and a few other ingredients she'd gathered from the bathroom. "Sit still," she said as we sat on the couch. She held the bowl in her lap and dipped a finger into the paste.

"I can do this," I said. "You don't need to..." I leaned back a bit as her finger approached my face.

"Just sit still, honey," she said, her words soft and drawling.

She dabbed the paste onto my stings and asked, "Now, where are you from?"

"New Hampshire," I said.

"I've been to Boston once. New York twice. Otherwise I've stayed in Mississippi."

"I've never been down South." The paste felt cold, a pleasant contrast to the hot welts. From the corner of my eye, I could see Belva and Carl settle onto the love seat.

"I could never stand the cold up North," Kara said. She wiped her hands on a paper towel and leaned back against the couch, shaking her head a bit to twitch her hair away from her face.

"It's not that bad, really."

"Boys," Kara scoffed. "Why is it you always have to pretend that nothing hurts and it's never cold?"

I had to smile. "Oh, I get cold," I replied. "I guess I just figure that it doesn't do much good to complain about it."

"Hmmm. So girls complain a lot?" She leaned forward, putting her hands on her hips in (what I was pretty sure was) mock anger. At least her voice was teasing, and the purpose of her lean seemed to be to get me a little closer to the cleavage that her v-neck t-shirt revealed. But I wasn't looking. No monkey business. I'd have to thank Gus for that rule.

"I didn't say that," I protested.

"Watch out, man," Carl called. "My money's on Kara for winning this argument."

"It's not an argument," I said, resisting the urge to roll my eyes at the stupidity of this argu...discussion. "Are you in college?"

"We're all at Ole Miss. I'm studying to be a nurse."

"She studies husband hunting," Belva chimed in.

"I'm gonna be a business major," said Carl. "Make some real money."

Melissa pushed through the screen door, bringing a slightly smoky smell in with her. "I hate campfires. One of you has to do the next one. The kids got marshmallows in each other's hair and just about fell into the flames. Their parents do nothing." She collapsed on the couch. "What happened to you, Ron?" she asked, seeming to notice my face for the first time.

"Wasps," I said.

"Oh, good. I didn't think you were the kind of guy who would go for a mud mask. Do we have any wine?"

Kara stood up and took a bottle from behind a stack of magazines. "Who else wants some?"

"Could you get my nail polish too?" said Melissa from where she lay. "I hate kids. I'm going to switch my major over when I get back to school."

Kara handed Melissa cotton balls and a bottle of polish, and I passed out cups of wine.

"What's your major?" I asked Melissa. The paste was getting dry and tight on my face.

"Preschool education," she answered.

"Well, I love kids," Kara said. "Do you, Ron?"

"They're okay, I guess."

Kara gave me a skeptical look. "Do you want kids? I want a big family, at least four kids."

"Me too," Belva added just as Melissa said, "No way."

I glanced at Carl, who rolled his eyes. Sometimes, I decided, stereotypes about guys could be used to one's advantage.

"I don't know," I said. "I haven't really thought about it much. I guess what'll happen will happen."

Kara shoved my shoulder playfully. "That is such a boy thing to say."

As I set the wine bottle back on the bookshelf, I spotted a checker set. "Want a game?"

Kara and I settled on the floor, and soon, between the fumes of polish, the stench of the milk curdling on my stings, and the cheap wine, I was feeling queasy. Or maybe it was just the awkward middle-schoolness of the whole scene: Carl and Belva feeling each other up on the couch, me playing a lame board game with Kara while covered in red dots.

"Hey now," came a low voice. There was a quick knock on the screen door, and the wranglers stepped in, Clyde first, the hugeness of him magnified by the confines of the cabin.

"Come in, why don't you," Melissa said.

J.T. shuffled his feet. "You ladies want to go to town? There's dancing tonight at The Comet."

"No thanks," they chorused.

"Aw, come on. Three of us, three of you."

"Match made in heaven," snarked Melissa. "It's late, and we've got to work tomorrow."

"Some other night. We're pretty tired," Belva said. I noticed that she'd untangled herself from Carl.

"If you're so tired then how come you're hanging around with these two pussies?" said Billy. "Playing checkers? And what the hell's wrong with his face? Is that zit cream? C'mon, girlie."

"Besides," Kara said to Clyde, ignoring Billy's comment, "aren't you and Cassie seeing each other?"

"I'll show you and your friends a good time," Clyde said with a sly smile. He'd hooked his thumbs in his belt loops and rocked back on his heels. "Don't you worry none about Cassie."

"Aw, she dumped him," J.T. said and gave his almost-giggle laugh.

"Shut up, you moron." Clyde didn't let his smile slip but rammed his elbow backwards, jabbing J.T. in the stomach.

J.T. scarcely registered the hit, only took a step away before speaking again. "Well, she did. Not that I'd mind much if I was you. That chick's a grade-A bitch."

Melissa waved a tissue-laden foot at him. "Don't you come in our cabin and use profanity."

"Fuck," said Clyde. "Now you've done it, J.T., you stupid asshole."

"Out," said Melissa. "Get out."

The wranglers retreated. Billy flipped me the finger as he left. Carl just laughed.

"I guess that's their idea of being romantic," said Kara. "I prefer flowers. Just a hint."

"Duly noted," I said, pushing a checker across the board.

Steve stopped by the kitchen the next morning after breakfast. "You fellows have the afternoon off," he announced. "Tonight we're heading into the Dollar, collect those pitchers that you earned us. You coming, Carl?"

"Nah. I'm taking Belva out."

Steve nodded. "Long as you keep the romance off the ranch. Oh, Ron, before I forget…" He passed me a postcard from Jane with a picture of the Empire State Building on the front. (C'mon, Jane, you can do better than a phallic monument.)

"I think I'll catch a ride in with you to the Dollar, Steve," Marc said.

Steve shook his head. I noticed he didn't quite meet Marc's eyes when he replied, "Sorry, no can do."

"Why's that?"

"Well, my car will be full up—"

"You sure it isn't my shithead brother telling people not to drive me anywhere?" Marc demanded, his voice rising to a near-shout.

Steve brushed a hand over his freshly-trimmed flat top. "I can pick up whatever you need from town."

"Get out of my kitchen," Marc said.

Carl and I exchanged a look, clearly sharing the same senti-ment: This was not a morning to be with Marc.

"You need help, Steve?" I asked. "Carl and I finished the mopping up."

Steve must have caught the desperation in my voice. "Sure, boys. I got some gravel to spread on the road."

As soon as the gravel was done, I took my lunch up into the woods past the river, settling on the bank of a little creek to read Jane's postcard.

Dear Ron,

Oh. My. God. Wyoming? What are you thinking? Come back. The city's fun. I've been spending a night or two a week on the couch at Laurel and Heather's. The commute's such a pain. I know the last few weeks have been tough, but there's nothing you have to prove. Stay in touch. Don't make yourself miserable.

Love,
Jane

Nothing I had to prove? The postcard, brief as it was, brought up a whole host of emotions that I'd been doing my best to repress. (I consider repression a hobby of mine.) I had plenty to prove. Everyone, even those who said they accepted me as transgender, didn't quite treat me like a guy, Jane included. To Jane, to Laurel, it was like I could only be a guy with a footnote attached to that term. Guy with past as girl. Guy who was socialized as a young woman. Guy who will never really be a guy. And how had my mom put it? Oh yes: *You're sick, Veronica. You need help.*

I didn't need help. I didn't need to run back to safety. I needed just to live as I was. That's all.

I lay back on the needle-strewn ground and stared up at the boughs above. Out here, I was Ron. A young man. Treated the same as Carl, more or less. Back in the East, everyone saw me as transgender. Someone who used to be a girl. I couldn't get rid of that. Out here, I could be who I was, right? Right. It was just my own insecurity that kept me wondering if I was matching up to standards. And I'd get over that. The longer I stayed out here, the more I would get comfortable with masculinity, with life in the West. Real life, not the coddled and over-intellectualized swirl of the East Coast. Out here, things were what they were.

I sat up and flicked a pine needle into the creek, watching as the current carried it away. Then I stood and followed the creek toward the top of the slope where the water disappeared in a pile of rocks as if the earth had sucked it down. Only then did I look around—I'd been fixated on the twist of water—and realize the vastness of the place about me. Without the line of the creek to walk by, I had no bearings. Any direction was all directions.

I hiked out above the timberline so that I could see the highway and the Fork below me, then I unfolded the free map and tried to orient myself. The map showed the North Fork River, a pale blue ribbon. A line of darker blue snaked its way across the landscape, marking the Continental Divide, a term I'd have to look up in my field guide. But the map was meant only for tourist families getting from point of interest A, to ice cream in town, to point of interest B. Triangles indicated a few major mountain peaks, but the ground where I stood was an undifferentiated swath of green. "Not to scale," the bottom margin noted. As if I hadn't already known that.

When I eventually wove my way down the slope, the ranch was deserted in the slanting late afternoon sun. I pulled open the door to the bunkhouse, tiptoeing inside, thinking: *Please be asleep, please be asleep.* I just wanted a quick shower and a fresh set of clothes; I didn't want to listen to Marc's complaints. As I eased the door shut, I heard the telltale sound of Marc's snores. Thank god.

I grabbed a towel, clean boxers, and a t-shirt, as well as a fresh compression shirt, and quietly made my way into the bathroom. The blast of hot water felt good. I did my best thinking (and made my best lists) in the shower. Tonight's was simple:

Go to the Silver Dollar
Don't make a fool of myself
Avoid Marc

That should do it. I soaped up again, wondering why I was wondering whether Cassie would be at the bar tonight too.

Then all of a sudden: "That you in there, Ron?"

Fuck. Number three was shot to hell. "Yeah," I called back. Then I heard the click of the bathroom door. Fuck again.

"Carl leave already?" Marc asked.

"Yeah." Now I heard the steady stream of piss followed by a flush. I rinsed off the last of the soap and waited under the shower. Should I turn it off and try to grab my towel? No, better just to stay in here.

"When you go to town, get me a bottle of Jack Daniel's."

"I can't, Marc. I'm underage."

"Well, fucking figure it out." He paused. "You shouldn't go to a bar if you're underage. Gus wouldn't be happy if he knew."

I stood there behind the shower curtain, the water drifting toward lukewarm. "Yeah, okay. I'm not going to drink anything. Steve said I could go."

"Fucking Steve. You gonna come out of there or what?"

"Yeah, in a second." I clenched my throat tight, trying to keep any quiver out of my voice. I wasn't afraid. I was just annoyed.

"What is it? You don't want me to see your tiny dick or something?"

Okay. A little afraid.

"You're such a pussy faggot," Marc went on. "*Oooh, I go to Harvard. Oooh, the girls think I'm cute.*" His voice grew closer, and I almost grabbed the shower curtain in a desperate attempt to cover myself. "This your towel? Maybe I'll take it, and your clothes too, huh?"

"Leave my stuff alone," I said.

"Get me a bottle of Jack Daniel's."

"Okay, fine, I will." Anything to get him to leave.

I waited until I heard the click of the bathroom door to peer around the edge of the curtain. There I saw that he'd balled up my clothes and towel and thrown them on the floor. I turned the shower off, dashed over, and grabbed them, drying off quickly and then pulling my boxers on before squirming my way into the compression shirt—at least he hadn't noticed that. As I stepped out of the bathroom, I heard the screen door snap shut then Marc's steps crunching away on the gravel. Thank God.

I buried Jane's postcard deep in the backpack under my bed. Not that she'd used the word "transgender," but I didn't want anyone to wonder about why I would be miserable here. I didn't want anyone to wonder about anything. I held my breath for a moment, making sure that Marc's footsteps had faded away entirely, then let my breath out in a slow sigh. Everything was fine. Everything was in its proper place. I unfolded the nearly useless tourist map on my bed and took the field guide out, thumbing through the index.

"Continental Divide." *Hydrological,* the entry began. Always nice to learn a new word. But what was it? *An imaginary line.*

That made me laugh because there it was in bold, bright blue on this map.

But then again, maps are just representations of the human mind, of how we understand the world. Maps aren't real; the land is. It's just that maps are useful for showing us what we can't see.

The field guide rambled on for a couple of pages. I toweled my hair dry and read through them twice. Apparently, to the west of the Divide, all water ran toward the Pacific. To the east, it headed for the Atlantic. The basic concept was simple, but the why of it was beyond me. I gave the tourist map one more chance, tracing that thick blue vertical line out of Montana and down toward Cody.

But there weren't enough details to make things clear. I couldn't tell which side I was on.

CHAPTER SIX

The Silver Dollar rested on the outer fringe of Cody. Twangy country music billowed out on air thick with popcorn fumes as the four of us—Clyde, Billy, J.T., and I—entered. Steve had ended up staying at the ranch to finish some paperwork, which made me nervous. Steve had the ability to calm people down. I'd seen him do it with Gus and Marc, I'd seen him manage Clyde and J.T. as well, and I feared I was going to miss his presence tonight. I'd ridden to town in the crew cab of Clyde's pickup truck instead, crammed in there with Billy, wondering why he smelled so minty until he spat a line of brown juice out the window.

Clyde barreled in like a jacked-up orangutan. Hair curled out from the V of his shirt—normally he kept it buttoned all the way up at the ranch—his chest seemed to be covered in a veritable pelt of brown-orange hair, resembling a rather unfortunate shag carpet my parents had installed in the den in 1972, the year I was born. (It, unlike me, was still a welcome presence in my parent's house.)

"There they are." Clyde pointed across the room. "Eight!" he bellowed, and the bar patrons all turned to stare.

We waded across the floor, and J.T. hauled over chairs and another table as Billy began introductions of the five Rimrock guys.

"That there's Randy. You want to watch out for him. He cheats like a—"

"Aw, shut up, you runt."

Billy cupped an ear. "Whaddya call me?" A waitress interrupted. I suspected her timing was professionally honed. "Hi, fellows."

"Hi, Stacy," said one of the Rimrock guys.

"What'll it be?"

"Eight pitchers," crowed Clyde. Sitting next to him, I eyed the tattoos on his forearm, anything to take my mind off the whiskey that Marc would demand upon my return. The largest tattoo, at least that I could see, was a skull wreathed with flames. Interesting.

Stacy nodded like a fourth grade teacher with a hyperactive boy on her hands. "Oh-kay. And who will be paying for these eight pitchers?"

"They are!" shouted Billy and J.T., pointing at the Rimrock team.

"All-righty. Eight on Rimrock Ranch."

"The losers," said J.T.

Stacy jerked her thumb at me. "I'm not running a kindergarten. He's got to go."

"Aw, Ron's a good guy. He looks little, but it's just 'cause he's an Easterner. They grow them all stunted out there," J.T. said.

"You from the East too, Billy?" a Rimrock guy shouted.

"Shut your mouth," Billy snapped.

Stacy rolled her eyes in what appeared to be a practiced move. "Fine," she said. "But you're taking the blame if there's a problem."

"There won't be a problem," said Clyde.

The beer came, and then, into what lacunae remained on the table, Stacy deposited bowls of hot, salty popcorn. Ten grubby paws dug in.

"Aw shit, here comes Cassie," said Clyde.

I turned toward the door and saw her navigating the sprawl of tables and chairs. She had her hair pulled back in a ponytail, just a wisp of it hanging loose across her forehead. It made me smile to see, and out of some subconscious instinct, I reached up to curl my own hair behind my ear, surprised for a moment to find it close-shorn. Eighteen years of long hair… I wondered when I'd lose that habit.

"Evening, gentlemen. Figured I'd claim a cup since I kept the clock," Cassie said as she drew near the table, standing beside my chair. She wore blue jeans and a plaid shirt, the sleeves rolled up to show her tan forearms. "Your barn door's open, J.T."

"Haven't been near the barn," he said.

"Your zipper, moron."

"Oh." He reached down to his fly. "Nice to know where you're looking, Cassie."

"At your brains, dumbass."

Clyde stood up and offered her his chair. "You gonna stay around for dancing tonight?"

"Give it a rest, all right?" she replied. "It's over." She walked past him and settled in a chair next to me.

A Rimrock guy leaned over the table toward her. "You oughta come out to our ranch sometime, we got a couple of horses you—"

Clyde stood up, shoving his chair back. "How about you shut up before I break your teeth?"

"Easy, there," said another Rimrock guy.

"Stop trying to pick her up then," Clyde said.

"Go fuck yourself," said the first Rimrock guy. He and his buddies grabbed a couple pitchers of beer and headed to another table.

"What'd you say?" Clyde called after them.

Cassie leaned back in her chair and looked up at Clyde. From this close, I could see the freckles on her nose and cheeks and smell something like hay or freshly-cut grass.

I redirected my gaze to my beer glass, thinking that I really didn't want to drink much. The Harvard basketball team had been big on parties (off-season only), and even then, with girls I knew well, I hadn't liked the out-of-control feeling that alcohol gave me. I already felt out of control enough with these wranglers.

"I'm not interested in your pissing contests," Cassie said. "We're done. Got it?"

"No need to be such a bitch," Clyde said. He took a couple swallows of beer. "Not like you got a line of guys waiting for you."

Cassie stared at him. "It should tell you something that I'd rather be alone than be with you. So quit acting like such a prick."

Clyde set his beer glass down with a thud. "I've gotta piss," he said and stalked away.

Billy jumped up and followed after him with a quick, "Me too."

Cassie gave me a wink. "And they say girls are always going to the bathrooms in pairs."

"Aw, you know Billy," J.T. drawled. "Anywhere Clyde goes, he's the first to follow." He refilled everyone's glasses and raised his mug to me in a toast. "First victory."

I drank timidly (keeping an eye on Stacy's whereabouts), wishing that Steve was there as a buffer between the wranglers and me. Clyde had looked angry enough to bust the place up. And on top of that, I still had to figure out what I was going to do about Marc's whiskey.

"Hey, Cassie," J.T. said at last, "why didn't you bring the other girls, Karissa and stuff?"

"Kara and Melissa, you mean?" Cassie cocked one eyebrow.

"Yeah, them."

"Well, Belva's with Carl. And Kara and Melissa wanted to go see some movie... *Sister Act*? Per your request, I did invite them along, but they made it, uh, clear that they preferred going to the cinema," replied Cassie, giving me a quick wiggle of her eyebrows. She looked so damn good, and for a moment that was enough to make me happy, but then I wondered about her implication: Was I in on the joke because I was smarter than J.T.? Because I wasn't a wrangler? Or because she saw me as more feminine?

I took a gulp of beer to hide my unease. Clyde had returned to his chair, tipping it back on two legs and staring at Cassie. I hoped he hadn't seen the wiggle of the eyebrows. Billy sat down beside him and lifted his beer.

"Yeah, well, you tell me this," J.T. said. "How come the girls like Carl and Ron more than us?"

"I mean, look at him." Billy pointed at me, leaning across the table. "What's he got that I don't?"

"He's right about their age," Cassie said.

"Girls like older men," said J.T.

"Bet you heard that from an older man."

"How'd you know?"

"What else? Uh, maybe Ron and Carl don't try to feel them up in the cab of a pickup truck, or—"

"Did she tell you I did that?" J.T. demanded. "'Cause I only put my hand on her thigh."

"Oh god. Spare me the details. For Christ's sake. They like Ron and Carl because they probably bother to get to know them. Here's a quiz." She leveled her gaze at J.T. "What's the name of the girl you felt up in your truck?"

"Carla," he said.

"Woo, boy," said Billy. "Even I know that's wrong."

"Well, damn. I'm close, aren't I?"

Cassie turned to me. "Ron. What do you know about Kara, aka Carla, aka Karissa?"

"She goes to Ole Miss, she's studying to be a nurse, she loves Wyoming but wants to settle in Mississippi, and her favorite movie is *Gone with the Wind*." I didn't know that last bit, but it seemed like a good guess.

"Shit. Are you two engaged?" J.T. said.

"I rest my case," said Cassie.

I felt heat rising to my face. Partly the beer, partly the realization that I'd just alienated myself. Maybe Carl would have known that much about Belva, or maybe he was just as bad as J.T. But even if he had known that much, he would have been smart enough not to go spouting off in front of the wranglers.

"Been meaning to talk to you about that bay—you rode him yesterday, didn't you?" Billy asked Cassie.

Within two seconds, they were immersed in horse minutiae with even Clyde joining in, laughing at something J.T. had said. At the back of the room, a man with a guitar and a woman with a fiddle stepped up on a small platform and started checking microphones.

"Test, one, two..."

Dozens of people stood up. Clyde grabbed the empty pitchers in his massive hands and lurched toward the bar as J.T. and Billy shoved the table against the wall, kicking chairs out of the way.

"If you're so good with the gals," J.T. said, leaning toward me with his beery breath, "go get some to dance with us." He gave me a shove in the small of my back, directing me toward a table of women.

Cassie stood and stretched with feline nonchalance. "Ask 'em yourself, J.T. You could use a little practice in the art of conversation. I'm going to take Ron back to the ranch."

J.T. smirked. "Yeah, I guess it's his bedtime, isn't it?"

Cassie put her hand on my shoulder. "Let's go, kiddo."

I let her steer me out of the bar, partly embarrassed to be rescued by her, partly grateful to be extracted, and partly dreading my outstanding predicament. How was I going to get Marc his damn whiskey? I didn't even know where the liquor store was in Cody, not that they'd sell to me if I did. Out in the parking lot, she unlocked the door of her maroon Jeep Comanche.

"Just shove that shit on the floor," Cassie instructed, headed for the driver's side.

I pushed the mélange of coffee cups, screwdrivers, and scrunched up paper—along with a mysterious box labeled Sweet Lumps—onto the floor and sat down.

"Whew. Those three. It's worse than babysitting Nancy's brats. I swear, J.T. is more than a decade older than you, but he behaves like he's thirteen."

"My brother likes to tease me that I was born forty years old," I said. It was one of Michael's favorite jokes.

Cassie eyed me appraisingly. "He might be right. I am surprised they served you in there though." A volley of shouts came from the bar, audible over the country music. "Good thing we left. Those three have more balls than brains."

"A six to three ratio, I'd guess."

She turned the key and the engine coughed. "You want to be a wrangler now that you're working on a ranch?"

"God no." I hadn't even thought about it. Though I guess I'd envied them, idly, in the way one might envy a golden retriever with a tennis ball or a cat by the fire. I wanted to have them accept me, but I didn't need to be exactly like them. They were jerks, and they seemed to revel in that. I wanted some of what they had—a bit of the swagger, a share of the ease—but I didn't want the whole package.

"First," I went on, "I can't ride a horse for a darn. Second—"

"You keep your brain in your head, not between your legs." She steered the Comanche onto Cody's main drive. "About riding, we can fix that if you want. Now, dinner." She pulled into the Burger King drive-thru. "Burger, fries, Coke," she said into the intercom, then lifted her chin at me.

"Same."

We inched forward. Three pickup trucks were in line ahead of us. I decided to go for it. "Um, is there a liquor store on the way back to the ranch?"

Cassie shot me a skeptical look. "What do you need at a liquor store?"

"A bottle of Jack Daniel's."

"Oh Christ." She rolled her eyes and eased the truck a little ahead. "Has Marc been giving you a hard time?"

"Not really," I said. "I mean, he's mostly fine in the kitchen. It's just that—" I didn't want to complain. I didn't want to seem weak.

"Let me guess. He's godawful in the morning when he's hungover. And he's fine when he's drunk, until he drinks too much and gets angry. And the worst is when he's sober and can't get his hands on any liquor." She tapped her fingers on the steering wheel, then leaned out the window. "Jesus. What'd they order? Twenty well-done burgers?" She inched the truck along.

"You've described him pretty accurately," I said.

She shook her head. "If he'd just try to get clean... Our father drank himself to death, pretty much. You'd think Marc would've learned, but he doesn't care. I should just let him pickle himself."

"He isn't that bad," I said.

Cassie gave a little chuckle. "You don't need to pretend. I know he's a bully. He's over-protective of me and a total asshole to everyone else. He's had a chip on his shoulder ever since he was young. My father... Well, it's not like any one of us kids was a real good scholar or anything, but my father made it clear he thought Marc was dumb as a box of rocks, especially when he opted for culinary school over college. So I'm guessing Marc's not much of a fan of Harvard students."

"Could be," I mumbled. I felt embarrassed about ratting on Marc but also relieved that maybe it was that simple: He was a drunk, and he was mean, and he resented me for my education. It had nothing to do with me seeming less like a guy. "I can deal with it," I said.

"You tell him if he wants a bottle of Jack Daniel's, he can talk to me." She revved the engine and at last pulled up to the serving window.

"Okay," I replied, feeling my stomach drop. That would not go over well with Marc.

The cashier handed Cassie the food and I sorted it out.

"You want me to hold your burger while you drive?" I asked as Cassie squeezed a ketchup packet on her fries.

"I can hold my own," she said. I had no doubt about that, really. Coke between her legs, burger in one hand, fries leaning against her thighs, she charted our course onto the North Fork Highway. "So, why'd you come out West?"

"Just wanted to try something new. I've lived my whole life on the East Coast."

"Uh-huh. And why Wyoming, why Cody?"

I shoved some fries in my mouth and tried to decide on what truth I would tell. "Just flipped a coin to figure out where to get off the bus, then went to find a job, and Gus found me."

Cassie crumpled up her burger wrapper and threw it behind her seat. "Doesn't seem like your style."

My style? How would she know my style? I wasn't even sure *I* knew my style. "What do you mean?"

"Every day you go out for a run, every day you go out for a hike up the Fork. When I'm down at the barn, I see you sitting out in front of the bunkhouse, reading and writing. You just seem... methodical."

"I didn't realize I was so boring."

"I didn't say 'boring.' There's plenty of interesting things about you. Like the other night. When you were on the court, you lost that anxious look you're always carrying around. You looked so focused. And, damn, can you play. I don't think you're boring at all."

I could feel myself blushing, embarrassed that I was so easy to read. "I haven't played basketball for a long time. I've missed it. I didn't even realize how much until I got on the court."

"I could tell, watching you. It was like when you're a kid, and you catch a frog, and finally at the end of the day you let the poor thing go, and it hops for freedom like you wouldn't believe. Plops back into that pond. You looked kinda like that frog."

"Good to know."

"A cute frog, mind you. Are you liking it out here?"

That word, "cute," caught me by surprise, and I felt a flush rise up my neck as I tried to remember any of the words she had said after "cute." "Uh, it still feels...unreal. Almost like I'm at a theme park or on vacation." That wasn't quite accurate, but I didn't feel like I could explain it to her. How this place felt like a goal, like a race to be won. I didn't want it to feel that way. I wanted it to feel normal. Maybe by the end of the summer, it would just be where I lived.

"Wyoming isn't a playground, though the tourists seem to think it is." Cassie took a sip of her Coke. "But I guess I under-stand. Aren't you on vacation from school?"

"Well, kind of. I don't mean I feel like a tourist, just that... You know how when you go on vacation and none of the conventions or habits or expectations of your regular life apply? That's how I feel." I searched around for a way to redirect the conversation and settled on taking a big bite of my burger. I stared out the window as I chewed. We'd long ago blown past the Wapiti Post Office, and I once again had no idea where we were. Somewhat close to the ranch. That's all I knew. "Why'd you come out West? Did Gus convince you?" I asked, steering the topic into safer waters and also focusing the conversation on her, which (as Carl would say) chicks dig.

"Other way around. I worked summers on a ranch near here when I was in college and convinced Gus that he should think about running a dude ranch. Timing turned out great. Gus was working some terrible job, selling copy machines or something."

"I can't imagine that."

"Yeah, he didn't take much convincing. He's always had an adventurous side to him. Plus, he likes being his own boss. When he was a kid, he spent half his time planning to run away, half his time running away, and the other half getting in trouble for it. And I know that's three halves, so don't correct me, buster."

"Wouldn't dream of it."

"That's probably the way me and Gus are most similar. I couldn't wait to get away from Jersey. Right after I graduated college, our grandmother died, left me and Gus a good bit of money, and we both ploughed it right into the ranch."

"What about Marc?"

"Let's just say he'd gotten on Granny's bad side long ago."

She let her foot off the accelerator, and we bumped off the paved road and over the cattle guard, pulling to a stop in front of the ranch's garage.

"It's been really nice talking with you," I said. "Thanks for the ride." As I opened the truck door, I remembered that Marc would be waiting for me in the bunkhouse.

Cassie hopped out as well. "I'll walk you down." As we passed by the barn, she said, "Anytime you want to get on a horse, you let me know."

"I haven't ridden in years. Those horses would toss me right off."

"I'll give you some pointers."

"That'd be nice," I said, knowing I sounded lame, but I was too coiled with tension about Marc to say something cooler.

We'd reached the bunkhouse. Inside, Marc sat with his feet up on the plaid couch, clipping his toenails. I made a mental note never to sit there again.

Before I could say anything, Cassie had brushed past me and pushed Marc's feet off the couch. "You trying to get Ron arrested? Sending him to buy you liquor?"

"Did you fucking tell her?" Marc shouted, starting to stand up from the couch. "What are you doing talking to her anyway? Didn't I tell you to stay away from—"

Cassie caught him with an arm across his chest, and he fell back against the cushions. "Don't pull that shit, Marc. He did what you told him to, but I saw the bottle on the ride home. The last thing in the world you need is whiskey." I tried to keep the surprise off my face as I registered her lie.

"I'm dying here, Cassie. Gus has me living with these two faggots—"

She shook her head. "Quit whining. You know why you're here. Gus'll fire you if you keep causing problems. Put some shoes on your ugly feet and come up to my place. We'll have hot chocolate and watch TV and give Ron some peace." She gave me a wink and a quick smile, then prodded her brother out the door.

Marc turned around as the door slapped shut and spoke to me through the mesh. "Don't fucking touch any of my stuff. I mean it."

I held up my hands in mock surrender.

Alone in the bunkhouse, I sat reading the field guide under the light of an antler lamp, trying once again to understand the Continental Divide. It was like a barrier, but not. It kind of followed the highest ridges and summits, but not exactly. It seemed to me that the Continental Divide was yet another case where we humans observed some natural phenomenon—the water flowed west here and east there—and felt the need to come up with an explanation, as in the fashion of myths. Or maybe I just hadn't paid enough attention in physics.

I snapped the field guide shut, not sleepy at all. The drive with Cassie had left me hungry for more conversation. I liked her. I turned the antler lamp off, plunging the bunkhouse into near-darkness. I liked her. And not just as a friend. When she put her hand on my shoulder in the bar, when she gave me those winks… Shit. I wasn't supposed to get involved with anyone. That wasn't part of the plan. Not that my plan was super specific (i.e., head West, live as a man). I just knew that living as a man was contingent on my not getting intimate with anyone. And I could survive that way, at least for a while. It was just that Cassie… I hadn't felt like this since I'd first met Laurel, this rubbery helpless feeling of a total crush.

Well, thinking about her wasn't going to help at all. Better to get my mind *off* of her. I shuffled from the front room over to my bed and switched on the lamp there. I had made a to-do list (of course I had) earlier in the day. Top of the list: *Write to Michael.* If I wasn't going to sleep, I should be productive. So I settled myself on top of my bed and propped the yellow pad against my knees.

Michael was the second youngest of my older brothers. (I was closest to him and Brian, who was nearest to me in age, but Brian was in his second year of law school and working for some firm this summer, so I had no idea what his address was.) Mike and I had been tight. He was often my babysitter when I was little. He was old enough to drive me around to basketball games when I was in elementary school and he was in high school. Now he was an accountant in Manchester, New Hampshire. I'd last seen him at…Thanksgiving? It seemed so long ago. And yet, I couldn't imagine when I would see him next, when there would be another family holiday where I'd be welcome. What a mess I'd made.

Dear Michael,

I don't know what, if anything, you've heard from Mom and Dad. And probably I should have written this letter a while ago. So I apologize and hope you'll keep an open mind.

You know I've always trusted you and relied on you for advice. You were the first family member I came out to as a lesbian—and I only ever came out to you and Brian. It meant so much to me that you accepted my identity (that you knew me well enough not to be too surprised) and that you agreed to keep it from Mom and Dad. You should have probably been the first person I came out to this time as well, but I went to Mom and Dad instead.

You see, I'm transgender. I'd just started to come to terms with this when I last saw you at Thanksgiving. Not long after that, I made the transition: I cut my hair short, changed my name to Ron, and asked everyone to refer to me as "he." I'm more comfortable as a guy. In fact, it felt so right to me that I was sure everyone else would understand too. But coming out to Mom and Dad didn't go well. I'm guessing that they've already told you, but they kicked me out. I have to take a year off from Harvard now since Dad won't cover the tuition or co-sign for loans, and the college requires that I prove I'm independent before they'll redo my financial aid package. But that's not what upsets me. I thought parental love was pretty much unconditional. Maybe I'm naïve.

I'm out here in Wyoming, getting a chance to live as myself where no one knows me.

I hope you can accept me as your brother. I know this is strange and maybe confusing. Ask me any questions you want. Just don't push me away.

Love,

Ron

CHAPTER SEVEN

At six the next morning, Marc still wasn't in the kitchen. Carl and I had crept out of the bunkhouse while Marc snored on, his alarm clock beeping shrilly, but that wasn't uncommon. Usually, however, Marc made it to the kitchen by six, surly and sour, but present. With one eye on the door, I told Carl about the Dollar and what Cassie had said to Marc.

"She actually thinks Gus would fire him?" Carl said.

"Yeah. Maybe. Should we go wake him up?" I asked, glancing at the clock.

"I'm not getting close to him," Carl replied. "Can you cook the eggs?"

I handled the sandwiches and then started scrambling eggs while Carl got the dining room ready. I'd just filled the last platter with bacon when Gus pushed through the doors.

"Where's Marc?" he asked.

I stared at Carl, who met my eyes, then glanced at Gus, shrugging.

The kitchen flapped shut with a bang, making me jump. I turned to see Marc, face flushed with exertion or anger. "Why didn't you wake me up, you fuckers?" he shouted.

"Keep it down," Gus said, stepping close to his brother. "The dudes are out there."

"They were supposed to wake me up," Marc protested.

Gus looked at Carl and me.

"We tried, man," Carl said. "We couldn't get you out of bed. Right, Ron?"

I nodded. It was true enough.

"You know who you smell like?" Gus leaned in, his face close to his brother. "You smell like Dad used to. Is that what you want?"

"Get off me." Marc gave Gus a shove. "You know what? I quit. I don't need this job, and I don't need you looking—"

"Yeah? And where are you going to go? You can't go back to Jersey. And you're supposed to be employed. If you aren't, your next hearing is going to be—"

"Just shut the fuck up."

"Do your job. Stay off the booze." Gus jabbed a finger into Marc's chest and then pivoted around, pushing through the swinging door and into the dining room.

The rest of the meal was spent sprinting out of the kitchen with food and into the kitchen with dirty dishes, dodging a soapy sponge that Marc hurled at me and letting his insults land unanswered. At long last, he sulked into the storage room. Carl high-fived me. "Maybe he'll be out on his ass soon."

Some small, empathetic part of me tried to chirp up that Marc had some serious issues and that it wasn't nice to wish bad things on other people. But I squashed that empathy down and gave Carl a grin. "We can hope."

Steve came in after the dishes were done. "The delivery truck's here. Carl, you unload. Ron, the stables need to be cleaned. And Marc, the two of us need to talk."

At the barn, I gathered my weapons—pitchfork, shovel, wheelbarrow, broom—and first tended to the dung heap (or what my medieval studies professor would call "the middens") before venturing down the dusty, dim aisle of horse stalls. There was something truly medieval about this whole place. I mean, how much had the world of horses changed since then? Saddles and stirrups and all these strips of leather. Jane could probably write a dissertation on the gendered implications of sitting astride another beast while bedecked in—

"You want to take that ride, kiddo?" Cassie's voice broke me from my reverie. I must have jolted a foot in the air.

"I thought you were out with the dudes," I said.

She lifted the cowboy hat from her head, wiped her forehead against her sleeve, then settled the hat again. "Nancy wants me to give her squirts riding lessons," Cassie replied. "But the two of us have got time for a short ride before the rugrats show up."

She didn't wait for me to answer, just went into the tack room and emerged with a saddle. I watched her walk past me and down the aisle. Watched her ponytail swing from side to side, brushing against her light blue shirt, just below the collar. Watched her hips, how they moved just a little...

"You gonna finish cleaning that stall and give me a hand?" She turned her head over her shoulder to peer back at me. I couldn't quite leap into action quickly enough to cover the fact that I'd been staring. Shit. I'd been staring. *Get a grip, Ron.* I plunged my pitchfork into the dung and sawdust. Cassie gave a peal of laughter, nice-sounding though. Not the mean bark I often heard from Marc.

I emptied the last wheelbarrow of manure, and by the time I had the pitchfork put away, she'd saddled two horses.

"You know how to get on?" she asked.

"Theoretically," I muttered, trying to channel memories of my horseback riding experience. When I was ten years old, I learned to ride. (Double digit gifts for Bancroft boys = .22 rifle. For girls—that is, me—riding lessons.) My teacher was Mrs. Thorndike, the proprietress of Tamworth Stables who smoked Swisher Sweets. (*Keeps the flies away*, she told me.) Now, almost a decade later, I put into motion her instructions on how to mount:

Hold the reins, not too tight. Grab the edge of the saddle, near the front.

Left foot in the stirrup.

Step up, swing the right leg over.

Silently curse the horse for shuffling as you settle, landing the saddle horn in your crotch.

"Okay there?" Cassie smirked.

"Fine." No family jewels to damage.

She swung onto her own mount, a dark brown horse with a black mane and tail. Mine was more red-chestnut with a splash of white on its nose and two white socks. "Let's go," she said.

As we ambled out of the barn, I had a moment of panic. What if Marc saw me riding off with Cassie? But the task of staying upright in the saddle soon occupied all my mental energy. Her horse led the way through the gate, across the bridge, and up the trail. A short climb, during which I found myself clutching the horn to stay in the saddle after nearly dropping the reins, and we emerged from the pines into a level plain of scrub.

Cassie twisted around to look back at me. "So you've ridden before but English saddle, I'm guessing. Let's see you make the horse walk."

I jabbed the horse with my heels, but it didn't budge. *C'mon.* I willed it to move. *You were walking just fine a moment ago.* I flapped the reins.

"Use your knees and thighs. Let the horse know you're in control."

Amazingly, the horse moved when I squeezed its sides, and as I lurched forward, I dredged up more of Mrs. Thorndike's pearls of wisdom. Straight back, hands front, thumbs along the reins, flipped over, like so, heels down. The horse shook its head, bit jangling as if it disagreed with me. Deciding we'd gone far enough, I yanked one rein to turn it around.

Cassie sidled her horse next to mine. "You are an Easterner," she said, clearly amused. "You ride all stiff, but that doesn't work on a Western saddle. Straighten those legs, like you're standing in the stirrups, but a little out in front of you. And drop your shoulders. Your hands can rest lightly on the horn." She reached over to flip the reins in my hands and gave my shoulder a playful shake. The warmth of that touch, even though it was just for a moment, went right through me. "Relax."

"I'm no good at relaxing." I was especially no good at relaxing when someone was staring at me. And really especially no good at relaxing when that person staring at me happened to be good looking and… I stopped my thoughts short. Concentrate on the riding, Ron.

She started her horse forward, and mine trailed dutifully along. *Follower.* "Better," Cassie said as she turned around to watch. "You want to feel the horse move and match that. Communicate with your knees and thighs, not your feet and hands. Unless it's an emergency." I lurched across the basin, and over the scents of horse and leather, I breathed in sage and the sharp resin of pine. "Ready to trot?"

"Sure." I squeezed with my thighs. Dug my heels in. Gave a crisp command: "Trot." I tried to feel masterful and convey that mastery. My horse trudged along. A sidelong glance showed a merry grin playing across Cassie's face. I kicked again. "Ambulate."

"'Ambulate'? That horse doesn't go to Harvard. Just give a little click." She snapped her tongue against the roof of her mouth, and her horse jogged off.

"Could you have told me that earlier?" I muttered, then clucked my tongue, and the chestnut picked up the pace. Ahead of me, Cassie trotted with ease. Though the horse's legs moved quickly, her own body hardly swayed at all. I, on the other hand, bounced all over, losing a stirrup and leaning precariously to gain it back.

At last, Cassie pulled to a stop and waved for me to keep going, watching me as I trotted past. "Straighten your legs out."

I did, trying to stand in the stirrups like she'd suggested. It was better. I didn't bounce around so much.

"And don't let your feet flap," she said, drawing even with me and putting a hand on my forearm. "Relax your arms. You're confusing the horse. If you kick with your heels and pull with your hands, it's like you're asking to stop and go at the same time. The horse doesn't know what you want."

That makes two of us, I thought. I wanted Cassie to keep her hand on my arm, and I wanted to run away. Well, I didn't *want* that, but I thought it might be safer. I squeezed my legs tighter, holding my feet still, and dropped my shoulders.

"And walk," Cassie said. The horses magically obeyed. "There's a nice lookout over here."

She led the horses to the edge of a promontory. High enough and exposed enough to reveal a view of the ridges and mountains beyond. One of those ridgelines was America's spine, the Continental Divide. According to the guidebook, it more or less followed the highest peaks and ridges, but from here, I couldn't see that any ridge was that much higher than the others. It could be the jagged line off in the purple-blue distance that was highest. Or it could be the dun-colored peaks that were closer to hand. That's the trouble with being a person with only a single perspective. How things look depends on where you stand.

"It's amazing," I said after a moment. "Even though we've been riding toward the mountains, they don't seem any closer. If anything, they seem farther away." I shifted my gaze to the valley, a twist of river slicing through. "I guess it's good to have some things always off in the distance."

"Sure," she said. "Wanting something's always more fun than getting it. Well, usually. There are some exceptions."

"What's that supposed to mean?" I kept my eyes fixed on the mountains. They were fascinating. Really. Quite fascinating.

"I think you can guess, Mr. Harvard."

I heard the teasing tone in her voice. The gentle wryness. Yeah, I could guess. I wrenched my stare away from the landscape. Cassie's face was shaded by the brim of her cowboy hat, so I couldn't see her eyes clearly. That made it a little easier.

"It can be tough to want something if you're not supposed to have it," I said.

"What're you, a monk or something?" She laughed and gave me a playful shove on the shoulder, her hand lingering just a moment longer than it had to. I tried to match her laugh, but it was hard to seem at ease. Every muscle in my body had tensed up, and I couldn't blame the riding for that.

"I hadn't considered that as a career path. No, I meant that Steve said that it was one of Gus's rules: No romance on the ranch." A lame excuse, but I was glad to have it.

Cassie edged her horse closer so that our knees touched, side to side. She leaned toward me (if I tried that, I'd fall right out of the saddle) until her hat brim rested against my forehead. Now I could stare into her eyes. Deep blue in the shade of her hat.

"I own just as much of the ranch as Gus," she murmured. "So I can make my own rules."

My watch gave two little beeps, marking the hour, and Cassie grabbed my wrist to look at the time. "Shit," she said. "We better head back." And just like that, her tone had switched from smoky and charming to all business. That was fine with me. Really. It was.

"Thanks for bringing me up here. It's nice to get away from the ranch," I said.

"No kidding. Look, if Marc keeps giving you a hard time, you let me know."

"Thanks," I said. "But to quote you, I can hold my own."

"Don't want a girl to help you?"

"No. It's not that. I'd say the same thing to Steve. But I'll take any tips you have on how to get along with Marc."

She turned her horse around and mine followed, slowly walking in the direction of the ranch. "I tried having a talk with him last night, but I guess I didn't help much. From the sound of things at breakfast, he must've gotten tanked somehow after he left my place." She squinted against the sun. "Here's my advice. Don't let him push you around. If you show a sign of weakness, he'll be all over you. Far as I can tell, that's how bullies work. Gus pushes him around, Clyde pushes him around, and in turn he wants to push you around."

I nodded. She was probably right. But that didn't mean it was going to be easy.

Two light-footed animals—deer, I thought at first—jolted out of some scraggly brush ahead of us, their white tails bobbing, their skinny legs gracefully picking their way downslope, their antlers sticking up like antennae from their heads.

"What are those?" I asked. Their orange-brown and white coats weren't like anything I'd seen before.

"Pronghorn," Cassie said, watching their progress. "Folks call them 'pronghorn antelope,' but they're not really antelope."

"Are you pulling my leg? Is this related to all those stupid jackalope skulls hanging up at the ranch?"

"Do I look like I'm fooling?" Cassie tilted her head back, peering out at me from under the brim of her hat.

No, she did not. I wrenched my gaze back to the pronghorns as they trotted away. "So they're not antelope? Or related to jackrabbits?"

"Nope. They're funny critters. They have a shape where you'd think they could jump, wouldn't you? But they can't, so they get stuck sometimes, fenced in by ranchers. I don't know what they're related to, just that they look like they're something they're not."

They disappeared downslope, fading in with the grays and umbers.

"Wow," I said. "They're beautiful."

"I love that look on your face. You are something cute."

I couldn't think of a reply to that, but I figured the flush of crimson on my cheeks said it all. We ambled down from the lookout, taking the switchbacks slowly.

"So what're these horses' names?" I asked.

"Names?" Cassie shot me a sour look (the first time I'd seen her look similar to Marc). "Why do they need names?"

"Don't horses usually have names?"

"Sure. My mother's horse is named Mr. Wiggles. That's cruelty to animals."

"The horse I rode as a kid was named Tubby."

"Exactly." She stared hard ahead as if the line of blue sky and gray scrub had mortally offended her. "God. That's why I had to leave the East."

"Because of horses named Tubby?"

"You know, out here, after the dudes leave, we drive these horses out to pasturage near the Big Horns. Turn them loose. In May we go back and round them up. They're all shaggy and more than half wild. Then we drive them back down to the ranch."

"Don't you feel bad that some fat Midwesterner's going to sit on their spine all summer?"

"You're a softie. I guess I used to. Now, though, I'll comb out all the burrs and mud, and I'll see how their ears prick at certain sounds and how they're impatient sometimes, and other times they eye the brush like they like it. And they aren't always pretty and glossy, but they're real horses. You know? They have work to do. It makes them real." She trailed off, shook her head. "They're independent out here. Not some kid's Patches the Pony or Mrs. Gardner's Prize Mare or whatever. They know they're horses. Does that make any sense? They know what they are."

"To do is to be," I said and thought of how I wanted something substantial, something real, not the theoretical of Harvard. "I guess when I think of horses back home, they're something elite and snobby, like yachts."

Cassie snorted, an almost equine sound.

"Or prissy," I continued. "There were a few girls at my elementary school who wanted ponies so they could comb their manes and braid ribbons into their tails. The same way some girls want little siblings or babies. And even at seven or eight, I knew that's not what babies are like—they aren't something you can dress in pretty clothes and coo at all the time. Horses, either. They're fussy and messy, and you're better off with a doll. I don't think most of those girls ever figured out the difference."

Cassie took her eyes off the horizon and settled a look on me. "You got sisters?"

I shook my head. "Just brothers."

"How the hell do you understand girls so well?" Her stern look gave way to a huge smile, thank god. If it hadn't been for that, I might have panicked.

"Just observant, I guess."

"Praise the Lord," Cassie said. "There's one sweet, observant guy in the world."

Some word of gratitude bubbled up in me, that she liked me, that she saw me as a guy, that I didn't have to act like one of the wranglers to get her to pay attention to me. Before I could get any version of that out though, she'd made some subtle directive, and her horse flowed forward, a trot, a gallop. Already distant, she lifted her hat and waved it above her head.

My own chestnut raised its head, jangling the bit. "Don't worry," I told it. "I have no interest in doing that."

Instead, we loped slowly across the basin. I practiced trying to stand in the stirrups, which kept me from bouncing so much, and gradually I grew closer to Cassie, though I suspected she was slowing down in order to let me catch up. Sure enough, when I was even with her, she lifted her hat and perched it on the back of her head. Now I could see the freckles on her nose, the pink of her lips, and the full denim-rich color of her eyes. She didn't wear any makeup. No earrings, either. There was nothing to look at except her, and that was fine with me.

I tried to do the same trick of getting my horse close to hers, but instead of a smooth nudge of my knee against hers, I managed to ram my toe into her horse's ribs, making it snort and bare its teeth at me.

"Oops," I said. "Sorry, Mr. No Name. No offense intended."

When Cassie threw her head back and laughed, her cowboy hat slipped off her hair. I snagged it before it fell to the ground, almost losing my perch in the saddle, and offered it back to her.

"Thanks," she said. "I owe you one. I hate it when my hat gets dented."

Back in the barn, Cassie stabled her horse with its tack on, saying, "I'll be back on him in a minute." Then she settled the chestnut, tossed me a brush, and removed the saddle. "Get the sweat out. Go nose to tail."

She carried the saddle away, and I heard thuds and scrapes from elsewhere in the barn as I carefully brushed the horse. I couldn't tell if it liked it or not. Sort of like petting a cat.

"Just don't bite me," I said.

"Hey, Ron! Come up here and give me a hand," Cassie called.

I followed the sound of her voice to a ladder that led through a trap door to the hayloft. Hotter up there, the air thick with sweet-smelling dust, I walked around a pile of boxes to where the bales were neatly stacked in rows that reached a few feet above my head.

"Whaddya need?" I asked when I saw Cassie standing near such a stack.

She put a hand on my shoulder and gently pushed me back against the hay. I felt it poke through my shirt, sharp and instantly itchy. Then she lifted herself up on tiptoe so that she was eye-level and kissed me. Even as I knew it would be better if I didn't, I kissed her back, pulling her toward me. I reached out to touch her neck, my fingers meeting soft flesh that was as warm and damp as the chestnut's had been. She pressed against me, her belly touching mine. I didn't want her to feel my chest, not even when I had my compression shirt on, so I leaned back into the hay, setting the pile teetering. *That's it, Ron. Dump bales of hay on the head of the girl you're making out with.*

Unconcerned, Cassie had her hands on my hips, then one hand under my t-shirt, and I felt her fingers on my compression top, pinching the Lycra. *Oh fuck.* I grabbed her hands with my own to stop her progress.

"What are you, Spider-Man?" she muttered, before tilting her head and kissing me again.

I kept her hands tightly squeezed in my own—hoping it seemed romantic rather than restraining—until at last, she leaned back, settling on her heels and looking up at me.

"What is it about you, Ron Bancroft? You're quieter than the guys I usually like. There's something about you I just can't put my finger on. But I intend to."

I hoped a smile would be enough of an answer.

"Toss down two bales, will you?" she asked. "Gus's kids will be here soon." She crossed the loft, her boots ticking against the floor until she reached the ladder where she paused and looked back at me, brushing a strand of hair behind her ear. "Remember what I said. I make the rules here too."

CHAPTER EIGHT

Whatever Steve had said to Marc that morning seemed to have had some effect. When Carl and I arrived at the kitchen that afternoon, Marc was almost in a pleasant mood.

"We're lucky none of the dudes got sick from those eggs you made," he told me by way of greeting. "Listen up, and I'll teach you how to cook."

Vats of water were heating up on the stove for pasta night. Marc took down a frying pan from the rack. "We're making meat sauce, alright? Go to the walk-in and get the ground beef."

I came out with the tray of meat. Carl shot me an amused look from the sink where he was scrubbing, the suds up to his shoulder. Marc was stirring another pot, so I turned the flame on under the huge frying pan and started to pile the meat in.

"No, no, no," Marc shouted, scraping the meat out with a spatula. "Let the pan get hot." We stood there for a few moments, then Marc tossed in some of the ground beef. "Hear that?"

The meat sizzled and bubbled against the pan. "Yeah."

"That's what you want. The pan should sing to you," Marc said, tossing in more meat. "The heat locks the juices in, so the meat tastes better, right? Let the pan sing."

I took his place at the stove, stirring the beef with a spatula. Marc went out back, probably to have a cigarette on the sly, and Carl came over to me.

"'*The pan should sing to you,*'" he said in a lisping voice, waving his hands around. "The guy's a faggot."

I offered a lame smile, choking down my resentment—mostly at myself, for being such a wimp. "Yeah," I said, forcing a little chuckle before Carl turned back to his dishes. I knew he didn't actually think Marc was gay. I knew he just didn't like him. I knew I shouldn't let it bother me. There was nothing I could do about it. Maybe that's what bothered me.

After dinner, Steve pulled me aside as I was cleaning tables. "Things go better tonight with Marc?"

"Much."

"Good. I think I know what the problem is. You know, the wranglers are together, and you and Carl hang out. Gus has his own family, and Marc ends up alone. That's why he gets upset, I think."

"He hangs out with Cassie sometimes," I pointed out.

Steve scratched at the stubble on his cheek, a *scrtch* sound that I envied. "Well, yes. But he and Cassie are…complicated."

"I've noticed."

"You have a sister?"

I shook my head. "Just brothers."

"Maybe if you had a sister you'd understand. Marc wants to protect her."

"I know plenty of brothers and sisters who don't have that dynamic," I said. I was getting tired of this sort of excuse.

"Well, Marc doesn't have anything else to protect. No car, no house, no wife, no kids. Just this job, which his brother gave him."

I recognized the patriarchy here—the subtle insistence that Cassie could be used, should be okay with being used, to bolster the self-esteem of her wretched little brother. I didn't have any patience for that. Maybe it was visible on my face because Steve held out a placating hand.

"I'm not saying it's right. I'm just saying that's what's happening here. Maybe we can help make things better. There's another basketball game tomorrow tonight, and I invited him to play. A little male bonding."

"Great," I said, without much enthusiasm.

Marc's greasy white t-shirt was already sweated through as he took warm-up shots the next evening. J.T. "limbered up" in a manner that would have made my former coaches wince (bouncing toe touches).

A blast from the horn. I gave a jolt of surprise and turned around in time to catch the malicious grin on Cassie's face as she once again stood behind the table by the bench, running the scoreboard. I tried to arch my eyebrow coyly in reply. No luck, but she smiled at my scrunched face anyway.

The stands this time were a little fuller. Belva, Kara, and Melissa occupied a bench near the top, and Nancy had brought her two boys. I could hear their kid voices screaming, "Go Uncle Marc!"

Carl dribbled over to the bench where Steve was tying his sneaker. "Can we ask the girls to play?" he said, gesturing with his chin toward the stand.

"Well, maybe…" Steve wavered.

"No way," Clyde said. "I want to win some beer. They'd just stink things up."

"No worse than Marc," said Billy, who was carefully extracting flakes of tobacco from his teeth and wiping them on his gym socks. Lovely.

We all turned to look at Marc, who had ignored the buzzer and kept shooting. As we watched, he gave the ball a mighty shove, and it trembled in a feeble arc, missing even the backboard by a hefty margin.

"Ah shit," said Clyde. "Least we've got Ron."

He lined up for the jump ball. Carl whispered to me, "Make me look good, man. Belva's watching. And don't pass it to Marc, whatever you do."

I tried my best, passing to Carl every chance I got. He scored on a couple of layups and looked smooth doing it, slapping me five as we headed downcourt. Billy and a Buckhorn Ranch guy tussled over a loose ball, the two of them rolling on the floor swearing, until Cassie honked the horn and Steve pulled them apart. He sent Billy to the bench, which let Marc in on the action. Marc took five jogging steps onto the court and then shambled to a walk. I could see his chest heaving just from that amount of effort.

We were up by ten. There were fifteen minutes left on the board. I pulled down a rebound and fed it to Carl, who landed a basket. The Buckhorn team tromped down the court, and I shot out my hand and stole the ball, racing in for an easy score. As everyone else trotted past, Marc hung out by mid-court. Either he was leery of the fray, or he didn't want to move too much. In any event, that made it five on four under the net. Buckhorn's shot bounced off the rim, and there was a scrum for the rebound, which J.T. won. I zigged loose, and he tossed me the ball, so I dribbled past Marc and put in a layup.

As I ran back toward the other end, I heard Marc yell, "Hey, pass it to me, you ball hog."

I rolled my eyes and kept running. I might have to listen to him in the kitchen, but I definitely didn't have to listen to him on the court.

Buckhorn scored. J.T. tried for a jumper and missed. Buckhorn scored again.

Clyde went to pass it in, and he called to me. "Drop another one in. Let's get some more pitchers."

But Carl missed an easy shot, and a Buckhorn player grabbed the rebound. I sprinted down the court, keeping pace with him, and got my hand on the ball as he primed to shoot. Stripping it away, I raced toward our basket.

"Hey!" Marc yelled. "I'm open."

Fine. I shot a pass at him, saw it spin through his hands, his fingers scrabbling, but he couldn't get a grip. The ball splatted in the stands.

He didn't turn to get it, just strutted up to me. "You're a real dick. Trying to show off."

I backed away with exaggerated innocence, my hands in the air.

Carl stepped up next to me. "Lay off, man," he said to Marc. "That was a good pass. You just flubbed it. Better luck next time."

"You're a dick too."

"Why don't we concentrate on basketball?" Steve said. He retrieved the ball from the stands and handed it to a Buckhorn guy, who passed it in.

"Thanks, Carl," I said as we jogged off.

"Yeah, well. Any chance to tell Marc he's a jerk is a chance I won't miss."

The fun had gone out of the game for me. I watched J.T. whang a shot off the backboard, watched him strain to catch the rebound, his whole body pushing to get him half a foot of air, and I couldn't even laugh. God, I hated Marc.

"C'mon, Ron!" Steve yelled. I gave a little hop and joined the melee beneath the Buckhorn basket. Someone tried for a layup, but the ball bounced off the backboard and I snagged the rebound, looking for a good pass. But only Marc was open, waving his arms at me. No way was I passing to him.

"Go for it, Ron!" yelled J.T. "Don't pass it to that moron."

I skidded around a Buckhorn guy, sprinted past Marc, heard the thunder of feet behind me, and lofted the ball. It kissed the backboard, rattling the rim. I landed on the balls of my feet as it passed through the netting.

Right in front of me, someone's hand shot up, palm open, facing me as if they were playing defense. Except I didn't have the ball. And the hand didn't stop.

A sickening pop filled my head, a flash like a light bulb exploding—sudden, small, incandescent—behind my eyes. Then a hot rush of blood. My neck snapped back and then forward. I cupped hands over my nose, felt the blood rush through, tasted iron and salt in my mouth.

"You fucking dickwad!" J.T.'s voice.

"It was an accident." Marc's whine.

"You okay, man?" asked Carl.

The buzzer sounded.

"At least we won." That was Clyde. "Two points. If we'd've lost, I would've pounded your fat ass."

Marc snapped back, "I'd like to see you try."

Someone clamped a hand on my arm. "Let's get you off the floor," said Steve.

I let myself be led to the bench and sat heavily, the motion making my head throb.

"What happened?" Nancy shrilled. That made my head throb too. I kept my eyes closed, tilted my head back, and tried to pinch my nose, but it hurt too much to hold it tight.

"Marc popped him one. Look at that sucker bleed. I didn't know such a skinny guy would have so much blood," J.T. said.

"Better get him a towel," Nancy replied.

Cassie's voice cut in. "Hey, Marc. Toss me your sweatshirt."

Soft cloth in my hands. I opened one eye.

"Here," said Cassie with a wink. "Apply steady pressure with this."

I held the cloth against my nose and eyes. Even that little bit of pressure hurt like hell.

"Hey!" Marc yelled. "Don't let him bleed all over my—"

"Then don't be such a prick."

"Cassie! Language."

"Sorry, Nancy. Then don't be such a penis, Marc."

My whole face felt as if someone had stuck a bicycle pump up my nose and given a few good strokes. Rubbery and distant.

"I can't find ice."

"We can get some at the store."

"Hey, Marc, why don't you clean up the floor where he bled?"

"Do it yourself."

"You caused it."

"I'm not touching his blood. That faggot probably has AIDS." Through the pain and swelling, anger began to vibrate, and I pushed myself up from the bench. But Cassie grabbed my arm around the bicep and pulled me back down.

"Marc, you are the biggest pussy ever," she said. "Sorry, Nance. Biggest vag—"

"Cassie!"

"Let's see that nose," Steve said.

I moved the sweatshirt away and tried to open my eyes. One just wouldn't. The other cracked reluctantly, showing me, as if through a soap bubble, Nancy, her face wrinkled in worry, and Marc, who mostly looked annoyed.

"Ugh," said Billy. "Pretty nasty."

"Thanks," I tried to say, but my lips were too heavy to manage anything beyond "ffnf."

"You're going to have a couple of shiners," said Steve.

I shrugged, determined to be nonchalant.

"His nose looks crooked," said Clyde.

"How can you tell? You can hardly see his nose, his whole face is so swollen."

"Maybe it was always crooked," said J.T.

"Did you feel a crack?" Steve asked.

"Something went pop," I slurred.

"I'll take him to the hospital," Cassie said.

"Better safe than sorry," Steve intoned.

"See you back at the ranch," said Carl, slapping me lightly on the arm.

"C'mon, champ," said Cassie.

"I'm fine," I insisted.

"Uh-huh." She put a hand under my elbow, and as I stood, two trickles of blood started up again. "You are as pale as a mushroom. Don't pass out on me." I shuffled along, my vision going to static around the edges.

Blood oozed down the back of my throat. When we got to the parking lot, I spat out a huge glob, remembering Coach Foster (god, I'd had a crush on her) ministering to a bloody nose of mine in eighth grade and saying, *Spit, don't swallow, or it'll make you sick*, and the other girls laughing. (I hadn't gotten the joke.)

Now Cassie led me to her truck. "You're still gushing like Old Faithful. Can't have you bleeding all over my truck. Here." She handed me the blue bandanna that had been around her neck.

I sank into the seat and clamped the cloth to my nose, breathing in, smelling through the blood the scent of horses and hay and something like cloves. It made my mouth water.

At the hospital, I filled out an intake form while Cassie amused herself with an ancient *Seventeen* magazine. "Is he a good kisser? Ten questions to help you decide. One, does he drool on you? Two, has he ever drawn blood? Just kidding, it doesn't say that."

"Damn," I muttered.

"What?"

I'd reached the line where it asked for policy number. "I don't have insurance."

"Don't your parents cover it?"

"No… Long story."

"Here I am thinking all Harvard kids are loaded. Well, don't worry. One or the other of my brothers will pick up the bill. I'll make sure of that."

I flipped the page to fill in the checklist of questions. Even Cassie's attempts at humor ("Has he ever sprained your tonsils?") couldn't dispel the growing sense of dread. Question 49: If female, are you pregnant? Is there any chance of pregnancy? Question 50: Do you have your periods regularly? Question 53: Any pain in your testicles?

In Massachusetts, I would have left them all blank and explained to the nurse or doctor that I was transgender. But out here… It would be better to lie. It wouldn't affect their medical advice on a broken nose, right? In some ways it was the truth: I felt no pain in my testicles. And I'd be really worried if I did. Phantom Ball Syndrome. There was no chance of pregnancy unless the Holy Spirit had made an unheralded visit. (Did most young Catholic girls live in fear of that visitation, or was it only me?) Just a small lie of omission, a few boxes blank.

My nose had stopped bleeding heavily, and Cassie's now-crusty bandanna sat crumpled on my lap. I finished the form and prodded my cheeks. I still couldn't open one eye.

Cassie looked up from the magazine. "I wouldn't touch that if I were you."

"I can't see very well." I fingered the swelling under my left eye.

She swatted my hand away. "Vision test. Is this girl cute?" She held up the magazine to a nondescript, airbrushed blonde selling either lip gloss or hair conditioner or mascara. The picture seemed to emphasize all three, and I couldn't read the fine print.

"Not my type," I said. Even through the throbs of pain in my head, I could manage a few clear thoughts. Thoughts like: *I should not be having this conversation with Cassie. I should not be wanting to kiss her. Clyde would kill me. Or Marc. Or both, one after the other.*

"Hmmm." Cassie studied the photo. "What is your type?"

I thought of Laurel. "A little off-beat, maybe artsy..." But Laurel wasn't really my type. I'd had a crush on her the first time I met her at the queer student group, but that was because she was brash and sassy and bold (and cute). I admired, even envied, all that about her, but it was part of what tanked our relationship: I was so much more broody and quiet and prone to introspection. I was also a guy. And she was a lesbian. So, yeah. Back to what Cassie had asked.

"Jock-y," I said. "You know, a little tough. Stands up for herself. And good to talk to. That girl doesn't look like much of a conversationalist."

"That's not what they're selling. But I'm glad you're not buying it." She riffled the pages of the magazine. "A little tough. A little outspoken. Who would fit that description?"

"I think you know the answer to that," I murmured. My nose itched and, without thinking, I scratched it, setting the blood flowing. "Crud," I said and clenched the handkerchief to my face.

A nurse approached and started talking to Cassie.

"Are you his guardian?"

"Do I look like his mother?"

"You never know, hon."

"I'm nineteen," I mumbled through the blood and fabric.

"Mmmm." The nurse took the clipboard from me. "ID?"

I fumbled to get my wallet out while still holding the bandanna to my face.

"I'll get it," Cassie said, dipping into my pocket and extracting my battered old black nylon wallet. "Classy."

"Had it since fifth grade." My heart had just about leapt out through my mouth when she put her hand in my pocket. All I could think was, *Fuck*. There were old IDs in there, IDs that said "Veronica." There were pictures too. Why on God's green earth hadn't I cleaned the wallet out? Probably the doctor would think I was having a stroke, the way my pulse was hopping around. Would I make more of a scene by trying to grab the wallet back from Cassie? What would she do if she saw my Harvard ID, the one where I still had long hair? *Shit*.

Luckily, Cassie just removed my current license and handed it to the nurse.

"Ron from New Hampshire," said the nurse. "You're a long way from home. Wait a moment, and we'll get you right in."

I felt a moment of relief before I saw that Cassie was pulling something else out. *Please, please, please.* "These your folks?" she asked, waving a picture at me, my parents at my oldest brother's wedding.

"Yeah," I said. "Can I have my wallet back?" I tried to keep my tone light, keep the tension out of my voice.

"What? You got a picture of your girlfriend in here or something?" She had a half-smile on, wicked and teasing, and in any other circumstance it would have been sexy. But she was still looking through my wallet. "Shit, you don't even have a condom."

"Ha ha," I said and held out my hand. She ignored me and slid the wallet back into my pocket. Slowly.

"Okay, Ron, follow me," the nurse said as she returned.

"Take your time," Cassie said, sitting back down and lifting the magazine. "I want to finish this quiz."

My Tour of the Cody Hospital:

1. A very much non-private curtained booth where I described what had happened.

2. One doctor, middle-aged, who poked my face and *hmm*ed.

3. A brisk walk to the X-ray room.

4. Back to the curtained booth—just to make sure there's no concussion.

5. Quicker than I could anticipate, he's got his stethoscope under my shirt. Under my compression shirt. Cold. I gave a sharp intake of breath that had nothing to do with his instructions. Exhale, he tells me. His hand is between my breasts. I don't dare move a muscle. *Can you breathe?* he asks. I manage a breath, another. He's looking intently over my shoulder. *Okay, sounds fine*, he says.

6. He's either very kind or very clueless. In either case, I'm very lucky.

"So, what's the damage?" Cassie asked when I reemerged.

"Fracture, but small. A clean break, shouldn't even make a bump."

"Good." Cassie squinted appraisingly. "You'd still be cute with a crooked nose."

"Thanks. I've got ice. And pain meds. And what are basically two Tampax shoved up my nose."

"Ha. I don't think I've ever heard a guy use that word without flinching."

I poked at the cotton wadded in my nostrils. "Must be the painkillers," I muttered. "These things are pretty good." "Well, don't let Marc see where you keep them. That's the last thing we need. I called for a pizza. We can pick it up on the way."

I held the ice against my face as we drove. It felt fine just to freeze out the world for a while, go slowly numb, let the adrenaline drain. I'd been lucky with the doctor. It made me realize how lucky I'd been in general. What a huge secret I was carrying around with me. What it might cost me if the truth came out. I hated that, but what could I do? I didn't want people to know. I didn't have an obligation to tell anyone. It was none of their damn business.

"You okay there, partner?" Cassie put a hand on my thigh and squeezed gently as she pulled out of the parking lot of the pizza place.

"Yeah." My leg had given a little twitch when she touched me. Even with the ice and the painkillers, I was still tense as hell, could still feel that doctor's hand on my chest.

"You should eat. You left about a half-gallon of blood at the gym." She put her hand back on the wheel.

I took a slice of pizza and chewed it slowly. My jaw felt sore.

"I'm sorry my brother's such a jerk," Cassie continued.

"It's not your fault."

"It probably is. He's the youngest, so Gus and I spent a lot of time beating him up or ignoring him. Probably made him all mean and drunk and fat."

"I don't think all that childhood stuff is what forms your personality anyway."

"Really?"

"Really. I think the most essential part of who you are is formed before you can talk. When all you can do with the world is just take it in, be subject to it. And we can't even remember those years, but we internalize them so deeply that they become the essence of our personalities, our fears, our weaknesses."

"Wow. Those painkillers *are* good."

I laughed. "You don't buy it?" Maybe I only bought it because I had known my whole life the truth of who I was while the world kept telling me I had it wrong. Whatever had made me myself, it happened before my childhood. It was something much deeper.

Cassie shook her head. I shifted the ice against my jaw so I could hear her clearly. "I think that childhood shit matters a lot. Like, if your father's a drunk and you're the oldest son and have to do all the crap your dad is supposed to. Or if you're the youngest kid in the family and you pretty much know you're a mistake..." She drifted off, staring through the windshield.

"And if you're the girl in the middle?" I prompted.

"You go to the stables all the time and learn that it's easier to love horses than people."

In the silence that filled the truck cab, I wanted more than anything to share some piece of myself, something true. Not to prove that I'd suffered as well but to show her that I trusted her. But there was only one true thing about me that really mattered at this moment, and I wasn't about to share that.

Cassie let the truck slow as she turned into the ranch driveway. "Don't mean to be overly dramatic. It wasn't like I was abused. My dad would slap us around some, but the boys more than me."

"I was lucky," I said. "I had a real happy childhood."

"Your parents still together?"

"They've been married for over thirty years."

"Long time." We bumped over the cattle guard. "They gonna come out and visit?"

"No chance," I said. "That's kinda why I left the East. They kicked me out." As soon as I said it, I knew I shouldn't have told her, but it felt nice to be honest for a change.

She looked at me, slowing the truck down even further. "I bet there's a good story there."

"A long one."

"I'm not Nancy," she said. "I won't pry."

"Maybe I'll tell you about it some other time," I responded, before I could determine whether that was a wise thing to offer or not.

Cassie just nodded and stopped the truck beside the Quonset garage, pulling up right under the jackalope skull.

I put my hand on the door latch. "Thanks for taking me to the hospital. It's been really nice talking to you."

"Yeah, well, therapy time is over."

"I owe you one," I said. "For the pizza and the ride and—"

"I'll cash it in. I've never kissed a guy with tampons in his nose."

Leaning awkwardly over the stick shift, I put a hand on her hip and brought my lips close to hers. I'd told myself I shouldn't do this. It would only lead to problems. But... Her tongue pushed between my lips, and pretty soon I couldn't feel the stick shift digging into my thigh, nor the ache of my jaw. I could only feel the warmth of Cassie. I found that I had slid my palm off her hip and between her legs—I hadn't meant to do that—and now she moved against me.

But when she twisted toward me in her seat, her head bumped against my nose, making me flinch.

"Sorry," she said. "Sex in a car is no good. I learned that in high school. About the only thing I did learn." She kissed me again, gently.

I stepped out into the glow the light on the garage offered. The lamp didn't make much of a dent in the darkness, just enough to illuminate the grill of Cassie's Comanche and half of the jackalope.

"That thing creeps me out," I muttered.

"It's just a skull," Cassie said through the window. "Just a poor, mixed-up creature like the rest of us. Get some sleep, Ron."

CHAPTER NINE

The painkillers made me dizzy, or maybe that was just Cassie. There were about a million reasons why I shouldn't be thinking about her the way that I was, why I shouldn't be imagining getting back in that truck and getting her out of those jeans. She was older than me, and she was my boss's sister, and my boss already hated my guts. Not to mention that her ex-boyfriend was a very large wrangler. Oh, and that she didn't know I was female. There was that too. Even I couldn't bear to write out a list delineating why this crush was a very bad idea.

Of all the reasons, though, there was only one I could control. I couldn't do anything about Marc or Clyde, or even Gus and his no-romance rule. But I could do something about Cassie not knowing I was female. I would have to if I ever did want to get her out of those jeans. And I did want that. A lot. Enough to tell her? Hadn't I planned to come out here and not tell anyone? Wasn't that the point? Maybe I could just make Cassie an exception to my non-disclosure rule… I kicked a rock that sat in the middle of the path, and even that small gesture made my nose ache.

I took slow steps toward the bunkhouse. Not a light from the barn or from the wranglers' cabin or the girls' house. None of their cars were around either. They must have gone to a bar or something after the game. That was fine. I wasn't in the mood for company. Or, to be honest, for anyone's company except Cassie's. I pulled open the bunkhouse door, shuffled across the front room, and flicked on the lamp by my bunk. An envelope waited for me on the blanket. My brother Michael's handwriting was instantly recognizable. Pausing to swap my bloody shirt for a clean one, I sat on my bunk and opened the letter.

Dear Ron,

Thanks for sending me your note. I hadn't heard from you in a while (last phone call was April?!) and was wondering what was going on. Mom and Dad said you had a rough visit home, but they didn't go into details. It sounds like you've had a lot on your plate lately, but hopefully you've landed in a good spot. (Wyoming? Really?)

I guess I'm wrestling with a couple of things. Part of me (the hippie part) wants to tell you to be yourself, to be free, be happy, do your thing. Part of me (the accountant part) wants to know the practical aspects: How do you intend to do this? Surgery? Change of name/gender? What's the legal status of all this? And then another part of me is curious and confused: How do you know this is what you want? Why not just be a tomboy, like you've always been?

Honestly, Ron, think about it. If I showed up at your doorstep and asked you to call me Michelle, not Michael, and she, not he, could you do it? Of course not. I'd be a six foot five, 240 pound guy, with stubble and a low voice, pretending to be a woman. Even if you wanted to be supportive, it would take some time for you to get used to it. I think that's what Mom and Dad need.

Are you sure this is who you are 100% of the time? Just to voice the part of me that's your older brother—you're only nineteen (almost twenty, I know). When you were little, you collected Barbies and you loved the color purple. You wanted to be an astronaut, and then you wanted to be a doctor, and you played the Wicked Stepmother in the school play. And didn't you have a crush on my friend Dennis when you were in high school? I guess I'm just thinking of all the things you were or believed yourself to be. You're young. Take your time. Think things through. (And in case you forgot any of what I mentioned, I enclosed some photographic evidence.)

I'm worried about you, Ron. Are you safe out there in Wyoming? I know you have to take a year off school, but come back East. I have friends in Manchester and Concord who could give you a job. Stay in touch.

Love,

Michael

P.S. Brian says hi. Didn't tell him much. Thought you'd let him know.

I shook the photos out of the envelope and onto the blanket. Yes, there I was, hair in a French braid, hugging a purple teddy bear about half my size, my smile broad enough to show that one of my front teeth was missing. And there I was in a black velvet dress and stage makeup, trying to look haughty and evil for the play, with a bored seventeen-year-old Michael standing next to me.

I looked at another picture, this one of Michael standing next to me at maybe ten years old when I was getting ready to head to YMCA camp. I looked just like him now. (Okay, his shoulders were broader and his face a bit leaner than mine, especially given its current swelling.) Somehow the resemblance reassured me, like I was meant to be this way. Maybe if I sent Michael a picture of me now, he'd see the same thing, this connection between us.

The last picture showed me with Michael and his buddy Dennis. I must have been fifteen, and they were still in business school. Home for a weekend, they took me along with them to a party. A crush on Dennis? We'd danced and gone for a walk in the dark... What I remembered of the evening was that everyone else was drinking and making out. I wanted none of that, and Dennis seemed like a safe bet. I'd always assumed he was gay, in fact.

I stared at the picture. I stood between the two of them, my hair in a ponytail, smiling hugely. Was I always pretending? Had I ever been myself? Was I still just playing a part now? Jesus. I did not need an existential crisis at this moment. I had enough on my plate.

I put the letter back into the envelope, shoved the pictures in too, and tucked them deep inside the backpack under my bunk. There were clear psychological implications there—monsters under the bed and all that—but I wasn't going into it. I wasn't going to think about his question: *Was I safe?* I could take care of myself. I didn't need anyone to rescue me. Right now, I was going to take a painkiller and fall asleep and not talk to Marc or Carl when they came in. Maybe Marc would be a bit nicer now that he had broken my nose. Yeah. Maybe Marc would be nicer, and maybe Cassie wouldn't mind that I was transgender, and maybe I'd wake up tomorrow without two black eyes.

No such luck, at least with the shiners. When I looked in the mirror the next morning, they were so dark and defined they looked like a baseball player's eye grease. But at least breakfast went smoothly. Marc simply ignored my existence. I dug postholes with Steve and then went for my run in the afternoon.

When I came back to the bunkhouse, Marc was nowhere in sight, and Carl was cranking out pull-ups from the bunkhouse rafters.

"How many can you do?" he asked, dropping to the floor beside me. He ran a hand through his thick dark hair.

"None." Visions of the Tamworth Junior High School gym, the day of the Presidential Physical Fitness Test. One Veronica Bancroft (five foot eight and maybe 118 pounds) with all forty-eight other members of the class cheering her on. If there was one girl who could do one pull-up, it would be Veronica. I could remember dangling from that bar, straining in utter futility. Telekinesis was my only hope. And in the end, I had to settle (like all the other girls) for the flexed arm hang. Twelve seconds. I doubted that would impress Carl much.

"None?" he asked, raising his eyebrows. "Man, you've got to get some muscle."

"I can do push-ups," I said defensively.

"Let's go."

We lined up on the floor and Carl counted. I tried not to stare at his tan arms, pistoning up and down. Thirty-nine, forty, fuck. My arms gave a wobble. Come on. I could manage fifty the last time I did a set, which was last fall… But now, just forty-four. I took a knee and watched Carl crank out a dozen more.

"You run too much," he told me. "You're like a stick. What do you weigh?"

"I don't know. Maybe 130 pounds or so?"

He laughed. "Peanuts. You've got to eat more. You're taller than me. You could hold some weight." He stood up and flexed one arm so that his bicep bulged. "Check that out."

"Nice," I said. My arms hurt already.

He checked his watch. "Shower time." He flapped his sweaty shirt against me. "I bet Kara would like it if you put on some muscle. Chicks dig it."

I gave an involuntary groan and sat on my bed to finish unlacing my shoes. The last thing I wanted was to impress Kara.

"What's your problem? She's cute. Not as cute as Belva, but still. You should quit being a faggot and get with her." Carl grabbed his towel and opened the bathroom room. "How's your nose, man?"

I prodded it. "It hasn't bled anymore. But it still kinda hurts."

"If I were you, I'd be looking for payback, you know?"

I shrugged. I didn't want revenge. I just wanted to be left alone.

"C'mon, man. Seriously? If I were you, this is what I'd do." Carl walked across the bunkhouse, pulled a half-empty jug of Jack Daniels out from under Marc's bed, took out his dick, and pissed into the bottle. Then he screwed the cap back on and shook it up.

"That could make him really sick," I said.

"What do I care?" Carl said. "The guy's an asshole. He punched you, he yells at us all the time for nothing, so why shouldn't I piss in his whiskey? He shouldn't be drinking that shit anyway. Step it up, man. Don't be a pussy." He strode past me into the bathroom.

I waited on my bunk until I heard one of the showers start running, followed soon after by the sound of Carl singing "Cold November Rain." I grabbed clean clothes and a towel. I was sweaty. My compression top clung clammily to my torso, and I didn't want to wriggle out of it in the bunkroom in case Marc came in. But I didn't want to wriggle out of it in front of Carl either. So I pushed open the door and hopped into the shower next to him to perform Ron's Dance of the Seven Layers.

The pelt of hot water didn't bring me any comfort or clarity, and the longer I stayed there, naked and soapy, the more I got to feeling miserable for no good reason. Or for lots of good reasons. I had breasts. I had no dick. None of this would change. I looked down at myself, and it didn't look…right. Or it didn't look how I wanted it to look. Or how others expected it to. If I were a guy, I could kiss Cassie without worrying about it. And maybe Marc wouldn't even be that much of an issue.

Did I want surgery? Did I want testosterone? Not so much as I didn't want to worry. I didn't want to hide. I wanted to be able to step out from behind this curtain and not be embarrassed.

On the other side of the curtain, I heard Carl turn the shower off. I imagined his bio-boy body: easy, steady, right, ready for a night with Belva. I lathered shampoo onto my hair and listened as he toweled himself dry, still singing Guns N' Roses: "*Everybody needs somebody…*"

Dear Michael,

Thanks for writing me. It feels good to have a line of communication open with home. (You can share this letter with Mom and Dad if you want.) I'll say that the one thing I miss out here is good conversation. There're lots of folks I can chat with but only one person I really talk to, and even that's not like having a best friend or a brother nearby. Anyway, it's okay. You know me. Never really been a social butterfly. More of a social moth.

And thanks also for the pictures. If I had photo albums at my fingertips, I'd send a few back your way. Here's what I remember from the family stash. How about the one of you, me, Brian, and Dad heading out to hike Mount Chocorua? I think I'm nine or ten, and we're posed in jeans and flannel shirts and orange hats because it's hunting season. Or the one of me when I'm twelve, and I'd gotten a pixie haircut—it was a school picture and had that terrible mottled background. I begged Mom to let me get my hair cut short, remember? And then when I did, a woman yelled at me for going into the ladies' room at DeMillo's because she thought I was a boy. Mom was so embarrassed. But I was thrilled—it meant other people could see what I felt.

Just flip through an album and you'll see: I've always been this way. Of course it isn't "normal," by which I mean typical or usual, but it's who I am. It's who I've always been. I just didn't have a word for it or know what to do about it.

I remember praying as a kid (You know those rosaries Grandma had given us?) that I'd grow up and be a man. I was young but old enough to know that what I was asking for was pretty unlikely. But the way I felt, I knew I wasn't supposed to be a girl. I figured God would realize the mistake and get to fixing it.

I guess what hurt the most about my last "conversation" with Mom and Dad was how they both thought I was throwing my life away, that I'd never be successful. I got some of that from your letter too—your feeling that I was making my life difficult. Believe me when I tell you that it is much more difficult for me to try to be a girl.

Thanks for trying to understand, and thanks for being open to having this conversation with me. Being out here, pretty much alone and unmoored, it means a lot to me that you're willing to discuss. I miss you!

Love,

Ron

Carl took a long time getting his hair and shirt just right (he was picky about how he rolled the sleeves of his t-shirt), so I managed to finish my letter before we headed up to the kitchen. To our surprise, Marc was nowhere to be seen. Instead, Nancy had taken over the helm. She'd dialed the radio to the gospel station and was crooning along to "Precious Lord" as she stirred tomato sauce. It was the most uneventful dinner preparation of the summer.

"Do you think Marc drank that whiskey?" Carl whispered as we finished mopping up. "And got sick and that's why he's not here?"

I shrugged. "Are you the worry wart now? Let's just be glad he's not here."

Carl headed off to find Belva, and I got the bunkhouse to myself. Time to read my field guide and stare into the bathroom mirror. The swelling in my cheeks had gone down considerably, though the black and blue bruises had spread across more of my face. At least it didn't hurt much anymore, just looked like hell. I stretched out in my bunk and fell asleep quickly—the lack of Marc's snoring helped—until a tapping at the window woke me.

I sat up. The window stood at the foot of my bed, and I leaned blearily toward the glass. Cassie was outside.

She held a finger to her lips and then beckoned me with her hand, mouthing, *C'mon.*

I pushed my covers off (again, boxers were a good choice) and stood. Carl lay in his bed, his arms thrown out spread-eagle. I pulled on jeans, grabbed a compression top, and stepped into the bathroom to shimmy it on. The Lycra felt cool and slick against my sleep-warm skin. T-shirt over that, then I grabbed my sneakers and tiptoed to the front stoop, easing the door shut behind me.

Cassie waited beside the path, her eyebrows furrowed as I tied my shoes. "What took you so long?" she whispered. "Doesn't look like you were doing your hair."

I ran a hand over my head; the back of my hair was standing on end. Oh well. "I have this shirt..." I mumbled, still half asleep.

"Oh yeah, I remember. Your Spider-Man suit." She wore blue jeans and cowboy boots and a zip-up sweatshirt. It was surprisingly cool outside. I could feel the skin on my bare arms prickle into goosebumps. "You wore it at the game too, didn't you?"

Before she could ask more questions, I stepped close to her and put my arm around her waist, pulling her warm body against mine, nuzzling my nose against her neck. "Nice night for a moonlit walk," I murmured, my lips against her skin. I hoped she'd let the topic of my shirt just fade away.

"Actually, there isn't much moonlight. That's the point. I wanted to show you my stars."

She steered us away from the barn and bunkhouse, down a gradual slope. We followed a fence line, our feet scuffing against tussocks of grass, my jeans catching on spiny somethings. I kept my arm around her waist, even though it made walking awkward, my hip bumping up against hers, both of us losing our balance when one of us stumbled on a gopher (or whatever the Wyoming equivalent was) hole. The night chirped full of desert scurry sounds.

Where the fence formed a corner, Cassie stopped and placed her foot on the lower rail. "There. Those are my stars." She pointed, indicating a section of the heavens. The sky overflowed; hardly a scrap of blackness remained.

"Uh, which ones?"

"They form a 'W,' like a crown."

Her fingers traced the shape, and I moved to stand behind her, sighting along her arm, resting my chin on her shoulder. "I see," I said. I didn't, but I didn't really mind if I didn't so long as I had my nose nestled close to breathe in the smell of her. "Why are these your stars?"

"They're my constellation, Cassiopeia."

I wrapped my arms around her waist. "What's her myth?"

"Same old. Mortal gets screwed by the gods. Literally and figuratively."

"So why'd you get named after her?"

"My father wanted a classical name. You know he was a Greek teacher, right? And my mom asked for a list to choose from. She figured 'Cassiopeia' could at least be shortened to 'Cassie.' I doubt she even knew the story—she isn't much into that stuff."

I loved the tough coolness of her voice and tried to keep my own words easy and level. "How'd they meet?"

Cassie leaned back against me, and my heart thumped against her spine. I hoped she wouldn't feel my breasts. Even with the compression shirt, my chest wasn't perfectly flat.

"He was a professor at a women's college in the South, the kind of place where girls bring their horses. My mom worked with the horses, and my dad worked with the girls. She had no interest in Greek, and he had no interest in the stables, but somehow they met. You know how small places are."

"Do I ever. Did you have to take Latin and Greek?"

"Course not. I think Gus tried Latin. He was the one always wanting to please our father. I hid out in the stables."

I unwrapped my arms from around her and settled my butt onto the top rail of the fence, my mind still half-gummed with sleep, awed by the star-smacked sky above.

"What does your dad do?" she asked.

"Contractor. He does road construction. Culverts, grading. Some of my brothers work for him."

"How many brothers do you have?"

"Five."

"Whew. Two is more than enough for me. You get on good with your dad?"

"Used to. Right now he's a little pissed off at me." I tried to sound casual, tried to match her easy tone.

"How could he be? You're clean cut, good at sports, you work hard, you're smart as hell…"

"You want to write me a letter of recommendation?"

"Sure. But first tell me what you did to piss him off. Or let me guess. Did you knock some girl up?"

"God no. He wants me to be a doctor, or to do something that's useful. And I like studying history. I want to go into research and academics. And he said if I wasn't going to do something prac-tical, it wasn't worth his money." I stared past where she leaned on the fence, glad it was dark, worried she'd catch me in this lie, worried that everything was starting to be a lie. "I guess I should just do what he wants."

"Of course not. It's like what you said the other day. To do is to be, right? You have to do your thing, or you can't be yourself." She left a brief pause. "You got a girlfriend back home?"

"Nope, no girlfriend. We broke up before I came out here." I paused and considered how much I wanted to say, how much I wanted to hide. It wasn't *hiding*. It was just keeping things to myself. "May was a rough month."

Cassie nodded, her facial expression unreadable in the night. "Are you on the rebound? Is that what you're telling me?"

I thought I'd heard a hint of sarcasm in her voice, so I replied, "About the same as you and Clyde. Or are you still dating him?"

"Not a chance. We had fun in the spring, bringing the horses in. And it was fine going to town to have a couple of beers. But he's one of those guys who thinks that just 'cause we're seeing each other, and just 'cause he's older than me, that means he can boss me around. I don't take that kind of crap."

I brushed her hair back where a strand had fallen onto her forehead. I wanted to say something like, *You're gorgeous*, or, *I think you're beautiful*. But words like that don't come easily to me. I can't even write them on my yellow pad most days.

So instead I said, "I'm glad you're through with him."

A smile spread across her face. It might have been teasing or disappointed. "I told you the story of my name," she said, reaching her hands under my t-shirt, her fingers running across the Lycra. I flinched at her touch and gently moved her hands away, intertwining my fingers with hers. "Am I ever going to get you out of this shirt?" I didn't want to answer that, so I kissed her, just a light kiss, lip to lip.

"That's a good answer," she said. "Your turn." She extracted her fingers and moved her hands to rest on my butt. "How'd you get your name, Ronald?"

"Just 'Ron.' It's kind of a long story."

"You've got a lot of long stories. That shirt. Your name. An ex-girlfriend."

"Seems like you have a few of your own," I replied, hoping I didn't sound defensive.

Cassie took a step back and gave me an appraising look. "You know where I live, right?"

I nodded.

"Good. If you decide you want to share stories, you can come on by. I'm not playing chase all summer."

She leaned toward me, her ponytail sliding over her shoulder to tickle my neck. Soft lips, mouth much warmer than the night air. I held her waist, feeling the crest of her hips, the gentle give of her flesh above that.

"Thanks for waking me up, Cassie. I kinda suck at this romantic stuff. Sorry." My hands were on her ass now, and I pulled her toward me for another kiss.

"No apologies needed," she said. "I'm just saying it's up to you if you want to stop by some night. Gus usually goes to bed by ten."

"And Nancy?"

"Eight thirty. She's a wild one." Cassie turned away and walked down the fence line.

I had just made a mistake. I could taste it on my lips, feel it with every jolt of my heart. Hell. Best thing would be for me to crawl back into my bunk and forget everything. Stick to washing dishes. But there was no way that was going to happen on a ranch this size, not with someone who reached me like Cassie did.

CHAPTER TEN

"Which one of you has been fucking with my liquor?" Marc asked, leaning close to Carl and me. The odor of the onions he'd been chopping oozed off him but didn't quite cover the smell of booze on his breath.

The kitchen had to be a million degrees with turkeys roasting in the ovens, and cakes and rolls cooling on the counter, and vats of water boiling on the stove, waiting for the potatoes that Carl and I were peeling. I shot Carl a glance, but he kept his eyes fixed on the peeler.

"I know someone's been at it. And it isn't the wranglers, so it has to be one of you." Marc held a chef's knife in his hand. Neither one of us said anything. "I don't know what you put in my whiskey, but if you fuck with it again, I'll kill you."

"Maybe it was Nancy," Carl said.

"You shut the fuck up," Marc raised the knife, and I scooted back a bit, casting my eyes around for a likely weapon. "It was one of you two. Was it you, Ronnie?"

"Don't call me that," I said.

"I'll call you what I want to, Ronnie." Crap. I'd just given him ammunition.

"Or was it you, Carlos?" Marc turned to Carl.

"Not my name, brother. I'm Carleton."

"Yeah? Well you look like a spic."

"Shut the fuck—"

Marc lunged forward. I grabbed a saucepan and swung it widely in front of me. Carl leapt to the side. There was a huge clatter as he knocked over a stepstool and a shelf's worth of trays. Potatoes went everywhere.

Marc sprawled, tangled up with the spilled mess of peels. I stood clutching the saucepan like a crazed lunatic before stepping over to Carl and offering a hand to help him up.

"Thanks, man," he said.

"Everything okay in here, fellows?" It was Steve. No doubt he'd heard the ruckus since the office was practically next door. "Can I borrow Ron for twenty minutes? One of the trucks…" He stepped through the screen door and took in the scene: The knife on floor. Marc still working his way out of the mess of peels. The scatter of trays. "What the heck happened here?"

"He tried to stab me, man," said Carl, pointing at Marc.

"I slipped," Marc said. "These two have been messing with my private property."

Steve looked from me to Carl to the potatoes. "Let's just stay calm. Dinner's in an hour. Marc, why don't you go talk to Gus. Ron and Carl will clean up here."

He held the door for Marc, who rose shakily to his feet and clutched the counter for support. "I'm going to find out which—"

"That's enough," Steve said.

He ushered Marc out, and it was just the two of us. Carl cranked the country music and started playing air guitar, laughing and shouting, "We got him. We got him good."

I set the saucepan down, my hands still shaking a bit. "Do you think he would have stabbed us?" I asked.

"Man, he was too drunk for that. Don't sweat it."

I started gathering up the spilled potatoes. Carl turned the music even higher, crowing the lyrics at high volume: "*Don't you tell my heart, my achy-breaky…*" To my surprise, I found that I knew the words too, and soon enough, both of us were singing along.

Carl was still laughing about how he'd made Marc snap when we headed back to the bunkhouse after dinner. He went to find Belva, and I went to my bunk where I found a letter waiting.

Dear Ron,

I meant it about writing regularly. You better put a letter in the mail to me soon. And don't just talk about the trees and the moun-tains and crap like that. I wanna know what's going on with you.

The city's great. You're missing quite the summer. We went out to an awesome club with Lily and Ann, who say hi, by the way, and also agree that you're crazy to be in Wyoming. There's a queer poetry slam that we all go to regularly. And this wonderfully cheesy lesbian bar that does country line dancing. Have you learned how to line dance yet? Seems like a Wyoming sort of thing. I love my internship.

Also, Heather and Laurel are together now. I hope it doesn't hurt you to know that, but I thought I should tell you. Laurel is doing some really amazing art. She made a dress for one of her fashion design classes that is unbelievable. She says hello. Write soon!

Love,

Jane

Heather and Laurel together. It didn't really hurt. Now that I knew, I suppose I could say that it felt inevitable. They were better suited for each other than Laurel and I had been—especially after I'd come out as trans. I was tempted to sit down and write back to Jane and tell her that not only was I not hurt but that I, in fact, also had a new girlfriend of my own. But that would likely only cause more problems.

I stared at the letter, rereading it numbly. A queer poetry slam, nights out with a group of lesbians. Even though I had run away from all of that, suddenly it sounded good—a cozy community, people who understood me when my own family did not. I hated to admit it, but I would fit in more easily line-dancing at a lesbian bar than down at the Dollar with the wranglers. Why could I not figure out which side I belonged on? Why did it have to be so difficult?

I barely turned at the sound of the screen door snapping shut, thinking it was Carl, but Cassie's voice caught me by surprise. "My stupid brother hit you again?"

"Nah. He got Carl this time."

"Christ." She paused in the living room. "This place is a dump. Is Carl here?" She stepped into the bunkroom, and I hastily stood up from my bunk, embarrassed by the scatter of legal pads, crumpled pages, and books that littered the bed.

"I don't know where he got to. Probably with Belva."

"Don't think I'm here chasing after you," she said. "I'm only here 'cause Steve asked me to grab some of Marc's clothes. I think he's spending a night or two up at Gus's house. Nancy wants to keep an eye on him. I should tell her not to waste her time. Gus says this is Marc's last chance. One more problem and he's gone."

"Steve thinks that Marc just needs to feel included. At least that's what he said before the last basketball game," I told her as I picked up all the clutter and slotted things into their places on the shelves.

"Steve's an optimistic fool. *Bless his heart*, as Nancy would say."

I laughed at her brief impersonation of her sister-in-law's voice; it was dead-on. "Nancy, she's—"

"Don't get me started."

"I somehow doubt she gives you a hard time."

Cassie flattered me with a sarcastic smile. "You should have seen the dress she made me wear at their wedding. Tangerine. Who on earth puts their bridesmaids in tangerine?"

"I can't picture you in a dress." I tugged my blankets straight and tucked the corners in tightly.

"I avoid them like the plague."

Somehow, that thought reassured me. "Hard to ride a horse in one, I guess."

"Yeah, it always drove my mom nuts when I was little. She wanted to dress me up and do my hair, and I was always in the barn. She was too, but in a different way. And when I was in high school, I spent all my time with boys who liked to fix cars, driving around with them, working in the garage with them. I was kind of one of them and kind of their girlfriend…"

I crossed the room to where Cassie stood. "…and then?"

"Then I figured I liked horses more than cars. And, in some ways, more than boys." She lifted her chin to me. "Present company excepted, I'd rather be around horses."

I bent down to put my lips on hers. "I'm flattered," I murmured and kissed her again. Her hands dug into the rear pockets of my jeans, pressing my hips against hers, and I leaned my head against her neck to kiss her, tasting the saltiness there.

The screen door banged. "Poker night with the wranglers!" Carl called as he burst into the bunkroom. "Oh shit. Sorry, man."

"That's okay," Cassie said, stepping away from me and flicking her ponytail back. "I'm just getting some of Marc's clothes. He's not sleeping here tonight."

Carl and I both watched as she strode the length of the bunkhouse, that heel-toe click to her walk, and picked out jeans and shirts from Marc's drawers. As she passed us, she gave me a wink and Carl a nod.

"Hold your cards close, partner," she said on her way out, and I wasn't sure which one of us she meant.

"Holy crap," said Carl once she'd left. "You getting it on with Cassie?"

"I wouldn't say 'getting it on,' I mean—"

"Nice one!" He held up his hand for a high five. "That'll piss Marc off for sure."

"That's not why I'm—. Not that I'm—"

"Chill, man. Look at you. Scoring with a girl who's older."

I said nothing, but I couldn't keep from smiling.

"Oh man," Carl said, grabbing a deck of cards from the shelf. "When Marc finds out, he'll lose his shit."

"You better not tell him. Or the wranglers. Are we going to play poker or what?"

"You're going to play? Mr. I-have-ten-books-to-read?"

"Let's go," I said. There was no way I was letting him go out on his own, not when he could spill the beans about Cassie and me.

Billy's lower lip bulged with tobacco as he scowled at his cards.

"Aw, just play already," said J.T.

"Don't rush me none," Billy said and turned his head to spit. "I'm out." He laid his cards on the table. We'd started out quarter ante and were up to a dollar. I wanted to go to bed, but every time I stood up from the table, J.T. or Clyde would pull me back. I was down six dollars but was considering this a win as nothing about Cassie and me had come out.

Clyde sloshed some more whiskey into everyone's glass. Mine was in danger of overflowing. I hadn't been keeping pace with the drinking. In fact, I was sober enough to realize I had a losing hand, so I folded. Pretty soon Clyde was raking the pot toward his side of the table.

"Whyn't you bring over the girls, Carl?" said J.T. He crossed the room, pausing to steady himself on the doorframe before entering the bathroom. In a moment, the sound of piss hitting water was audible.

"They all went into Cody to see *Batman Returns*." Carl's words were spoken with the careful deliberation of one approaching total inebriation.

"Those girls," said Billy. "They won't give me the time of day." He spat again and pointed his finger at me. "You been with that Kara yet?"

I shook my head. "Nah, she's not interested."

Carl leaned over the table. "She's not, but I know who is. Ca—"

"Shut up!" I yelped.

"What's that?" Billy said, all innocent. "Who's interested in Ron?"

"Cassie," Carl said. "Oh come on, Ron," he pleaded when he saw me glaring at him. "You were kissing her in the bunkhouse.

How long is that going to be a secret? You can't take a crap around here without someone finding out."

Somehow, that thought did nothing to reassure me.

Clyde shuffled the deck with a loud rippling noise. "Cassie, huh? I had her figured for a dyke."

J.T. emerged from the bathroom, zipping up his fly. "Just 'cause a girl won't suck your dick doesn't mean she's a dyke," he said. Probably the smartest words I had heard from him all summer.

"I guess she likes 'em little," Clyde said slowly. "Easier to push around." He dealt out another round, setting each card down with a slow, deliberate click, his eyes locked on mine. I made myself match his stare. I'd learned a few things from handling Marc, and one was that backing down didn't solve anything. It just meant he'd keep on shoving.

I didn't go any farther than staring though. I wasn't stupid enough to reply to his comment and start an argument. When Clyde finished dealing, I picked up my cards and studied them. "This hand stinks," I muttered.

Next to me, J.T. put his cards down. "If you're gonna fool with Cassie, you better learn to play this game better."

"How is poker going to help with Cassie?" I asked, flicking a glance at Clyde, glad to see that he was staring at his cards and not at me.

"You learn to watch people. Read 'em." I could smell the whiskey on his breath as he leaned close. "Like Billy, see how he's pulled his eyebrows close?"

Across the table, Billy jerked his head up. "Shut it, J.T."

J.T. ignored him. "That means that he likes his hand. He pretends to scowl, trying to cover it up. But really he's happy."

"I said shut it," Billy snapped.

"You ain't gonna do a thing about it," J.T. drawled, picking his cards up. "Matter of fact, you don't do much unless Clyde tells you to. Ain't that right, little man?"

"I'll do something real soon if you don't close your mouth," Billy said.

I wanted to leave. It was one thing when the three of them picked on Carl and me. That felt like teasing, the kind I'd seen often at school. But this drunken, card-stoked fighting with each other seemed more dangerous. Add Clyde's feelings for Cassie to the mix, and it got even more unstable.

Clyde watched Billy and J.T., running a finger along his jawline. "Can it, Billy, and let's play," he said at last. Then he turned to stare at me. "You fucked her yet?" The look on my face must have made the answer apparent. He grinned. "Didn't think so. She's just playing with you. Take my advice. Leave her alone."

"You hoping she'll come back to you?" J.T. said.

"She'll be begging for it soon. Ron's not going to give it to her, right? She doesn't want him. She just wants to make me jealous. She'll come back to me. I know how girls think." Clyde clicked his cards against the table and leaned back, staring at me, eyes hard, a smirk on his lips. "Girls want a real man, not a little boy."

"I don't think you understand women at all, actually," I said, the words rushing out. "I think she's pretty darn over you." My stomach tangled in a mix of anger and fear. Clyde was as much of an asshole as Marc was. I wasn't going to let him walk all over me, but I also knew if he started a fight, I was going to be in a lot of trouble.

"Guess we'll find out, won't we?" Clyde said. He laughed, braying at me, but his eyes were still narrowed, showing no sign of humor.

"I'm in. And I raise," Carl said, pushing some bills into the center of the table.

"Overconfident," J.T. said to me. "Anyone that plays like that is either bluffing or a fool. In this case, I think Carl is just drunk. Can't hold your liquor too good, huh?"

Carl laughed in response.

I'd always thought J.T. was the dumbest of the three, but he seemed to have a decent understanding of people. He was certainly right about Carl: The guy was totally drunk.

"We should go to bed, Carl," I said, standing up, glad to have an excuse for leaving the table.

"You're just going to fold?" Clyde said. "You forfeit what you've put in. But it's fine by me if you want to wimp out, little boy."

I wasn't going to rise to his bait. I was done with these three. "It's late. C'mon, Carl."

"Stick around, Ron," J.T. said. "I haven't gotten to figuring you out yet. And I can tell you're hiding something."

I set my cards on the table, face up. I was leaving even if Carl wasn't coming with me. "I'm not hiding anything," I said. "I'm an open book. I'm just not sure you know how to read."

Back at the bunkhouse, I washed my face and settled into my bed. My hands were still shaking with frustration. Why had I gone to play poker? I flopped against my pillow and stared up at the rafters. Did I want to be a man like those guys? No. Couldn't I be a kind man, like Steve, just a little gentle? I was pissed at Carl for spilling the beans but also had to admit he was right: It would have come out sooner or later, which made me worry about certain other things that in all likelihood would come out sooner or later.

I grabbed my yellow pad and pen, then paused to massage away the beginning of a headache. Why had it seemed like a good idea to drink with the wranglers? Jane would laugh her ass off at me if she knew. Laurel too. This was just the sort of scene they had probably imagined when I told them I was headed West: an abrupt encounter with the full bilious weight of real American masculinity.

Well, fuck. I was here, and I was glad I was here, and I was living as a guy. So I didn't want to be a wrangler and didn't want to even be like the wranglers. So they saw me as a little boy and not a man. That was fine. Things were going well. After all, I'd met Cassie. And that was a good thing, right?

That was a mess, actually. Like everything else.

There was only one thing I knew to do at a moment like this. Make a list.

<u>Ways to Resolve This Situation (aka My Life)</u>:

1. I don't tell Cassie and stop seeing her.
   Problems with this:
   a. I want to see her.
   b. The ranch is too damn small.
2. I don't tell Cassie and keep seeing her.
   Problems with this:
   a. It would go badly, eventually.
3. I tell Cassie.
   Possible results:
   a. She freaks out, I'm fired, or worse.
   b. She doesn't freak out but isn't okay with it. Awkwardness and fear.
   c. She's fine with it. Bliss.

Option 3c was clearly totally and completely implausible. But it was also the only happy ending. And telling her was the right thing to do. Otherwise, given the range of listed outcomes, it was clearly better to leave, and I didn't want to leave.

It wasn't just Cassie either. Despite the craziness of Marc, despite the discomfort of the bunkhouse and the wranglers, I felt a resonance with this place. The beauty of it, the strangeness of it, was just beginning to feel okay. I liked Carl and Steve, and even if we wouldn't ever be best friends, I felt I could trust them: Steve to be fair, Carl to have my back when it came down to issues with Marc or the wranglers. I wanted to be here.

The only trouble with achieving option 3c was that, apart from its implausibility, it meant I had to act. And act courageously. I wasn't so good at that. My last courageous act had been to get on a bus, go West, and, now that I thought about it, that was just as cowardly (i.e., running away from Laurel rather than actually working through our problems) as it was courageous.

So I had to tell Cassie. The sooner the better. Even though I didn't want to. Even though I'd come here to live as a guy, not to be out as transgender.

Gus met us in the kitchen before breakfast to explain that he was giving Marc a day or two off to "collect himself," as he put it. He gave Carl and me a little talk about everyone getting along and playing nicely with each other and so on.

Carl, intent on making the most of the time without Marc, had the radio blasting as he washed dishes. I gathered ingredients from the stockroom and hoped I wouldn't screw things up too badly. How hard could it be to make chili for fifty or so people? Certainly that was the easier of the two tasks I had ahead of me today.

The chili turned out okay—or at least none of the dudes complained, and Carl apologized repeatedly during breakfast and dinner for talking about Cassie and me in front of Clyde. I shrugged it off as no big deal. As we were heading out after dinner, he said, "Belva and I are going into town. Clyde's taking Kara, so I think all is forgiven, man. He's moving on."

"Yeah, great," I replied. I was not about to propose a triple date. "Have a good time. Don't stay out too late. It's just the two of us for breakfast." I stopped myself short. If I nagged any more, I'd sound like my mother. "Unless you think Marc will be back tomorrow."

"Who cares?" said Carl, waving as Belva approached. "As soon as he finds out about you and his sister, he's going to blow his stack. He's gone, man."

I wished I had an eighth of his confidence. Alone in the bunk-house, I showered, changed, and ran through some possible lines:

There's something you ought to know, Cassie
I want to tell you something about me
You see, I'm not really a boy
I'm a guy now, but I haven't always been
Maybe I should have told you earlier
I don't want you to be upset

It was like writing a terrible play. I couldn't settle into a scene. I couldn't imagine how the dialogue would go. Or I could; it just all went badly.

I tried to find Cassie's stars as I left the bunkhouse and walked up the slope to her place, but everything up there was a hopeless muddle to me. I climbed the steps to her above-the-garage apartment, empty-handed, but then again, what would I have brought her? Chocolates? Jane would have some crazy suggestion like a wildflower bouquet accompanied by a recitation of Proust.

I knocked softly on the door.

"Come in," she called.

I pushed the door open and found her flung across a couch, watching a baseball game. Her apartment was one big living space up front, the kitchen right ahead as I walked in. A counter with stools separated this from the main area, which held a table and chairs, the couch, a coffee table, a recliner, and a shelf crammed with paperbacks. That was nice to see. I didn't trust a home without books in it.

"Grab me a beer from the fridge. Get one for yourself too," she called without moving from the couch.

She wore blue sweatpants and an old t-shirt, faded green, that made her hair look more golden than usual. She was barefoot and, with the short sleeves of her t-shirt, I could see a clear demarcation: the tanned forearms and hands, the milk-whiteness above the elbows exactly where her rolled sleeves rested when she was riding.

"Quit staring and pass me that beer."

I handed her the bottle and sat on the other end of the couch, near where her feet were stretched out.

"I wasn't sure you'd come over," she said, taking a slug of beer.

"I didn't want you to feel like I was just fooling around."

Cassie let the bottle dangle, the neck held between two fingers, her arm off the side of the couch. She watched me closely for all that she looked relaxed. "Whaddya mean?"

"I mean I like you. I like talking to you and getting to know you and…" I couldn't quite keep eye contact. I mentally rehearsed the lines I'd written down earlier. *There's something I want to tell you...* *There's something you should know about me...* But I couldn't get the words out. Instead I said again, "I wanted you to know I'm not just messing around."

She pulled her knees to her chest, freeing up the middle of the couch. "Come over here," she said, and I scooched toward her until I was almost leaning against her shins. "That's gotta be one of the nicest things I've ever heard. Who would've thought that a guy would be the one to talk about commitment? That is what you're talking about, right?"

I nodded. *Tell her.* "That's what I mean. And I—"

She put a hand gently to my face, fingers on my cheek. "Before you say anything else, there are a few things you should know about me."

That was supposed to be my line. Cassie held her gaze steady, leaning into me as she spoke. "I'm a bitch on wheels. At least that's what most guys say. You can ask Clyde if you don't believe me. I haven't had that many boyfriends. I'm pretty choosy, but I like you, Ron Bancroft. I like you a lot. You're not like anyone I've met."

I opened my mouth, but she plunged on, letting her hand trail down from my cheek to my neck and then to my shoulder. "I'm not real patient. I don't take any bullshit. So don't even try lying to me. And I've never dated anybody as young as you."

"I'm almost twenty," I said. "And—"

She shifted, sitting up and reaching a leg over my thighs so that now she straddled me, her butt resting just above my knees. "And I'm twenty-nine. That's a big difference, kiddo."

From outside, I heard a door slam, a pause, then another slam. Cassie looked out the window, and I followed her gaze, but the glass just gave way to the utter nothingness—stars upon stars—of the Wyoming sky.

"Will Gus care? Should we tell him?" *Just tell her.*

Cassie leaned in and her lips brushed against mine. "He'll be happy as hell. He always thought I was a dyke. Matter of fact, I heard Nancy-pants complaining that I was a lesbo just the other day because I don't want to marry a guy like Clyde."

Shit. Hearing her say "dyke," "lesbo"—all my reluctance came welling back up.

She kissed me again. "Are you sure you've thought this through?"

"You're making rational thought difficult," I said.

"Good," she murmured, her lips close to my ear.

She wasn't going to take this well... But I had to tell her. When I'd disentangled a bit— somehow my hands were under her shirt, against the cool skin of her stomach, a position not ideal for the revelation I had in mind—I leaned my head back against the couch cushions and looked up at her, her hair scattered over her shoulders. She paused now and tucked it behind her ears. Her eyebrows arched as if in expectation of a sarcastic comment.

"There's something I want to tell you, Cassie."

She tilted her head, and her hair fell loose again, partly obscuring the wary look that flashed across her face. "Is this going to be heavy? Should I get another beer?"

I put my hands gently on her wrists. To anchor her. To anchor myself too. I felt like I was going to float away. "It's important to me, and I hope it doesn't upset you. I probably should have told you this earlier."

She shifted off my lap to sit next to me on the couch.

"I was born female, and I was raised as a girl." I gulped some air, not wanting to go on but knowing I had to. "I never felt like a girl though, so about a year ago, I started living as a guy."

I watched her face and wished I hadn't. It was like I could see her receding, like a wave pulling away from the sand. Only she wasn't going to come rushing back anytime soon.

"Are you joking?" she asked.

"No. I'm transgender. I haven't had surgery. I don't take hormones—"

"So you're a girl."

"Not anymore. I'm a guy."

"Does anyone else know this?"

"Not out here."

I waited for her to ask the questions I'd come to expect: when did I know, how had I transitioned, what did my parents think. But she just drew her knees against her chest and sat there, curled up at the other end of the couch, not exactly looking at me.

"I don't think you should tell anyone. They'd kill you." She definitely was not looking at me. "In fact, I don't think you should be here at all. It isn't right. You shouldn't fool people—"

"I'm not trying to fool anyone. This is who I am. I'm a guy."

She shook her head. "But you're really a girl, underneath."

I knew what she meant. Underneath my clothes. Underneath, my body, as if that determined who and what I was. Yes and no—I wasn't not my body, but my body didn't mean what others seemed to think it did. "I'm sorry if I upset you."

"I just had no idea."

A silence drew out between us. I couldn't think of anything else to say. "Should I go?"

"Yeah," she said, still not looking at me. "I think you should."

Outside, I retraced my steps back down the hill from Cassie's place, wishing there was someone I could write to. But Michael wouldn't understand, and Jane would just chide me for getting involved with someone I hadn't come out to, and Laurel, for obvious reasons, was not a possibility. The best option was to scrawl what I felt on a scrap of paper and shove it in a beer bottle, chuck it in the Fork, and hope someone sympathetic would find it. But it would have to float a long way to reach anyone who'd understand.

CHAPTER ELEVEN

After a night of no sleep, I decided the proper course of action was to leave Cassie alone and hope she wouldn't tell anyone else. For the next few days, I just fumbled through my routine, wishing that Cassie would stop by to talk to me, but she didn't.

Marc came back from his days off in a grumpier mood than ever. Granted, I did manage to break two dozen eggs while we were cooking breakfast one morning, but that was only because Carl had spilled a pot of soapy water on the floor by the sink, making me slip all over the place. Marc had blown his stack at both of us, flinging a colander against the wall in his rage. I hoped that Gus would hear and intervene, but no such luck. At least Marc had aimed at the wall and not at us.

On the Fourth of July, Gus planned to take the dudes to a scenic outlook to watch Cody's fireworks. I watched from the porch of the lodge as Steve and Gus loaded the dudes into the vans. Cassie stood there, leaning against a hood of a van, talking with one of the dudes, her cowboy hat tipped back on her head. It hurt just to look at her, so I went back into the kitchen. Steve asked if I wanted to come along with the dudes, but it felt better to be alone. It had barely been a week. I should give her more time before trying to open up the conversation again.

Carl drove off with Belva, and I walked down the slope toward the bunkhouse. As I crossed the road, I saw Clyde's big black truck kicking up a cloud of dust, and I guessed that he and Kara were heading out as well. There was a light on in the barn, and I paused for a moment, staring at the open door. Maybe Cassie hadn't gone with the dudes. Maybe she was in there. Maybe she was waiting for me to talk to her.

Maybe this would be a turning point. Maybe Marc would straighten out and be nice. And maybe my father would call me in a couple of weeks to wish me a happy birthday and tell me I was a great son and that he was proud of me.

Or maybe I'd just crawl into my bunk in the dark and shimmy out of my compression top under the covers, afraid that someone would walk in on me.

"Pies!" Marc shouted as he came out of the storeroom the next afternoon. "Twenty of them. The dough is in the walk-in. Get rolling. Do you know how to do it by now?"

I didn't bother to answer him and set up my station at the counter, arranging pans and flour. My mother had taught me how to make pie crust. Marc used butter, but she favored Crisco. We used to roll out a dozen or so pies every Thanksgiving when we hosted all my brothers and their families at our big old farmhouse in Tamworth. Those were some of my favorite times. Even though I always got stuck with babysitting my little nieces and nephews, it was nice to have everyone together.

I went to the walk-in and retrieved the wax paper-wrapped balls of dough, wondering if I'd ever go back for another holiday. I started working the dough with the rolling pin, remembering the inevitable game of touch football on the lawn and the inevitable post-meal squabble over who got the best napping spots.

A sudden clang jarred me out of my thoughts.

I looked up to realize Marc had smacked a metal bowl on the counter across from me.

"Clyde says you're giving my sister the business," he said, scowling.

I ignored him, pushing the edges of the dough thinner. If it wasn't even, some of the crust would burn and some would be undercooked. (Exhibit A: Veronica Bancroft's very first Thanksgiving pie, circa age eight—the one my brothers insisted was the most delicious of them all despite its cosmetic defects.)

Marc tumbled apples onto the counter and began to peel them, the knife nicking smoothly under the skin.

"Have you been messing with Cassie?" he pressed.

"It's none of your business."

"She's my sister, stupid. Of course it's my business."

Carl came over and started hanging clean utensils on the racks. "You should get a girlfriend of your own, Marc. Then you wouldn't worry so much about what we're getting up to."

I shot Carl a quick grin.

"And you should shut the fuck up," Marc replied.

As I bit back the remark I'm sure Cassie would have wanted me to deliver—that she was no one's business but her own—I wondered if my brothers would have been like this with one of my boyfriends. If I'd ever had any boyfriends. I could see Michael trying to be my knight in shining armor. I would have hated him for it.

"We're both adults," I told Marc, carefully transferring the crust to the pan. Of course, I could have told him that it was over between Cassie and me, but I didn't want to admit that—not to him and not to myself.

"Barely, in your case." He sliced the apple quickly, letting the severed segments fall into the bowl, and picked up the next piece of fruit. "Let me put it to you straight. Keep your hands off her, or I'll make you wish you had."

"It's up to her to—"

"No, it's not. I don't like you, dipshit. And I don't want you around Cassie. Got it?" He set the apple down. "Think you can handle the pies, Ronnie?"

"I know I can."

"Well, good." He seemed torn between displeasure at my confidence and pleasure at my compliance. "It's steak night. Potatoes are in the oven. When they're done, put the pies in. I'm going to go get the coals ready. When I shout, bring out the steaks, Carl. They're going to the dudes straight off the grill." Marc wiped his hands on his apron and then, moving quicker than I thought him capable of, leaned across the counter and poked me hard, once, right on my sternum. "Hands off. Got it?"

He slipped through the screen door with a nonchalance I felt certain was feigned. In a moment, the smell of lighter fluid wafted in. I finished two crusts and started rolling more dough.

Carl peered out the door and then came over to peel apples. "He's pissed, man. Nice work. I just saw him stalking off toward the bunkhouse. Wanna bet he comes back shitfaced?"

"I'm not stupid enough to bet against that. I'll get the pies in and then set the tables." We both glanced at the clock over the sink. Thirty minutes until dinner time.

Baked potatoes meant sour cream, chives, and butter on the tables. Steaks meant an extra knife. I had it all set and stepped back into the kitchen to check on the pies. Carl stood nervously at the screen door.

"What's up?" I asked him.

"Don't the coals look ready?" He pointed outside at the grills. "Yeah."

"So why hasn't Marc asked for the steaks?"

"How the hell should I know? Where is he?"

"I'll go look for him if you bring the steaks out." Carl pointed to the clock. Ten minutes.

I hated steak night. The day before, the dudes had gone to the ranch next door and watched roping and branding and whatever other show the cowboys put on and then learned about the care and feeding of a high-quality beef steer and—skipping over the slaughter stuff—got to pick out their own genuine Wyoming free-range steaks. I yanked open the walk-in door. Yes, there they were.

Trays of beef, each with a little plastic marker in it indicating its dude's name and preferred degree of done-ness.

On a good week, steak night sent Marc into a tizzy. And this week had been far from good. I hefted the tray and kicked open the screen door.

Carl jogged up to me. "Found him. He's drunk off his ass."

"What a shock."

Marc, gesticulating with a barbecue fork in his hand, wavered near the grills. "Gimme the steaks." He yanked the tray from my hands. "Carl's supposed to bring them. You set the tables."

"Tables are set," I told him. "Dinner's supposed to be in five minutes." I turned back toward the kitchen to see Carl hurrying out with another tray of steaks.

"Get those on the grill," Marc snapped.

I left them to it and went back to get the potatoes onto serving trays.

Billy poked his head through the swinging doors. "Ring that bell, Ron boy. It's steak night, and I'm starving."

I pushed past him into the dining area with pitchers of water. "We're running a little late."

I hustled back into the kitchen to get the pies out of the oven, and, hearing Marc's shouts, spared a glance toward the grills. Carl was out there picking steaks up from the grass while Marc waved a towel in an attempt to fan the listless coals. Suffice it to say, things didn't look good.

"You gonna ring the damn bell?" Billy said, pushing his head through the door again.

"You do it."

He stalked off, and in a moment, I heard the clanging. I started the dudes with potatoes and salad and rolls, explaining that the steaks would be right out. I hoped. But a dash to the screen door revealed Carl trying to extract steaks from a now blazing inferno with no sign of Marc. I pulled the pies from the ovens, and Carl, sooty, came into the kitchen and set down a tray of blackened steaks.

"Can you take those out, Carl? I forgot the A-1, and they're going to need something to choke that charcoal down."

He didn't look pleased at the thought of facing the dudes with the desiccated lumps of meat, but he pushed through the doors and I dashed into the storeroom, right into Marc.

As if he'd been expecting me, Marc grabbed me by the shoulders and tossed me against the file cabinet, making the cheap metal flex resoundingly. *Whang.* Another shove that drove the breath out of my chest.

"What the—"

He pressed up against me, his hard, warm gut pinning me to the cabinet. I squirmed, an insect on a pin. Waves of a sour liquor smell coiled off of him. With one hand he got my shirtfront twisted up in his fist.

"I didn't trust you from the first time I saw you," he spat.

"What the fuck—"

"Meeting Gus in the bus station. Saying you go to Harvard. You're a lying piece of shit. Telling us you're nineteen when you look like you're ten. I bet your license is fake. I bet everything about you is fake." He rammed his fist against my chest as if he would drive it straight through.

"Jesus Christ, Marc," I managed. "Get off me."

"You're probably lying to my sister about everything too."

"I don't know what you're talking about." I tried to wriggle away but couldn't move. "Just calm down, okay?"

"You shut up. Just shut up." Spit flew from his mouth and landed on my face. "I'm gonna find out the truth. Everything about you."

I got my hands up and pushed against him to no effect. "Let me go!" I shouted, abandoning any attempt at dignity.

"What the hell is going on?" Suddenly Gus was standing in the doorway to the kitchen.

I had never been so glad to see him. Marc dropped me immediately, stepping back, and I pushed myself upright, steadying myself against the filing cabinet.

"He's been messing with Cassie," Marc squawked. I stayed pressed against the cool metal of the filing cabinet, out of range of Marc's fists.

"You're drunk," Gus said. "What did I tell you?"

"This little shit. With our sister! Don't you remember—"

"I remember what I told you three days ago: You screw up once more, and you're done." Gus's hand landed heavily on Marc's shoulder, and though I expected Marc to fight, to lash out at me or Gus or both, he merely slumped down, hunching his back and staring at the floor. "I can drive you to the bus station and get you a ticket back to Jersey," Gus said. "Or I can drive you to the detox clinic in Cody. Your choice."

The screen door snapped shut behind the two of them as Gus led Marc outside. Just like that.

Carl peered into the storeroom. "You okay, man?"

I went back into the kitchen, still buzzing with adrenaline, and stared out through the mesh. Gus had his arm around Marc's shoulder.

"That guy's not just an alcoholic," I said. "He's fucking nuts."

"Took you long enough to figure that out."

I let out a long exhale. Did Marc actually think I was hiding something? Did he have some reason to think I was a liar? Or was he just mad at me about Cassie and spouting all kinds of crazy crap?

"I think he's going. For good," I said. I could just see the white of Marc's t-shirt as he stood beside Gus's truck.

"Sweet," said Carl. "Nice work, man."

I did feel relief as the truck pulled away from the lodge. Some relief. And some worry about Cassie. Would Marc's departure change anything between the two of us?

CHAPTER TWELVE

It was quiet in the bunkhouse now. I slept better without Marc's snores and had plenty of time to read all the books I wanted. It was nice to come back after a run and, knowing Carl was off with Belva, shower unafraid. It was nice to work at the kitchen, just Carl and me. And even if it was a bit more work without Marc there (and even if the meatballs weren't quite as good), that was fine. The asshole was gone.

But I was still worried about Cassie. I missed her and wanted to talk to her even though I knew the best thing was to let her be alone. She wouldn't be the first person whose friendship I had lost by coming out. On my afternoon runs, I berated myself for ever telling her. Hadn't I come out West in order to leave all that transgender stuff behind? No matter how fast I ran, I couldn't escape the only clear conclusion: I never should have gotten involved with her in the first place.

Steve checked in on the kitchen often, and one night Nancy came to help us. She gave the kitchen such a scouring, she seemed to be more interested in exorcising any remains of Marc than in sanitizing the surfaces. I caught glimpses of Cassie at breakfast and dinner, but she never gave me a look, let alone stopped to talk. Almost a week after Marc left, I was mopping the floor in the dining room when Steve came by.

"Howdy," I said. "I'm almost done."

"Take your time," he replied. He helped himself to a cup of coffee and sat at one of the empty tables.

I rinsed the mop and squeezed it out, then set to scrubbing a sticky patch.

"What's on the to-do list today?" I asked. I had discovered weeks ago that Steve was almost as much of a list-keeper as I was.

"Ah. Today. We'll see." He stared past me, out the window, and I turned to see what he was looking at: a line of horses crossing between the guest cabins and the office as they headed for the trails above the river, an unmistakable ponytail twitching against a sky-blue shirt at the rear of the group.

"Everything okay?" I asked. Steve was usually chatty, sharing details of the weather report or what we'd be working on.

He blew on his coffee and stared into his mug. "I'll tell you when you finish mopping."

That sounded ominous. I picked up my pace, slopping water a bit, but Marc wasn't there to complain, and Steve didn't seem very interested in what I was doing. At last I wheeled the mop bucket into the kitchen and shed my apron before returning to the dining room.

Steve set down his mug and shot me a quick glance before averting his eyes.

"Gus wants to see you in the office."

"Okay," I said. Maybe one of the guests had gotten food poisoning. Or maybe Gus finally had something to say with regards to Cassie. I'd been waiting for that shoe to drop ever since Marc had mentioned it to him.

Gus sat at his cluttered desk—top strewn with screwdrivers, gears, a doorknob—while Steve stood behind his own tidy workplace.

"You mind telling me what the hell's going on?" Gus demanded, a flush rising up his neck and splotching across his cheeks.

I pulled in a breath, not sure what to say, but before I could reply, Gus barreled on.

"Do you think this is some kind of joke?"

"No," I said, hesitating.

"You think you're playing a game, coming out West and pretending to be a boy? You think I'm dumb? You think I wouldn't figure it out?" He shoved back his desk chair and stood up, leaning over the messy surface at me.

My heart stuttered as disbelief shivered through me. How did he know? He couldn't know. It felt like I was sucking air through a straw.

"Pretty funny, huh?" he continued. "Come on out to Wyoming and have a good laugh. Well, you can clear off my ranch. Right now."

"I wasn't trying to fool—"

"Steve. Drive him out of here in thirty minutes."

"Let me—"

"Get your stuff, Ron," Steve said. "I'll pick you up down there."

The bunkhouse waited, empty as Pandora's box. It wasn't like a robbery scene—my stuff wasn't spilled out everywhere—but I could still tell someone had been through it. My neat rows of socks disturbed. The corners of the sheets mussed where someone had checked under the mattress. The notebooks and letters shoved back on their shelves but out of order. The backpack was under the bed but with some of its pockets unzipped. Who had it been? What had they found? A photo, a journal entry, the tampons? And what had they felt at that moment: Surprise, confusion, disgust, triumph?

I sank onto the bed, feeling deflated. Gus knew. Steve knew. Everyone would know soon. They'd all have a good laugh while I'd be out on my ass.

I stuffed the contents of my drawers into the backpack, grabbed my toothbrush and shampoo, my shelf of library books. The yellow pad with my latest list of lines I'd never get to use on Cassie.

God. Cassie.

Part of me said, screw it. Her brother was the one kicking me out. But that wasn't fair. I knew Cassie wasn't the one who had said anything, and she'd likely have to take a lot of crap from Gus and the wranglers and everyone else once it was known that we'd been involved and that I was transgender. Or, as Gus had put it, that I was pretending to be a boy. Or, as they'd all say, that I was a girl.

I had to try to write something to her. I sat down on the bottom bunk and put the yellow pad on my knee.

Dear Cassie,

I'm sorry I have to write this in a letter rather than say it in person, but Gus is kicking me off the ranch. Somehow, he found out that I'm transgender, and he doesn't want me working here anymore. I don't know what I'll do next.

I'm sorry things have ended this way. I was hoping that maybe, with time, we'd have a chance to talk. I'm sorry that I upset you, and I'm sorry if you feel like I was trying to fool you. I wasn't. I felt drawn to you the first time I saw you and even more every time we talked.

And I'm sorry if this—my being found out, my being fired— makes your life more difficult. I certainly didn't mean for that to happen.

I really like you, Cassie. I admire your confidence, enjoy your sense of humor, respect your attitude toward life. I want to get to know you better, but I guess I've wrecked my chance of that. I'm sorry.

Please know that, no matter what Gus thinks, I just wanted to come out West and live a simple life as a guy. I count it as the best part of the journey that I got to meet you.

Yours,

Ron

There was more I wanted to write, but I knew time was running short. I put the note in an envelope, wrote "Cassie" on the front, and jogged to the barn, tacking the envelope to a beam beneath yet another jackalope skull. How many of those stupid things did one ranch need? I hoped she'd find my letter before she heard anything from someone else. I took one last look at it there, and a little doubt skittered across my mind: What if it *had* been Cassie who had told Gus? Not a chance. First, she would have been shooting herself in the foot. And second, it didn't seem like her style. Not her. But who then?

I couldn't worry about that now. I had larger issues to contend with.

When Steve pulled up, I heaved my backpack into the bed of the truck and settled into the passenger seat, staring straight out the windshield. He drove silently through the ranch, and my mind alternately gabbled—*What next? What the hell are you going to do now?*—and seized up, unable to accept what had just happened.

At the threshold where the drive met the highway, Steve stopped the truck even though there was no traffic.

"Which way?" he asked.

"What do you mean?"

"Which way do you want to go? Right, I can take you to Yellowstone. There's restaurants and hotels, you could get a job as a dishwasher pretty easy. Or left, back to Cody. I can drive you to the bus station."

I looked to the right. I'd been a fool to think I could do this, to think I belonged here. Time to go back to New York and tell Jane and Laurel and everyone else they'd been correct.

"Left," I said. Let's get this over with.

He pulled out. Soon the wind was guttering through his open window, a waffling sound that echoed the nausea roiling in my stomach. I was going back to Cody. Back to the bus station. And from there? New York was my only anchor point. And even then, Laurel was with Heather, and I'd be living at Jane's parents' house until I could get a job and money and live somewhere else. Was that so bad? It wasn't terrible. At least I wouldn't have to worry about being discovered all the time. But I wasn't ready to settle into that known world. I wanted the unexplored. I wanted to write my own terms.

Mountains and cliffs whipped past. I tried not to look, tried to stare at the indifferent ribbon of asphalt. But my eyes kept getting drawn over to the woods, with their pine needle-strewn shade, steep slopes of pebbly rock—pumice, I knew from my field guide, or tuff, volcanic rock pocked full of holes, not like our solid New Hampshire granite. I felt a growing hollow in my gut, an emptiness that would take a long time for me to fill.

I was going to miss this place. I had barely gotten to know it at all. It didn't seem fair to be kicked out so abruptly, to have to slink back East. Maybe I'd let Steve drive me to Cody and then look for another job there. Or get on a bus and go even farther West.

Steve took his foot off the gas and aimed the truck toward a rest area where two RVs wallowed by picnic benches as a kid sat squirting yellow mustard onto his plate. Steve nosed into a parking spot and shut the engine off but made no motion to get out, just sat there drumming his fingers lightly on the steering wheel. I put a hand to the door latch, wondering if I should just get out now, hitch a ride with one of the RVs (if they'd have me), and avoid whatever unpleasantness was coming.

"I'm sorry things turned out this way," he said finally.

I shot him a quizzical glance but took my hand off the door latch. "Me too." I shrugged. "I guess it's mostly my fault."

Steve nodded but still stared out the windshield, not looking at me. A sensation rose in me, one I hadn't felt since I'd arrived in Wyoming except for a brief moment with Cassie: It came from the knowledge that the person next to me knew I was transgender and felt uncomfortable and that everything between us would now and always carry this patina, this tarnish, this film of dissonance. There was the me I knew I was, and then there was this other me. The past me. The one I wanted to be done with. Why couldn't I get away from it?

"You should have told us right away," said Steve.

"Gus wouldn't have hired me."

"Maybe, maybe not. But if he did, and if he knew—" Steve paused. He couldn't even name this thing between us. "—then folks would have gradually accepted it."

"It doesn't work like that. If you didn't know me and the first thing I told you about me was that even though I live as a guy, I'd grown up as a girl, you wouldn't want to get to know me. You'd dismiss me right then."

"Some people would. They're the jerks. Some people wouldn't." He ran a hand over his flat top and finally turned to face me. "I understand why you didn't. I just don't think that was the right choice. Look, what's done is done. I have a friend from the Lions Club. He's the ranger who oversees this district. This is the busiest time of year for the Forest Service. Do you want to stop in and see if he has a job?"

"Not washing dishes?" I said, letting a little smile edge onto my face.

"Not much need for that in the Forest Service."

I stared out at the cliffs that rose beyond the parking lot, rust-red and looming. I knew I wasn't done with this place, and it wasn't done with me. "That sounds good."

Steve turned the key in the ignition and guided us back to the highway.

I rubbed my palms against the thighs of my jeans, my fingers trembling with relief. "I feel terrible for the mess I made. Especially for Cassie."

"You've put her in a real pickle. But she's a strong girl. She'll pull through. That's why you should've told us, first thing."

I felt a flash of annoyance. What could this straight man know about coming out? "Okay. I know I screwed up, and I do feel really bad. But honestly, it doesn't work like you think it does. I don't want people to hate me for what they think I am without knowing the real me beyond that."

"If folks are going to hate you for being what you are, they'll hate you sooner or later, whenever you tell them. So why not be up front?"

"If they don't know, they'll be okay with me. Like Carl and the wranglers."

"They'll hate you more once they find out. 'Cause then you're not just what you are, you're also a liar."

"It's not a lie. I'm just waiting to tell the full story until it's a good time."

"Well," said Steve, drawing the word out. "No time like the present."

Scenery flicked past. Drowsy beef critters. RVs. Buttes. Sage scruff. The truck's wheels sizzled on the pavement, and the air played shimmering tricks on the road ahead. Now water. Now tar. Now sky.

"Thanks for taking me to your friend," I said.

"You're one of the best workers I've ever had," Steve replied. "And I think you'll like Pete. Real nice fellow. Salt of the earth."

There's a phrase you didn't hear back East. It was easier to imagine Jane saying, *a real mensch*. I missed Jane, even though I could also imagine her saying, *I told you so*.

The truck started to slow in advance of a parking lot where cars towing pop-up campers and a few RVs sat beached before picnic tables. A brown and green building hunkered at one end beside a sign: Shoshone National Forest, Wapiti Ranger District, Visitor Information.

Steve turned the truck down the dirt road behind the visitor center, straight between two split rail fences, spewing up dirt clouds as we went, obliterating the world behind us. Ahead, I saw a semicircle of dark brown buildings. The one in the center boasted a flagpole out front and a radio antenna on top.

Steve stopped the truck by the flagpole and hopped out.

"Okay?" he said as I shut the truck door behind me. "I'll see if Pete's here."

"Okay."

Steve brushed his hand over his flat top, stared at me a moment as if on the cusp of saying something else, then turned to head into the building. The metal of the truck's hood ticked without rhythm. A line of cottonwoods behind the building suggested that the river ran through there, invisible to me. We'd gone maybe thirty minutes on the highway, but the land here was different. The cliffs beyond the Fork jutted up red, with darker gray streaks. And there were no pines here, just cottonwoods and willows.

I stared down the drive. Our dust clouds had settled back to the earth. Did I want to be here? Yes. I wasn't the same as when I'd first arrived. I'd come out here with something to prove, and I felt like I'd proven it. If someone hadn't gone digging through my stuff, they never would have known.

So I could pass. I could live as a man. I knew that now, and that made a difference. It meant that I didn't have to come out. It also meant that I could, if I wanted to.

The door opened and Steve emerged, followed by a man in the green jeans and tan shirt of a forest ranger.

"Pete," said Steve, "this is Ron."

I held out my too-small hand. Pete stood several inches shorter than me, round-headed and with what remained of his white hair styled in a regrettable comb-over. His cheeks rose in two knobs as he grinned, his eyes squinting behind his square plastic-framed glasses (just like my dad had worn in the mid-'80s, with a bar over the nose bridge). He looked pleasantly gnomish.

"Nice to meet you," I said.

"Steve tells me you're looking for work."

I nodded and resisted looking at Steve as Pete let a pause grow in the conversation.

Then he asked, "What sort of work do you like?"

"I've been washing dishes, cleaning the kitchen, helping Steve with odd jobs—"

"Ron's the hardest worker I've had," Steve chimed in. "Doesn't need supervision. Does what you ask for."

"It won't be glamorous," Pete began.

"That's fine," I replied.

"Well, then. My campsite manager could use a hand. It's high season now until Labor Day, and he's been real busy since his assistant had to leave."

"I can help out."

Pete grinned wider, his eyes wrinkling up behind his glasses. "I haven't even told you the details! Clean up campsites and the rest areas and picnic spots. Tend to things around here too, the grounds and the buildings and the stables. Pay's not much, five bucks an hour."

"Sounds good. Is there a place for me to live here at the station?" I felt a little quiver in my voice, a little buckle of my chin, as if I might start crying. Suddenly I wanted to disappear. I *had* disappeared. I was in the middle of nowhere with all my possessions sitting in the back of someone else's pickup truck, banking on a stranger having a place for me to stay. I just wanted to sit down for a little while, figure things out, write a few good lists.

I cleared my throat. "I don't have a car either."

"That shouldn't be a problem," Pete said, a little gently. "We've got a couple of options for living quarters, the bunkhouse or a cabin."

Steve shuffled his feet and leaned against the hood of his truck, catching my eye when I looked over at him, giving me a little nod.

I cleared my throat again. My arms hung stupidly by my sides, but there was nowhere else to put them. I felt Pete's gaze on me, Steve's too. Waiting. Wanting something from me.

"Uh... You should know that I'm transgender. I was born and raised as a girl. I'm biologically female. But I'm living as a guy now. It shouldn't matter, but I thought you should know."

Pete nodded, his head bobbing steadily for a few seconds. "You're right. It shouldn't matter. But I'll put you in the cabin by yourself. That'll be better." He pursed his lips in thought, and I waited for some questions. There were the usual suspects:

Which bathroom do you use?

What was your name as a girl?

How'd you know?

But he just nodded again, and that heavy feeling of suspense went out of my limbs, leaving me slack with relief.

"All righty," said Pete. "That's set. I'll go get some paperwork, and we'll settle you in." He turned to go back into the office. "Forest Service is big on paperwork," he added, looking back at us with a wink.

After I grabbed my backpack from the rear of the truck, Steve offered me his hand.

"I'm glad you told him."

"Thanks for the introduction, and thanks for not telling him yourself."

"It's your business. But I think you did the right thing." He took his wallet from his pocket and began to count out bills. "You almost made it to the halfway point. And you more than earned your pay. 'Specially putting up with Marc." He passed the money to me.

"Thanks." I thought about asking him to tell Cassie something, but I had no message to give other than what I'd already left for her.

"Good luck," Steve said. He reached into his pocket once more and took out a business card with the ranch's logo. On the back side, he scribbled a telephone number. "This is for the phone in my apartment, not the office. If you need anything. But I think you'll be in good hands with Pete."

I stuffed the card in my pocket and shook his hand again. He waited long enough to say goodbye to Pete and then drove away, dust swirling behind him.

CHAPTER THIRTEEN

"Let's give you the lay of the land," Pete said.

I grappled my pack on and followed Pete around the half circle arc of the ranger station while he narrated the provenance of each brown building: the stables, a couple of small cabins, two larger bunkhouses for the trail and fire crews, and finally, a very small log cabin set back behind and to the side of a plain old clapboard house. The cabin was old enough to be off-kilter, with a front porch that seemed tenuously tacked on.

"Here you are," Pete said, holding the door for me. "Used to be a coal shed," he explained. "But it's cozy. The fellow who was helping Walt had to take off a couple of weeks ago, family emergency, so I'm real glad Steve brought you by."

Inside, one room. Fridge, counter, sink, stove, cabinet along one wall. A table—Formica-topped and patterned so like my grandmother's that I could suddenly smell her perfume—with two chairs. A wood stove with a rocking chair nearby. A double bed. "Bathroom's back there," said Pete as he fiddled with the curtains over the sink. Past the bed, I nudged the door open. A little cramped but all mine.

"Looks great." I leaned my pack against the bed.

"Not too small?"

"Bigger than what my friends are subletting in New York."

"Let me introduce you to my wife."

We walked back across the brief interval of grass between the buildings. "Laundry's in there," Pete pointed to a shed alongside the house and then opened the front door. "Hello! Margaret?"

"Back here!"

We crossed a pleasant living room with a wood stove and a couch and entered a kitchen where Pete introduced me: "Ron, this is my wife, Margaret."

She had her hands in a pile of pie dough and appeared to be the very model of a grandmother: plaid apron, graying hair in a bun, reading glasses perched on top of her head.

"Ron's going to help Walt out. He'll be living in the coal cabin."

She scooped up the dough, swaddled it in wax paper, and washed her hands before offering a palm to me. "A pleasure to meet you."

"Margaret's a sort of station mother—"

"Grandmother if you keep hiring them this young," she said with a laugh. "I cook dinner every night. Twenty-five dollars for the week, and you boys help with the washing. You need sheets and towels?"

"Yes, please," I said. I glanced at Pete briefly, but he was busily cleaning the lenses of his glasses. Repressing a sigh, I thought of Steve's advice. "I told Pete this, but I should tell you too, just so you know… I'm transgender. I live as a boy, but I was born and raised as a girl."

"Well, okay," Margaret said, looking a little confused. "That's fine."

I still didn't want to tell people this—I wanted to just be a guy, nothing else. But maybe Steve had a point. I couldn't decide what was right or what it was that I wanted: to change how I saw myself or to change how the world saw me. And I didn't know if either was even possible.

Margaret gave me a reassuring smile. I maintained that Steve was a little naive about the risks of coming out, but maybe I'd underestimated the potential benefits.

"He doesn't have a car," Pete said in a delightful non sequitur, steering the conversation back onto safe terrain. "Someone can get you to town soon, Ron, but maybe we can set you up with food for a few days?"

I left their house with arms full of linen and groceries.

"Dinner at six thirty," Margaret called after me.

Bed made. Books on shelf. Clothes in the dresser near the bed. Toothbrush in the bathroom. Oatmeal in the cupboard. Milk in the fridge. I found my hands trembling as I put away the peanut butter, the loaf of bread, the package of cookies Margaret had forced on me despite my protests, saying nothing more than "growing boys," a phrase I appreciated given my awkward coming out.

I checked my watch: two in the afternoon. I missed my routine. My turkey sandwich. My jog down the ranch drive. The little creek up amid the pines. I missed Carl, his joking and easy banter. We'd been a good team against Marc, standing up for each other. What would he think of me now?

I sat on the bed, soft, sagging under my weight, and took deep breaths, surprised to hear a sob jerk at my throat. I was so damn stupid. I lay down, felt the bed sink to envelop me. I could tell myself that this was better—better job (Who wouldn't want to be a forest ranger?), better place to live, better boss—but the truth was, I had screwed up.

The worst part of it was the position I had put Cassie in. Up until this morning, I had hoped that with a few more days, maybe a few short conversations about something innocuous like the weather, things would have been okay between us. It would have taken time, but it might have worked out. Right now though, I imagined she'd be leading a group of horses back into the barn. Finding my letter. Worse, I could imagine later tonight, the teasing, the snide remarks. What the wranglers would say.

At least Pete knew. That felt...good? A relief. Like I had more control over things, even if that was just an illusion. In fact, it had felt nice to talk openly to Steve, to realize that this could be a fact between us. In some odd way, I almost wanted to see the wranglers and Carl one more time to say, *This is who I am. Transgender.* Not to taunt them, not to imply (as Gus had feared) that I'd tricked them, but just to say, *This is me, and I lived with you. I'm not ashamed of who I am.*

But if I wasn't ashamed and if I wasn't trying to fool them, then why hadn't I told them? In truth, I didn't want to see them again. It wouldn't be pretty.

I sat up and dug my knuckles into my eyes, rubbing at existential grit.

Then I took the yellow pad from my pack and clicked my pen.

Dear Cassie,
    I am so sorry.

I saw her, that wink, that half-grin, that easy beauty she had: t-shirt and blue jeans and ponytail gorgeous.

I am so sorry.

But it was too late. Soon, she'd probably hate me as much as Marc did.

Trading jeans for running shorts, I laced on my sneakers. Outside, a daytime moon ghosted above the red cliffs. The North Fork guttered and roared. The fence line by the stable led to a bridge, which crossed to a dirt road. I shambled from walk to jog, from jog to run, the river behind me, the road rising in the distance to a stand of pines. A thread of sweat edged from my hairline toward my cheek, but the thin air sucked it dry, leaving the rasp of salt on my skin. Far away, the violet mountains continued on. This place was too good to leave.

A few hours later, the trail crew rolled in, driving mint-green Forest Service trucks. Laughs and the clang of metal as they unloaded a trailer at the stables, steering the horses inside. Margaret began to ferry stacks of plates from her house to the picnic tables, and I went to help. The men waved to her and then clambered into their bunkhouse. The horses, loose now in the pastures that ran alongside the station and down the long drive, nickered and jostled and tossed their heads. (She'd have found the note. She'd have read it by now. She knew…)

I set two pitchers of fruit punch on the table.

"Smells delicious," Pete said.

Margaret rang a bell and each brown building disgorged its men, still in the grays and greens and tans of the Forest Service uniform. Pete and I stood to the side as they queued up, and he narrated.

"That's the trail crew." Young, vaguely military with their similar buzz cuts, I counted seven of them. "They're here most nights. Sometimes they head out on a hitch for a few days to fix up some backcountry spot."

He paused, and in that pause I reflected on how much I savored words like "hitch." Words that didn't exist in the Eastern vernacular. Words that—unlike theoretical jargon—sounded like they meant it.

"There are 1.75 million acres of wilderness in this forest," Pete mused. "That's a lot of territory to cover."

It sounded bigger than the whole state of New Hampshire.

"Ah, here's Walt." Pete waved to a man who cut from the stables across the station's yard to us. Green jeans and khaki shirt like everyone else, but he had a long beard, square at the bottom, which reminded me of a Civil War general. Tweak the clothes a little bit, and he'd look plausibly Amish. And if you put him in grungy jeans, flannel shirt and Birkenstocks, he'd be a perfect fit for hippie Harvard Square. Despite the clunky work boots, he walked with a lilt, rising up on the balls of his feet with each step.

"Walt, this is Ron. He's going to be your assistant."

"All righty." Walt grinned through his beard as he held out his hand. "Where are you from, Ron?"

"New Hampshire."

"No kidding. I went to college up there."

"Ron's been working at a ranch," Pete said as we joined the dinner line. "Friend of mine brought him by, thought he'd do well here. You'll get him set with a uniform and show him the ropes tomorrow?"

"You bet." We took plates of chicken and green beans and sat at a picnic table where Margaret joined us and dug in.

"So," Walt began once we'd demolished our dinner, "where in New Hampshire are you from?"

"Tamworth," I said, not expecting anyone to know my speck of a town.

"Home to Mount Chocorua." My surprise must have been blatant because Walt laughed. "I've hiked that a few times. I've hiked most of the White Mountains. Green ones too."

"Even *I've* hiked Mount Chocorua," said Pete. "Back before the Kancamagus Highway was built, before either of you were born."

"How do you know the area?" I asked.

"I had cousins from Massachusetts who had a summer place up on Lake Winnipesaukee. I grew up down in Meeteetse, Wyoming, but I still got out to that lake at least once a summer," Pete said.

Just hearing the names "Chocorua" and "Winnipesaukee" made me lonesome all over again. "I love that lake," I told them. "I went to YMCA camp there when I was a kid."

"Little busy for my taste," said Walt. "I'm a North Country boy myself. Went to college in Hanover."

"At Dartmouth?"

"Only college in town." He wore a look I had familiarity with: the half-pride, half-chagrin of dropping an Ivy League name.

"Are you in college, Ron?" Margaret asked.

"I just finished my sophomore year at Harvard."

Walt laughed. "You've got the most over-educated crew this side of the Continental Divide, Pete."

I laughed too. "Which side of that are we on anyway?" I pointed to the where the North Fork ran behind the station. "Does that river flow east or west?"

Walt said "East" just as Margaret said "West." More laughter.

"Should I get the map off the wall?" Margaret teased. I was about to tell her, yes, please, when Pete waved her off.

"It actually goes both ways. Besides, it's not on the map, really." He took his square glasses off and wiped the lenses. "This river, or at least its tributaries, starts up in Yellowstone. Some of them flow west. But down here, it flows east. How does it manage that?" He shrugged. "Beyond me." Darn. I'd been hoping for an answer. "This station is a little dot." Pete jabbed his finger against the picnic table. "In the middle of a great big forest. And you and Walt are going to be driving all over, east and west and up and down. Any given day, you'll be on both sides of the Divide."

"I think I'll enjoy that," I said.

"Well, now." Pete pushed his plate away. "Since you're from New Hampshire, I expect you play cribbage. And since you go to Harvard, I expect you play well."

He went to retrieve his board just as the fire crew rolled in, a line of F-350s painted mint green. Soon they were grabbing plates and heaping food on.

Walt stood up, brushed a few shreds of chicken from his beard, and called out, "New guy, working with me. This is Ron, everyone." I waved as Walt settled back next to me. "That fellow with the mustache?" he said, pointing out the one older looking man on the fire crew. "That's Gary, the crew captain. He keeps them on their toes. These fellows are considered the best handcrew in the Shoshone National Forest. Unless there's an all-alarm call to fight a fire, we won't work with them much. They spend most of their time in the backcountry, and we're strictly front country. Except on our days off, if you want. You like to hike, Ron?"

"I love it. I haven't gotten out much this summer. Just little stuff."

"Things are on a different scale out here. Not the beaten down trails like the Whites."

"I barely have a sense of it," I said. "I've gotten up on some of the buttes, but…" I waved generally to the mountains, the horizon, the beyond. "Not really anything. I need a trail map, something that really shows the detail."

"I'll get you the quadrants tomorrow," said Walt.

Pete settled back down, placing the cribbage board between us, and began to shuffle the cards. The margin of the sky took on the orange brush of evening. Margaret brought out pies, and the trail crew squared off against the fire crew to play volleyball. Walt watched Pete and me play, and by the time the streetlights flickered on, illuminating the center of the station, I'd lost colossally.

Walt stood and stretched. "Time to help with the dishes."

I'd kind of hoped to be done with dishes for the summer, but at least I knew it was a job I could do well.

I hadn't set an alarm, but out of habit I snapped awake at five. A run on the same road as yesterday. My footfalls on the packed dirt seemed to say, go, go, go, and I couldn't decide: *Go, keep running, head to those beckoning mountains*, or, *Go, get back, you know where you belong.*

Except I didn't know where I belonged. Maybe I was asking for the impossible. I didn't want the presumptive acceptance of New York or Cambridge where, when I came out, people would give me that, *Oh, transgender, I have a couple of transgender friends.* As if that one word could capture everything about me, explain my every nuance. But I also didn't want the anxiety of being hidden and secretive out here, or of trying to determine who was safe to come out to. Granted, Pete and Margaret and Steve had been fine with it, or maybe just too polite to say they weren't. But how many people would react like Gus had instead?

In the station yard, the fire crew was working out. Push-ups and jumping jacks, crunches and pull-ups. I watched them go through their routine as I stretched, one leg propped up on a fence rail. Returning to my cabin, I found four maps stuck into the frame of the screen door, and, after showering, I ate oatmeal and spread the quadrants out on the double bed.

Thin brown circles converged into peaks or wavered away to suggest declivities. Green to indicate cover, white to show where you'd be exposed. The twisting blue line of the North Fork. Little black squares denoting structures. The ranger station's buildings like ants clustered on a crumb. I resisted but then gave in. West of the station, there was the ranch, two dots. The lodge and the office? Was this an old map before more had been built? Or were some things just too small to include? After all, who needs to know that there are ten tidy cabins, two bunkhouses, and a garage? In the mass of contours rested the Xs of benchmarks and the dashed hurry of trails, the tiny dots of humanity having disappeared.

I stood up from the bed and found that with a little distance, even the thin lines of river and road were subsumed by the overwhelming wilderness.

"I guessed you're a size 31-33, right?" Walt's voice startled me. I turned to find him at my door, holding a folded stack of uniform clothes.

"Close enough."

He tossed the jeans to me. "Medium shirt. What's your shoe size?"

"I have hiking boots."

"Need to be steel toe. When you work for the Forest Service, everything's got to be done to regulation."

"Eight."

Walt's eyes dipped to my feet. "Small for someone your height. I'll see what we've got."

I pulled on the uniform. Feet and hands, always the giveaway. And the lack of beard. And the high voice. And the narrow shoulders. Not to mention the heavy chest on an otherwise skinny guy. I sighed and buttoned up the jeans. *Just relax.* Maybe I should tell Walt too.

But really, I didn't want to deal with this crap. I thought of how my brothers joked about our father's "sex ed" talk (I'd gotten a longer and less relevant one from my mother), which they'd summed up as follows: Keep it in your pants. That about captured how I understood gender—there was what was in your pants, and then there were your pants. Look at what I wear, look at what I show you as I move through the world. That's my gender. What's under those clothes? That's my business.

Walt whistling "Oh! Susanna" preceded his return with a pair of brown boots.

"Okey-dokey. You're looking official." He handed me a baseball cap with the Forest Service pine tree logo. "Bet you're wishing for the Smokey Bear-style hat. But they don't just hand those out." He puttered around the cabin as I laced the boots on. "Pete only wears his sometimes, like in the Fourth of July parade. They had me dressed up as Woodsy Owl. Be glad you missed it. I got my beard caught in the zipper." He fingered the dark brown whiskers that reached almost to his chest. "All set? Got lunch? Okay!"

The trail crew had already loaded up, and we waved them off. Then Walt began my orientation. "Half a dozen mules plus a few horses, for those who prefer. I'm a mule man myself." He kept up a steady stream of banter as we walked past the stables. "We'll clean out those stalls before they get back. Now, let me introduce you to Guinevere."

Guinevere turned out to be his truck, a mint-green Ford Ranger with its rear filled with rakes, shovels, a disheveled cooler, brooms, a chain saw. "I like to be prepared," Walt said, "even though I was never a Boy Scout. Yep. And don't be fooled. Guinevere is a conservative lady. Strong on the brakes, a little slow to accelerate, but she'll get you there."

I strapped myself into the passenger seat and Walt tooled on out to the highway. Between his exhaustive explanations and our morning of activity, I was prepared to write up the following job description:

1. The Shoshone National Forest has five districts. Ours is Wapiti. (Walt said it right too.)

2. Wapiti District has ten campgrounds. They are:
   a. Big Game
   b. Wapiti

    c. Elk Fork
    d. Clearwater
    e. Blackwater
    f. Newton Creek
    g. Rex Hale
    h. Eagle Creek
    i. Pahaska
    j. Threemile

3. Not to mention scenic views, rest areas, and visitor information centers.

4. According to a system controlled by (from what I could ascertain) Walt's peculiar logic, we drove up and down the highway and stopped at said locations where our job was to:
    a. Clean: self-explanatory—rake fire pits, pick up litter, trim low branches.
    b. Record: make notations of area usage, both human and critter.
    c. Teach: find tourists and make sure they know the rules.

At Rex Hale, our second campground of the day, Walt explained the teaching aspect of the job.

"The Forest Service calls it 'interpretation,' which I kind of like," Walt said as we approached a couple who had set up a tent next to their car. "I imagine it as though nature speaks another language, and we have to translate to everyone who comes through." He straightened his cap, brushed his beard (I already noticed its tendency to pick up twigs and pine needles), and fixed a smile on his face. "Howdy, folks. Going hiking?"

"Sure are," the man replied.

"Up to the lookout? You got a map?" Walt handed them a Forest Service map, the glossy kind you could get for free at a visitor center that showed depressingly little detail, as I knew from experience. He traced the trail with his finger. "You should get a better map than this one if you're going any farther, but this'll get you to the lookout." He peered over the woman's shoulder to where their green tent rested next to a small gas stove and a red cooler. "There food in that cooler?"

The woman nodded.

"I'd use the cables then." Walt pointed. There were pulleys and lines strung between two trees. "You can just run it up there, keep it away from critters. Or put it in the box." He indicated a metal cube with an intricate latch.

"Isn't it fine in the cooler?" the woman said, eyeing the box suspiciously.

Walt rummaged in Guinevere's bed and produced a cooler of his own. He held out the lid, which had one mangled edge and a large puncture like a gunshot. "Bear got this one," he said. "Probably a black bear, not a grizzly."

The woman's eyes widened. "Oh. Well, we'll put it in the car."

"They can do a number on those too. I've seen cars opened like a can of anchovies. Let me show you how to string it up."

Back in Guinevere, we drove on to the next campground where Walt wrote a warning to some campers who had left food all over a picnic table. "Sure way to train the bears to come here often," he grumbled as we packed away the chips and cookies.

"Are they really a problem?" I shared the tourists' skepticism. In New England, wild animals were a nuisance, like deer in the garden or mice in the basement, but not a real concern.

"Used to be worse, but yes, they're still a problem. It's better since we got the dumpsters locked down." He showed me the system of handles and chutes that kept the bears from getting in. "The real problem is, they're so darn smart. And trainable. We used to tell people, just wear a bell when you hike, and that'll warn the bears away. We thought bears didn't want to run into humans any more than humans wanted to run into bears. But what happens? The bears learn: Bells mean hikers, and hikers mean peanut butter sandwiches. Soon enough, ring a bell and you get a bear." He paused, leaning on his rake to watch a father coax two young kids out of the car. "Sometimes I think they're smarter than most tourists."

We ate lunch at a campground perched along a creek. I'd lost track of which one we were in and had stopped trying to keep up. Walt told more stories about campers and bears.

"I always carry bear spray," he concluded.

"Bear spray?" I was pretty sure he was luring me on as the rookie on the crew, like with Gus and the jackalope. "Would I lie?" Walt looked like an Old Testament prophet with his beard slightly afloat in the wind. He tossed his empty lunch sack into Guinevere's cab and fished around behind the seat, eventually extracting—and brandishing triumphantly—a black cylinder with a trigger on top and Bear Protection Spray written in silver and red. "It's like pepper spray," he said, handing it over. "But the nozzle releases it in a big mist, not the thin line like mace for muggers."

I turned the can over to read the warnings. "It works?"

"On grizzlies. Humans too, for that matter. But not on black bears."

I handed the can back, and Walt jiggled it in his palm.

"I guess for it to be useful, I should wear it on my belt. But I don't want to look like a—"

I braced myself to hear that one syllable drop, to take a step back from Walt who, despite my self-admonishment that emotional distance equaled safety, I was beginning to like.

"—total dork," he finished. "But then again, why fight it?"

Yeah. I liked him.

Back at the station by three, we cleaned out the stalls, and then Walt took me to the office.

"Let me show you how to file a daily report." He cleared a spot on a desk and took a carbon paper form from a tray. "Black or blue ballpoint. Press firmly," he intoned. "These go to the head ranger's office. Permanent file." He paused and gazed thoughtfully at the blank sheet. "If you see any bears, write it up on the big board." I glanced at the corkboard hanging over the desks. The last sighting had been on July third at Big Game.

Walt put pen to page, and I read over his shoulder: *As dawn, with her rosy fingers, spread over Wapiti, I took young Ron, that clever trainee, forth to learn the craft of woods and field.*

I laughed. "Nice Homeric humor."

"Gotta keep myself amused. Speaking of which, you're done for the day. Relax."

CHAPTER FOURTEEN

The next morning, Pete stopped by my cabin and brought me books from the Cody Forest Service Office, *Bear Country* and *Wildlife of the Absarokas*, as well as a bunch of pamphlets on wildflowers, hiking trails, common birds, and a dozen other topics he thought might be useful when I spoke to tourists. He also delivered a sack of groceries.

"Brought you a calendar too, and a quilt," he said. "This place looked a little bare. Do you want another chair?"

I was touched by the gesture. "I'm fine, thanks. I'm not expecting guests."

"You lonely?"

"I was around people all the time at the ranch. It's kind of nice to be by myself for a bit," I lied. I was lonely, but all the people at the station could be here in my cabin with me, and I would still feel lonely. I wanted—someone who knew me. Jane or Laurel, or even Michael. Or I wanted to be forgiven—to have Cassie here and to have her tell me it was all okay...

Pete took off his glasses and cleaned them on his shirt tail. "Yes. You're something of an old soul. Truth be told, you remind me of what I was like at your age."

"Really?" I'd heard that from a couple of aunts before but never from an older man.

"Really. I recognize that mix of utter determination and complete uncertainty."

"Thanks," I said, not sure (true to form) if that was the right response.

I hung the calendar on the wall behind the table. The July picture showed elk moving through a verdant valley. I crossed off the days that had passed, putting a little dot on the day I'd left the ranch. It felt odd to put Xs through the boxes. At school, I counted down to vacation, but what was I counting toward here? What was the next end point, the next road sign?

Well, in four days, my birthday: the big 2-0. The end of my teen years. I didn't want to tell Walt or Pete. I didn't want a fuss that would only make me feel bad for myself.

It was Walt's day off, and he'd asked me to mow the station's grass and clean the visitor center. An easy day. The fire crew had just finished their workout. The morning sun stretched across the cabin's porch as I waited for the grass to dry while reading through *Bear Country*, my yellow pad ready to take notes.

I knew what I should be doing instead. I should be writing to Michael, and Kate back at Harvard. I should tell them where I was. I should tell Jane what had happened and give her my new address. But I didn't want to admit that I'd screwed up. I didn't want Jane to worry (or feel vindicated, for that matter), and I didn't want Michael's suspicions—that being trans meant a difficult, unsuccessful life—confirmed.

I settled on writing short postcards to Jane and Michael and Kate, giving them my new address at the ranger station but saying little about why I had a new address. As I wrote, I felt something new itching at me, something beneath the guilt and regret: It was a little bit—okay, more than a little bit—of anger. I had been fired, and I didn't deserve to be fired, so why was I the one feeling guilty? And beneath that anger, a curiosity: Who had found out that I was transgender, and how? Had it been Nancy? Carl wouldn't go through my stuff, I trusted him more than that.

Would Clyde bother? I imagined I was below his interest since he and Cassie were through.

Getting up from the rocking chair, I brought the postcards to the office where Pete was filling in a logbook.

"Is there a phone I can use?" I asked. "For a local call?"

"Right over there," he said. "Dial away." He stood up from the desk and left the office.

I extracted the business card that Steve had given me. He probably wouldn't be in his apartment now, but I called anyway.

"Hello?"

"Steve—it's Ron. Is this an okay time to talk?"

"Ron! You bet. I was just getting my work boots on. I have a whole lot of postholes to dig without you around to help. Everything okay?"

"Everything's fine." I fiddled with a pen on the desk. "I was just wondering if you could tell me… Who found out? About me?"

"Oh…" I imagined Steve running a hand over his flat top. I could practically hear the ruffle of his hair. "Well, that was Marc."

"Marc? I thought he went back to Jersey."

"No, Gus brought him to, uh, a clinic in Cody, you understand? After a week there, he got a day out to visit his family…" Steve sighed. "Well, he went through your things. I don't know what he found, but he found something and came running up to Gus."

"So is he still at the clinic?"

"No, no. He's back in the kitchen here."

"Oh." It took the breath out of me, the thought of him back at the ranch, everything restored to normal, and me banished like some sort of criminal. "I see. Thanks, Steve. I just had to know."

"I understand. Hope everything's good at the station."

"It is. I hope it's all fine at the ranch."

He paused. It was definitely a pause. "Yep. It's fine."

I mowed the grass and raked the clippings into the compost, Steve's words in my head the whole time. Marc. Just the thought of him turned my stomach, the way he had pushed me around.

And now he was back there, back in the kitchen and the bunk-house, and I bet he thought he'd won—well, hell. He had. But I was still here. He hadn't driven me out of Wyoming. That counted for something. I gripped the rake so hard I thought I would break the shaft. God, I hated him. I wanted to show him... I wanted to go back there and tell him... What, exactly? How crazy was I? I knew I should count myself lucky to be away from the ranch and to have a job here.

What I needed was a long run, so I laced on my sneakers as soon as I finished raking. As I ran, I started writing an overdue letter to Cassie in my head.

Dear Cassie,

I have regrets enough to fill a book. I should have told you sooner. Maybe I should have told Gus at the start of the summer—that's what Steve says. But that's all unchangeable.

There are some things I don't regret. And the biggest one is going to work at the ranch because that's what let me meet you. I've been thinking about it—what are the chances? The chance I'd get off the bus in Cody, that Gus would find me and have a job to offer, that we'd meet and be drawn to each other, neither one of us being people who easily fall into relationships. It's kismet. It's fate.

I hope you can forgive me. I can't stop thinking about you. Days at the ranch, I often looked forward to nothing besides getting to talk to you. To have you explain how you were training a horse out of a bad habit or tell a funny story about one of the dudes. I feel like I've barely gotten to know you. Maybe it's hopeless now. Maybe I should just let it go. But it's worth asking, given how I feel about you: Would you write back? Would you still want to stay in touch with me? If so, Steve can get you my address.

Yours,

Ron

After my run I wrote that letter, and a dozen more just like it, and crumpled each one up. I couldn't send them to her. I didn't want to be a stalker. I didn't want to pressure her if she wanted to be left alone. My wastebasket overflowed with never-to-be-sent mail, yet I couldn't stop writing letters—as if I might sometime soon find the words to win her back, or the words to make me feel better.

On my birthday, a siren went off at the ranger station just as Walt and I were loading up Guinevere.

"Holy smokes. That's the fire call," he said.

I watched as the trail crew and fire crew spilled out of their bunkhouses like ants from a hill that'd been kicked. Pete rushed from the office and found Gary, the fire crew chief. The two of them conferred over a clipboard Pete held.

At last, Pete cupped his hands to his mouth. "All in! All in!"

Everyone, even Margaret, gathered around him. Gary chewed one end of his moustache.

"All hands fire, up in the Sunlight Basin. Gary'll muster the fire crew. Trail crew, you take Truck Three. Walt and I will follow, and we'll rendezvous at the Sunlight Station. Margaret, Ron, you hold down the fort."

Within fifteen minutes, nothing was left of them but a dust cloud over the driveway. Walt had tossed me the keys to Guinevere and told me to keep things clean.

Margaret had already commandeered Pete's place in the office. "This paperwork will eat you alive if you don't stay on top of it," she'd said as she hurried off. "You let me know if you need anything, dear."

I went through our routine at the campsites, cleaning and talking with tourists. When I came back to the station, Margaret gave me a haircut on her porch, and now I understood why all the guys on the trail and fire crew looked the same. She only offered one style: high and tight. I read the bear book that Pete had loaned me and tried not to feel sorry for myself for being alone on my birthday. For being left behind at the station with Margaret. Had Pete thought I couldn't handle the work of a firefighter because I was transgender? Or maybe it was just because I was new. It was like being a kid again, watching with envy as my older brothers headed off to go hunting with my dad, leaving me at home with Mom to make cookies.

When the mail arrived, there was a manila envelope sent express from Kate, which I opened in my cabin.

I unfolded a packet of pages to reveal a rainbow letterhead reading "PRISM: Helping GLBT Youth." Kate had put an orange sticky note on the first page.

Hope everything's okay out there. Thought you might give this a try. I'm checking with the deans, but I think they'd let you return this fall if this organization gave you a grant. President of PRISM is a Harvard alumnus. We spoke, and he says he'll try and get the board to decide and find the funds quickly, maybe within a month. Let me know what you think. –K

Beneath the rainbow letterhead, the pages contained a breezy description of the struggles of GLBT kids: lack of parental support, homelessness, depression, drug abuse, bullying at school. Then, like a single bright ornament dangling on this sad tree, the final paragraph contained their statement of purpose: *PRISM's mission is to help GLBT youth get back on their feet, restore their pride, and continue their educations to become tomorrow's leaders.*

I flipped through the rest of the material. Kate had sent the full application for a grant. The forms asked whether I needed the money for housing expenses, for clothes, or for tuition. There were essay questions, pages of personal information to fill in.

This was it: a chance to go back to Harvard without missing a beat. I hadn't let myself think of it before, of how nice and easy that would be, to return to Cambridge, to say that all this time out here was a dream, a dare, a game—a joke to tell over one of Au Bon Pain's ridiculously expensive coffees. It wasn't like I had an alternate plan for the fall. It would be crazy not to give this a shot.

Next semester… It seemed so soon. I went to the calendar and looked ahead at August and September. Labor Day: Pete had said that was when the season ended. And that was pretty much when Harvard would start up again. Just six weeks from now.

As the sun was starting to set, I heard Margaret calling me, "Ro-on! Want some dinner?"

I headed over to her house where she'd set a small table for two.

"You didn't need to cook for me," I said.

"If I hadn't," she replied, loading a plate with a baked potato, broccoli, and a chicken breast smothered in cheese and onions, "you'd be eating ramen right now, correct?"

I paused. "Possibly." That was exactly what I'd been planning to prepare. "But I can cook and bake. My mother taught me."

She filled her own plate, and we sat at the table. I slathered my potato with butter, and Margaret cut her chicken into bite-size pieces.

"Of course. I keep forgetting. Most boys wouldn't have learned to cook. But you—"

"I grew up as a girl," I finished. "I learned how to sew on a button and iron a dress shirt. Though I might argue those are useful skills for *anyone* to know."

"We don't have to talk about it."

"I don't mind," I said. I didn't. Kind of.

"Well, I just think it's very fortunate that you look so much like a boy." She paused, digging her fork into her potato. "Was that a rude thing to say? I'm sorry."

"It wasn't rude. And you don't need to worry about offending me. Honest." I swirled my broccoli in the lake of melted butter my potato had produced. "I'd rather talk about it and get a chance to explain myself than have people make assumptions."

Was that true? Yes. I'd rather not have to talk about it at all, but I guess I was starting to realize that was an impossible dream. I was transgender. I could live as a guy. But passing as a man didn't erase my trans-ness.

I asked Margaret a few questions about where she'd grown up (Montana) and how she and Pete had met (she'd been working in Veteran's Services when he came back from Vietnam). And she asked me how I'd ended up in Wyoming, and there we were, back in the land of gender. (Why did all roads seem to lead here? Or was it just me? Never mind. It was just me.)

"I had a blowout fight with my parents, my dad mostly," I began. "They kicked me out for being transgender. So I went to live with my girlfriend, but we broke up. And then I got this crazy idea that what I needed was a chance to go someplace where no one knew me and where, I don't know, people were *real*." I paused and fiddled a bit with the last piece of broccoli on my plate. "It sounds so stupid. But I was thinking of the explorers and cowboys and just heading West and trying to be a man."

"That's not stupid. You're following a grand tradition. Did you find what you were looking for?"

I laughed. "Not yet. But I've learned an awful lot."

The evening ended with me standing in front of my cabin's mirror, telling myself that I could still pass even if I was twenty. Some men have baby faces their whole lives, right? No, I looked fifteen. And the older I got, the harder it would be for me to be taken for a guy. Especially if I went back East where androgyny was more the norm.

Great. Happy birthday. Have an existential crisis.

Over the radio in the office the next afternoon, Pete said the fire was contained and that they should be back in another day or two. "Hope it rains soon, otherwise we'll have more of these," he said before signing off.

I recorded the work I had done and filed all the reports like Walt had shown me. Margaret brought in the mail. She went to Cody for groceries, and we had another dinner at her house, then played cribbage on the porch.

The sun had set behind the cliffs as I headed back to my cabin, and I had just stepped inside and snapped on the lamp when I heard tires crunching on the driveway. Just one car, it sounded like. I went outside and saw Margaret on her porch craning her neck to look down the drive. A blue pickup truck pulled to a stop in front of the office—then Steve stepped out.

"Ron?" he called.

I walked over.

"Hi, Steve." We shook hands. "What brings you here? Pete's on a fire call."

He brushed his hand over his flat top, shifting his weight from foot to foot.

"Everything all right?" I asked.

"Well, see, I wanted to let you know that Cassie's had to leave the ranch. I thought about calling, but it seemed important enough to tell you in person."

"Why'd she have to leave?"

"It's been a tough time for Cassie since you… I think between Marc and Clyde, things weren't going so well for her, if you know what I mean."

I wasn't certain I did, but I knew I didn't want to imagine the possibilities. "I'm sorry to hear that. You think she's all right?"

"She's tough. And she owns half of that ranch. Her name's on the deed right next to Gus's. So if I know Cassie, she won't be gone long." Something in Steve's tone made me worry even as he tried to reassure me.

"Thanks for telling me."

"Yep. Well, I wanted to let you know, see, that Clyde has been giving her some trouble, and I've heard him mention your name more than once too. Thought you should know."

"Does he know I'm here?" I asked.

Steve shrugged. "I haven't told him, that's for sure. I'm guessing he thinks you headed back to the East Coast."

Like a coward. Well, I hadn't. "Where did Cassie go?"

"Down on the South Fork, close to town. When you have her talent, it's easy to find work with horses."

"Can you give me her address? I'd like to write to her."

Steve brushed at his hair again. "I'm not so sure she'd like to hear from you."

"Okay. I understand," I said. "Could you maybe at least ask her?"

"I can do that," Steve replied. "But I'm not joking. Watch yourself. You saw how mean Marc can be, but he's a terrier compared to Clyde. Clyde's a big dog."

And I was a squirrel. "Yeah, I know. Thanks, Steve."

I watched him drive away and then walked back across the dark grass to my cabin. Moths clustered around the one streetlight that illuminated the station grounds. There was a light still on in Margaret and Pete's house, and I thought about stepping inside to maybe talk things through. But I didn't feel like saying much of anything. What kind of trouble could Clyde have given Cassie that would make her leave the ranch? I didn't want to think about it, how often the two of them had to work together in the barn. How hard it was to avoid someone at that small a place. And it was all my fault. I had put her in this mess. Now I had to see if I could help her out.

I wasn't expecting the package that Margaret brought the next day when I returned from my run, but I recognized the handwriting immediately. I took it to my cabin and tore it open. Inside, there was a letter on top of crumpled newspaper.

Hi Ron,

I got your address from Jane. She's told me some of what you've been doing. I'm sorry things ended so abruptly between us, and I hope it isn't too tough for you out there. Given what you're up to, I thought this might come in handy. Be safe. Happy birthday.
Laurel

Digging through the newspaper, I unearthed the same brown paper bag that I'd last seen in New York and drew out the vial of greasy testosterone and a bunch of syringes, as well as a note in Laurel's handwriting:

I talked to an FtM in my art program, and he said you should start with half a cc every other week. He's been taking the stuff for over a year now. He goes to a doctor at a gay clinic here in the City. He showed me where to inject it.

Next to this was a drawing of a butt with two dotted lines dividing one of the cheeks and an "X" marking a quadrant. Right there.

I tried to imagine this FtM friend of hers, this gay clinic, the world of queer people on the East Coast. I imagined them pierced and tattooed and with crazy, dyed hair, getting comments tossed at them on the subway, on the sidewalk. Was I the one playing it safe? Was I the one taking the easy route out, trying to pass my way through the world of straight people? Trying to be invisible? I turned the vial over in my hands, watching the greasy, viscous liquid slide around. How come everything I did felt like wimping out? How come I could never quite measure up? I wasn't queer enough for Laurel. Wasn't straight enough for Cassie. Wasn't girl enough for my parents or guy enough for me.

I chucked the vial back into the paper bag. I didn't need it. But I also had to admit that I *did* want it. I wanted the facial hair, and the muscle, and the lower voice. I just didn't want the message that went along with it, the implication that right now, without it, I wasn't sufficient, wasn't enough, wasn't really a man.

I thought about the cutting replies I could send to Laurel. I thought about how I might ship the whole package right back to her. But in the end, I just stashed the vial and the syringes in the cabinet beneath the bathroom sink.

The better news came in a phone call that afternoon: Steve calling from the ranch to give me Cassie's address.

"She said she wasn't sure if she wanted to hear from you, but she also wasn't sure she didn't want to hear from you."

"That sounds like Cassie."

"Sure does. Just be careful, okay, Ron?"

Pete and Walt and the trail crew returned the following day. The whole ranger station smelled like an old barbecue grill as we cleaned and stored their sooty gear. I asked Walt for details, but for once, he wasn't verbose.

"Fighting fires is the most boring thing in the world," he said. "It feels like I just smoked a whole forest. I can't wait to take a long shower."

Even if he downplayed it, I envied him. I wanted to go on the next fire. After all, I did the same job, more or less, as Walt did. And I ran everyday—he never did that. Maybe Pete would take me on the next one.

But when I asked him at dinner that night, he just licked his chapped lips and said, "That's Gary's call to make."

"The fire crew had to stay up in Sunlight for another couple of days," Walt added. "There's still some spots to put out. Don't see why you want to join in to tell the truth, Ron. A lot of boring digging, that's what firefighting is."

"Do you think Gary would let me go?" I asked him and Pete.

"There's a physical test," said Walt. "If I passed it, you can pass it for sure."

I wanted to ask for more details, but Pete was quicker.

"How were things around here while we were gone?" he asked. "Did Margaret find work for you to do?"

"We got along fine," I said. "But I'd rather join you guys next time."

CHAPTER FIFTEEN

A troop of Boy Scouts had made a mess of Clearwater Campground, and Walt and I set to cleaning it. Once we'd handled the litter (they'd apparently eaten nothing but potato chips and then shredded the bags, according to Scout tradition), Walt decided there were two dead trees that we ought to take down.

"Widow-makers," he said, pointing to the bare limbs that stretched over a trail and campsite. He dug two chainsaws and a jug of fuel out from Guinevere's bed and checked how sharp they were.

"I don't know how to run one of those," I told him.

"A New Hampshire boy who doesn't know how to chainsaw?"

"I'm more for the books."

"Books are better than chainsaws, I'll grant you that. But chainsaws are real helpful. At least sometimes."

Couldn't argue with that logic. Truth was, I'd always wanted to learn how to use a chainsaw. All my brothers knew, of course.

Walt rolled his shoulders, gearing up for a nice, long lecture. "Forest Service regulations. Wear a brain bucket." He tossed me a red helmet and then led me through the paces:

Clear perimeter of people and possessions
Plan path of descent

Gauge angle of back cut

Remove obstacles to prevent hang ups

He felled both trees, and I worked at limbing them, slowly, the weight of the saw making my shoulders droop. Sweaty, I took a break and tied my bandanna biker-style over my head before clamping the helmet back on and starting to cut again. Walt gave me a thumbs up as he refueled his saw and headed across the trail to start cutting up the other trunk. The buzzing echoed in my wrists and shoulders, the whole world muted by the earphones I wore. The air tasted of sawdust and exhaust. I tried to imagine how I would explain this experience to my friends back at Harvard. *Yeah, I worked as a ranger in Wyoming. Chainsaws, grizzly bears, you know.*

Walt's saw stopped buzzing, and he began to stack what we'd cut. I put my saw down and followed suit, glad to give my muscles a break, even gladder to take my helmet off for a moment.

Walt came over and sized up the work I'd done. "We'll come back with one of the big trucks to haul it all in. It's time to head back to the station." Stretching his shoulders, he started gathering up the gear and carrying it to Guinevere.

A van towing a pop-up camper circled around the grounds, and a man leaned out the window, peering into the available sites. Spotting us, he waved and pulled around. He looked to be in his fifties, brown hair graying at the temples. Next to him, a fat beagle draped itself across his wife's lap.

"Howdy there," he called. "What's the best place? Is the next campground any better?" He leaned farther out the window and stared at the fallen tree. "Did you saw that down yourself, young lady?"

I blinked in disbelief. Before I could reply, he continued.

"Are any of these sites reserved, or can we just pull in?"

"Anywhere you want," I said. "And I'm not a lady."

"Oh." The man settled back against his seat. "Hard to tell sometimes nowadays." He rolled his window up and drove along.

Behind me, I heard Walt shifting wood, and I turned to help him.

"You should have seen your face when he called you young lady." Walt chuckled. "Don't worry, someday you'll be able to grow a beard like mine."

It would be easy enough just to laugh along and laugh at my own private joke as well. Or…

"Not any time soon," I said. I snatched the sweaty bandanna from my head, wondering if that was what had made me look more feminine. Then I launched into my usual speech. "I'm transgender. I was born and raised as a girl, but I identify as a guy." My heart thudded painfully as I stumbled through my declaration, though I couldn't help noticing it came out more succinctly this time. But I wished it didn't feel as if I were laying my life on the line every time I came out to someone.

"Huh," Walt said. "No kidding. That why you left off working at the ranch?"

"Yeah. They found out. But Pete knows."

"Thanks for telling me."

"I don't want to make things awkward between us."

"I don't think I would have ever guessed. I mean, you look young, but—"

"Thanks," I said, settling onto the stump I'd created.

Walt sat down on the grass next to me. The scent of sawdust and tree resin reached me with each inhale. Above us, a few birds circled the campsite, and Walt began to explain how to tell the difference between a hawk and a vulture from their silhouette. I kind of listened, but most of my attention was on the tree stump and the rings that were now exposed: dark brown lines encircling the yellow heart of the tree, thin and wavery like the lines on a topographical map. Years and years circling around.

We each hefted a saw into the back of the truck and started down the highway toward the station, stopping only to empty the trash at the visitor center. In short order, we pulled up in front of the stables, and Walt dug out two files, tossing one to me and proceeding to show me how to sharpen the chainsaw blade. We worked side by side, set up on Guinevere's tailgate.

"When I left college," Walt began, "I'd already gotten into med school, but I deferred for a year and worked on a ski mountain all winter, just bumming around. I'd always wanted to. A year became two years, then three. And pretty soon I had to go back to my mom and tell her I wasn't going to med school, that if I did, I'd be miserable because that wasn't who I was. I wanted to ski and live outdoors, and here I am almost twenty years later, still doing just that. I know it's not fair to compare career choice to gender, but I think it's kind of the same."

"Yeah, I see that. Both are some essential part of who we are, no matter what other people want or expect. So you're still a ski bum?"

"Every winter. Drive from here down to Colorado or Utah, get a job for the season on some mountain or other. It's the life."

"Bet your mom wasn't happy about that decision."

"She had a conniption. Or two. She's forgiven me, or gotten used to it, I guess. How's your mother handling things?

"Part one, the same. We haven't reached part two."

"She'll come around. Might not be happy about it, but she'll see that this is who you are and that it doesn't make you a bad person. In fact, you seem solid to me."

"Thanks, Walt."

"And heck, you go to Harvard."

I did, kind of. I'd get back there sometime... Maybe sooner if I filled out that application Kate had sent me. I'd sat down and looked over the essay questions a couple of times. But ever since Steve had given me Cassie's address, I found that I was more interested in writing a letter to her (for real this time) than in finishing the application.

At the second campground we cleaned the following day, I found a bear box that had been ripped free of its bolts, the metal peeled loose at one seam. I picked it up, surprised by its considerable weight, and hauled it to Walt.

He whistled. "Woo-ee." His finger traced the ripped bolt hole, the jagged edge of the metal. "Grizzly. Look at that. We'll show Pete once we're back at the station."

I returned to my raking. The campsite sat empty in the late morning hours, everyone off hiking, or horseback riding, or touristing along the highway. In my almost two months out here, I'd seen buffalo, lots of birds, rabbits every morning on my run. The pronghorns with Cassie. I couldn't imagine a bear lumbering through here. But there must be dozens of creatures in this forest that I'd never catch a glimpse of—maybe even a jackalope or two.

Walt delivered the box to Pete as if it were a reliquary.

Pete poked at it. "Six years of research, design, and testing. This is conclusive proof that the bears are smarter than we are."

"At least where peanut butter is concerned," Walt added.

Pete checked his watch. "Ron, you want to drive this in to Cody, drop it at H.Q.?"

I knew that he could just as easily do it, but I guessed he was giving me the excuse to go into town. "Yeah, I would."

I thought of the address Steve had given me, the one I still hadn't done anything with. "I haven't been to town for weeks. My library books are overdue. Is it okay if I run a few errands?"

"Well, Forest Service vehicles are for Forest Service business only. So be sure to pick up some essential supplies. We always need light bulbs, for instance." Pete winked.

"Mildred's ready for you," said Walt, holding the door as he led me to the garage. It felt like a coming-of-age ceremony, the official bestowing of a truck. "She's older than Guinevere, so go easy on her. And she's only a 4x2, so stay on the paved road."

He walked me around the Ford Ranger, its mint-green hue faded by years of sun. I got in, he placed the busted bear box on the seat beside me, and then I gave a toot of the horn and rolled out onto the highway.

The ranger station in Cody sat just off of Main Street. After delivering the box to a decidedly uninterested secretary, I drove through the center of town. Cody boasted a few commercial streets, and though it paled in comparison to Boston, it was far livelier than Tamworth. Besides, after weeks out in the boondocks, anything would look like a metropolis. There was a pizza place, a doughnut shop called Hole in the Wall, lots of tourist traps selling racks of postcards. In the Western wear store, city slickers in Hawaiian shirts were trying on cowboy boots.

I bet you'll be too embarrassed to wear those back East, I wanted to call out to them as I drove past. *Plus, they'll give you blisters.*

I pulled onto a side street and checked my map one more time, then steered toward the South Fork.

Even though they were two branches of the same river, the South Fork didn't look anything like the North Fork. Muddier, seemingly slower. It even looked like it was running the other way, but that had to be an optical illusion or me getting turned around. I knew this river would drain into the Atlantic eventually. The landscape, too, had shifted drastically, more rust-colored, more classic desert with its free-standing rock formations evoking castle turrets or Grecian columns.

When I reached the right street, I turned Mildred down a long drive that curled around gracefully, leading to a modern-style timber house large enough to be called a mansion. Well before I'd reached it, I slowed down in front of a vast red and white barn, which looked like a refugee from the Vermont countryside. Next to it, barely beyond the barn's shadow, stood its quarter-size replica, identical in every facet down to the spacing of the windows, the styling of the latches, and the hayloft door. Horses stood in the field around the barn, swishing their tails vaguely.

Cassie's Comanche was parked next to the smaller barn. The sight of it made me smile. I pulled my truck into a shady area and turned it off. I didn't get out though. Now that I was here, I wasn't certain why I'd come. So Steve had warned me, so he had told me that she was having a tough time with Clyde and Marc. What was I supposed to do?

Something. I was supposed to do something. Not give up.

I got out of Mildred and went to the door. I could see curtains on the window, a couch and a table inside. I knocked. No answer. I was embarrassed by how relieved I felt.

It was four in the afternoon. She should be done with work soon, I hoped, not knowing what her work was or whether it followed a nine-to-five sort of schedule.

I took out my yellow pad and wrote a note:

Dear Cassie:

Thanks for sharing your address with me. I'd really like to see you. I'm in town for the day, which doesn't happen too often. If you want to, and if you have time, I can meet you at the pizza place on Main Street. I'll be there at 5:30. And if you don't want to see me, I understand. Maybe it's easier if I write you a letter, but I really would like to talk in person. Steve came by and told me some of what's going on.

There was so much more I wanted to say, but I didn't want to sound desperate or condescending. So I signed the note and slipped it under the door.

Back in Cody, I picked out a stack of books at the library: *The Sun Also Rises*, which I'd liked in high school, and, though they didn't stock Judith Butler, which was all that Jane had ever recommended, I did find *Bastard Out of Carolina*, which Laurel had suggested to me a while ago. I sat in a comfy leather chair (I would have checked that out too if they'd let me) until it was a quarter past five.

A queasy feeling came over me as I headed to the pizza place: What if she didn't come? Should I have left her my address so she could write me? What if she *did* come? What on earth would I say to her?

I took a booth at the restaurant and tried to remember what toppings Cassie had ordered on the pizza we ate when she was driving me back from the hospital. God, that seemed so long ago. I settled on pepperoni and mushroom. I ordered a large (Why not be optimistic?) and sipped on a grape soda while I waited, watching people stream past the window and resisting the urge to take out a book and start reading. Then five-thirty passed. So did a quarter to six. The pizza came. I let it cool. I ate a slice. Finally I took out *The Sun Also Rises* and started to read. I didn't remember much of my high school discussions about the book, but I found myself totally absorbed: This guy, who couldn't have sex like he used to, was tantalized by an exceedingly macho culture. I could definitely relate.

Then I heard those footsteps—heel-toe, heel-toe—clicking across the linoleum. When I looked up, she was sliding into the booth across from me, her ponytail swinging.

"Cassie," I said. "It's so good to see you."

"How have you been?" she asked.

I'd forgotten—the pitch of her voice, the exact old denim color of her eyes. I felt like I could just melt right there. "Pretty good," I managed. "And you?"

"All right. Been better. Been worse."

Her eyes flicked around the pizza place, pausing on my face, then flicking away. I wondered how she thought of me, if she saw me as Ron or if she just saw a transgender, a former girl.

"A uniform?" she said. "You working for the Forest Service now?"

I nodded—I'd forgotten I had on the khaki shirt with the green badge on the sleeves. "Has Clyde been around to bother you?" she asked.

I shook my head. "I don't think he knows where I live."

"Keep it that way."

"What's going on, Cassie?"

She waved a hand as if batting away a fly. "Calling me all the time. Showing up where I live to yell at me. He even followed me around the grocery store the last time I went shopping. So I spent a long time looking at tampons. Ha."

Even though she tried to keep her tone light, I could hear the strain beneath it. "That's not right. You should call the co—"

"Don't tell me what to do." Every trace of smile drained out of her face. "You have no idea what it was like after you left." She picked up a piece of pizza and ate it slowly, not looking at me. "Marc's one thing," she said at last. "I know how to handle him, and Gus at least keeps an eye on him. All I hear from Marc is how he was right and I was wrong and what a loser you are and how I should always listen to him." She took another bite of pizza. "He's never liked a single guy I've dated, not that's he's known about most of them."

Marc. The thought of him made my tongue curl. "What's his problem?" I asked, sounding angrier than I meant to. "I've got brothers. They sometimes try to tell me what to do, but they're never jerks like Marc."

Cassie wiped the grease from each finger, slow and deliberate. "Maybe it has to do with him not being able to protect me, or protect my mother, when he was young. My father wasn't kind when he was drunk."

"I'm sorry." She shrugged, and I felt a heavy embarrassment settle on me. "And what about Clyde?" I asked, wanting to know and not wanting to know.

"Just be glad he hasn't learned where you are. He sure spent a lot of time telling the other guys what he'd like to do to you. And it wasn't pretty. He made sure I heard what he was saying."

"Sorry," I muttered.

"Yeah. Not as sorry as I am. I thought it might make things easier if I got back together with Clyde."

I fought back a yelp of surprise. She had gotten back together with Clyde? But I realized it was really not my place to be jealous, so I tamped that down and said, "Jesus. I'm sorry."

"You can stop saying that," Cassie snapped. "I just figured it would shut him up some if I…you know…slept with him and… well, you know. He and I had been together before, and it wasn't that bad. But he's such a bastard." I could see the flex and clench of her jaw. "Once he gets his hands on you, he doesn't like to take them off. That's the trouble. I had to leave."

"Where are you working now?"

"Got a job with an old woman who's got more money than she knows what to do with. She does dressage. I work the horses. It's good enough."

She bit off the words with finality as if expecting me to contradict her.

"I wish things had worked out differently," I said. "Maybe I should have told you earlier, I don't know. I haven't been able to stop thinking about you."

She held up a hand like my mother used to do when I was whining: Enough. "No hard feelings." She tipped her head back to look at me for a long moment, her chin lifted and her eyes gazing into mine. "That's why I came into town today. Just to say this loud and clear. No hard feelings. No feelings at all."

It was as if someone had let all the air out of my lungs. I tried not to show the disappointment in my face and just nodded. "Got it. Thanks for coming to see me."

I watched her as she walked out of the pizza place and down the sidewalk. Close, and impossibly far away. My heart had been racing the whole time I talked to her, faster than if I'd been running at a sprint. Now it seemed to have stopped entirely. I looked at the remaining pizza, but the thought of eating another slice turned my stomach. I paid the bill, scooped my library books under my arm, and headed out.

Mildred was parked down past the hardware store. Tourists milled about on the sidewalk in front of postcard racks or restaurant windows. At least I had gotten to see Cassie. It was better than—

"Hey! Veronica!" The shout came from behind me.

I spun around. It was Clyde, his long legs in blue jeans, the white sleeves of his shirt rolled up to show his tattoos. A cowboy hat pushed back on his head. I turned back around and kept walking.

"Hey, Veronica! Don't run away."

I stepped down from the sidewalk and, barely glancing at the traffic, jogged across to the other side of the street. *Don't turn around. Just ignore him. Maybe he'll give up.*

But his voice persisted, trailing behind me. "Why won't you talk to me? C'mon, honey. You wanted to be my friend before." There were people on the sidewalk, in the stores. They'd help me, right? "I didn't know you were still in town. I'd've liked to visit. Looks like you found Cassie, or did she find you? You two dykes still screwing around?"

I walked faster, keeping my eyes on Mildred. But Clyde kept right up with me, his speech unceasing. "Where you living, Veronica? Nice uniform you got. Think it makes you look like a man? Doesn't fool me a bit, little girl."

Shit. He'd caught sight of the Forest Service logo. If he put two and two together… The heels of his boots—tack, tack, tack— caught up to me, and I spun around.

"Leave me alone." I stared up at him. His mouth hung open, and he panted from the pursuit, from eagerness, his lips bared in a grin of vulpine cruelty and amusement. "I'm not bothering you, so just—"

"You bothered me plenty, you lying little cunt. You had your laugh."

People walked around us like we were islands in a stream. "Just go away, or—"

"Or what? You'll scream? You think these people will help? You want me to tell them what the problem is? Hey, folks!" He shouted the last bit loudly. "Gotta girl here dressed like a boy. Girl who thinks she can just—"

I turned my back on him and took two quick steps before he caught up and shoved my library books from my arm. I bent to pick them up, and he kicked them away. Classic bully move.

"I don't see anyone rushing to help the poor little dyke, do you?" he sneered.

I left the books where they were. "All right, you've had your fun," I said. "What do you want?" Maybe passersby wouldn't tell him to shut up, but surely they wouldn't let him beat me up right on the Main Street of Cody, right? Clyde seemed to be having the same thought. He bore down on me like it'd be me he kicked or shoved next instead of my books. But he kept his fists clenched at his sides. "I want you to leave Cassie alone. She's mine. Next, I want you out of this town. Out of this state."

"You can't tell me what to do," I said, my voice shivering more with fear than anger.

"Me and Cassie were together long before you ever came to the ranch. She knows what's good for her. And that isn't you." He took a step closer, and I fought my instinct to run. "So fuck off, little girl, or I'll make you wish you had."

He turned around and stalked down the sidewalk. A few people watched him go. A few stared at me. I could feel the heat radiating off my face as I bent to pick up the library books. My head down, I scurried to Mildred, then to the station, then to my cabin. To my relief, the door had a decent lock.

Later that evening, I took out the manila envelope Kate had sent me and spread the application across the Formica table, rereading the application questions. With a sigh, I realized that I had been holding out some hope that Cassie would want to get back together with me. That I could make things work here. But that wasn't going to happen—in their own ways, Cassie and Clyde had both made as much clear. And if I was giving up on that, I really should apply to get back to Harvard. I needed an escape hatch. Here it was: my metaphorical note in a bottle that the trusty North Fork would carry all the way to the Charles River.

Question One: PRISM gives grants to those individuals who will positively affect the GLBT community. In 250 words or less, explain how would you use a grant to create such a positive effect.

It seems strange to say, but the way I will most influence the GLBT community and be an advocate for transgender rights is by leading a normal life, and PRISM would let me do that. Too many people think of transgender people as talk show material, not part of the normal world.

This summer in Wyoming, I've seen the power of being a good worker and a good citizen. I've also seen how none of that matters if the people around me are bigots or if I don't come out. I want to let people know I am transgender and then proceed to show them that I'm also happy, well-adjusted, and capable. I don't want being transgender to limit what I can do and where I can go. My ability to have this freedom, this feeling of safety and comfort, depends on me and people like me. I have to stand up and live as I am with the expectation that people will treat me decently. If I don't respect myself, if I'm not open and comfortable and confident, others won't respect me.

Funding to finish my Harvard degree would be a tremendous step. A Harvard diploma is a sign of success and a stamp of legitimacy. Achieving that, I would show that being transgender doesn't mean I must be marginalized or unsuccessful.

Question Two: In 400 words or less, explain why you need and how you would use a PRISM grant.

Almost a year ago, I came out as transgender. It was both the most natural and the hardest thing I've ever done. Though raised as a girl, I've always felt like a boy. I just never knew what to do with that feeling. When I finally started living as a guy, in the fall of 1991, it was a huge relief: professors, classmates, folks on the street all called me "he." Because I felt so good about this, I expected others would as well. I thought my family would see that I was happy and understand that this was what I wanted.

But when I went home in the spring of this year to tell my parents that I was living as a guy, they were shocked and horrified. I had hoped we could discuss things, but my mother burst into tears and my father grew furious. He told me that if I wanted to stay in the family, I would be their daughter, not their son. They have made it clear that they will not support me financially if I, in their words, choose to live as a guy.

Therefore, I am now in the process of proving I am independent from my parents: I am taking a year off without familial support, and I will reapply for financial aid the following year. Even in doing so, I expect that I will be asked to cover a portion of my tuition, and

I am not yet in a position to do that. I am applying to PRISM to help me close this funding gap and to support my return to college in the fall, if the deans allow it.

Writing the essays was almost calming. I looked again at the calendar, all the boxes with their red "X"s. Kate had said it would take PRISM about a month to get back to me. And it was just over a month before students would be returning to Harvard for orientation. What were the chances that this could happen?

I put down my pen. It was a full five minutes before I thought about Clyde. A full ten before I checked the lock on the door again. Cambridge was looking like a decent option.

I folded everything into an envelope and set it on the table. Tomorrow I'd bring it to the office to mail it, express.

The firefighters were working out the next morning, same as they always did, when I came back from my run. Gary had set them up into pairs to run through a series of exercises: push-ups, pull-ups, sit-ups, and some tires that they had to run through for agility. It reminded me of watching the high school football team getting ready in the preseason, except the firefighters were definitely in better shape.

"Morning, Ron," Gary said when I walked over. "How far did you run?"

"To the second bridge and back," I replied. I'd thought of Clyde the whole time, couldn't shake the feeling of him chasing me, what he'd do if he caught me.

His eyebrows shot up. "That's at least six miles. What can I do for you?"

Six miles. I hadn't thought it was that long. I just knew I needed to keep running until my brain shut up about Cassie and Clyde and Laurel and my parents… Actually, six miles seemed pretty short.

"Pete said I needed to talk to you if I wanted to help out," I said. "In case there was another fire, so I could go along."

"Uh-huh," Gary said, pausing to scan his crew and shout, "Switch up!" The pairs dashed to the next station. "You need to be eighteen."

"I just turned twenty."

"Okay. You sure look younger than that. And you need to pass minimum physical fitness requirements. You got the run down, no problem. The rest is five pull-ups, fifty push-ups, and then the weighted carry." He jerked his thumb to the side of the fire crew's bunk where sandbags almost the size of my torso were stacked up. "In backcountry firefighting, there's always a ton to carry. Tools and gear, for sure. But sometimes, on a crew, you end up having to carry each other, if you know what I mean. You up for it?"

I knew I wasn't. "I can try," I said.

"Go for it."

I started with the push-ups, grateful, at least, that the other firefighters were involved in their own training and weren't paying too much attention to me.

Gary shouted again, "Switch up!" Then he counted for me. Thirty were easy. The next ten were slower. The last ten—well, I got them done.

"Okay," said Gary. "Grab that sandbag. You want to get some of the weight on your shoulder, then run it around to the other side of the bunkhouse."

Picking up the sandbag, I hugged it awkwardly. I tried to get at least a part of it up on my shoulder, but it was all I could do to keep my arms around it and not let it slip to the ground.

"Go ahead!" Gary urged.

I managed a trot. More accurately, a walk that looked like a jog, and then I dumped the sandbag on the far side of the bunkhouse.

"Just pull-ups," Gary called out.

I walked from the bunkhouse back onto the central lawn where a thin metal pipe connected two wooden posts.

"Switch up!" Gary called.

"All done, chief!" one of the crew replied.

"Go for a run—a two miler!" Gary ordered. The crew jogged off toward the river.

I wished I could join them. Two miles was nothing. I could run all day. But that metal pipe… I jumped up and took hold of it. *C'mon, Ron. Just five pull-ups. Five.* I had never done even one. I flexed my arm muscles. Nothing moved. I strained, gritting my teeth. Nothing. I dropped to the ground.

"Well," Gary said, giving me a once-over as if he had misjudged me. "Maybe next time try the pull-ups first and then the rest of it."

"I've never been good at pull-ups," I said sourly.

I could hear the whisk of Margaret's broom as she swept her porch. Maybe I should just help her with that chore and forget about firefighting. I could hear Cassie's voice: *no feelings at all.* The cold plunge of those words, signaling the end of any hope I had of being with her. I could picture the vial of testosterone under my sink, Laurel's suggestion that I needed it to be a man. I was who I was. I was who I had been. That was never going to change, and I didn't want to keep hiding it.

"I'm transgender," I said. "I was born and raised as a girl, but I live as a boy. So I'm biologically female. That's why pull-ups are tough for me."

Gary had a sudden interest in his clipboard. "Huh," he said. When he lifted his gaze, he gave me another once over. "I wondered. A fellow your age and size should be able to do at least five pull-ups, no problem. There's a different fitness standard for girls," he said. "I think it's twenty push-ups and a flexed arm hang for—"

"I'm not a girl," I said. "I'll do the boys' standards."

"I won't tell anyone," Gary said, not quite meeting my eyes. "It doesn't matter to me."

"It matters to me," I replied. "But thanks, I appreciate the chance. Maybe I can join in the training?"

"Of course." He paused, frowning down at his clipboard and then peering at me. "I just want to get this straight. You're really a girl, but you want to look like a boy?"

I took a deep breath. Patience. "I'm really a boy. It's just my body is female." The first of the fire crew was returning from the run; I could hear their footsteps echo on the bridge. "Thanks again, Gary," I said.

He fiddled with the papers on his clipboard and extracted a pamphlet. *So You Want to be a Firefighter?* was printed across the front of it. "This has got the basics," he said, handing it to me. "You can study up. The physical fitness standards are in the back. Both sets."

"Thanks," I said and took the pamphlet. I was afraid I'd left him confused, but I didn't know what else to say. At least he hadn't been hostile.

I flipped through the pamphlet, trying not to hear condescension in his voice. *Study up.* Like that was all I was good for. The pamphlet had a glossary and a few diagrams detailing tree-cutting, hose-handling, and rescue techniques, as well as the physical requirements. Five pull-ups? That sounded impossible.

Walt and I spent the day in the campgrounds before returning to the station for a supper of Margaret's lasagna. As much as I disliked Marc, I had to admit that his lasagna was better. It was, perhaps, the only good thing about him. Walt was telling some long story to Margaret about the bear boxes, and then the crews squared off for volleyball. Walt and I hopped in for a bit before deciding to play a game of checkers.

As we set up the board, I saw Gary go over to the table where Pete was sitting. I couldn't hear what he was saying, but I did catch him looking my way and Pete looking too.

The evening light faded, and the crews quit their game. Walt had trounced me, of course. I couldn't keep my mind on the board.

"Everything going okay?" Pete said as I walked past where he was sitting.

"Yeah, fine."

Gary had cleared off with his crew. Now the only folks outside were me and Pete and Margaret, who called softly, "I could use a hand with the dishes, fellows."

So Pete and I filled up the sink with soapy water. I washed and he dried.

"I tried the firefighter fitness test today," I said.

"Gary told me."

"I came out to him."

"He told me that too." Pete kept rubbing the dishcloth around and around a bowl that was long since dry. "It isn't easy, is it? No, that's a stupid question. Of course it's not."

"Is he upset?"

"I wouldn't say 'upset.' Confused? He's bothered by something, and he doesn't know what. I think—" He took the plate I handed him. "I think he's like most people, and he wants everything to be simple. You know, stay within the lines. How can I say this and be fair to Gary?"

I had to admire Pete. He was the rare sort of individual who cared about fairness no matter what the situation was.

He muttered to himself for a bit and said at last, "For instance, Gary's the sort of person who doesn't mind foreigners and immigrants at all. Wouldn't discriminate against them or be rude. But he does want them to speak English. Does that make sense?"

"That makes perfect sense," I answered. Assimilation. Be who you are, do what you do, but act "normal." Keep your weirdness in the closet. I understood that entirely: It was about making people like Gary comfortable, and to hell with how it makes people like me feel. I didn't have much sympathy for that position, even if I wasn't looking to dye my hair teal like Laurel.

Margaret was spooning leftovers into Tupperware containers. "It's also that you're so...unique, Ron. I've never met someone who looks like—who is a boy but used to be a girl. Am I saying that right?"

I appreciated her delicacy, how I was "unique" and not "strange." "You've got it. There's quite a few of us on the East Coast. But yeah, it takes some getting used to."

"Gary thinks it might be better if you didn't join up with the fire crew," Pete went on. "Easier, you know?"

"I see." I worked the sponge over a plate. "I can understand that."

"Well, yes," Pete said. "I can understand it too. But that doesn't make it right. I told him that if you passed the test, you'd be coming with us. Easier doesn't always mean better."

I locked the front door of my cabin (though I felt silly doing it, I couldn't shake the thought that Clyde might figure out where I lived) and started to get ready for bed. After brushing my teeth, I took out the vial of testosterone that Laurel had sent and turned it over and over.

This oily stuff was my ticket to a whole different body. No more period. A lot more muscle. Deeper voice. Facial hair. I wanted that. I had wanted it back in Cambridge, back in New York City, back for as long as I could remember. But I had also wanted to prove that I was enough—that Ron Bancroft, as I had been born, was a man.

It was hard to reconcile. On the one hand, I looked the part. On the other, I couldn't meet the expectations. Gary had expected me to be able to do those pull-ups. There was no reason I shouldn't be able to. And Clyde was only able to push me around because I didn't have as much muscle as he did. I ought to.

I'd been holding myself to an impossible standard. Choosing not to take testosterone was like deciding to live without electricity: Sure, it was possible, but what was I trying to prove, and to whom?

I drew the liquid into the syringe, watching its greasy gradual flow. Referring to Laurel's diagram, I pinched up some flesh and cleaned it with rubbing alcohol. I twisted around, the needle like a harpoon in my hand, my butt as white as Moby Dick. Don't wait. Just jab.

"Ah!" A momentary sting as the alcohol entered, then, oddly, nothing.

I thumbed down the plunger and felt the spread of liquid into my muscle, drew the needle out, and pressed a wad of toilet paper against my butt for a few moments. No blood. No mark. I pulled on my boxers, brushed my teeth, and got into bed with *The Hobbit*, the same as I had always been.

CHAPTER SIXTEEN

Each morning, I ran six miles by myself, then joined the fire crew for their exercises. The push-ups gradually got easier, and the agility drills weren't that hard to begin with. It was just the damn pull-ups. Sometimes I saw Gary watching me as I dangled there, every fiber straining, yet nothing moving. Mostly, though, he ignored me, which was fine. I figured he'd get used to me at some point.

A fire call came in late one afternoon when Walt and I were just back from the campgrounds and sent the crew off for a few days. Walt laughed at me for keeping on with the exercises even without them around, but after the first morning, he started joining me. He was slow on the push-ups but rattled off the pull-ups like they were nothing. Unfair. At least he helped me though, holding my legs and giving me a boost.

He also offered praise I didn't deserve: "You're getting better. You're pulling yourself an inch higher. At least an inch!" I told him that I'd started taking testosterone a week ago, but I knew I wouldn't see changes for a while yet, to which he encouragingly replied, "Probably get a pimple or two really soon." Great.

Two belated birthday cards arrived in the mail while the crew was out, one from Michael and the other in a yellow envelope, addressed in my mother's tightly looped cursive, neat and precise like the elementary school teacher she was. I tore the envelope open to reveal a card with an elephant clutching a bunch of balloons with its trunk. Pleasantly gender neutral. Probably purchased at the Shaw's in North Conway, although if my dad had done the shopping, he would have bought it at the Dollar General, unless Home Depot was now stocking birthday cards. I started to open the card, hesitated. Did I want to read what it said? Could I just leave it propped on my table, its cheerful elephant and bright colors suggesting an aura of goodwill I didn't want to disturb? No. That was beyond cowardly. I opened the card.

Dear Ron,

Michael told us that you are out in Wyoming, and we hope you are safe. Dad and I are very worried about the path you are on. We wish very much that you not make rash decisions or do anything that can't be undone. It's hard to understand what you are thinking or feeling. Your announcement took us by surprise, and I, for one, felt hurt that you wouldn't even discuss it, that you expected us just to accept that you were now a boy, as if it could be true because you said it. Dad and I have talked about it, and we think you could benefit from seeing a psychologist. Maybe there isn't one out there in Wyoming, but we would pay for your bus ticket back and also for the sessions with a doctor who can help you understand what it means to be a girl. We're worried that something's gone wrong, and we want to help you make it right. We love you so much.

Mom and Dad

I held the card in my hands, not quite believing what they had written. *As if it could be true because you said it.* They thought I should be fixed. Like I had some disease they could cure. *Something's gone wrong.*

Yes, something had gone wrong, but they weren't trying to understand me at all. They just wanted me to fit their idea of how I ought to be: a girl.

I put the card back in the envelope and tossed it onto the table. I had no idea how I would answer them, so for the moment, I hung on to the one positive aspect I could muster—at least they had reached out. At least they wanted to talk.

The tourist season was in full swing. The days consisted of clear skies and warm weather, though the nights were still cool. A whole week flew by. I turned the calendar over to August, with its picture of buffalo grazing near a hot spring, and I gave myself another shot of testosterone. I knew from the support group I'd been to in Boston that it would be at least a month and maybe longer before I'd see any changes: My voice hadn't cracked yet. I still got my period. And I dangled from the pull-up bar the same as ever. It didn't help matters that another all-hands fire broke out, leaving me with Margaret at the station as everyone else drove off.

With that time on my hands, I had no excuse not to write to my parents.

Dear Mom and Dad,

Thank you for the birthday card. I know this isn't the life you want for me. I know you don't want me to be a boy. I know you don't think I really am a boy. Maybe to you this is a phase I'm going through. Or maybe to you I'm just mentally ill and need to be fixed. But there's nothing about me that's broken. I've felt this way my whole life. I just haven't had the words for it.

For the record, I did see a psychologist when I first came out. My friends at Harvard found me a support group to go to, and a psychologist came to one of our meetings. You know what we talked about? Whether I should start taking testosterone. Whether transitioning my body to be more male would help me feel more at home with myself. Myself. Because I'm a boy.

After that meeting, I decided not to start taking hormones, and I don't regret that at all. This is who I am. I was hoping that when I came out to you, I'd have the chance to explain more, but you weren't willing to listen. You just wanted me to go back to being a girl. I can't. I'm not a girl. I'm not a lesbian. I've tried that, and it didn't work. I don't know what else to tell you except this, and I hope you will love me as I am, not as you wish me to be.

Love,

Ron

I let that letter sit on the table in my cabin for a while. What I'd written was true, but there was so much I was leaving out. How could they not understand that this was me—hadn't they known me as a tomboy? Didn't they remember how I'd begged for a short haircut all through elementary school? And what I wrote about testosterone… Obviously I'd changed my mind since Cambridge. But I didn't want to tell them that, at least not yet. It would only alarm them more.

After two days of rereading the letter, I finally sealed it into an envelope and sent it off.

I checked the mail religiously over the next few days, wondering when I'd hear anything from PRISM. In the evenings, Margaret and I played cribbage. At last the crews returned from fighting the fire, and the normal routine resumed.

I was raking the dry grass of the yard, waiting for Walt to emerge from the stables, when a small pickup truck rattled down the station drive, paused in front of the office, and then puttered over toward my cabin. A Jeep Comanche.

Cassie stepped out, tipped her hat back on her head, and nodded to me. "Nice spot," she said.

"I like it." I couldn't help it; my heart was just about leaping out of my chest. I gripped the broom with both hands. Why was she here? Good news? Bad news? "What's up?"

I tried to repress my hopes, tried to keep my mind a blank slate. Knowing she could say anything, not wanting to want what I wanted—and feeling the slightest resentment because of that fact. I'd tried so hard to get her out of mind, and she just kept popping back up.

"Promise you won't laugh?" She leaned against one of the posts that held my porch up, her thumbs hooked in her jean pockets. God, she was gorgeous.

"Promise."

"Last night, I woke up out of a dead sleep. You know that feeling, when you can't remember where you are, and it's all dark, and you feel like you could be anywhere?" She tucked a strand of hair behind her ear.

I nodded. "I've had that quite a bit. There should be a word for it."

"Bet there is. And I bet it's French."

I offered her the one chair on the porch and went inside to drag one out for me. "Want a cup of tea or anything?"

"No thanks." She sat down and stared off across the station. "So, anyhow, last night. I got up. I knew I wouldn't be able to get back to sleep, so I went outside to the barn. I was missing the ranch. I hate being close to town. It never gets real dark. I looked up at the sky, and I saw my constellation, and that reminded me of you."

In the pause between her words, I could hear the North Fork rushing along behind the cottonwoods. I wasn't sure what to say.

Cassie continued on. "I was thinking about that night we were out there on the ranch, and we were talking about my name, and I asked you about yours, and you said it was a long story—"

"I should have told you then," I interrupted.

But she just talked right over me.

"—and I realized I don't know your name."

I thought back to that conversation and, strangely, what I remembered most vividly was the smell of the sagebrush on the night air, the now-and-then sounds that came from the dark, the scurryings and scatterings of invisible life. My name—my birth name. I'd heard it recently, from Clyde, but I didn't want to mention that to her. I didn't want her to worry about Clyde any more than she already did.

"I realized that, and…" For the first time I heard hesitation in her voice as if she were nervous. "I said to myself, Cassie, if you keep thinking of him… If you're out working horses and you find yourself wondering, 'What's Ron doing?' then maybe you should go find out." She shook her head, still looking away from me. "I'm not used to being such an idiot."

"You're not an idiot," I said, trying not to sound smug.

"You're laughing," she said.

"Just smiling."

"Why?"

"Happy. That's all. I'm happy that you're sitting here talking to me."

"So. What was your name?"

"Veronica. Now *you're* laughing."

"Darn right. I can't picture you as a 'Veronica.'"

"My mom's always been into saints."

"Veronica." She squinted at me as if trying to fit the name to my face. "Does it feel funny to hear that name?"

"Yeah. I wish I could say it doesn't feel like mine anymore, but it's hardwired." Across the station, I saw Walt emerge from the stables, leading a mule toward the trailer. "Is everything going okay for you?" I asked. "Are things good?"

She gazed at me, gave a slow blink. "Okay? I suppose I'm okay. But no, nothing's good. Clyde's taken to calling the lady who's hired me, and Gus is no help. I think Nancy's finally gotten to him. He calls up and wants to know if I'll go to church with them. Church!" She rolled her eyes. "He hated church when we were kids. I don't see why he'd think I'd want to go now." Abruptly, she stood and rubbed her hands on the thighs of her pants. "Complaining won't do any good."

So that was that. She'd woken up wondering about my name. Now she'd learned it, and she was leaving.

"Can I make you dinner sometime?" I asked, before I lost my chance and my nerve.

She squinted at me. "Are you asking me on a date?"

"Only if you want it be," I said, worried about moving too fast, scaring her off. "We can be just friends."

"Hmmm." She nodded slowly. "No. A date might be fine. Tuesday at six?"

"Awesome." I wanted to hug her, to pull her close, but I sensed that might be too much. And it would be just plain stupid to offer her a handshake. So I just shoved my hands into my jean pockets and grinned. "I can't wait."

Cassie being Cassie, she of course had the perfect gesture as she headed back to her Comanche: a tip of her hat, a little bow from the waist, and, as she straightened up, a quick wink.

The next morning, I gave myself my third shot of testosterone and tried not to worry too much about what I would cook Cassie for dinner. When the fire crew ambled out of their bunkhouse, stretching and laughing and groaning as usual, I trotted out onto the station yard to join them. We did jumping jacks and limbering-up exercises to start, and then Gary split us into stations. I rotated through the agility drills and sit-ups, then found myself, as usual, hanging from the thin metal bar.

Up, up, up. Think positive. (Margaret had recently given me a stack of books to read, mostly murder mysteries, but tucked in their midst was a slim volume on the power of positive thinking. I wasn't sure whether she had intentionally included this or not, but I figured it was worth a try.) *I can do this.*

I squeezed my shoulder blades together, felt my biceps flex and... Yes, my elbows bent, more and more, and I was actually moving up. It felt like my shoulders were going to explode—my whole body was quivering—and that's when I noticed that the fire crew had gathered around me, shouting and cheering, "You got this, Ron! C'mon!"

I ignored the tearing sensation in my biceps, pushing away the memory of my junior high self just dangling there, and somehow managed to crank myself up until my chin was even with the bar. Then I let myself drop to the ground. I wasn't sure I'd ever straighten my arms out again.

"Nicely done!" That was Pete, calling from the porch. All the cheering must have drawn him out of the office.

There was a round of applause from the crew, a few loud whistles, and then Gary called out, "We've still got half a workout to go. Let's move it!" He looked less than entirely pleased.

One down. Four to go.

CHAPTER SEVENTEEN

When I borrowed pots and pans from Margaret to cook dinner for Cassie, I also got a good earful of advice on how to roast a chicken. She even drove me into Cody to take me grocery shopping as if I couldn't be trusted to pick out potatoes on my own. Then she helped me carry the bags into my cabin, suggested that I give the place a good mopping, and wished me luck.

"Is she older?" Margaret asked as she headed out the door. "I caught a glimpse of her when she pulled in the other day."

"She's older," I said, "but that only makes her better."

"Oh my. I see you've been practicing your lines." She gave me a wave and went back to her house.

At six sharp, Cassie's Comanche rolled around in front of my cabin. I could feel the entire station's eyes on her as she disembarked, dressed in black jeans and a crisp white shirt that looked like it had never been near a horse.

She carried a brown bag with a six-pack of beer inside, which she shoved into my hands at the door. "Smells great."

I opened a beer for each of us and shoved the rest in the fridge. "Let me tend to the bird." I didn't have an apron, and I was wearing my nicest shirt—the one button-down I'd bothered to bring on this adventure—so I extracted the chicken from the oven rather cautiously. I pored over Margaret's instructions, double-checking that the critter was done. Nothing killed romance like food poisoning.

"'Exudes clear juices when poked.' Check. 'Thigh joint feels loose when jostled.' Check." I set the bird on the stovetop. "How's your week been?"

"I'm ready to toss the old lady I'm working for out of the hayloft. She's so dang fussy. 'My horse sneezed. This barn needs to be dusted.' You'd think they were her children. Yech. Your week?"

"Lots of RVs," I said, telling her all the funny stories about tourists and bear boxes that I could think of as I put together the salad.

"I haven't seen a grizzly bear in a while," she said. "They come down by the ranch in the springtime. There's something there they like to eat…" She broke off, tapped a finger against the glass of her beer bottle. "Clyde called me this week. He call you?"

"I don't have a phone."

"That's good."

"What did he want?"

"To tell me I'm a stupid cunt. To let me know that he knows where I live and where you live."

My hands paused in their lettuce tearing. He knew where I lived? Was he lying to Cassie? Or had he followed her out here? Or followed me?

"Do you think he knows that we've—" I stopped short of describing what it was we were doing, not wanting to name it, knowing how much power could rest in a label.

"Seen each other lately? Who knows? Probably. Small town life. Plus, he follows me around whenever he can."

"So what'd you say to him?"

"I told him to go fuck himself and that if I ever caught him by my place again, I'd have a gun ready." She gave me a smile, and although it was a little grim, it was still a smile. And she still looked gorgeous.

"I'm so glad you're here," I said, feeling much more than that but not trusting myself to put it coherently into words.

I set the salad on the table, and Cassie took a seat. The cabin was so small—my chair backed up against the side of my bed, and hers was wedged against the bookshelf. As I started to carve the chicken, my thoughts circled back to Clyde. What would I do if he showed up here? I would probably just run away. In fact, that seemed like a very good idea.

Well, not really. At this moment, I didn't want to go anywhere. "White meat or dark?" I asked Cassie.

"How about a little of both." We dug in. "Good chicken," she said.

"Margaret's recipe. It is pretty good, but my mom used to make the best roast chicken."

"You say that like you're never going to see her again."

I tried to keep my tone light. I really didn't want to talk about my parents. "Currently, that's about how it feels. I might be okay with that."

Cassie took another bite of chicken. "Believe me, I understand how frustrating mothers can be. There've been years when I've barely talked to mine. The mother-daughter dynamic—now there's something they should study at Harvard," she said, pointing her fork at me.

"It's not just my mom. It's my dad too. They both think that I ought to live as a girl. Like it's just some switch I can flip." I wasn't sure how Cassie would take this, or how much she wanted to talk about my past, about my having been raised as a girl. I wasn't sure how much I wanted to talk about this... But there it was. There I was.

Cassie went to the fridge for another beer and laughed when she opened the door. "If there was any doubt about whether you're a boy or a girl, this fridge answers the question. Nothing but milk and condiments. Boy all the way."

"Well, most nights Margaret cooks for everyone," I said, half-defensive over her teasing and half-delighted that I'd passed this (admittedly ridiculous) test of guy-ness. I pointed through the screen door to the station's central grassy patch. I'd heard the fire and trail crews pull in while I was cooking and knew they'd be eating sometime soon.

"Sounds nice," Cassie said. "But I'm sure this is better."

She speared some overly crispy potatoes and read the book spines on the shelf beside her. "*Bear Country. The Wildflowers of the Shoshone National Forest.* You're taking this ranger thing seriously."

"That's what I tend to do, for better or for worse. I've never really liked television."

"Me neither, except for sports. Plus, the reception out here is crappy." She flipped through the book on wildflowers. "Don't you at least read novels?"

"Of course. They're over by the bed."

She stood up and went to peruse the stacks, such as they were. "*The Hobbit.* Never got into fantasy. Oh, I liked *Their Eyes Were Watching God.* Read it in college."

"What was your major?"

"Arts and Sciences. Whatever that means. At the end of four years, I'd taken just about everything. Went in wanting to be a vet, hated physics, which was a requirement. Wanted to be an English major, but all the girls were reading poems and looking for husbands. Not my thing."

"I wouldn't think so."

She plunked back into her chair, thumbing through the volume. "But the college let me graduate anyhow. Nice of them. They probably just wanted to get rid of me. I loved the classes. I wish I could have joined a frat. They had all the fun. The sororities were lame."

"You sound like you were as much of a tomboy as I was."

She raised her eyebrows. "Probably not that much."

"That's not what I meant," I muttered, looking down. When I flicked my eyes up at her, she looked annoyed, or displeased. "Does it bother you that I'm transgender?" I asked, figuring there was no point in being coy about it.

"Bother me? No, it doesn't bother me," she protested. "Ah, hell. I don't know what to think. I'd be lying if I didn't say that I wished you weren't. I wish you were just a guy. That'd make things easier."

"Don't I know it." I ate the last forkful of potatoes on my plate. Thought for a moment about her words, how often I'd wished the same thing. How often I'd insisted to Laurel or Jane that I was a guy despite the "transgender" label. "But I'm not just a guy. Are you okay with that?"

"I've never dated a girl before," Cassie went on, looking out through the screen door. "I've never slept with a girl, never kissed a girl."

"I'm not a girl."

"I know." She rocked back in her chair, shifting her gaze to me as if waiting for me to challenge her. "I know. You're not a girl, and you're not just a boy. You're Ron. I've said it before, and I'll say it again. There's something about you. I get within three feet, and I can hardly keep my hands off of you."

"You did a pretty good job the last couple of weeks at the ranch." I was surprised by the resentment that snuck into my tone.

"Christ, Ron. I was… I didn't know what to think. My whole life, everyone's thought I was a lesbian. Even the boys I've dated have said that. My mom once tried to send me off to some place to get 'cured,' for Christ's sake. When I found out about you, I didn't know what that meant about me."

"I understand." I thought I did, anyway. "This past year, I was dating a girl who had always identified as a lesbian. But it was tough for her to be with me because we weren't a lesbian couple, not really. Even though we weren't straight either."

"Yeah, that's it. I'm not sure which side it leaves me on."

"I ask myself that all the time." I stared down at the tabletop, tracing the pattern in the Formica with my fingertip. Why did it matter so much? Why was being in-between, being neither, being both, so impossible? "Does it bother you that much? About your sexual orientation?"

I heard the thud as she rocked forward, dropping the front legs of her chair back to the ground. "I've given sexual orientation a lot of thought these last few weeks, and I've decided all that crap doesn't matter. I'm sexually oriented to you."

She stood up, stacked our plates, and went to the sink, running water and squirting in some soap, leaving me to gape at her for a moment. Had she just said…? I wanted to grab a yellow pad and write down that line, preserve it forever.

"Let me do that," I said, pulling myself together and standing up. "I'm the professional—"

"I'm just letting them soak," she said, turning the water off. "You can do them later. I don't intend to let you get up for quite a while."

With that she stepped over and gave me a gentle shove so that I toppled over onto my bed. I reached out with my foot and kicked the door shut, muting the sound of the crews playing volleyball on the yard. Cassie straddled me on the bed, sitting with her butt on my hips, smiling down at me as I reached up to undo the buttons on her shirt, slipping my fingers inside and unclasping her bra.

"You did that real easy," she said.

"Lots of practice."

"I suppose you know your way around bras more than most guys." Now her fingers worked at the buttons on my shirt. "Oh, right. Spider-Man," she said when she had gotten down through the layers to my compression top.

"This takes some effort," I said, twisting the tight shirt up and over my head. Once I'd gotten free of it, I saw Cassie looking down at my chest. Gently, she ran her fingers along my sternum, between my breasts.

"Now I see why you wear it," she said. "Even after you came out to me, I just couldn't picture you having breasts."

I waited, quiet, hoping that she wasn't bothered or turned off or… No, I guess she wasn't as she leaned over, her hair tickling against my neck and stomach, and took my nipple in her mouth. I guess she wasn't bothered at all.

I put my hands on her hips and gently worked her jeans lower, pulling her hard against me. It felt so good to touch her, to have her touch me, skin against skin. I'd been imagining this for weeks, but my fantasies had been tinged by fear and doubt. None of that now. Just her tongue against my belly, her tugging at my jeans. Both of us laughing, standing up from the bed to shed our pants, clutching each other, grappling, a teasing sort of wrestling as we fell again onto the bed, my nose buried in her hair, drinking in the smell of her, the taste of her, better than I had dared to hope for.

Work the next day felt almost comically easy. By lunchtime, Walt and I had cleaned the Big Creek campsite and hiked up to a little promontory that jutted out, giving a view of the tent sites below. Cassie was all I could think about the whole morning, and Walt seemed to read my mind.

"So, the young lady yesterday?" he said as we took in the view. "Girlfriend or friend-friend?"

"Girlfriend, I hope. Maybe."

She'd woken up when it was still dark out, given me a kiss that I was barely awake for, and said she'd stop by soon. When I got up I saw that she'd written her phone number on my yellow pad—and also amended my to-do list so that it read:

Buy shoelaces
Write back to Michael
Write to Jane
Fill out report on fence repairs
Change your sheets before Cassie comes to visit again
Buy Cassie chocolates (And by the way, who is Jane? Should I be jealous?)

And the rest were too embarrassing to report—though every time my thoughts returned to them, I felt a jolt of desire.

"We'll see how things go," I told Walt as we sat down to take a break.

"Yes, indeedy. She looks like your type."

"What does that mean?"

"She looks like someone who it'd be fun to cross swords with. Someone who wouldn't let you off easy or accept slipshod work."

"You make her sound like a boss."

"No. But good girlfriends hold you accountable. To them. To yourself."

I agreed with him, though I had to admit the description fit Laurel too. I owed her a letter, or at least a postcard, especially since I was actually taking the testosterone she had sent. "You have a girlfriend?"

"Back in Colorado. She's a teacher. Real sweet. I move around so much, it's hard to count on anything, but she's a keeper—son of a gun!"

Walt just about slipped off the promontory, he lurched to his feet so quickly. I followed the line of his pointing finger. There, below us in the campsite, two black bears—one large (the mama, I guessed) and one small (the baby)—ambled through the tent pads, past the idle Guinevere, right up to the dumpster. Sniffing, lumbering, the mother bear stood up and pawed at the lever.

"Ha," whispered Walt. "Bear proof."

Clank. Even from above, we could hear the catch of the lever dropping into place. It opened a chute whose door you had to pull open. Which the bear did.

"Darn it," Walt murmured. "Well, she won't be able to reach in…"

She didn't have to. We both watched the mama bear lift the cub and drop it in the dumpster.

"What the…?" I breathed.

A few moments later, she reached in again and snatched the cub out by its scruff. Only now, the cub had assorted items of garbage clutched in its paws, which the two of them tore to bits and then, holding the choice pieces in their mouths, ran off.

"Now I've seen it all," Walt said.

"Pete'll never believe it."

"Shoot. This forest has gone crazy. Bears that can break into dumpsters. Mothers forcing their cubs into lives of crime. What's next, transgender rangers?"

"Definitely a sign of the impending apocalypse," I replied.

"Sure enough. Maybe we better build bunkers instead of bear boxes."

Later on, as Walt regaled Pete with the tale of the bears, I filled out our report form, in triplicate, noting the "use of offspring as retrieval mechanism."

Walt tapped the page. "Write down a suggestion: Make the 'bear proof' signs bigger. Maybe the bears just can't see them."

"Better start with a literacy program for bears," I said. "The problem might be that they can't read a darn thing."

"Careful, or I'll sign you up to tutor them," Pete said, taking the form away from me.

CHAPTER EIGHTEEN

There hadn't been much rain all summer. I had watched the level of the river get lower and lower, and that morning I helped Walt rig up Guinevere to hold a big water tank.

"Got to keep the dust down," he said. "You're on your own for the campgrounds. Try to get to Pahaska." Off he went, the truck spreading a steady sprinkle of water along the dirt road and parking lot.

I loaded rakes and shovels and trash bags and climbed into Mildred, driving out to the farthest campsite first. That took me along the highway past the ranch—Gus's ranch—and I couldn't help slowing down as I drove by. What would they do if I showed up there? And what would I say to them? Some part of me wanted to tell Marc and Gus that I was still in Wyoming, that they hadn't gotten rid of me. That Cassie had chosen me over them. But the less they knew, the better.

When I returned to the station, Pete waved me over to the office. "Got a message for you." He passed me a pink sheet of paper, one of those headed, While You Were Out. It read:

Cassie called. Meet her at 7:30 at Castille Ledge.

"Thanks, Pete."

"She called just before you rolled in. You know where Castille Ledge is?" I shook my head. "Go up the road, just past Lazy D.

There's a Bureau road on the right. Turn there, it climbs pretty steep, and stop when you get to the stand of pines. You'll see a pull out and a little trail." He smiled at me. "I'm guessing she wants to catch the sunset with you. Nice spot for it."

I almost called Cassie to ask her if I should bring anything but decided that if I had to ask, it would be lame. So instead I crossed over the Fork and gathered up a fistful of wildflowers, purple cone-shaped ones and little yellow ones like buttercups. I returned with them just as Margaret called for dinner, and all the crews saw me and hooted with laughter.

"Who's the girl?" one firefighter said.

"Tell me what line you used!" another called.

I laughed it off and took a plate of meatloaf and green beans.

"It's quite something," Walt said. "Out of all these guys, you're the only one going on dates that I see."

"What can I say?" I managed around a mouthful. "I've got something they don't."

By seven, I had changed and climbed into Mildred, flowers on the seat beside me, and headed up the highway. I turned onto the Bureau road, the ruts jouncing me, the open window letting in the smell of sagebrush. Now and then a jackrabbit skittered across the open ground. The road climbed, switched back and back again. At last I reached a thick stand of pine and saw a little pullout, big enough for a car or two to park. It was empty, but I was early (a typical Ron move; Laurel had complained that I was compulsively early to everything), and so I gathered up the flowers and followed the little trail through the pines, their scent heavy around me.

The pines ceded ground to a gravelly shelf that opened onto a ledge. To the side of the piney patch I'd hiked through, a cliff of yellow crumbling rock thrust up, not quite sheer but nothing that I would want to climb. I walked to the lip of the ledge—the valley spread out below, sere and serene, the sun dipping low already. It was a great spot.

My gut fluttered with a mix of anticipation and anxiety at the thought of sitting there with Cassie. Would she come soon, or would she be late like she was to the pizza parlor? What if we missed the sunset, or—?

"Hi there, Ronnie."

That wasn't Cassie's voice.

I pivoted. Clyde stood in the shady margin between the pine trees and the cliff. He walked over now, slow and insouciant, like a well-fed cat.

There was nowhere I could go. Dropping the flowers, I took a few steps away from the edge, steps that only brought me closer to Clyde.

"What do you—"

Before I could finish, he landed a punch in my stomach. It felt like his fist had made contact with my spine, he drove it in so hard. I fell to the ground, landing awkwardly on my knees, doubling over so my forehead rested on the dirt. I could barely think. Saliva drooled from my mouth, my stomach fighting to heave up.

Clyde grabbed my bicep, his long fingers curling easily around my arm, squeezing tight. I took one breath, another. Okay, okay. He probably just wanted to scare me. Mess with my head. Shove me around a little bit. Deep breath.

"I told you not to bother Cassie."

Clyde's fingers worked their way farther into my muscle, and he yanked me up to my feet. The key was not to cry. The key was to get away if I could.

Tires rumbled on the road beyond the pine trees. Clyde and I turned our heads. Could it be Pete or Walt? They knew where I was. They'd see my truck. Maybe even a tourist. Someone, anyone… I pulled against Clyde's grip, but it was useless. He just dug his fingers in more, both of us staring at the trees. Footsteps, and then Clyde's face split into a smile. Billy appeared, a white plastic cooler dangling from one hand. The sinewy wrangler walked toward us and tossed the cooler to the ground.

"Little problem, Clyde," he began.

Then, puffing with exertion, Marc emerged from the pine trees.

"What the fuck did you bring him for?" Clyde asked Billy.

"He wanted a ride into town," Billy said. "I couldn't get rid of him—"

"I thought I'd crash your little party," Marc said. He bent down, opened the cooler, and took out a bottle of beer, twisting the cap off and taking a long swallow. "Far as I can see, I've got more right to be here. This little bitch messed with my sister."

Billy took out a bottle too, and the sounds—the *fitz* of the opening, the tinny clang of the cap hitting rock—reached me, preternaturally. My every nerve jangling, I watched utterly transfixed as Marc walked toward me, the long brown neck of his beer bottle held loosely between thumb and forefinger of one hand, dangling below his gut. I stared at Billy—what had I ever done to him? Did he just do anything Clyde asked him to?

I didn't want to look at Marc, but he stopped right in front of me, angry red acne scars standing out against his otherwise pale cheeks.

Marc took another slug of beer and then casually, almost slowly, lashed the back of his hand across my face.

If it hadn't been for Clyde's grip, I would have fallen to the ground. As it was, my knees gave out, and my feet scrabbled uselessly. *Don't fall down.* Clyde's hand burned into my flesh as his fingers pulled, pressing into the muscles of my arm. I tugged against his grip until I could support myself, my stomach still spasming, my ears roaring.

Marc grabbed my chin and forced my head back, my eyes staring straight up into the sunset-shot sky. Sparks popped across my vision. The oyster of thick saliva that had pooled in my mouth slid down my throat, spinning queasiness as it settled in my gut. I had forgotten how Marc smelled, that mix of old fried food, last night's booze, and cigarettes.

He had his mouth next to my ear, his words unavoidable. "I'm gonna kill you, you fucking bitch."

My breath barely came in gasps, my muscles clenched and fluttered, my neck strained back. A word or two bubbled past my lips, but even I didn't know what I was trying to say.

"Me first," said Clyde, and I felt his grip shift on my arm. "You're not even supposed to be here, shithead."

"Fuck off," said Marc, but he let go of my face and scuffled his feet in the gravel to stand behind me.

Clyde was still holding me from the side. Then Marc's forearm—slick, sweaty—came down across my neck like the safety bar on a roller coaster, squeezing my windpipe until my breath wheezed. He yanked me closer to him, my spine up against the hardness of his belly.

Clyde let go of my arm. I heard him snag a beer from the cooler and exchange a flow of words with Billy.

Then Marc's voice was in my ear again. "You think you're pretty clever, huh? You're about to find out what happens to little girls who want to play with big boys."

I could feel the scratch of his stubble against my ear. My vision blinked with red, spots swimming across it. I closed my eyes for a moment of relief, then snapped them open. That moment of darkness, the thought that I might pass out, scared me more than the pain.

Now Clyde walked back toward us, swigging from his bottle, coming closer, flinging the empty away from him out over the ledge. I saw its arc rise and fall, waited, but didn't hear it hit the bottom.

The edges of my vision grew staticky, matching the ringing in my ears.

Clyde was standing over me now. "I got a question for you, Ronnie. How do dykes fuck?"

I twisted in Marc's grip, trying to stand up straight, trying to get a good breath, trying to kick out at him before he got any closer.

"Hey, Billy. Help us hold her," Clyde shouted over his shoulder. He turned back to me. "I'm just thinking, whatever it is you do, you're not very good at it." His hands worked at the front of his pants, his belt buckle, the buttons on his fly. He had his dick out in his hand. I yanked my gaze up to his face, the sneer there. "So

I'm going to show you how you ought to be fucked." His hand moved on his dick. I could see the motion in his shoulder, but I refused to look down. Clyde grabbed the front of my shirt with his other hand. "When I fucked Cassie, she was awful glad to see this dick. She just about—"

"Shut the fuck up!" Marc's voice exploded in my ear.

His arm clenched tighter across my neck, then went slack. I coughed violently for an instant.

"Don't you talk about my sister, you—"

Marc shoved me in the back. I hit the ground hard and crumpled onto the gravel, one knee and both hands taking the impact. I couldn't catch a scrap of breath. Someone kicked me but not hard, almost as if by accident, and I heard the small-dog scamper of Marc's voice.

"You telling me you—"

I pushed myself up, scuttled on my hands and knees until I managed to stand. One quick glance back: Marc toppled Clyde, who fell easily, his pants down around his ankles. Billy had jumped onto Marc's back, pounding the top of his head with a fist.

I didn't stay to watch, just ran into the pines, heedless of the path, scrambling through the undergrowth. Across the road, I plunged into the forest on the other side. I didn't want to waste time trying to get back to my truck. It felt safer to lose myself in the woods. I half ran, half slid down a steep slope until a barbed wire fence brought me up short. I crawled through, the barbs snagging my shirt, and crashed down more of the hillside until I reached the banks of the North Fork.

I squatted next to a big droopy cottonwood, trembling and sobbing, snot running from my nose.

My knee stung where I'd landed on it. I could see through the hole in my jeans that it was bleeding but nothing major. I gulped deep breaths that didn't seem to fill my lungs. The rushing of the river panicked me, sounding like someone running toward me.

I pushed myself to my feet, wobbling, grabbing the tree for steadiness, the world around me swaying. Then I bent over and vomited, retching long after my stomach had offered everything up. I rinsed my face in the cold water of the Fork and finally caught my breath. I had no idea where I was. But this river would get me where I wanted to go.

The sun folded down behind the cliffs. The sagebrush I now walked through flared yellow, orange, then flattened to gray. I walked on, feeling soreness in my knee and ankle. Maybe I'd turned it while running. My stomach where Clyde had punched me and my neck where Marc had held me both throbbed with pain. What girl had they gotten to call—Belva? What did it matter, except to let me know that they all hated me? *Stupid, stupid, stupid*, I berated myself, and the Fork shushed me.

Headlights slashing the twilight told me where the highway was, but I felt safer walking on the riverbank, my feet slopping now and then in the marshy spots, darkness settling around me like a weight on my shoulders. In a grove of saplings, something scrabbled in the roots, and my body jerked involuntarily, wincing away. It was impossible, or at least unlikely, that they were following me. I told myself that. But I still paused to listen, my leg twitching in place like the needle on a sewing machine.

I reached the bridge behind the station, crossed it, and approached my cabin, weary but still alert. The grounds were empty. One streetlamp, cluttered with moths, bled pale light on the office. A window in the trail crew bunk glowed as did Walt's porch light. Plenty of shadows to lurk in. *Breathe*, I told myself.

I opened the door to my cabin, bolted it behind me, and fell onto the bed. Wrung out. Tired beyond the physical. Sore in that space behind my eyeballs.

I knew I should eat something. Have a glass of water, at least. I flicked on the lamp and filled a mug and lifted it to my lips. The porcelain of its rim clicked against my teeth when I heard a knock on my door.

"Came around earlier and you weren't here," Walt called out.

I opened the door and he stepped inside, still in his uniform, and my heart went thudding again. Some part of me was still running down that slope. Some part of me was still on that ledge, tasting the sneer on Clyde's face.

"I was going to see—Hey. Are you okay?"

I set my mug down, trying to think of a reasonable answer. But my mind was like wet cardboard. I nodded, my head feeling too heavy for my neck.

"What happened?" Walt gestured vaguely at me.

I gazed down to see my jeans torn at the knee, congealed blood visible on the flesh beneath, muddy calves and boots. One side of my face throbbed where Marc had hit me, and I still felt the ache of my stomach. But Walt couldn't see that, couldn't see the help-less flutter of my mind ratcheting through the same images, loud and persistent as a card in a bike's spokes—and the urgency there still, the feeling that maybe I'd stopped running too soon, that the only safe choice for me was to sprint back to the East Coast.

"I met some guys from the ranch," I said finally. Talking was hard; my throat kept tightening up around the words.

Walt stroked his beard. It must be like having a cat, that beard. I swallowed, feeling the stickiness of cloying saliva, the edge of sickness.

"You look hurt," he said.

His tone of voice did it. He sounded just like my brother Michael would have, as if he'd like to go and beat the shit out of them for hurting me. I swiped at my eyes, found that my cheeks were gritty with sand. I must look like a wreck.

"I'm okay."

"Ron. If they—"

I sank onto the edge of my bed—I just couldn't stand anymore. "They just roughed me up. Shoved me around some. I'm okay."

"Do you at least have some iodine for that cut?" He gestured to my knee.

"I'll be fine," I said. "I don't need any help. I just need... I'll be fine."

"The last thing I want is an assistant with gangrene," Walt said. "I'll let you do the cleaning, but let me at least get you a first aid kit." He looked around as if the cabin might inform on me. "And some food." He left without waiting for my reply.

I lay back on the bed, but as soon as I stretched out, my stomach muscles twitched as though electricity surged through them. Marc. What a bastard. But I should probably thank him: If it weren't for his pig-headedness and general asshole nature, I might still be up on that ledge, Clyde and Marc and even Billy—would they all have… Would they have let me go? Or after they were—through—would they have pushed me off that cliff? I could feel myself falling, the dark spin of descent, enough to make me dizzy.

I sat up and walked to the bathroom where I washed the grit from my face and hands. In the mirror, a purple-red bruise was rising up near my left ear. The rest of my face seemed pale beneath my tan, making me appear jaundiced.

I unbuttoned my shirt, pulled off the t-shirt beneath, and stood in just my compression top to take more of an inventory. On my neck, I could see red marks—they looked almost like burns—where Marc had held me. I felt them gently. They might be bruises tomorrow. On my right arm, high up above my elbow where my skin glowed pale, bruises had already flowered, purple. They looked like USDA stamps on the edge of the steak: blue on marble white. Clyde's thumb, darkest, on the inside of my arm, and two of his fingers written there on my flesh.

I saw him, his dick in his hand, a smile—pleasure—on his face, telling me what he'd do. I gripped the edges of the sink, ready to be sick again. But the nausea passed. In the mirror, there was just me. Stupid fucking me.

I pulled my t-shirt back on and caught a glimpse of the clock as I walked out: ten p.m. How long had I been up there? How far had I walked? Even though I was normally in bed by now, I felt strangely alert. A layer of fatigue ran under that, but sleep felt endlessly far away.

"Hey," Walt called through the door. "I brought you some soup. And some iodine. But I don't recommend combining them."

I unbolted the door and opened it. "Thanks."

We sat at the table. Walt had made himself a cup of tea and one for me as well, and he talked while I ate, his words a pleasant, normalizing blanket.

"One of my skiing buddies talked me into doing search and rescue with him for a season. This was years ago, up on a remote mountain in Colorado. Good money. We lived in a pretty comfy basecamp, a cabin kinda like this. I'd ski all day until it was my turn to be on, and then I'd go sit in front of the radio and wait for a call. Play solitaire. Read books. I even learned how to knit. Just waiting for something to happen. And I realized one day that I had to quit because I was sitting around hoping for someone to get hurt so I could go rescue them. There's something wrong with that. I felt like I might be asking for it, you know, if I kept wishing ill on others. So I quit."

My soup had cooled to the point where I could eat it, and I risked a spoonful, my stomach still tight and queasy. I liked Walt's stories. I could never tell if they had a point or not. He blew on his tea, leaned back, and stared at the rafters. I wanted him to keep going even though I knew he was just talking to distract me.

"Did you have any rescues?" I asked.

"Oh, we had a few. Skiers with broken femurs. One guy had to be helicoptered out. The call I really remember though... I was in the radio room with the head of search and rescue, and we were playing chess, and the radio starts up all *kshr-kshr* static, and then this little kid's voice: 'This is Troop 123, radioing to Mountain Search and Rescue.' What a voice to hear, all tiny and trying to be official. Turns out, he's with a Scout troop, and they're up on a ridge, doing a traverse, and their troop leader fell and broke his arm. You can hear it in the kid's voice, he's terrified. And so the head of search and rescue listens and asks the kid, 'Do you know where you are?' Kid says he does. 'You know how to get down?' Kid says he does. 'Okay, we'll see you at the bottom.' Dead silence. Then you can hear a few clicks, like the kid is pressing down the button on his radio and not saying anything. Click, silence, click, wind. And then his voice comes over again, 'What about our troop leader? He broke his arm. How's he gonna get down?' All wavery, I can tell he's barely holding it together. And my boss just says, 'Did your troop leader walk up there on his hands?' Tiny little voice replies, 'No.' My boss thumbs the button, 'Then he can walk down just fine.'"

Walt took a big slurp of tea. "I hated that job."

"I guess I see your boss's point. What would you have done with a broken arm? Splinted it? He'd still have to walk out." I took a sip of tea, mint. The taste spread across my tongue, sweet at first then a little bitter. Maybe I'd let it steep too long. "He didn't really need to be rescued."

"Yeah. Isn't that always the problem though? The folks who need to be rescued are never the ones who ask." He lifted the bottle of iodine and gave it a little shake. "Promise you'll clean that cut on your knee? And any other injuries you have?" He set the bottle down, gathered the mugs and soup bowl, and headed out the door. "See you tomorrow."

CHAPTER NINETEEN

Overnight, the bruises on my neck darkened. I skipped my morning run but hesitantly joined the fire crew for their calisthenics—my quads and calves burning from my frantic scramble down the slope—and did my push-ups, wondering with each rep why I hadn't gone to town as soon as I'd woken up and hopped the first bus headed East, with or without PRISM's scholarship money. I had to admit: I was scared. After Walt left last night, I'd bolted the door and slept fitfully, jerking awake at every small noise.

Back in my cabin, I looked at the marks on my arms. Clyde's fingerprints. Did they hate me just because I was transgender? Would they have attacked me even if I hadn't been with Cassie? Probably Clyde would have. But maybe not Marc. And at least Carl and J.T. hadn't been there—that meant something, in a way. Not that I would trust them if I saw them around. God, I didn't want to be paranoid. I didn't want to live in fear. But what would keep Clyde from trying something else?

And what reason did I even have for staying here? Pride (stubbornness, Jane would say). I had come out here to prove a point, and if I left, slinking back to the East Coast, I would be admitting—especially to people like my parents—that transgender folks couldn't hack it in the "real" world. Despite what I'd written in my PRISM application about wanting to live a normal life (and "normal" for me definitely involved more final exams than fire-fighting), it was hard to imagine letting Clyde and Marc chase me out of Wyoming, away from the wide-open skies, the Fork, the Divide. Hard to imagine letting all that go.

Pride, and Cassie. Should I call her, or would I be scaring her for nothing? We were back together, right? That hadn't been just a one-night fling. It was the start of something. Or it could be. Or was I just making things up out of a desperate hope? Maybe she'd been curious as to what it would be like to sleep with a trans-guy, and now that she knew... *Jesus, Ron. Get a grip.* My mind was moving at a hundred miles an hour in three directions, and it wasn't helping me. Nor was it helping Cassie.

I pulled down the sleeves of my shirt. There was nothing I could do to cover the bruises on my neck. For lack of anything better to do, I picked up the *So You Want to be a Firefighter?* pamphlet and read it for the eight millionth time.

Walt and Pete had gone up to fetch Mildred where I'd left her, and after they returned, Walt and I spent the morning painting signs for the campgrounds. He asked once about whether I had used the iodine, and after I rolled up my jeans to show him the cut—neat and clean and under a bandage—he let it go at that. Each campground got a new placard for the winter. I handled the brown background, and Walt handled the yellow letters. My lunchtime sandwich tasted of turpentine, and Walt declared that we'd both be brain damaged if we inhaled any more fumes, so, with Pete's help, we loaded bear boxes into Guinevere.

"We're going to drive to Clearwater and bolt down this new bear box design, try it out," Pete said as we packed into the cab with Walt driving, Pete in the passenger seat, and me on the hump. We zipped down the highway, and Pete enumerated the design features of the new box. In short, it was heavy as heck.

"I'll give it two days," Walt said cheerfully.

"Cynic. The bears won't figure it out until next summer," Pete answered.

Walt pulled into the campground. "Only because the tourists leave out easier pickings."

"Sad but true," said Pete.

We opened the crates and assembled the boxes, cranking heavy bolts into metal plates along each seam. When put together, it took both Pete and me to carry one.

Walt fit a masonry bit onto a drill. "We have to sink anchors into the concrete pads for these. Otherwise the bears will just pull them loose. I'll drill if you two keep putting them together." He set off to the other end of the site, and soon we could hear the vague grind of progress.

"So, Walt told me you had a run-in with some folks from the ranch?" Pete said. He took off his square glasses and cleaned them on the tail of his shirt, squinting at me. His gnomish face furrowed with concern.

I guess I wasn't surprised that Walt said something to Pete, but I was still a little peeved. "It's nothing."

"Really? Do you want to talk about what happened?"

I didn't. I did. What was there to hide? Somehow it touched upon my competence, my right and ability to be here—even though objectively, I knew it wasn't my fault.

I sighed. "They were mad because of…who I am, I guess. And what I've done. One of them had dated the girl I'm seeing now, and the other one was her brother. Anyway, they got me out in the woods. Roughed me up some. But I got away from them before they could really hurt me." I decided to leave out the part about Clyde's dick, about what he'd threatened to do.

Pete seemed to pick up on the omission. "Okay," he said. "By 'rough you up,' do you mean…?"

"Nope," I answered, a little sharply. "No big deal."

"Ron. We have laws out here. It's not the Wild West anymore. And you have rights."

I paused in my wrestling with the bolts. Rights. We talked about those a lot at Harvard. Civil rights for gays, lobbying the government in Cambridge, holding marches and rallies. But rights out here? I didn't want to be rude, but I was fairly certain I didn't have any. At least not as a transgender person.

I cranked the wrench around, staring at the bolt's progress through the metal as if it demanded my full attention. "They didn't rape me if that's what you're asking, though I think that's what they intended to do. I got punched and yanked around some. Nothing worse than a typical basketball game. Even a women's basketball game."

Pete didn't match my grin. He took off his Forest Service cap and scratched his head. The breeze pulled a few wisps from his comb-over, and he smoothed them down. "Okay."

A truck dragging a horse trailer pulled into the site's corral and began to unload.

"Popular trail up there," Pete said. "Nice views. I remember, oh, six or seven years ago, I rode out with a few friends of mine. Nice day, and then heading back, one of the horses got spooked and my friend fell off, cracked his head on a rock. No blood or anything, he was just laid out cold for a few moments. We were all standing over him, asking him, 'You okay?' and he just brushed us off. I remember what he said, to the word: 'I'm fine. That damn horse just rung my bell.' Like it's something to be embarrassed by. Rides in with us, won't go to the hospital. Dead in bed the next morning. Stroke."

I set the wrench down. "I'm not too embarrassed to tell you, Pete. It's the truth. I'm fine."

He held up his hands in mock defense. "I was just telling a story."

I looked away from him, studying the trail that wound up from the campsite into the trees. "I think Steve was right," I said at last. "He said that people would resent it if I wasn't upfront with them. They'd think I was fooling them. I didn't agree with him then, but I think I do now. If it were all out in the open… Maybe Clyde would have hated me anyway, but me keeping it secret—I don't know. I think it made me more of a target. Like I was ashamed of being transgender, and that made it something they could really hurt me about. A liability instead of just a fact."

"Steve's a smart fellow," Pete said.

"You know, at the start of this summer, I wanted to come out here and just live as a guy, just be myself. But I guess I'm realizing that this is who I am: not quite a guy."

"Oh, I don't know. I'd say the same thing but different. You're a lot more than just a guy."

His words surprised me, and I felt a thickness in my throat as I said, "Thanks, Pete." I bit down on the inside of my cheek. I did not want to cry. "I just feel like I've been really stupid."

"You can't be a human and not be stupid sometimes, and from what I've seen you're smarter than many," Pete said.

Before I could say anything in response, Walt slung the drill back into Guinevere's toolbox. "Let's anchor these suckers, give the bears something to play with."

Four big bolts, driven through the box into the cement. I didn't see how it would budge and told Walt that.

"Coat it with peanut butter. Or salmon."

"Or Cheez Whiz. They love that," said Pete.

Walt raised his eyebrows. "That's just unhealthy. Even for a bear. If they want what's in it, they'll get in, rest assured."

We were anchoring the last box when Pete turned to me abruptly. "So, all in all, you glad you came out West this summer?"

I gave it a moment of thought. I could feel that, once I returned East, as I might be doing soon if I ever heard from those PRISM people, I *would* be glad I'd come out here. Close enough.

"Yeah," I said. "I am. It's been amazing."

"He paused too long. He doesn't like it," Walt teased.

"Well, I bet it hasn't been easy. But…" Pete set down the torque wrench and kicked the box to test its permanence. "I for one am glad you made it out here. I've never met a transgender person before. Not that I know of, anyway. I think it's important."

"Thanks," I said.

"Have I told you about my brothers?"

I shook my head as Walt started gathering up tools and spare bolts, plunking them into the toolbox as Pete launched into his story.

"Three of us brothers, raised in Meeteetse."

"You the middle one?" Walt asked, and Pete nodded. "Knew it."

"May as well have been triplets," Pete said. "Did everything together. There was one year we were all in high school together—senior, sophomore, freshman. We even went on triple dates. Back when cars had those nice big seats." He shut Guinevere's gate with a decisive click. "By the time I graduated, it was Vietnam. My older brother was drafted, and my younger brother and I enlisted. My mother just about killed us. I think we had some idea that we'd all end up in the same unit, but we didn't."

I slid into the cab, the others bookending me, and Pete continued on.

"Anyway, we were all over there, we all made it back. That's the point. We did everything the same: same schools, same sports, same food, same war, even the same girls on occasion."

"Not at the same time though?" Walt asked as he waited to pull out onto the highway.

Pete ignored him. "My older brother became a high school teacher. Teaches for over two decades, then out of nowhere, charges of sexual assault. It turns out he'd been inappropriate with several of the girls in his classes. He's still in jail. On the other hand, my younger brother was about to head off to law school, and the summer before, he's living with my parents. One night, they catch him sneaking his boyfriend into the house through the darn window. None of us knew he was gay. They kicked him out."

Walt floored it to merge between two RVs. For a moment, there was no noise except the friction of our tires, the roll of us across the earth. Three men in a truck cab in the middle of nowhere.

"Why does one brother turn out so different from the others?" Pete said. I could tell he wasn't looking for an answer, even if I had one. "Here's what gets me. My parents go down all the time and visit my older brother in prison. He'll probably live with them when he gets out. But my younger brother? He's a lawyer in Seattle, and they still don't talk to him. Won't acknowledge him at all." Pete shifted toward me. "That's why what you're doing is so important."

"Me? I'm just trying to…" I shrugged, not sure how to finish that sentence anymore. Make it through a year? Live as a guy? Get back to where I belong? "…live my life," I said.

"Aren't we all?" said Walt.

"You come out West, you work hard, you let people know who you are and what that means, and you do your job well. That'll change people's minds," Pete said.

"Or at least make them think," Walt added.

"I'm not on a mission."

"You don't have to be. You don't have to do anything special. You just have to be yourself."

As we pulled into the station, coming to a rest beside the office, Pete paused before getting out. "The sheriff is a friend of mine. We're in the Lions together. I could give him a call. He can come out here, and you can talk to him. Nice fellow."

I shook my head, thinking about what Walt had said about the bear boxes, how after all that fuss and bother, they wouldn't work anyway. The police would be the same. It was just window dressing, a placebo, something to make me feel better when I should just admit there was no real solution.

"If you let them get away with this, what'll they do next?" Walt said quietly. "I don't mean to scare you, but—"

"I know," I sighed. "Let me talk to Cassie first." I felt I owed that to her. After all, her brother would be one of the people I'd be implicating.

"Phone's all yours," Pete said.

I dialed Cassie's number and let it ring and ring—maybe she was in the barn or out on a horse. But it was almost dinner time. Maybe she was in the shower. Maybe someday soon I'd take a shower with her… But for now, I just hoped she was okay. That Clyde wasn't there.

At last she picked up, her voice wary, even in greeting. "Hello?"

"Cassie, it's Ron."

"Oh, good. What's up, kiddo?" Her lightness seemed forced, or maybe that was my own tension coming through.

"Look. Clyde tricked me, yesterday… He got me to go out into the woods."

"Oh god. Are you okay?"

"Yeah." It was just that my voice kept catching, and my chin was quivering, and for the second or third or four hundredth time since last night, I felt like pretty soon I'd be crying my eyes out. "I'm fine." How many times had I said that? And how many times had it not been true? "I'd rather talk in person. Can I come over?"

"Of course. You know where I live."

I was surprised Walt and Pete let me leave the station without an escort, though Walt did give me a can of bear spray.

"Works fine on humans too," he reminded me.

And Pete said that I was to wake him up when I got back to the station, no matter what time it was. "And no matter how nice Cassie is, don't spend the night, or Margaret and I will be worried sick."

"You sound like my mother," I said, teasing. Then added, "Thanks."

I tuned the truck's radio to the country station for my drive into Cody, wanting some noise to distract me from my thoughts. I'd get to Cassie, and I'd explain what happened, and… Then what? Then she'd understand that it was time for me to go back East? Or she'd let me call the cops on her brother? All the songs on the radio were about cheating women and broken hearts, and I found myself yelling at the speakers, "What about the asshole guys?!"

And that's when I knew I had to turn the radio off and figure this shit out.

Soon enough, I was in front of the mini-barn, knocking on the door. I saw Cassie peer through the window before letting me in.

"Has he been by?" I said as soon as I entered.

She shoved the door shut behind me, flipping the latch locked in a way that would have been normal in Boston but was seldom done out here. She wore an old gray t-shirt advertising a rodeo from 1988 and a pair of blue jeans with a rip in the knee.

"No, not today. A lot of phone calls, and when I'd pick up, no one would answer. I stopped picking up since you called."

She pulled me in for a hug, and for a minute or two we just clung to each other, my nose buried in her hair, her face pressed against my shoulder. I could feel her breathing, the flex of her ribs where my hands wrapped around her, could feel her palms pressed into my shoulder blades. At last, she let her arms fall, wiped her eyes against the sleeve of my t-shirt, and took my hand, leading me from the entryway into the living room.

Stairs climbed against one wall to a loft-like second story, and the living space on the main floor was open up to the rafters.

In the kitchen, she took two beers out of the fridge, handing one to me and then settling at the table. "So, what happened?"

"They got one of the girls to call the station and pretend to be you, asking to meet me out on some ledge."

"Jesus," Cassie said. She looked grim, her fingers picking at the label on the beer bottle.

"So I went. Stupid. But I went."

"How were you supposed to know?"

"I just should have...called you or something. Anyway." I let out a slow exhale. I didn't want to tell her. Didn't want to relive it. But she should know. "I got there. Clyde showed up first. Before I could even really figure out what was going on, he just punched me in the gut. I don't know why I didn't run away as soon as I saw him. But after he punched me, that's when Marc and Billy showed up."

"Oh shit," Cassie said. She quit shredding the label and put her hand on top of mine, cold and a little wet from the beer bottle. "Ron. What'd they do?"

"Well, Marc hit me too, and then he got me in a chokehold. And Clyde, Clyde..."

There was no warning, just a sudden flood of snot and tears and me choking on all of it. Coughing and crying and dissolving into a mess right in front of Cassie. I buried my head in my arms. I didn't want her to see my face. I heard her chair scrape back against the floor, then felt her hands on my back, rubbing small circles there. Squeezing my shoulders gently.

"It's okay, it's okay," she said, but I could hear the doubt in her voice. "Do you want to tell me what he did?"

I lifted my head up and propped my hands against my temples. I was glad Cassie was standing behind me; it made it easier to talk. "He took out his dick, and he said he was going to rape me, and then he said he'd fuck me the way he'd fucked you." Her hands stilled on my back. "I'm lucky he said that because it pissed Marc off big time, and then the two of them started fighting and I got away. I just ran through the woods, back to the station."

"Oh, Ron. I'm so glad you got away."

"I just feel so stupid." My voice was thick and weepy. "It could have ended so differently. I could have..." And I was blubbering again.

"Is it okay if I hold you?" Cassie said.

"Please," I said. "Please."

And she wrapped her arms around me, her hands clasped over my chest, and bent her head down so that it rested next to mine, rocking gently back and forth. I put my hands over hers and took deep breaths until I felt calm again.

Then I opened my eyes and reached to grab a napkin. I blew my nose and rubbed my cheeks dry. "Sorry," I said.

"What on earth are you apologizing for?" She sat back down across from me.

"All this...feels like my fault. Like if I hadn't come out here, and I hadn't tried to pass as a guy, then—"

"Then I never would have met you." She gave me a stare that was half-teasing, half-dead serious. "Ron. Are you okay?"

I thought about that. Really thought. "No," I said. "But I'll get there."

"What do you need?"

I laughed, afraid I would start crying again at any second. "You. And a little time to pull myself together."

She gave me a little time. And she gave me herself too. Another long hug, then the two of us settled on her couch. Stretched out, spooning each other, Cassie behind me with her arm wrapped around my stomach.

After a while, I started in on the rest of it. "Pete wants me to call the cops, but I didn't want to without talking to you first. Marc's your brother."

Cassie scoffed, shaking her head. "He's a piece of—"

"And even if he weren't involved, I don't know. Calling the police—I mean, it's Wyoming. How are they going to treat me? I don't know if it's worth it."

"What's the other choice?" Cassie asked.

"Go back East. I guess." That was a solution for me, at least, especially if PRISM came through.

"Uh-huh. That's an option." It wasn't disapproval in her voice, just disappointment. She pushed herself upright and stood up from the couch. "Let me call Gus and try to explain things to him. He's thick as a brick, but this might finally sink in. Maybe he can do something about it, get rid of Marc and Clyde without getting the cops involved."

As good as that sounded, I thought it was pretty unlikely, but I wasn't about to say so. Instead I just watched her walk to the phone, pick it up, and then pause.

"It's too late to call tonight. He'll just be grumpy and half asleep. I'll call in the mor—" Cassie set the phone back down, her head cocked toward the door. "What was that?"

I'd heard it too, shuffling and thumping outside, not quite as regular as footsteps. "Could it be the horses?"

"Not at this hour." She shoved her feet into her boots. "I hope it's not a bear," she said as she stalked across the room and headed up the stairs. "Easier to see from above," she called.

I pressed my face to the glass of a window in the living room, but all I could see was the dark hulk of the barn.

From upstairs, Cassie yelled, "Shit balls! That bastard." Her footsteps came hurtling down the stairs, and I jumped up, astonished to see her holding a double-barrel shotgun.

"Is it a bear?"

"Worse. Clyde." She cracked the gun open, poked two shells inside, and set it, still broken open, on the coffee table. Then she went to the window, opened it a foot, and yelled, "Get away from here, you shithead."

From the darkness, Clyde brayed, "You gonna make me?"

"Shut up!" She slammed the window down. I could see her trembling, the quick quiver of her fingers before she spun around, her back to me, and stared down at the phone. She briefly touched a hand to it, then crossed her arms over her chest.

I imagined what was going through her head: whether or not she should call the cops, whether she could handle this by herself. What the cost would be either way, and who would pay it. When she looked over her shoulder at me, she was biting her lower lip, pinching it till it was just a pale line.

Call, I wanted to tell her. *Even if it means turning your own brother in too. Call. Just get Clyde away from you, from us.*

But before I said anything, before I could even move to stand next to her and put a hand on her arm, there were dull thuds on the door.

"Open up!" he bellowed. A brief rattle of the knob, a pause. Then a splintering of glass that made me wince. When I looked again, Clyde's hand was reaching through the shattered pane to turn the knob.

He stepped inside, seeming to fill the whole foyer. The sight of him froze me stiff. His hair was matted down like he'd been wearing a hat all day, and the smell of whiskey that radiated from him matched Marc's levels.

"I warned you," he said to Cassie, not seeming to notice me. "I gave you a chance to get back with me, to prove—"

"Get out." Cassie's voice came out like the growl of a dog whose tail had been twitched one too many times. "Out. Now."

Clyde stepped farther in, banging against the coat stand and sending it crashing to the floor. I wished there was a way for me to get to the gun—I'd left the bear spray out in Mildred.

"I don't think so," Clyde said. "I think I'll just..." He trailed off as he stepped into the living room and caught sight of me, standing stock still like an idiot next to the couch.

"Veronica," he said, the name slow and deliberate. He dropped one hand to his crotch. "How you doing, bab—"

But Cassie had reached for the shotgun, snapped the two halves together, and set it to her shoulder in a gesture that could only—even in the hideousness of the present moment—be described as sexy. Then she leveled it at Clyde. "Go away."

"I'm not done with you. Or you."

I met his gaze as he backed out of the house.

Cassie half lowered the gun and walked slowly toward the door. An engine revved, once, twice. The spit of gravel as tires spun, a roar of open throttle—and then a devastating crunch.

"You goddamn bastard!" Cassie hollered as she broke into a run.

I sprinted after her, emerging into the darkness in time to see Clyde's truck T-boned into Cassie's Comanche. His tires spun as he reversed, his larger vehicle seeming unscathed. Cassie fired the shotgun with the muzzle pointed straight up in the air, a massive blast. Now she leveled it at Clyde's truck.

Behind me the phone started ringing. I was amazed I could hear it over the buzz in my ears. Clyde had rolled his window down and was shouting at Cassie now. She ignored him to face me.

"Ron, will you get that?" she said, as plain as if we were in the kitchen and she had her hands covered in bread dough.

I dashed inside. "Hello?"

"Cassie?" A woman's voice, older sounding.

"She's, uh, busy."

"Who is this?"

"Her friend."

"What on earth is going on down there?"

I guessed it must be the owner and craned my head to see out the window. Indeed, there were lights on in the big house at the end of the drive.

"There's been an accident," I said. From outside, I heard the rip of tires in loose gravel, a lesser crunch of metal, then the rush of an engine, loud and, at last, diminishing.

"Put her on the phone. Now."

"Just a moment."

I walked to the door. "Cassie? It's for you."

"No shit." She handed me the shotgun. I held it as one might hold an infant with a soiled diaper while she spoke into the phone. "No. Yes. I understand. Shouldn't happen again. Yep. Well, that's not— Okay then. Tomorrow." She slammed the phone down. "Christ." For a moment as she stood there, a hand to her eyes, I thought she was crying. But then she shook her head and caught a glimpse of me. "Oh man. Give me that."

I gingerly passed over the gun. She broke it open and set it on the table.

We both went out to look at the Comanche.

"Least he hit the passenger side," she said. "You'll just have to go in through the window next time you get in my car. I'm guessing that door won't open."

"How come his truck was fine?"

"He had a plow mount on. Kind of like a battering ram. I think he planned the whole thing in advance. That's pretty good for Clyde."

"Everything okay with your boss?"

"I'll figure it out." She tucked some loose hair behind her ear. The banter and the surety seemed like a thin veneer. Brittle. I wanted to put my arms around her like she'd done for me. I wanted to tell her that it would be okay, but I wasn't so sure myself.

"How could I ever have dated that shithead?" she said. She picked up the gun from the table, set it back down. "How could I have been so fucking stupid?"

"Remember what you just told me," I said gently. "It's not your fault. It's not my fault either. Clyde's a total asshole, all on his own. Should I call Pete?" I asked, wanting to offer her something, anything. "The sheriff's a friend of his. They're in the Lions together." Whatever that meant.

"Call Pete," Cassie said and sank down onto the couch.

CHAPTER TWENTY

The bruise on my face had lightened from purple to red, but that wasn't what excited me as I peered into the mirror the next morning. There it was: a whisker. Just one, on my neck, next to the fading bruises. It was a start. Someday I might even need to buy a razor. The thought was enough to give me the courage to face the sheriff.

The sheriff was, as Pete had said, a nice fellow. Nice, but still a sheriff. I'm one of those people who breaks out in a sweat at the sight of a cop, even if I haven't done anything remotely wrong. He came out to the ranger station with another officer and sat behind Pete's desk, asking me questions while the other fellow took notes. They took pictures too, of my neck and arm, and when they had left, I sat there and thought back over the whole story I had told them, the story of my summer: how I had ended up here by chance, how I had fallen in love.

I was willing to blame some of what happened at the ranch on myself. Maybe Carl and I shouldn't have tried to provoke Marc. Maybe I should have come out earlier to Cassie and Steve, and even Gus. But that was it. I couldn't blame myself for anything that Clyde had done. I had a right to be here, to live peacefully and not bother anyone, and to not be bothered.

The sheriff asked a few questions about my being transgender but only a few. It was as if, to him, the matter was barely relevant. Or it made him so uncomfortable he didn't want to mention it.

After the interview, I stepped out of the office and found the sheriff and his assistant still there, talking to Pete, all three of them cracking sunflower seeds in their teeth.

"All right there, Ron?" Pete asked. I nodded. "So what happens next?" he said, turning to the sheriff.

"I'll go into town and get a statement from Ms. Cassie Ridley." He flipped a couple of pages in his notebook. "There's paperwork to be done, SOP. But I'll be heading out to the ranch soon." He spat out a sunflower shell and nodded to me. "I'll keep you posted."

Their brown and green squad car swirled up the dust as it drove away. "Could use some rain," Pete muttered. He clapped me on the shoulder before heading into the office.

Already the morning was warm. The fire crew was cleaning their trucks and checking their gear. I still hadn't done more than one pull-up. Somehow I was stuck there. Just one and then I'd dangle, helpless, every single day. This morning, I hadn't even felt like trying.

Walt pulled up next to me in Guinevere. "Let's get moving. Campgrounds won't clean themselves."

By the afternoon, Cassie hadn't called, and I didn't want to bother her. I was pretty certain that between the sheriff, her boss, and her brothers, her day had been even worse than mine. I was feeling pretty miserable as I got ready for bed, in part because of the letter I'd received from my parents.

Dear Ron,

Your father has said I am the better scribe, so this note is in my hand, but we wrote the letter together. We are, in so many ways, very proud of you. From your grades and work at college, to your athletic successes, to the lovely friends you've made and even your courage to go out West. I would never have dared to, at your age.

But it is hard to accept that you suddenly want to be a boy. From your perspective, I'm sure it was gradual, a process and sequence. We certainly knew you were a tomboy. But we remember your sixth birthday party when you asked for a Barbie doll, or the Christmas when you begged me to make you a dress like the one your cousin Louisa wore. What were you then if not a girl? We had such hopes for you, for marriage and family and everything that has brought us happiness in our own lives. We still want that for you.

It seems to us like you are making your life very difficult. Can you be happy? Can you be successful in a career? Will you ever find someone who will want to settle down with you, or will you always be lonely? We don't ask this to be mean. We do believe in you, and we know you are capable of amazing things. And we do want you to be happy. But won't trying to live as a boy always be an obstacle? Won't it keep you from living a full life?

You've always been headstrong and stubborn (How could you not, being the only girl with all those older brothers!), and it feels to us like you might be rushing into something and trying to prove a point. You are still so very young—how can you possibly know that this is what you want?

We decided to take our own advice and go to a psychologist, a family one, and she was very helpful. She said that breaks in personality like yours often happen after big changes, like a divorce or a death in the family, and that likely you going away to college caused a big divide in your life. Who would you be in this new place? Who were you without your family around? And Harvard is such a pressure cooker: It was all too much.

Your father and I admit that we were wrong to cut off support and wrong to say you should leave. You need to be around your family. We know who you are. We can help you understand yourself. Please come back home. We will support you in a year off of college, time that you can spend here in Tamworth, with us. You need to reconnect to the real Ronnie, the beautiful, smart girl we raised. Won't it feel good to be around people who really know you?

Love,
Mom and Dad

A few days ago, I might have been able to write them a strident defense of my life out here. I could have told them about the ranger station. I could have described my work with Walt and maybe even said something about Cassie. But right now, I was in no mood to dissemble, to pretend things were going just swimmingly.

Instead, I read the letter twice through, my emotions rushing from angry to sad to simply hollow.

It was so hard to read what my mom had written about me, to try and understand what they were thinking. Did they actually believe that the stress of college could turn me into a boy? That made no sense.

I set the letter down on the table. My parents probably thought they were being helpful. But there was no way I was living as a girl again, no way I would exchange that for their love, or their money.

Cool air filtered through the screens on the windows, and I listened to the sound of insects whining out there, the more distant sound of the North Fork rushing along. This side of the Continental Divide, it drained, like all the rivers of my childhood, to the east. If I had a bottle, I'd slip a note inside. I'd heave it on the current and let it be carried away:

Help. I'm at the Wapiti Ranger Station, and I want to go home. Except I don't know where the hell that is.

No word came from the sheriff the next day, and at dinner Pete seemed to read my agitation.

"These things take time," he said. "But it'll work out. Just be careful until you hear anything."

Nervous, I went to the office and dialed Cassie's number.

"How'd it go?" I asked.

"Fine, I suppose. Easier to talk to the sheriff than to Gus."

"Did you go out to the ranch?"

"Hell no. I called him, thought he deserved fair warning. For being considerate, I got a lecture about being loyal to family."

"I'm so—"

"Don't say it. It's not your fault."

I drew in a deep breath and closed my eyes. "I've caused you so many problems. And I just want to say that I understand if it's just not worth it to be with me—"

"Oh for Christ's sake. We're in horseshit up to our necks, so the solution isn't to pile on more manure." She paused for a second. "Unless you're trying to dump me nicely."

"Never," I said, the word coming out more forcefully than I meant it to. "Not at all. Cassie, I want to be with you—"

"You still thinking you'll head back East?"

I had to pause. "I don't know," I said at last, which was true but not the whole truth. "On top of everything else, I just got an awful letter from my parents. It's just…" I sighed into the phone. "I don't know how to fix this."

There was a moment of silence. "Some things can't be fixed," she said at last. "But sometimes things aren't broken in the first place. Give it some thought."

"I will," I replied. I already was: What if PRISM did approve my grant? If the money came through and the deans gave me permission, would I really go back in just a few weeks? And if the deans didn't give permission and I had to wait another year, wouldn't it be even harder to leave her if I stayed out here in the meantime?

"I wish you were here, Cassie." That much was definitely true, and it was all I could bring myself to say right then.

Her sigh came through the phone line all staticky. "I've got a few loose ends to tie up in town, otherwise I'd drive out there tonight."

"What sort of loose ends?"

"Oh, you know, I got fired. The owner doesn't want gunshots around her precious horses. She gave me a week, until the end of August, to get my things together. Nice of her, I guess."

"I'm so—"

"Don't say it. You didn't make Clyde come out here. Besides, I'll figure it out."

"Where will you go?"

"I'm going to ask some outfitters up in Montana. But I don't know."

"That makes two of us, I guess."

"Think you can get into town this week?"

"Course. I'll call you tomorrow after I've talked to Pete." I pressed the phone against my ear, closed my eyes. "I just feel like if I weren't transgender, none of this would be happening."

There was a long pause on the other end of the line. "None of this would be happening," she said at last, "if Marc and Clyde weren't Grade A dickwads. You want to talk about gender, talk about that. How do two grown men get away with acting like wild animals?" Another pause. "I've got to get packed."

"Thanks, Cassie. I'll call you soon."

Walt and I had been up on the office roof all morning doing some minor fixes to the radio antenna. (Walt doing the fixing, and me doing the passing of tools.) Now Pete was inside making sure the thing worked, and Walt and I were painting more campground signs in the slants of sunshine by the office.

I looked up at the sound of a truck coming down the drive; it was too early for the trail crew. A red truck with Wyoming plates approached, maybe some friend of Pete's or a tourist? I dipped my brush into the can, then dashed mud-brown paint against the wood.

When the truck pulled to a stop, Clyde stepped out of the cab, his mouth wide in a grin as he caught sight of me. "Veronica…"

"Oh shit." I dropped my brush.

"There a problem?" Walt said, eyes darting between Clyde and me.

"Just here to see my friend." Clyde lifted his chin at me.

Walt tilted his head like a hawk considering a mouse. "That so?"

"Go away, Clyde," I said, fighting to keep my voice level.

"Doesn't sound like you're much of a friend," Walt told Clyde. "Why don't you—"

"Are you two faggots together? Is that possible, Veronica? Can you be a faggot and a dyke? I just came by to let you know I hadn't—"

"You need to leave." Pete had opened the office door and stood on the top of the steps. There was nothing imposing about him, a modest gnome of a man, his comb-over disheveled, his glasses flashing in the sun. "Don't make me ask you again."

Clyde's smile widened. "You the boss? Do you know about Veronica?" He pointed at me. "Do you know that it's a she?"

"I know that Ron used to live as a girl if that's what you're asking. And now I am telling you to leave. This is federal property, and you—"

"All right. You can shut up, old man." He didn't move an inch. "I heard you called the cops, Veronica. You scared?" I made myself meet his gaze, look at his stubbly cheeks, how one side of his lips curled up in a sneer. "You ought to be. I'm not done with you, Veronica."

"Go away," I said, teeth clenched. "I hate you."

Clyde cackled. "You're a fucked-up little girl who needs to be taught a lesson."

Next to me, Walt took a step toward Clyde, but I spoke up before he or Pete could say anything.

"I am who I am, Clyde. You're not going to change that. So just go away."

He sauntered back to his truck and flipped his middle finger at Pete. "The Forest Service can kiss my ass." Revving the engine, the wheels spun ruts in the road, and then he barreled down the driveway.

"Let me make a quick call to the Sheriff," Pete said, turning around and heading back into the station.

Dear Ron,   *August 21, 1992*

Allow me to introduce myself: I'm David Starmer, director of PRISM (also a former Winthrop House resident!). The board has reviewed your application, and we are all very impressed. Of course, I'm sorry that your family has rejected you, but I am glad to have

*the opportunity to get acquainted with your story. We want to sup-
port your going back to Harvard. We want to help you succeed. Too
many GLBT youth become homeless or unable to finish their educations and end up in risky situations when they are, like yourself,
suddenly turned out of family and home. There is no reason why an
intelligent and talented person should have to forsake college and
settle for lesser employment and lower ambitions.*

*Before we finalize our offer, I'd like to talk to you on the phone.
I've been in touch with Kate over at Harvard, and she's working
with the deans' office there. Once we have spoken and gone over
some details of the grant, I'll also make an appointment to talk with
the deans. I don't want to speak too soon, but I am confident that
we can get you back to Harvard this fall. Give me a call at the number below anytime during office hours.*

Sincerely,

David

I'd torn the express mail envelope open right in the station as
soon as the letter had arrived, and now I sagged down into Pete's
office chair. Holy cow. I could go back. I could go back this fall.
And "this fall" was only a couple of weeks away.

There'd been a seismic shift in my personal cosmos over the
course of this summer. I'd always thought the future was my
friend. My whole life, whatever I'd really wanted, I'd been able to
get. It had always been the case that when I thought about what
came next, I saw success, excitement, fulfillment. Even greatness.
But recently, I looked ahead, and it made me flinch. It felt a lot like
walking into a sandstorm. I was inclined to turn my back on it.

Now, though, maybe things would work out.

I spun a slow circle in Pete's chair, pushing against the floor
with my toes. This letter… I could go back East, I could pick up
more or less exactly where I'd left. Wouldn't that show my parents? They thought they held the cards over me—money, the
chance to go back to college—but this would let me write them
a nice, succinct note (maybe even a postcard) throwing their

stupid offer right back in their faces. I could just picture myself returning to Winthrop House or roaming the endless stacks of Widener Library. And the stories I'd tell Jane...

I brought the spinning chair to an abrupt halt and dialed the number on the letterhead, not seeing any reason to hold off; a receptionist blabbing a slew of names, then hold music.

"Ron, thanks for calling me," David said when he picked up.

I forced a smile on my face. My mother always insisted that you could hear a smile across the phone. "Hi. Good to talk to you."

"I can't believe you're out in Wyoming! We've got to get you back East."

He made it sound like a rescue mission. Granted, I was the one who'd been fantasizing about sending messages in bottles. But something about hearing David put it this way felt wrong, presumptuous.

"Thanks," I said anyway. "I'm glad you liked my application."

"It must be so tough to be transgender. When I came out, it was just gay and lesbian. I worry some about all this fractionalizing and how marginalized some groups..."

I cradled the phone against my ear as he told me the same old story about how there wasn't really anywhere transgender people belonged.

"...seems like gender identity isn't the same as sexual orientation, but transgender gets put into that category with gays and lesbians, and I do see how they relate..."

It reminded me of the tale of the piano that my elementary school music teacher used to share. All the instruments had families: brass, woodwind, percussion, string. But the piano didn't fit into any of them. It was kind of a string instrument and kind of percussion. The poor guy, Mr. Barker, had to teach a room full of rustic New Hampshire kids who had no interest in his banter, yet he'd stretch the story out, about how the piano would go and ask the violins if it could stay, and they'd send it off, and then the snare drum would do the same. And in the end, the piano was all lonely because it didn't quite fit into any established category.

Meanwhile, David carried on. "…we're seeing more and more transgender kids on the street. And you make a great role model. Harvard student, that's perfect, and Kate says you're well adjusted."

"Thanks," I said. "That's nice of her."

"Well, I just wanted to speak to you and say how impressed we were. Sorry it took so long to get back to you, but I had to convene the board. Our foundation's rules call for an in-person interview, but we've agreed that this phone call will suffice. There's just one more hoop to jump through. Kate said the Harvard deans have to approve the funding and make sure you can still declare independence."

"Okay, sounds good."

"I have to say, you really sound like a young man over the phone. I'd never guess."

"Thanks, David," I said. "I appreciate that." I tried to keep any sarcasm out of my voice. Why was this the default praise given to transgender people? Yes, I wanted to pass, but the whole point of passing is so that gender is invisible, see-through. I'd like to be known for who I am beyond that.

"I hope we'll see you soon," David said and hung up.

I stepped out of the office into the afternoon sunlight. Everything seemed a little brighter than it had that morning. Walt was down at the far end of the station with the fire and trail crews, washing all the trucks. From this angle, it looked more like they were having a good-natured water fight with the hoses.

When I waved to Walt, he shouted to me, "Take a break, we're all set." Then someone from the trail crew turned the hose on him, full blast.

Settling on my front porch, I let myself bask for a moment. Harvard in the fall… It could happen. But what about Cassie? Well, she was going to have to move, wasn't she? And my ranger job was only until Labor Day anyway, and that was just a couple of weeks from now. Just like the first day of classes. What courses would I want to take? If I could get into that elective in… Deep breath, Ron. It hasn't happened yet.

I summoned up Margaret's positive thinking book. Slow down. Focus on the present, my to-do list.

I took out my yellow pad.

Dear Mom and Dad,

Your letter was really tough to read. I know to you it seems like I am choosing something, but this isn't a choice at all. It's who I am. Trying to live as a girl made me miserable and confused. Things are much clearer now that I'm living as a guy.

You might be right about some parts of my life being difficult because I'm transgender. Yes, some people will hate me for that reason. But that doesn't mean I won't be successful. Just today, I got a letter and then had a phone call with a foundation that will fund my Harvard education. There are people out there who believe in me.

The fire siren shrilled, making me leap ten feet in the air. I hustled out onto the station lawn.

"Oh Lordy," Walt moaned. "This again. Maybe it's a small one."

I tried to build up a feeling of indifference. They could go off to their fire. I would stay here, no problem. It would possibly even be better to stay here. After all, there was a chance I could see Cassie. I didn't need to go with them. I'd be going to back to Harvard soon. (Maybe.)

The fire crew stood around, waiting for orders.

Pete hustled out of the office and came over to talk with Gary.

"It's an all-hands call, forest-wide," he announced after a minute. "Central office has set up a base camp. They want all crews there, extra hands. We'll muster and then disperse."

"Okay. Team One, load up," Gary called. The fire crew leapt up and swarmed around one of the F-350s, opening their gear lockers and starting to load tools. "Pete, do you and Walt want to ride with Team Two?"

Pete held a radio in his hand, tapping its antenna against his leg as he watched the truck being loaded, then brought his gaze to me, to Gary. "No. I'll call trail crew in. They can go with Team

Two. Walt and Ron and I will follow after. Close things down here, then pick up some extra saws and fuel."

Gary shook his head. "Ron hasn't passed—"

"I'll vouch for him. He's more than strong enough, just in different ways than pull-ups."

Gary stepped close to Pete, leaning in so his mouth was next to Pete's ear. "He can barely lift that sandbag off the ground. He's not going to be much good in an emergency." It didn't seem like he was really trying to muffle his words. They came across loud and clear to me anyway.

Pete shook his head. "I have complete confidence in him. He's going."

Gary threw his hands up. "Fine. As long as you keep an eye on him."

Walt tugged my arm. "Let's get those chainsaws."

I followed after him toward Guinevere, turning now and then to look back at Gary. What a bastard. He was nice enough to my face. I hadn't realized he thought I was that weak, that useless. Still, at least Pete had some faith in me. Hopefully not misguided.

"Mark my words," Walt said. "You might be eager to get out and fight that fire now, but give it a few days and you'll be wishing you were back here."

We trotted over to one of the sheds where the crew stowed gear. Most of the shovels and saws had already been loaded up, and the shed loomed empty except for a stack of sandbags. Walt perused the remaining saws, and I hefted one of the sandbags, dead weight in my arms. It didn't feel any easier than it had a month ago.

We loaded Guinevere with five-gallon jugs of water, picks, shovels, axes, mattocks, chainsaws, and gasoline.

Walt tossed me some shit-brown pants and a canary-yellow shirt. "Heavy but fireproof. Sparks won't catch it. Here's our brain buckets," he said, tossing over two red plastic helmets. "Get dressed and let's get going."

Before I put on the clothes he'd given me, I stopped by the office. Pete was alternately responding to the squawking radio calls and filling in paperwork. When I asked to use the phone, he just nodded, and I dialed Cassie's number. It rang three times and then an answering machine picked up—not a recording of her voice, just a mechanical greeting: *No one is available…* I hoped this didn't mean she'd already moved out.

After the beep, I said, "Cassie, it's Ron. There's a forest fire, and we've all been called to fight it. I don't know how long I'll be gone. I really hope everything is going okay for you. I'll call as soon as I'm back. And… I'll be thinking of you." I hung the phone up. I hadn't said an eighth of what was really on my mind.

As I walked past Pete's desk, I paused, waiting for him to finish a radio call. "Thanks," I said. "I appreciate what you told Gary. I hope I can do this."

"You'll not only be fine," he said, setting the radio on his desk, "you'll be a real asset to the crew. I believe in you, Ron."

CHAPTER TWENTY-ONE

Next thing I knew, Walt and Pete and I were in Guinevere (I got the hump seat again), driving away.

"What should I know about firefighting?" I asked.

"You'll get blisters," Walt said. "Keep them clean."

"Drink lots of water," Pete offered.

"What else? Oh, don't wander off anywhere," Walt added. "And don't take off your helmet until it's time to sleep."

Those seemed like guidelines I could handle, but I was still nervous as we blew through Wapiti and paused in Cody for Pete to dash into the ranger station there and load a few more supplies in the truck. We headed south, climbing up a steady incline, the mountains rising before us. The road curled in switchbacks, and Guinevere groaned a little on the hairpin turns.

"Look at that." Walt pointed through the windshield, and as the road curved around, I could see a big plume of smoke—white and thick enough to look solid—rising in the distance. "Thar she blows."

We climbed up and up, eventually turning off the main road and passing a big ranch, no buildings visible but plenty of cattle out grazing. Walt pulled the truck over at a rustic picnic area that had been turned into a sort of command unit. Mint-green trucks were parked everywhere like flotsam washed up on a beach over the winter, and men milled around—everyone in the same brown pants and yellow shirts.

"I'll check us in and get our orders," Pete said.

As Walt wandered through the crews, I sat on Guinevere's bumper, worried I'd lose her if I walked away. Everything and everyone looked so similar. I couldn't see the spire of smoke any longer, but now and then a breeze brought the hint of something burning. I felt jittery, sitting there waiting, worried that something would happen to Cassie while I was gone. I worried that the deans wouldn't let me come back on PRISM's funds. But then, I also worried that they would. I worried that Pete had taken me along out of obligation, and I wouldn't be able to hack it.

Wilderness firefighting—it struck me as exactly the sort of thing I shouldn't be doing at this critical juncture. But despite my concerns, part of me couldn't wait.

We spent the night sleeping on the grass next to Guinevere. As soon as it grew light, we joined a clanking caravan of trucks that jostled off the highway and onto a dirt road that soon degraded into a rutted track. Walt shifted Guinevere into four-wheel drive, and we slumped and banged our way along until the truck ahead of us pulled over.

"Thank goodness," said Walt, letting the truck rattle to a halt. "Poor Gwen." He patted the steering wheel affectionately.

At the tailgate, Pete drew out three packboards. Each had shoulder straps attached to two thin planks, a minimalist version of a backpack.

Pete started lashing on the gear with thick nylon cords. "Not as pretty as those fancy backpacks campers use," he said as he strapped on a chainsaw and then a five-gallon jug of water. "But you tell me how you're going to shove a chainsaw into one of those things and not gouge it full of holes."

I could see his point, though the packboards looked far from comfortable. He passed me and Walt rope and ties, and we strapped the rest of the tools—shovel, mattock, pick, ax—to the boards, then the sleeping bags on top, the cherry of the sundae.

"Gonna be heavy," Pete said.

He caught my eye, and I nodded. I guessed he was wondering if I was up for it. Maybe he was having second thoughts about taking this transgender kid into the wilderness too. But if he was going to carry one of these packs, and I figured he was on the far side of fifty, then I could handle it just as well.

The caravan of trucks transformed into a caravan of men, each with a packboard, each in a yellow shirt and shit-brown pants. Our red helmets dangled and bobbed from our packs. I hiked bent over for a while, ignoring the forest around me, futilely trying to shift weight off the shoulder straps that were currently cutting off circulation to my arms.

Then Pete showed me how to reach back and lift the boards with my hands to give my shoulders a break. "Take it slow," he said. "You've got about eighty pounds on your back."

I could feel the strain with every step, feel the tug of the weight through the straps. But I could also feel my body responding. My quads were thicker now, my shoulders weren't just skin and bone. The weight wasn't easy, but I could take it.

Pete paused to catch his breath. "There's not far to go. We just can't get to the spot except on foot."

"That's 'cause it's wilderness," said Walt from behind me. "Nothing motorized allowed in the wilderness."

"Even during a fire?" I asked.

"That's the rules."

To distract myself, I tried to pay attention to the forest: lodgepole pine on both sides, the narrow trail now growing steep underfoot, lots of deadfall in the woods. It was hot despite the shade, and the woods smelled of warm resin, spiky and pleasant. Soon, though, the drone and whine of chainsaws intruded on the peace.

"Almost there," said Pete. It took a while for the noises to grow louder, for the smell of oil and exhaust to replace the pine scent, but then we arrived in what was evidently a hastily-made clearing dotted with stumps.

"Take a load off," said Pete. "I'll check in and get back to you. I've gotta see where our crews ended up in this mess."

Walt and I shrugged off our packs. "This could be a while. Get comfy," Walt said, stretching his arms. "Fire's a whole lot of hurry up and wait. Then hurry some more. I'll see if I can get us some food."

We ate granola bars, and I watched rangers—or whoever they were—mill about. In all the yellow and brown, I spotted only one woman, youngish, with a ponytail under her Forest Service cap. It must be lonely to be the only woman on a fire crew. Lonelier than being the only transgender person? Probably. Or differently. Others would know she was the only one, and that could make it easier or harder, depending. That made me think of Cassie, which made me worry even more. I rummaged around for water, my mouth gone mealy and dry.

In the distance, the chainsaws buzzed on, and distant splintering could be heard.

"My back…" said Walt. "I'm getting old for this stuff."

"Plenty hard on a young back."

"That pack probably weighs as much as you do. Still, I tell myself, if Pete can do it, then I can do it."

I laughed. "That's just what I was telling myself."

"That makes me feel better," said Walt. "To know that all of us are just trying to macho up to the next guy. We're a bunch of lemmings."

"Then why do you do it? I mean, I understand why *I'm* doing it. But you don't have anything to prove."

Walt laughed, and then, as the wind brought a gust of smoke into the clearing, the laughter shifted to coughing. "Nothing to prove?" He hacked some more, spat to the side. "I'd say one of the paradigms of modern American manliness is the feeling of having something to prove yet having to look as if we have nothing to prove." He coughed some more, took a long draw of water. "Tell me again, why is it you want to be a man?"

I rolled my eyes at his teasing. "I just hate being told I can't do something. I hate being thought of as lesser." I picked up a twig from the forest floor and idly began stripping the bark from it. The shreds came loose easily, and the wood crackled beneath my fingers. No wonder this forest was burning up. The wood was as dry as the Sahara. "Who doesn't, I suppose? I mean, if Cassie, my girlfriend—" I paused over that word, liking how it sounded, hoping she would too. "—had been at the station this morning, I'm sure she'd want to come out here. She wouldn't take a 'no' from Gary."

The smoke had dissipated, and Walt stretched out, leaning his head against his pack. "If you want my advice—and I don't know why you would—trying to please others, trying to meet their standards, rather than asking what it is that *you* want to live up to, that's a recipe for unhappiness."

I peeled a few more twigs and watched the milling crowds. Now and then I caught sight of someone from our fire crew. They waved at me, but I stayed sitting near Walt. I thought about his advice, about why I had been so mindlessly pursuing some masculine ideal all summer. What was it that I wanted? Approval from an outside source? Or some feeling of satisfaction within myself? And why hadn't I been smart enough to understand this difference until now?

More smoke blew through the clearing, and Walt and I were coughing when Pete returned. Gary trailed after him, head bent over a clipboard, muttering.

"My team's on the anchor point," he said. "We're digging full out, all night if we have to. Gonna swing around, try to meet your line."

I stood up and brushed needles from my pants, sneezed. The smoke was making my eyes water. Gary pointed to his clipboard, and I saw a topographical map there with a thick black line arcing across it.

Pete reached over with a ballpoint pen and drew a little "X." "That's us. We'll get to digging. See you tomorrow, Gary."

"Sooner, I hope." He tucked the clipboard away before I had a chance to really understand where we were.

Suddenly things were happening. Pete rattled off instructions: Water over here. Leave the sleeping bags there. Here's a whistle for emergencies or if you get lost. This is the staging area. Return here at the sound of the air horn or siren.

"Orange ribbons mark the line. I'll be down to join you shortly. I'm running the water wagon." Pete helped us settle the pack-boards on our backs. When he leaned in to adjust the straps on my shoulders, he said in a low tone, "Are you going to be okay with this, Ron? You let me know if it's too heavy or—"

"I'll be fine."

I followed Walt out of the clearing where he pointed to an orange flag staked in the ground. "Here we go." It marked a trench, maybe five feet wide and no more than three feet deep, that we followed. "This is the line," he explained. "We're trying to create a break in the path of the fire. Take its fuel away so it can't burn across."

"How much can we dig? Won't it just go somewhere else?"

"They'll set it up so that we steer the fire toward bare rock, or they'll burn back fires and then steer the fire where there's no fuel left for it."

"Steering a fire?"

"It's a science. You saw Gary's map. They've got it all planned out. We just do what we're told."

We started to pass groups digging, standing in the trench and tossing dirt out. Walt waved to a few of them. Then the noise of chainsaws picked up.

"Helmet on," Walt called to me over the hum. Some crews were limbing trunks. Others were preparing to fell trees or dragging the brush away from the line. "They might burn that later," Walt called. "Depends what the fire does."

I watched the crews tug at branches and push trunks downslope. "Glad I'm not doing that."

"Wait until you're digging."

Soon we reached the end of the line, passed the last crew working with their shovels, and hiked until we reached another orange flag where we unloaded our packboards.

"It goes pick, mattock, shovel," Walt advised. "Ax for roots." He stood for a moment in his red helmet and beard, tugging on his leather gloves.

"You look like you're ready to audition for the Village People," I teased.

Walt laughed. "My favorite!" He hefted the pick and swung it over his shoulder. "*Macho, macho man!*"

Another crew hiking past us stopped to stare, and I started laughing too before swinging my own pick, the impact shuddering through my arms.

"*I've got to be a macho man!*"

As the afternoon wore on (we gave up on singing pretty quickly), I resisted the temptation to look at my watch, knowing that would only make time slower. Other crews leap-frogged us, heading farther along to dig. The pair who had been working south of us came into sight, and our trenches grew closer, connecting in a crumbling of dirt. It reminded me of digging snow tunnels as a kid: Mike on one side of the drift and me on the other, hoping we were scraping away toward each other.

Pete came by, lugging a packboard with jugs of water. "Get a drink," he called. He peered into our trench. "Looking good."

It looked like a hole in the ground to me. I soaked my bandanna, drained and refilled my canteen.

"Any blisters yet?" Pete asked.

"Just hot spots," I said, pulling off my gloves to examine them.

"I got tape for you when they blister," Walt said.

We dug on. I snuck a glimpse at my watch: only three o'clock. We had a couple of hours of daylight left. The chainsaws roared closer, and above their growls, I could hear the sinews of the trees tear and splinter. More light filtered down on us. I spared a bit of admiration for the sawyers, who could drop a tree with a precision I had never imagined possible, landing it in the six feet of open space available so it wouldn't get hung up in another tree's branches. My biceps ached, and I could feel a blister swell and split, smooshing warm wet into my glove. Walt kept on digging, but I rested against the handle of my shovel for a moment, trying to catch my breath in the smoky air.

It felt like I was in some alternate reality—like somewhere between the station and the clearing, I'd stepped through a portal. Nothing like Narnia, of course. But otherworldly, nonetheless. Maybe it was the smooth wood of the shovel handle. Maybe it was the anonymity and uniformity of our shit-brown pants and red brain buckets. Maybe it was the rigor of the task at hand—but I felt pared down to my core in a good way. Simple. Necessary. Just digging. Just right here. Even though I had no idea where "here" was. I thought of the note I would write: *I've gone off the map again. Look for the large plume of smoke. Head up the crummy dirt road. Wander into the woods some distance. Listen for chainsaws. I'm somewhere in there, looking like everyone else.*

There wasn't a stream around here for me to float a bottle in. And that was fine. I wasn't looking to be rescued from anything. Quite the contrary.

I scraped my shovel against the bottom of the trench. Or maybe it wasn't the bottom. Maybe we had farther to dig. "How do you know how deep to go?" I asked Walt.

He seemed grateful for the pause. "Look at the dirt. The top stuff, what's loose—that's duff, all the twigs and needles and pinecones. It's the first to burn, the fastest to spread the fire. Next down—" He ran a gloved finger along the side of the trench, marking the dark, almost black soil. "organic layer. Got lots of stuff in here: worms, bugs, beetles, which means—"

"Oxygen."

"Right. Fires love that. Now, next layer. See those white threads?"

I leaned close and saw little filaments, like frost across a cold window, spread through the brown dirt.

"From fungus and mushrooms. Even that'll feed a fire. Now below that—" Walt and I squatted down, getting to the nadir of our trench, "inorganic. What they call mineral soil. Clay. Rock. Nothing to burn. We scrape down to that, we starve the fire."

"That's a lot of soil to move."

"Well, where they can, they've got bucket loaders and bulldozers doing the digging. Here, they've got a couple dozen guys. I'd guess we equal one bucket loader." He rolled his neck and cracked his shoulders. "You like Nietzsche? 'That which does not kill me makes me stronger'?"

"The Harvard crew team has a shirt with that motto. I've never liked crew."

"Me either. I like to keep far from things that might kill me, and I figure I'm strong enough to do what I want to. Nietzsche was a little obsessed with masculinity if you ask me."

"I'll second that," I said.

I wished I had my yellow pad with me to jot down a note on that conversation. Somewhere in Wyoming on some mountainside, a conversation between two shovel-bearing Ivy Leaguers about the uber-mensch. Two guys, digging down through the soil, scraping away to get to the solid core, the heart of the matter—the stuff that wouldn't burn.

We dug on. The chainsaws passed us, and when I lifted my head out of the trench, I saw the forest had disappeared. Stumps only. The brush line pushed back twenty or thirty feet on each side as if the sawyers and their swampers were hordes of locusts, the forest the crop they were bent on obliterating.

Pete walked through again, his round cheeks crimson with exertion, offering water and granola bars. At his urging, I checked my fingers, finding two split blisters and a third rising between thumb and forefinger.

"Clean it well," he said, handing me an alcohol wipe.

"Tape it up now." Walt bit off a strip of silver duct tape and applied it tightly. "Better than a Band-Aid. Don't take it off for a couple of days." He taped his own fingers, and then we were back at it.

More digging, until finally the air horn sounded, tiny and distant. "Thank god. Dinner," said Walt.

I felt my shoulders trembling with relief, feeling immensely grateful that Walt didn't put on a show of machismo, pretending that nothing hurt. We groaned as we climbed out of the trench, whined as we shouldered the packboards, and talked hopefully of food as we followed the trench back toward the staging area. Streaming in from the woods, a general herd assembled. I mindlessly followed along, reaching a clearing where a pile of sleeping bags waited. I grabbed two, tossed one to Walt, and we searched out a relatively flat spot and leaned our packboards together. Then we joined the line for food.

Beef stew. Hunks of bread. We ate in a silent group. Some of the fire crew from our station joined us, soot-stained and sweaty. My fingers were silver with duct tape, and, self-consciously, I peered around, glad to see that others' were the same. I wondered if the tape really was better or if Band-Aids just looked prissy in the wilderness.

After a second helping, I felt a little more alive. A little. By my watch, it was only eight, but I was exhausted. Dusk was creeping in and with it a little breeze, which carried a breath of smoke as if our next-door neighbor had decided to barbecue.

Gary, who was sitting on a stump, lifted his head and gave a sniff. "Getting hotter," he said. "If the wind shifts too much, we'll have to head out tonight." Grumbling from all around.

"Might as well get some sleep now," Walt said.

I unrolled my sleeping bag as Pete came over with a gallon jug of water that we split three ways.

"Don't bother washing," Pete said. "Just drink it." He took a swallow himself and then said, "Big fire. Gary said they've worked about a mile from the anchor point, and if we can dig for most of tomorrow, the lines will meet. They want to keep it from getting into a ravine over to the west."

I drank from the jug until I thought my stomach would pop. My throat still felt dry as I passed the water to Walt and then stretched out on top of my sleeping bag. I could barely keep my eyes open. For the first time in days—weeks, it seemed—I was tired enough that my growing litany of worries couldn't even keep me awake. I took my boots off and rolled my shirt and pants to use as a pillow, then crawled into the sleeping bag in my boxers and t-shirt. The slick nylon felt almost wet against my hot and dry skin.

Propped on one elbow, the sky dusty gray above me, I looked down the line of bodies next to me—all of us in green sleeping bags like rows and rows of string beans. Walt with his beard outside the bag. Pete with it zipped up to his nose, his face softer without the squarish glasses. Men next to them, and next to those men, more men. Every bean-like body with a pair of boots by his head, a red helmet next to that, the line stretching far, far, far underneath the smoke and the sky that conspired to blot us out.

Lying there, I imagined my effacement. The only thing I possessed was my fatigue. But so did everyone else. There was nothing on me that was mine. No book to mark me as a scholar. No map to show me where to go. No yellow pad on which to jot my notes. But the man to my right and to my left—they knew me, didn't they? The closest I had to an identity.

CHAPTER TWENTY-TWO

"Oh, we're in for it," groaned Walt, unzipping himself from the sleeping bag as smoke rode in, bilious and yellow-cast in the morning light. "My aching back. God, I think I slept on a rock all night."

"Are you like this first thing every morning?" I asked as I wriggled back into my pants, trying to be discrete and quick.

"Until I have coffee."

"Let's hope they're serving it."

They were, along with glutinous oatmeal. "Reminds me of YMCA camp," I said. "We used to hang our bowls of pudding upside down and see whose would fall first." I felt better—not that I felt good—but better, seeing the guys from our fire crew groaning and stretching and complaining. My shoulders and back and hands and—everything—hurt. But so did theirs, it seemed.

Pete slurped his coffee, and now and then belches of smoke puffed through the clearing, bringing not only an acrid odor but the prickling sensation of dry heat. "Put a wet bandanna over your nose and mouth today. And drink as much water as you can hold. Otherwise—"

"Beef jerky," Walt said. "Otherwise you'll look like beef jerky. You just won't taste as good."

Pete stood up and walked over to Gary. The two of them bent over a clipboard for a while. Then Pete held a radio to his ear. I could see him nodding as Gary jotted down notes, then they came over to where Walt and I waited with the fire crew.

"Wind doesn't look good," Gary said. "My crew is going to hop on the line, here." He held out the clipboard and pointed to a spot on the map. Then he took out a marker and drew a new arc, a smaller "U." "We're going to try and reach this ledge."

"Walt and Ron, come with me," Pete said. "You're back to where you were yesterday."

By the time we got to where we'd left off with the trench, the smoke had settled in to stay. The breeze pushed it around but never cleared it out. The morning light shone eerily through it, the sun a red-orange ball even though it had cleared the horizon long since. As we dug and hopped up the line, the terrain grew steeper, the trees spindlier. The sawyers buzzed around us, laying the ground chewed up and bare.

"Seems like a terrible waste," I said to Walt as we both paused for water.

"Better than if it all burns."

Our voices were muffled by our bandannas. We looked like old time train robbers with the red triangles over our faces—that is, if you crossed train robbers with pirates who were burying their treasure. Even with the bandanna, my nostrils burned from the bitter smell. I was glad to have the trench to navigate by. Without it, the world would have been totally disorienting: smoke everywhere, stumps and bare ground all around.

At last, we caught sight of a rock outcropping in the near distance.

"Hallelujah," Walt said. "That must be where we end the line."

A group of half a dozen guys jogged past us, and I recognized Gary among them, carrying a pick and a shovel. I waved, but they didn't wave back. We set to digging again. Now and then, as I raised my head and peered through the smoke, I could see the ledge, the fold of forest below the sheer drop.

Eventually the trench grew shallow, our shovels scraping rock two feet down.

"Bare bones," Walt declared. "That ought to stop it."

Suddenly the air horn wailed: once, twice, three cries.

"Shoot," Walt murmured, stilling his pick mid-swing. "Get a move on, Ron."

All around, a frenzy of men packing up tools, grabbing water jugs, pushing a last trunk down the slope. The air horn shrieked again, insistent. Around us, men were half-jogging with chain-saws; others were running with tools in hand, their packboards flapping empty on their backs.

Beneath his handkerchief, Walt muttered indistinctly.

"What's going on?" I shouted to him.

"That's the move-out. Urgent. Mean's the fire's coming." He spoke in little bursts.

My breath came ragged too, from the smoke and the sense of panic. I grabbed the pick and the shovel and clambered out of the trench.

The horn wailed again. "Stick with me, Ron," Walt shouted as more men poured past us. They ran heedlessly. I saw some-one trip over a tree root and clamber back up. Saw another man toss aside the jug of water he'd been carrying and start sprinting. Another blast of the horn.

"Let them run," Walt said. "Let's just keep near the trench. Don't lose our heads."

We settled into a half-jog, the trench to our right, the steep slope to our left. The ground all around pocked with tree stumps. On the other side of the trench, more crewmembers ran past.

"Hey, Walt! Ron!" one of them called. "Get a move on!" Then he took off.

Walt coughed and jogged a little faster. "Haste makes waste," he muttered and coughed some more.

We came to a spot where a group of sawyers worked on one last tree, a big pine on the edge of the slope. The trunk leaned at a precarious angle, about thirty degrees from the ground.

"Got hung up," one of the sawyers said, gazing at the upper branches, which were snared in the boughs of pines farther down the slope. "We don't have time to fell all those trees," the sawyer said. "Plus, it's too steep to get down there. Shit."

"Let's move!" a familiar voice said behind me. It was Gary, jogging along with a chainsaw in his hand. "Get that trunk out of here. C'mon!"

"How?" the sawyer protested, the horn wailing again.

"Gary," Walt said, his tone low and warning. "We've got to clear out. Fire's coming."

"We've got to move this trunk. One tree like this is all it'll take for the fire to breach the line," Gary said, pointing to the tree. "Everyone get on. C'mon, climb up. If we're all on it and we give a good jump, that ought to break it loose."

I wasn't going to question him. I had no idea how to make a pine tree move, and he was the fire crew boss. The sawyer and his crew scrabbled up.

"Pretty doggone stupid," Walt muttered under his breath, but he climbed on next to me. I could feel the trunk sway and tremble as we all stood there.

"One, two, three, jump!" Gary said. We all leapt in the air, and we all came crashing down. The trunk did too, breaking through the branches, slamming into the ground, and starting to roll down the slope away from the trench.

Leaping clear, I landed on my feet, then tumbled forward before standing and catching my breath. The sawyers were already grabbing their gear and heading off.

"You okay, Ron?" Gary said.

"Yeah, fine." I looked around. "Where's Walt?" Smoke billowed through the trees, obscuring everything for a moment. No slope. No trench. No Gary. Then it cleared, and I could see the trunk we'd been standing on halfway down the slope, and someone in a red helmet and yellow shirt curled up next to it.

"Walt! Walt!" I called, panic making my voice screechy.

To my relief, the figure raised his head, then a hand.

"I don't think I can stand up!" he yelled back. I watched as he tried, getting to a knee and leaning against the trunk, then slipping and sitting back down.

Looking around for the best route, I took a step away from the trench and started to edge down the slope. The horn blasted again. There weren't any more crews running past.

"Stay here," Gary said, grabbing my shoulder and yanking me back toward the trench. "It's not safe." He pulled a radio from his belt. "Call in. Ask for Pete. Say we're at 3.48 or so." He crouched low and started picking his way down the slope.

I thumbed the call button on the radio and said what he'd told me to.

"We'll send a crew your way," came the reply.

Gary was halfway down. Walt was trying to stand again.

"I'm coming," Gary said. "I got you."

Gary looped his arm under Walt's shoulder. Smoke wallowed all around until I could barely make them out. When it cleared, Walt was crouched down again. Gary was trying to lift him, carry him like a groom would carry a bride over the threshold. No way. Even if he could hold him like that, he couldn't get him up the slope. It was too steep.

No time to deliberate further. I clipped the radio to my belt and started down, mimicking Gary's crouch.

"Get back, Ron," Gary said when he saw me coming. "I'll get him up." But he'd set Walt down, and I could see Gary's chest heaving from just the few steps he'd managed to take.

Ignoring the order, I slid a few feet down the slope and landed next to them.

"Let's lift him," I said. "Chair carry." Gary gave me a look of surprise, and I shrugged. "I studied the pamphlets."

We each slipped an arm under Walt's knees, our hands joining, then the same behind his back, so our arms made a sort of chair and Walt was sitting between us—though that makes it sound nicer than it was. Truth be told, he was heavy as hell, and the slope was impossibly steep. But we started up. One step, another.

Walt shifting this way, then that. I knew he must be hurt bad because he wasn't even complaining.

"Hey!" someone shouted from the top of the slope. "You need a hand?"

I looked up. It was just a few more feet.

"We got it!" I called. Gary gave a grunt.

Step, another step. Walt groaned. But we reached the top and set him gently down. Eight or so guys waited for us. We helped Walt onto the stretcher that six of them were carrying.

Pete appeared out of the smoke, handing me a water bottle that I glugged gratefully.

"Okay?" he said. "We've got to move!"

And we did, at as close to a run as we could. Along the trench, through the staging area. The litter crew swapped in and out, new men taking their turns. Then we were barreling down the path we'd climbed up yesterday. (Just yesterday?) More men around us, and then, at last, through the smoke, a mint-green truck. We'd reached the road.

"We made it," someone said.

Walt lifted his head and peered around. "Thank god," he said. "We're coming, Gwen!"

"I've got to find my crew. We're parked farther up," Gary said to Pete. He put a hand on my shoulder. "Thanks, Ron. I couldn't have done that without you." And he took off running before I could reply.

Pete and I helped Walt into Guinevere, and then Pete got behind the wheel to begin a jolting trip down the mountain, picking up a few rangers still on foot and letting them sit in the bed of the truck until we'd bumped along to their vehicles.

"We'll get you new shocks, Miss Guinevere," Walt cooed. "And all new oil."

"Don't worry about the truck," Pete said. "How're you doing?"

"I heard a crack. That could've been the tree. Or my ankle." He groaned as the truck took a curve in the road. "All I know is that I'm not taking off this boot until I'm in a hospital. Gonna be mighty swollen."

"What the hell happened?" Pete asked.

I gave him the short version of the tree trunk conundrum and Gary's idea to jump on it to get it loose.

"Goddamn stupid," Pete muttered. "Lucky more of you weren't hurt."

"Well, we did get the trunk down," I said.

Pete shook his head. "Good thing you came along, eh?"

"I'll say," Walt chimed in. "Guess I owe you one now."

When we hit the tarmac below, it was instant relief. No more jostling of sore muscles, and even the air that blew through the windows seemed cooler and less smoky. We drove for a while, descending around the hairpin turns.

Then Pete pulled off onto the shoulder along with some other trucks. He and I got out to look.

"There's our line," Pete said, pointing.

I found what he meant: a dim gray gash through the green of the surrounding forest, anchored by the exposed bedrock of the mountainside. The smoke was the only sign of impending danger to the forest, but it had been hanging around for days now and no longer seemed so threatening.

Then suddenly the fire appeared, racing over the peak and spilling down the mountainside where we'd been. Liquid in their fury, the flames poured out, gushing onto one tree and flowing to the next. I could hear it—or maybe I just imagined I could—a roar, like a seashell to the ear. Beneath that, a crackling that sounded like twigs in a campfire. But I knew my scale was off. The fire was at least a mile away, and I was hearing the sound of trunks snapping.

"Here it comes," Walt said, watching from the truck. "The moment of truth."

The fire approached our line like an ocean wave lapping at the shore, and I was certain it would engulf the next row of trees. But it receded, wavered, advanced again, and fell back, leaving a swath of black where it had just been.

The men around us erupted in cheers.

Pete grabbed me in a hug, thumping me on the back. "We did it! We did it!"

Even Walt was hanging out of Guinevere's window, slapping the side of the truck.

Pete took a few calls on the radio, and I stared out at the forest, the swath of black, the blanket of green. Smoke hung heavy in the air, stinging my eyes. I was ready to go back and take a shower. Walt had been correct: One fire was enough. But I'd done it. I'd been there, and it had made a difference.

"Heading home," Pete said, "by way of the Cody Hospital."

We got back in the truck, and for a while we wound down the same curves we'd come up the previous day. Then Pete took a different turn, and we followed a ridgeline through dense stands of pine. Forest Service signs marked trailheads and campgrounds, names I didn't recognize. At one hairpin turn, I caught sight of a bright blue sign with yellow lettering: Continental Divide.

For a second I thought about asking Pete to stop so I could finally take a look at the damn thing. But I knew we should get Walt to the hospital—and, moreover, I found I didn't care anymore. It didn't matter which side I was on. I knew right where I was.

CHAPTER TWENTY-THREE

We got Walt checked in to the hospital and wheeled off for X-rays. Pete and I sat in the same seats Cassie and I had occupied two months ago. I left the *Seventeen* magazine untouched.

"Got an offer for you," Pete said to me. "How'd you like to stay on? After Labor Day, things get quiet. We close down half the campgrounds. But a couple of weeks later, it picks up a bit for hunting season. Then we close the rest of the campsites. A bit of activity for Christmas tree season. Then snowmobiling."

"There's a tree season?" I said.

"You can get a permit to cut your own, but a lot of folks poach… I was wondering whether you'd consider sticking around through the fall and into winter."

"Would the crews be here?"

"They leave after Labor Day. So does Walt. It'd be just you, me, and Margaret at the station. We'd get you trained in how to plow, get you certified to write tickets and issue permits, all that. Plus, we'd set you up with plenty of firewood. The cabin would be cozy."

"Thank you. I hadn't realized I could maybe stay on," I said. "There's a possibility I could go back to Harvard this fall."

"Wonderful," said Pete, his voice full of warmth. "I expect it's not much of a decision then."

But I wasn't so sure. It felt like the fire had burned away a whole lot of mental clutter, and as I sat in the hospital lobby, I tried to remember what I'd been thinking about before we drove off to dig the line. I had been certain that if PRISM came through, I would return to the East, right? Did it make a difference now that I had a job offer out here? Did I want to stay or go?

But instead of being brimful of anxiety, I felt like I finally had the space to make a choice, to ask what I wanted, what felt right— not what I ought to do or what I had to prove, but what worked best for me.

Pete spent some time on the radio with Gary over in a corner of the lobby, figuring out where all the trucks were. I thumbed through magazines until eventually Walt was delivered to the lobby, his foot in a big white cast.

He maneuvered himself out of the wheelchair and onto his crutches.

"Clean break," he told us. "And not the ankle. About three inches above. So I'll be out of this in a month, tops."

Back at the station, Margaret greeted us, wrapping Pete in a big hug despite the ash and smoke that clung to him.

"You, young man," she said, turning to me, "are a popular fellow. I feel quite like your secretary." She handed me a veritable sheaf of pink message slips.

My fingers left gray smudges as I leafed through them. A call from Kate. A call from the sheriff's office to let me know they had Clyde in custody. Another call from the sheriff's office: Marc was in custody. Something about charges against them that I didn't understand. Another call from Kate. A call from David Starmer. Another call from the sheriff's office, asking me to call them. And last, a call from Cassie. The message in Margaret's tidy cursive: *She hopes you're well. She'd tell you to call, but she doesn't have a number.*

I went through almost a whole bar of soap in the shower, and the water swirled down gray until I'd washed my hair three times.

By the time I toweled off, the sun was about to set. I was sure that Margaret and Pete would welcome me to dinner, but I was grateful for a little time alone, grateful that it was too late to call the police, too late to call Kate. I heated a can of soup on the stove and was falling asleep before I had finished eating it.

My cabin smelled smoky when I woke up the next morning, a residual odor from the dirty clothes that littered the floor, or perhaps the scent exuded from my memory. The full sun was already up. I seldom slept this late. But then, no one else seemed to be stirring at the station just yet.

I put on water to boil and contemplated my nearly empty fridge. Maybe I could go into Cody today—I realized I could go in and not worry about Clyde... That was a nice thought. He was in custody. One more item I didn't have to factor into my decision-making.

There was a knock on my door and I turned, expecting to see Walt chipper and ready to head off to the campgrounds even on crutches. But instead it was Cassie, the sleeves of her white button-down shirt rolled up to her elbows.

"Hey there," she said.

I opened the door and wrapped my arms around her, a smile spreading across my face. It felt like it had been a while since I'd smiled this much.

"It's good to see you." I stepped back. "I'd invite you in, but my cabin smells like an ashtray. You want a cup of coffee on the porch?"

"Sounds great. How was the fire?"

"Didn't see much fire, just smoke. I bet my snot's still gray."

"Lovely." Cassie settled into the chair on the porch, and I dragged the rocking chair outside, then went back in to pour her coffee. "I don't have any milk, sorry."

"What the hell happened to your hands?" she asked as I passed the coffee to her.

I held up my duct-taped digits. "This is Walt's blister remedy."

She looked skeptical. "Let me know if it works." She blew on her coffee and took a sip. "You heard all the news from the sheriff?"

"I got a bunch of messages, but I haven't called yet."

"Marc's headed back to Jersey. The charges out here mean he's violated his parole or what-have-you. My mother is none too happy, but that's par for the course. And it seems like Clyde's going to do some sort of plea agreement, that's what the lawyer I met with said. He's got a prior record, God knows what, so the lawyer said he'll get some time."

"Good," I said. "What about you? Have you found a job?"

"It's a tough time of season," Cassie said. "Just about the end of the summer. It's kind of a dead spot between now and when hunting starts up. They'll hire some wranglers and guides then and maybe hire on hands to help drive the horses out to winter grounds." She blew on her coffee again. "Between what rumors Clyde's spread and whatever my former employer might be saying, I'll probably need to look far afield to find something."

"How do you normally spend a winter?"

"On the ranch. Steve and me, mostly. There are hunters through November, then it gets quiet. Gus goes back to Jersey with his family. I keep a couple of horses. Steve likes to snowmobile around, and then he goes down and spends a couple of months in Florida looking after his mother. That's when it gets real nice and quiet. I love it. I'm going to miss it."

"It isn't right that you can't be there," I said. "It's your home."

"I'm not going to beg Gus. I'm not going to make him feel like I owe him something, like he's done me a favor. I can take care of myself." She took a swallow of coffee. "No offense, but this tastes like kitty litter." She set the mug on the porch railing and rocked back in her chair. "I wonder if Steve would buy out my share of the ranch. I don't think Gus has the money—"

"Ron! Phone!" Margaret called from the office.

"Sorry," I said. I wondered if it was the sheriff, or PRISM, or Kate. Whoever it was, I would've preferred to keep talking to Cassie.

"Take your time," Cassie replied. "You mind if I use your shower? I spent last night in my truck."

"Help yourself to whatever. And you know you could have stayed here. Margaret knows who you are."

"I know. I just didn't want to show up unannounced in the middle of the night."

I wouldn't have minded that at all.

As soon as I picked up the phone receiver, Kate was shouting at me.

"Ron! Where've you been?" I could picture her on the other end of the line, her little office hot and sticky in the Cambridge summer humidity.

"Wyoming."

"Oh my god. Your voice is so low. And I know you've been in Wyoming. Why haven't you called me back?"

"My voice isn't that low," I protested. If it had changed, Cassie would've said something. "It's probably just scratchy from all the smoke. I've been off fighting a forest fire."

"No way. You're unbelievable. Well, the deans approved the funding. You can accept the PRISM grant for this year, and it won't interfere with you declaring independence. There's some details, paperwork, you know, but we can go over that when you come back. Classes start in just over a week."

There was a gap, a perfect silence, unmarked by the distance between us.

"Wow," I said. "That's…amazing. I didn't know if it would happen or not."

"I know!" Kate sounded like she had just won the lottery. Somehow I couldn't match her enthusiasm. "Do you need help with a bus ticket? I can call the company and see—"

"Thanks," I said. "I think I can manage it. I've got a decision to make first though. It's not going to be an easy one. I'll call you back soon, I promise."

When I returned to the cabin, Cassie was looking at my stack of books, her damp ponytail leaving a dark blot on her gray t-shirt. She grabbed a novel off the shelf and read the back cover.

Kate's words kept tumbling in my mind. I could go back if I wanted to. Classes started in a week.

"What's the news?" Cassie said as she flipped the book open.

Before I could reply, a flurry of pages came loose from the novel, and both of us stooped to pick them up. They were a random assortment of postcards and letters. Probably I'd jammed them in there in my hurry to leave the ranch.

Cassie grabbed a few. "Hey, is that you?"

It was the clutch of photos that Michael had sent me, and she was pointing at a picture of him and me: I was maybe ten and wearing a softball uniform, stretchy gray pants and a red jersey. My mother had made me take my hat off for the picture, and my hair was done in one long braid flipped over the front of my shoulder. Michael stood on one side of me, my mom on the other.

"That's my brother," I said, pointing, "that's my mom, and that's me."

"Wow. Little Ron." She stared at the picture. "You look a lot like your mom. Have you heard anything else from your folks? They must miss you… And you've got to miss them, a bit."

I shrugged. "I miss the idea of them. I miss how we used to be." I sat down on the edge of the bed and picked at a loose thread in the comforter. "I haven't written them back. I don't even know what to say."

"Tell them you have a hot new girlfriend."

"I don't think they'd find that encouraging. Just evidence that I'm a lesbian, which, come to think of it, might be a bit better than being transgender."

Cassie sat down next to me. "I understand tough families. You can work this out."

"You don't understand what it's like to be queer though. To come out."

She quirked one eyebrow at me. "Honey. I'm sleeping with you. Don't you think that makes me a little queer?"

I laughed. "I have got to introduce you to my friend Jane. You two would really hit it off."

She flipped through the other photos. "You don't mind if I look, do you?"

I didn't exactly relish the idea of her seeing me as a little girl, but what did I have to hide? "Of course not."

"You sure?"

"Go for it. The one of me on stage dressed as the Wicked Stepmother is a little embarrassing, but I'm sure everyone has embarrassing photos from when they were ten."

"I sure do," she muttered. "Braces and everything. God. It's just..." She held up a picture of me, dressed for an older brother's wedding—I couldn't even remember whose anymore. I had on a yellow dress, and my mother had brushed my hair out and poofed it up for the occasion. "I look at this, and I can't believe it's you. Does it feel like that's you?"

"That's me. I hated those shoes." I knew what she was getting at. "There's no sense pretending that I wasn't once a girl. I was. I'm just not anymore." She flipped through the rest of the pictures, and I looked at them over her shoulder. "I think that's one thing I've learned living out here. I can go somewhere new—I can start over where no one knows me—and I'm still myself."

She'd reached the picture of me as the Wicked Stepmother, and she laughed, cackled practically.

"Yeah, yeah," I said. "I'll admit it, even looking at that picture. I have no desire to pretend I'm something I'm not. That was me then, this is me now."

Cassie set the pictures on the table. "Well, I like all of you," she said, pulling me close.

She was still warm from the shower, still smelled like horses. I wasn't going to let go of her for a while.

"So, what was the phone call about?" Cassie asked after we'd disengaged.

I started smoothing the quilt on my bed, not quite ready to return to such real world matters. Cassie gave a little laugh and flopped down on the bed right after I finished tidying it.

"Thanks," I said. "You're really helping."

"I am. You need help relaxing and not sweating the small stuff. Like a wrinkly bed. Who called?"

"Kate, my advisor at Harvard, wanted to tell me that the deans approved the funding source. I can go back to school this year."

"That's great," she said.

"In a week, actually," I made myself add.

"Oh!" She raised her eyebrows, obviously flustered. I wasn't sure that I'd ever really seen Cassie caught off guard before. "Well—great!"

"Yeah, it is, I guess." I looked past her, at the books on the shelves, the little collection of pretty rocks I'd gathered. The thought of packing it up, of leaving this place, just when it was starting to feel like home, shook me. "I'm not sure what to do, to be honest. I mean, where do you think you'll go?"

I opened the front door. The air was still cool with morning. Across the swath of grass, I could see Walt, propped awkwardly on his crutches, fiddling with a lawn mower by the garage.

"Like I said," she answered. "Wherever I can find work."

I glanced at where her truck was parked, the back covered with a tarp tied down with ropes. From this angle, I could only see a corner of the side Clyde had crushed in. "Does it drive okay?"

"Good enough," she said. "It'll get me there. And once I'm there, I'll worry about getting back." That sounded vaguely familiar to me. "When will you head off to Harvard?"

I picked at some of the duct tape on my fingers. "I don't know," I said. "I might not go."

"Are you kidding? What the hell else would you want to do?"

"Stay here. Pete says there's plenty to do. He offered me a job even after the summer season is over."

Cassie shook her head. "The snow will be up past this window, kiddo. You're going to stay here and play checkers with Pete and Margaret all winter?"

"I was kinda hoping I'd get to see you too."

She shook her head. "Long drive to Montana, if I even end up there. The park roads are closed in the winter."

"Then you'd better be closer by." I put my hands on her hips, and she leaned back against the kitchen counter. "Let's go to the ranch," I said. "Let's talk to Gus."

She gave me a long, slow smile and put her hands over mine. "I don't think that's going to work. You don't know Gus."

"It's worth a try. I'm slowly learning that my expectations are often flawed."

"All right." She gave a long exhale. "It's just easier, in some ways, to say screw all of them, I'm out of here."

I laughed. "I think I said those very words when I left the East Coast in June."

CHAPTER TWENTY-FOUR

I walked around Cassie's ruined Comanche, surveying the damage: a crack in the windshield, the passenger side door caved in a foot or more, the hood on that side all crumpled as well. "I can't believe it runs. Want to take Mildred, my truck?"

"No. I think it reinforces the point. Besides, it's just aesthetics."

I crawled across the driver's seat and stick shift. At least the seatbelt still worked. We pulled out onto the highway, a few cows idly watching our progress. The Comanche rattled nonstop and the tires, to me, felt wonky.

"Insurance says it's totaled," Cassie explained as she kept to an unusually moderate speed on the highway. "One more thing to deal with."

Up in the forest above the Fork, I caught a flash of yellow amid the green. "Leaves are turning already," I said.

"Autumn comes quick. Goes quick too. It's winter that stays around forever," Cassie said. "You sure about this? What if things don't work out between us, and you end up stuck out here in a tiny cabin with snow up over your head? I told you, I'm not an easy girl to deal with."

"So you say. I want to be here. I'd prefer to be here with you, of course, but I want to be here, no matter what."

"Is this like your firefighting thing, you've got to prove something?"

"No," I said. "Not at all. I'm just happy here." I paused, remembering that first to-do list I made on the bus. Strange. I felt no urge to make one now. "I'm not the same as when I first got here. I think I like who I am a lot more now. And that's just three months here—imagine what a year will do for me."

Cassie didn't say anything as she swung the truck onto the ranch drive. I was afraid the cattle guard would do the old Comanche in, but it lurched on, past the jackalope gate.

"Those things," I muttered. "Did you know I kind of missed them? Maybe I'll get one to hang in my cabin."

We bumped along, pulling in at the Quonset-style garage. It was all the same: the ranch vans, the barn, the bunkhouse…

"Is this not the most beautiful spot?" Cassie said, yanking the parking brake. "Your ranger station is fine, but this…"

She was right. The ranch was wilder, higher up. Pine trees instead of cottonwood. The Fork rushed in roils of rapids here, not the lazier flow by the station. Not that far away but so different.

"It is beautiful," I said. At that moment, though, fear was creeping up on me. I couldn't quite believe that Clyde wouldn't come out of the barn at any second. But his truck was nowhere to be found. In fact, there was just one battered sedan sitting outside the wranglers' cabin, a car I didn't recognize.

"I guess we should do this," Cassie said. I had never seen her so hesitant. But I had to remember that Gus wasn't just a boss or a business partner. He was her older brother. How would I feel if I had to confront Michael? As it was, even writing letters to him had been a challenge, and Michael was a lot warmer and more welcoming than Gus.

Up the three steps to the porch of the office, Cassie opened the screen door and went inside. I carefully shut it behind me without the tiniest clack—no need to peeve Gus at this critical moment. Inside, Steve's desk was as tidy as always, though his chair was empty, while Gus's desk seemed to have been overcome by a tsunami of paper.

He stood up abruptly as we entered, his chair scraping back across the floor.

"You have some nerve coming back here after getting my brother into trouble," Gus said, leveling a finger at me. "Get off my ranch. I think I've said that to you before."

"It's my ranch too, Gus," Cassie retorted. "And I want him here with me."

"I'll talk to you later, Cassie." He pointed at me again. "Get off my ranch."

"Let's all talk now," I said. Energy born of anger and fear coursed through me. I wasn't backing down in front of Gus again, wasn't going to smile and apologize and play nice.

Gus didn't budge. "You know what Marcus is facing thanks to you? A couple of years of prison time, that's what, for parole violations, and that's not even counting the charges out here. Get off—"

"Do you have any idea what your brother did?" I exclaimed. "Or Clyde? They lured me out into the woods. They beat me up. And Clyde would have raped me if I hadn't gotten away. Maybe Marc would have too. I have nothing to apologize for where Marc is concerned."

Gus gaped at me like a fish that had been hauled out of the water.

Cassie laid her hand on my forearm. "Gus," she said. "Listen. You tried to help Marc, but he didn't want to be helped. You remember Dad. It's the same sort of thing. You can try and try, but until he wants help, until he wants to fix his problems, nothing will happen. Don't blame yourself for that." She took a deep breath, and her fingers pressed lightly against my arm. "And don't blame Ron either. Clyde deserves whatever he gets. If you knew half the things he did, you'd want to skin him alive."

"I'm sorry you feel that way," Gus said. But he didn't sound sorry at all. "I understand why you're upset, but I've got a ranch to run."

"I believe it's my ranch too."

Gus sank into the chair behind his desk, his forearms landing on a stack of paper, setting off a small avalanche that he ignored. "What do you want, Cassie?"

"I want to be here for the winter."

"No. Why don't you go back to Jersey—"

"Don't you dare boss me around, Augustus. You're my brother, not my father. How much of this ranch do I own?"

"You know how much." He leaned back in his chair, crossing his arms over his chest.

"Half. Granny left me just as much money as she left you. So, that's the score. You buy me out, full cash, by tomorrow, or you let me back here. This is my home." She pulled a chair close and sat down. I could see her jaw clenching and releasing as she waited for Gus to reply. I wheeled the chair from behind Steve's desk and sat down as well.

Gus stared out the window. "Cassie. I think you're screwing up, big time. I talked to Mom on the phone just yesterday. She's beside herself. Worried about Marc and worried about you."

"I'm guessing she's more worried about Marc than me," Cassie muttered.

"You're twenty-nine. She wants to know when you're going to get married and have kids."

"That worked out great for her, didn't it?"

Gus's eyes flicked between Cassie and me. "You're making a mistake. Go back to Jersey. Mom could use your help, I'm sure. There are horses for you to work with. Nancy and I'll be there soon enough, and I bet some of your friends from high school are still around. We can introduce you to—"

"No." Cassie leaned forward, resting her hands on Gus's desk. "Ron's the person I want to be with. Period. And this ranch is the place I want to be. Period."

"He's gonna cause problems," Gus said, tilting his head to me.

"I worked hard for you, Gus," I said. "I did good work. I've got a job now, and I get along with my boss and my co-workers. I'm not a bad person, and there's nothing wrong with me." I'd been wanting to say that for a long time. To him, to my parents—to anyone who doubted it.

"If anyone has a problem," Cassie continued, "it's Clyde and Marc. So stop defending them. I'm your sister. Always have been, always will be. Stop trying to punish me. Do you really think I'd be happy going back to Jersey and letting Mom and Nancy find me a husband?"

I thought I caught a ghost of amusement on Gus's face. "No. I guess not." He shuffled some papers around. "Steve'll be glad to have you back... He's been worried about the horses."

Cassie picked up a pile of mail from his desk and started to leaf through. "He ought to be if you've got J.T. in charge of the barn."

"J.T. and Billy took off right after Clyde was arrested. Who knows if they've got records too or what. I hired three fellows off of Andy's ranch. They're used to cattle, not people. Horses either, really," he admitted a bit sheepishly.

"Oh God," Cassie said. "You do need my help. I'll head down to the barn now."

"I'll unload your truck," I said as we both turned toward the door.

She reached in her pocket and tossed me the keys. Out on the porch she took a deep breath. "It's so good to be back." We both stared out at the pine trees for a long moment. "I've got to see what those idiots have done with my horses," she said. Then, on tiptoe, she gave me a nice, long kiss. "Thank you for unloading the truck. And thank you for not reorganizing my entire apartment. Otherwise, make yourself at home."

I brought in her boxes and suitcases and duffel bags, stacking them just inside the door. I didn't want to be a creepy voyeur, so I limited my snooping to the spines on the bookshelf: murder mysteries, *The Bell Jar*, *Jane Eyre*, and a lot of titles about horses. The living room occupied the whole width of the house. On one side, its windows gave a view up the slope, into the pines that cloaked the North Branch. On the other side, I could gaze across the guest cabins and the span of sagebrush desert that stretched toward the highway. What would this place be like in the winter? The river silent under ice, the blue of the distant mountains sheeted over with white.

And the two of us, to look out over it all. I couldn't wait.

The kitchen countertop was a mess of bottle caps, pens, scrunched receipts, and a beige phone. I hadn't been around a phone with real privacy for a while, and I knew I ought to call Kate, explain what was going on. But instead, I filled a glass with water at the kitchen sink and glugged it down. Then I picked up the phone and punched in the digits engrained from childhood: 603...A silence on the line, a little whir, and click.

"Hello?"

"Hi, Mom? It's Ron."

"Ronnie? Is that you?" A pause. "Is everything okay?"

"Yeah, it's me. It's Ron. Everything's great, Mom," I said. I crossed the room as far as the cord would allow me and looked out at a scrubby pasture where four horses whisked their tails and nibbled at the ground.

"Let me put your father on." I heard a click as she set the phone down. "Timothy! Pick up the phone!" I could just picture her voice echoing off the wooden banister, bouncing up the shag-carpeted stairs to my father's home office.

In a moment, another click and he said, "Hello?"

And my mother back on her own extension. "Tim, it's Ronnie. Ron. You there?"

"Hi, Mom and Dad," I said cautiously.

"Are you ready to come home?" my father said.

My words came a little thicker than I wanted them to. "No, Dad. Not now. Probably not for a while." I wrapped the phone cord around my index finger tighter and tighter as I said, "I got a scholarship to cover tuition at Harvard. And I have a job offer out here. I might stay out here."

"What?!" my mother exploded.

"Have you lost your mind?" my father said.

For a moment, the two of them talked over each other, a staticky chaos. Then my father won out.

"Ronnie, listen to me. We've all made mistakes in this process. I'm sorry for being so stupid and telling you to leave. And I'm sure you're sorry for some of the things you said and for running away—"

"I'm not sorry, Dad. Not a bit. I like it out here. It hasn't been easy, but I'm figuring it out."

"Ronnie," my mom said, and I could hear the tears in her voice. "Are you safe?"

"Yeah. I'm fine. I'm twenty. I'm an adult."

"What have you told them out there? Do they know you're a girl? Are you still trying to pretend you're a boy?" my dad said.

I wound the cord tighter. I could feel it digging into my finger, slowly cutting off the circulation. *Don't get angry, don't get angry.* "They know exactly who I am," I said, making my words slow and cold. "At least the ones who care about me."

There was a pause. I heard my mother blow her nose, and I had to fight back a surge of my own tears.

"I love you both," I said at last. "But I won't be coming home for a while."

I hung up the phone and sank onto the couch. I cried and paced and cried a bit more, and when Cassie came back, smelling of horse and hay and cursing about the idiots Gus had hired, the two of us cuddled on the couch until the sun set.

Cassie dropped me off at the ranger station the next morning. The first thing I did was tell Pete that I accepted his job offer.

"Wonderful!" he said, shaking my hand. "Did you tell Cassie about how you saved Walt?"

"I didn't save Walt," I protested.

Pete shook his head. "I can see I'm going to have to tell her that story myself. You certainly won't do it justice."

Margaret, who was filling in a massive ledger (trying to calculate the hazard and field pay owed to everyone who fought the fire) chuckled and beamed at me. "Does your girlfriend know how to play Hearts? It'll be so nice to have a couple around this winter."

"We're not exactly your quintessential straight couple," I said, returning her smile. "I think Cassie might prefer poker."

"I've always wanted to learn," Margaret said wryly.

It was almost Labor Day weekend, which Pete had said would be mayhem, every campground packed. "But after that, *whoosh*, as if someone pulled the plug on the drain, and all the tourists go swirling back to the Midwest," he warned.

Walt and I put extra trash bins in the popular campgrounds and then wrestled a wood splitter into operation. He was determined to leave me with an ample supply of fuel for the winter.

Margaret was planning a farewell party for the trail crew, who would pack up as soon as the weekend was over, and for the fire crew as well. Some of them would be heading back to college or other jobs, while a few would stay on through the fall on a consolidated crew run from a different station.

I'd just invited Cassie to come over and, with that phone call through, I dialed Kate's number.

"Ron!" she exclaimed when she picked up. "Have you got your bus ticket yet?"

"Actually, I was wondering if PRISM would let me defer for a year. Could I come back next fall instead?"

"What? I thought the whole point was to get you back to school this year. What's the deal?"

"Change of plans," I said simply. "I'm going to stay out here."

"I can't promise anything. You might lose the scholarship if you defer."

I nodded to myself. I might. "I'm okay with that," I replied.

There was a pause in which, I suspected, she must be wondering if I had lost my mind. "I'll talk to the deans. And PRISM. You're crazy, you know that?"

"Yeah. I know. Thanks, Kate." And I was thankful. Who knew what a year would bring? Maybe I'd transfer to the University of

Wyoming. Maybe Cassie would be moving back to Cambridge with me. I had the sense now that anything could happen—and instead of being scared of that possibility, I was excited.

"You're welcome. And give her my regards."

"How'd you know?"

Kate laughed and hung up.

Later that day, I put a postcard in the mail to Laurel.

Thanks for sending me the birthday package. It took me a while to admit it, but it was just what I wanted. I'll be spending the year out here in Wyoming. I hope everything at Harvard goes well for you.

And another to Jane.

You're going to say I'm insane, and I might be, but I'm staying out here in Wyoming for a while. I met a girl, and she's amazing, and I think you'd really like her. Come out and visit? Wyoming could use a few more queer folks, to say the least.

There was a lot more I could write, a lot more that I wanted to put onto paper about how Jane (and Laurel) had been right: I wasn't *just* a guy. I couldn't run away from everything that makes me who I am. And I did miss my queer friends. They did understand me better than (almost) anyone else.

But right now, all I could hear was the sound of truck tires on gravel.

I greeted Cassie at the door with a kiss. "How are things at the ranch?"

"It's a miracle those morons Gus hired didn't burn the barn down," she groused, then gave a broad grin. "It's good to be back."

Dinner, one final volleyball game, then Margaret brought out a huge cake. Pete announced that I'd be staying the winter at the station, and immediately I was deluged with advice about how to survive. As I listened to Gary's tips on where to snowmobile, Walt and Cassie argued fiercely about the merits of mules versus horses. I was happy to let the two of them duke that one out.

"You show me a trail you wouldn't take a horse on, and I'll show you someone who doesn't know how to ride a horse," Cassie said.

"It's all about the point of balance," Walt insisted, pushing his empty cake plate away from him.

"Riding a mule is like riding a washing machine."

"I'd show you how smooth these mules are if I didn't have this cast on my leg," Walt protested, shaking his foot at her.

"How did you get that? Falling off a mule?"

"It's getting late, and Walt and I will have campgrounds to clean tomorrow," I interrupted, not wanting Walt to tell the story of his leg. I'd just get embarrassed. I picked up a few plates, Cassie grabbed the rest, and we brought them into Margaret's kitchen.

The next morning, I woke when it was still dark and gently reached out a hand. Cassie was there next to me, and I ran my fingers along her thigh. I still couldn't believe it. I was here. She was here. I looked at the calendar on my wall. There were months and months ahead when we would both be here.

I rolled out of bed and rummaged around for my running shorts. Maybe I'd have to get a pair of snowshoes if the winter was all that Pete said it was.

"What're you doing?" Cassie mumbled, squinting up at me.

"Going for a run. Want to come along?"

She fell back on the pillow. "Hell no. I'll brew some coffee that doesn't taste like dung."

Her coffee was good. After my run, I skipped the fire crew's workout to sip it with her.

"You gotta do tomorrow with us, Ron," Gary called when he saw us on the porch. "Tomorrow's the last day of workouts."

I raised my mug to him. "Count me in."

Cassie went inside to take a shower before heading back to the ranch. I sat on the porch for a few more minutes, watching her battered Comanche disappear. I could hear the sound of the wood splitter roar to life, and I knew that in a moment Walt would come and set me to work.

There was just one thing I wanted to do, one last note to write. This one I was sure of. I'd send it down the North Fork in a bottle, let it drift along toward the East:

Never mind. Cancel the rescue. You can save someone else.

ACKNOWLEDGMENTS

This book was a long time in the making, and many people were crucial in its formation. I want to thank early readers Lexi Adams Wolff and Patricia Lothrop, who offered both helpful criticism and enthusiastic support. The earliest reader, as always, was my beloved spouse, Ilona, who read and commented and cheered me on and who has looked at this manuscript more than anyone other than myself. I am also extremely grateful to my agent, Alison Fargis, who has been my champion again and again and who didn't give up on this one, though the journey was long!

Of course, the book wouldn't have come into the world without the wonderful people at UNO Press. I am so thrilled they chose this book for the Lab Prize. Chelsey was a superb editor, and this book is better for her insight into character, among other things. GK and Abram shepherded me and the manuscript through the process with great care and attention to detail.

And, before all this writing and book production, the real stuff happened, and I want to thank the folks who I met out in Wyoming. There was a real dude ranch from which I really got fired, and there was a real ranger station that did really save me and teach me a ton about myself. The head ranger there was a fellow named Mick, and he is one of the best men I have ever met.

Author of *Revolutionary* ("A remarkable novel" —*The New York Times*), ALEX MYERS was born and raised in western Maine. Since high school, Alex has campaigned for transgender rights. As a female-to-male transgender person, Alex began his transition at Phillips Exeter Academy (returning his senior year as a man after attending for three years as a woman) and was the first transgender student in that academy's history. Alex was also the first openly transgender student at Harvard, and worked to change the university's nondiscrimination clause to include gender identity. After earning a master's in religion from Brown University, Alex began a career as a high school English teacher. Along the way, he earned an MFA from Vermont College of Fine Arts. He currently lives in New Hampshire with his wife and two cats.